OZARK WEDDINGS

DISCARD

ANITA HIGMAN
& JANICE THOMPSON

BARBOUR
PUBLISHING

ISBN 978-1-60260-806-1

Cover design: Kirk DouPonce, DogEared Design

Published by Barbour Publishing, Inc., P.O. Box 719, Uhrichsville, Ohio 44683, www.barbourbooks.com

Our mission is to publish and distribute inspirational products offering exceptional value and biblical encouragement to the masses.

Member of the
Evangelical Christian
Publishers Association

Dear Readers,

It is such an honor to share *Ozark Weddings* with you. All three love stories are set in the beautiful state of Arkansas. I hope these novels give you many hours of entertainment, but I also pray your heart will be lifted up in the process, and you will come away knowing the love and hope that God offers us through His Son, Jesus. Please visit my Web site at www.anitahigman.com and drop me a note. I would love to hear from you.

Anita Higman

Dear Reader,

It is with great delight that Anita and I offer our readers these lyrical and romantic stories. These three Arkansas-based tales were crafted to captivate your imagination and to offer you a glimpse of this amazing state where hot springs flow and rivers sing. Beyond that, however, we hope you are captivated by the love stories. . .not just the ones between hero and heroine, but the eternal story, which is sung over us each day by the very One who created us to love and be loved. He alone is worthy of our praise.

Janice Thompson

LARKSPUR
DREAMS

Dedication

To three amazing women. . .Kim Watson, Kristen Clark, and Sylvia Thompson. What treasures you are to this world.

Much gratitude goes to my daughter, Hillary Higman, for her honest input and support.

Thanks goes to Val Vogt for helping me understand the life of an artist.

Anita Higman

To all of the "Larkspurs" in my life. You know who you are. Your creative spirits uplift, encourage, and bring a smile to this face when I need it most.

Janice A. Thompson

Chapter 1

*W*hat a scene! Lark sat in her Hummer. The move in day of her rich neighbor certainly had a sitcom quality to it. She leaned in to watch him. Mr. New Guy gestured to the movers about his leather furniture, but they held to their standard modus operandi—the heave-ho method. And Lark could tell her dear, old friend, Skelly Piper, had the new guy cornered with his zucchini brownies and the highlights of his hernia operation.

Is that truly a pair of boxers flying up in the breeze? Apparently they had blown out from an open carton and were doubling as a kite. The offending object finally landed in a tree and began flapping like a white flag. *So how does a guy look manly while retrieving unmentionables from a blue spruce?*

Just as Lark was about to find out, her eyes followed a new addition to the bedlam. *Oh no. Not Picasso!* Her pet duck had yet to be approved by the planning commission, and he was waddling about on her new neighbor's walkway being loose in more than one sense of the word.

I'd better go help Mr. New Guy out. She rolled the window down and let her Christian rock music soar free into the air. With her brightest smile, she waved to her new neighbor. Skelly Piper saluted back, but Mr. New Guy sported a croaking sort of smirk that seemed to be directed at her.

Lark cut the engine and strode over to the two men. "Hi." She hugged Skelly as he said his good-byes.

"Oh, and see ya at the fall festival, kiddo." Skelly shuffled off, bowlegged. His thick hair stuck up on his head like a clump of silver grass. But he had his usual warm smile as he glanced back at her.

Turning to her new neighbor, Lark couldn't help but notice God had been quite charitable with his appearance. He had a striking presence with his hazel eyes, short brown locks, and a "surely he must lift weights" kind of build. *Hmm. Early to mid-thirties, same as me. Same medium height. But who wears a suit to move in?* And his tie looked like it would work equally well as a tourniquet. Lark also took note that Mr. New Guy held the bow on the sack of brownies as if he were holding the tail of a dead skunk.

Lark extended her hand to welcome him. "I'm Larkspur Wendell, your next-door neighbor."

"I'm Everett Holden III," he said like a maitre d' with an attitude. He slipped his Blackberry into his suit pocket and shook her hand.

The word *mannequin* popped into Lark's head, but his fingers and gaze lingered a moment longer than she expected.

One of the movers sneezed loudly, and all at once the assessing moment dissipated. They quickly freed each other's hand.

Everett looked down at his ultra-polished wingtips.

Lark wondered if he could use them for rearview mirrors. Picasso toddled over to her. "And who let you out?" She shook her finger at the duck as he dipped his head in shame.

"You actually *own* that flying outhouse?" Everett asked without a speck of humor.

"I'm sorry he left a bunch of his. . .doodling artistry all over your walkway. But you know, he doesn't usually get out. Perhaps someone *let* him out."

Everett straightened his already immovable posture. "Well, *I* certainly didn't do it."

A belch reverberated out of one of the movers. She tucked her giggle away, folded her arms, and nodded in the direction of the two guys lugging a couch up the steep steps to the house. "I rest my case."

"Okay," Everett said. "Mutt and Jeff over there might have accidentally done it since our gates are next to each other, but generally you *do* keep that thing penned up, right?" His brows furrowed a bit.

"I assure you, Picasso's not been trained as an attack duck." Lark could barely hold back her mirth. She took a treat out of her pants pocket and tossed it to Picasso. He rewarded her with a few happy mutterings.

"So do you run a game preserve back there?" Everett asked.

"No. Just one sweet, little mallard that thinks I'm his momma." His face grasped her attention. "And what do you do, Mr. Everett Holden III?" *I can't wait to see what this amazingly uptight guy is going to say next.*

Everett smiled as if it were a new expression he was trying out. "I'm an accountant, and I'm going to work out of my home. I spend most of the day behind the computer, but it suits me. I like quiet. Well, actually, I require it." He raised his head and made a little sniffing noise.

Lark tried to smooth the folds of her angora sweater. She gave up and looked over at Everett's gingerbread cottage. She couldn't imagine him buying such a dainty, rosy-colored house. "You certainly bought a pretty place to live."

He glanced at his home and then nodded. "It should be an excellent investment."

Lark waited for him to say more, but he just stared at his house. Many homes in the neighborhood were Victorian with pocket gardens, but she also loved the charm of the whole town with its galleries, trolleys, and quaint shops. For now, though, she couldn't help wondering if her new neighbor had also been captivated by the delight of Eureka Springs.

Everett tapped his shoe against a rock.

Okay, it's time for me to leave. "I've kept you too long. I'm so sorry." She turned to go. "By the way, we all have get-togethers around the holidays."

"Holidays?"

Surely Everett hadn't forgotten Thanksgiving would be arriving in just a few weeks. "You know, Thanksgiving and Christmas?" Lark said.

Everett shifted his weight as if he were losing patience. "I realize *what* holidays. I'm just not used to spending them with anyone."

Lark could feel her mouth gape open. What could she possibly say in response to that? She looked back at Everett. "Oh, but to spend Christmas alone sounds so. . .I mean. . . wouldn't it be lonesome?"

"I don't know. I've not spent a lot of time thinking about it." Everett straightened the sleeve of his suit, making Picasso think he had a treat. As her duck waddled toward his shoes, Everett took a conspicuous step away.

"I always have guests over around Thanksgiving, so I hope you'll be one of them."

Everett looked up at the sky as if he were expecting bad weather. "I really hate to obligate myself right away. But thank you."

What a peculiar response. "You're welcome," Lark said. "By the way, you'll enjoy your new neighbors. They're down-to-earth, generous, and practically like family."

"That's nice. Uh, so, do you mind?" Everett pointed at Picasso's handiwork. "You know, hosing that off my walkway?"

Lark jolted back from her reverie. "Oh yes. I'll clean it up."

Everett nodded.

"I'll say bye for now," Lark said.

"Good-bye."

Lark turned to leave, but when she heard the pounding of piano keys, she glanced back. The movers lifted an old, high-back piano down from the truck. "Do you play?"

"Excuse me?" Everett asked.

Lark motioned toward the instrument. "The piano. Do you play?"

"No. I don't." His frosty countenance softened, giving him a boylike appearance. "It was my mother's."

"Well, it's a pity. With some lessons I'll bet you could make it come to life."

"I don't think I have enough aptitude."

"All you need is the passion. Then everything else falls into place. . .like colors on a canvas." She wondered if the piano made him nostalgic. She could tell he had a smile aching to be released. A good sign. It meant Everett had a warm, beating heart under his cool, starched veneer, and a handsome man with heart would make good cocoa-sharing company on a cold evening.

Lark wiggled her fingers in a wave and headed toward her backyard gate, which she could see had indeed been left ajar. Without any commands, Picasso followed Lark. She sang to him softly as he waddled next to her along the limestone path. Before shutting the latch, Lark glanced toward Everett. He'd been caught gazing at her. Why did his interest give her so much pleasure?

Quickly Everett turned away and headed toward the delights of Mutt and Jeff.

"Well, what do you think of our new neighbor?" she whispered to her duck. "I think he reminds me of my old university professor, Dr. Norton." Picasso paused to look up at her and then toddled on his way with his tail feathers wagging. Lark recalled her professor had craved such a private life he eventually left his career. In fact, he'd become so withdrawn, one by one everyone left him to his lonely existence. "We'll watch out for our new neighbor, won't we, little fellow?" Picasso continued to have nothing to say on the subject, so she secured him in his large habitat and blew a kiss in his direction.

A gust of crisp, autumn air turned Lark's mind to the church's fall festival. She wished she'd remembered to invite Everett. She could tell he needed to get out. *Maybe I can ask him later.*

Lark scooted into her old tire swing and gazed up at the cornflower blue heavens. *Such a nice color, God.* She shoved off toward the sky.

Just as Lark wrapped up her prayer, she realized she'd reached the highest point she'd ever gone in her swing. She felt suspended in midair like a cloud. As if the day had stopped just for her to enjoy a moment longer. Lark slowed her speed and then locked her arms to let her body drift low. She'd always loved swinging that way when she was growing up. Her parents did, too. Right alongside her.

Lark stopped her swinging and shook her head. She pondered how one thoughtless act of an intoxicated driver could affect her life so deeply. Sending her mom and dad to heaven early. She sighed. *I miss you both so much.*

Lark refused to dwell on the parts of her life she couldn't control, so she released her sorrow as she took in a deep breath. The late October air smelled of earth and foliage and wood smoke. Mmm. Her favorite time of the year in Arkansas. And so magnificent with the autumn leaves setting the hills ablaze with gold and orange and crimson.

She picked up an acorn from her little pile and then released it again. The nut struck the mound and then rolled off in an unexpected direction, making the whole stack of acorns scatter as well.

Lark thought having a brand-new neighbor was like her tiny acorn drama. She wondered how God would allow Everett Holden to change her life. Neighbors always did. At least, *Lark's* neighbors always did. Or did she change *their* lives? She wasn't sure in the end who influenced whom more. It appeared all of humanity bounced off each other, with each movement and word affecting the whole like a loose nut pouncing on a mound of acorns. Whether acorns or humans, the conclusion remained the same. Life was pure adventure. One never knew for sure what would happen next.

Chapter 2

Everett handed the movers a check and shut the door to his one-hundred-year-old house. *Ahh. Quiet at last.* He looked at the stone fireplace and polished wooden floors. In spite of the ornate qualities of the exterior, the home suited him well, and he liked the idea of moving to a quiet, woodsy village amidst the Ozark Mountains. Best of all was the convenience factor, since his biggest client lived in Eureka Springs.

After making some serious money as an accountant, Everett looked forward to reaping the benefits. But he wasn't about to lose what he'd gained, so that meant no distractions. Living in a smaller community would help. His Realtor had promised him that in spite of all the tourists, the neighborhood was so quiet, one could hear a pin drop. *Perfect.*

Except for that woman next door. Larkspur Wendell certainly could be a potential distraction. *And attractive enough to cause a traffic pileup.* What was it with those brown eyes of hers anyway? She had a probing gaze, which made one wonder if she knew everyone's shadowy secrets and fully intended to use them. Yes, there was mischief written all over her lovely face. If he ever planned to get any work done, passive resistance and neutrality would need to be his watch-words when it came to Lark. He almost chuckled, but instead walked over to the piano and closed the lid.

Everett heard the doorbell and thought it might be the movers coming back to give his furniture one more bash with their crowbar, but a quick peek told him it was his neighborly distraction instead. He opened the door with his passive resistance intact. To his surprise Lark stood before him dressed in a bee costume. "May I help you?"

Lark smiled as one of her shoulders came toward her cheek in a shy kind of shrug. Was that her perfume drifting over to him?

Everett loosened his tie a bit.

"Hi. I know you're unpacking and all."

Good calculation.

Lark reached up to adjust one of the antennas on her head. "But our church is having a fall festival later this evening. And I wanted to invite you."

"It's hard to take you seriously. You're dressed. . .like an insect." He held back a chuckle.

"Tell me, Mr. Holden. What do you *really* see?"

What does she mean? "I see a lady dressed like an insect."

A warm smile inched its way across Lark's face. Her hair floated around her in the breeze as she wiped the strands from her eyes. "Well, you also see a neighbor who wants you to feel welcome."

"Okay." It was a struggle for him to drum up any animosity since Lark seemed so sincere.

"I give away candy and run the win-a-goldfish game," she said. "That's why I have on this costume. I have to be there early to get set up, but here's the address if you decide to come. We'll also have a cakewalk, a white elephant sale, and plenty of hot dogs." She offered him a folded piece of paper along with a packet of chewing gum.

Everett accepted both items, but he wasn't going to bother asking why she was dressed like a bee instead of a goldfish. He figured her answer would be as tangible as her gauzy wings.

"You're certainly—"

"Listen." Was that one of his headaches coming on? "I *will* be looking for a church in this neighborhood, but right now I've got to get my office set up and get back to work. Maybe some other time." *Do I really mean that?* He'd been a Christian since childhood, but sometimes he had to admit his church attendance had taken a backseat to his work.

"No problem. But don't work too hard. If you're not careful, Mr. Holden, you'll miss the *joie de vivre*." Lark whirled around, just missing his face with her wings. Oblivious to her near hit, she headed down the walk humming something he'd heard in Sunday school when he was a kid, "Go Tell It on the Mountain."

Everett watched her go as he placed his hand on his arm where she'd touched him. *What did she mean?* He'd miss the "joie de vivre"?

Before he closed the door, he noticed a man sporting a bomber jacket and a ponytail rumble up to Larkspur's house on a motorcycle. He looked like something off a billboard promoting filterless cigarettes and a tattooed lifestyle. Why did some people generate noise just by existing? The thunder from his bike echoed through the canyons. *Who does he remind me of anyway? Oh yeah. My brother, Marty.* He hadn't heard from him in years and suddenly wondered what had become of him.

The revving of the engine forced him to refocus his attention on Lark. She slipped on her suede jacket and hopped onto the back of the guy's bike as if she'd done it many times. *Must be her boyfriend.* He told himself that when he did have the time to date again, it would be with a woman who had her feet firmly planted on the earth's surface.

Everett put a stick of the gum in his mouth before he remembered he hated candy. Hmm. He hadn't chewed licorice gum since he was a kid. Kind of an odd, sweet flavor. He stuck the packet in his shirt pocket and headed to the stacks of boxes in his office. But the second he hit the office door, he knew what he would do next. He'd look up the meaning of joie de vivre in his French-English dictionary.

After the festival, Lark removed her coat and bee wings. She smiled, remembering how the faces of the children lit up when they'd won a goldfish. *And I still can't believe The Salt and Light Band played all my favorite songs.* She'd also been pleased to see so many new people in the crowd. And some were interested in checking out the church on Sunday morning. *What a success.* She sank into the couch, exhausted but content.

Lark closed her eyes for a moment and thought of Everett. At the festival she'd glanced around looking for him, but she knew he had the perfect excuse for not attending. He was still busy unpacking. *I wonder if he'll ever become a part of the community.* She certainly couldn't imagine him wanting to spend the holidays all alone.

Lark thought of Dr. Norton again and pulled down one of her yearbooks from the university. She flipped the pages back and forth until she found her professor's photo. She studied the picture. So forlorn with a hint of something else. Desperation? She touched his photo. Rumor was, he'd not only lost his wife and friends because of his reclusive lifestyle, but he'd also died a lonely death. Only three people had come to his funeral, including herself. Strange, he'd willingly chosen his solitary way of life. Lark wondered what trauma in Dr. Norton's past had made him so self-destructive.

But there was still hope for Everett. She vowed to rally round her neighbor. Whatever it took, she'd help him out of his solitary existence.

Chapter 3

E verett woke up feeling as animated as dirt. During the night he'd conjured up his usual array of nightmares.

Is that the doorbell? He realized the constant ding-donging had awakened him. He rarely slept in, but he'd stayed up late clearing out boxes. By the time he'd finished, he dropped from exhaustion. No time to grumble. He'd see to the door, get rid of whoever it was, and then get busy finishing up his office.

Everett stumbled over a shoe, nearly smacking his head on a bedpost. His brain whispered the word *caffeine*. And lots of it. *No time right now,* he told himself as he yanked on a pair of old jeans and a T-shirt. He made his way to the front door, but just as he opened it, a Pets Lovers of America van sped away from the curb leaving a trail of blue smoke. There on his porch sat a large cage. A parrot, the colors of a Hawaiian shirt, sat perched on a twig. Everett leaned down to the level of the bird's eye. "Who are you?"

The animal scooted across the branch and crooked his neck upward as if to size him up. "Who are you?" the parrot repeated.

Great. A yapping parrot. Was it a delivery gone awry? Well, maybe the feathery varmint really belonged to Larkspur, the lady with the duck. And if not, maybe she'd at least want to take it off his hands.

The last thing on his agenda, though, was to get entangled in Lark's day. His head began to throb. He threw on a coat, picked up the parrot, and headed next door.

Everett's attention turned toward the street. Okay, so why was there a Fayetteville television van parked in front of Lark's home? How could he have missed seeing the vehicle before? Everett marched to Lark's house, bypassed the bell, and hammered on her door with his fist.

A man with a goatee and a notebook opened the door. "Lark does have a doorbell. You must be Everett from next door. I see you brought Igor."

Who is this guy? "I'm afraid I don't understand any of this—"

"I'm afraid," the parrot repeated with a noisy mocking sound.

The man with the wimpy beard laughed. "Well, both of you come on in. Lark's in her loft. We just finished the interview up there. We wanted to be where she creates."

"Creates what?" He set the parrot down and glanced around inside. Sunlight poured in through the large windows. Immense paintings hung on every wall. Countryside scenes were filled with people caught up in everyday life.

Everett gazed at a painting of a girl wearing a sun hat and playing with a lamb. The word *realism* came to mind from a required art class in college. Even though the picture depicted life a hundred years ago, it looked welcoming and real enough to make him want to step into the landscape. And he also caught the unmistakable influence of the Ozarks in her work. *Fascinating*.

Then he remembered what Lark had said about joie de vivre. In French it meant the "sweetness of life." Those words seemed to describe the painting completely. He felt himself falling into some kind of emotional black hole. *Back to reality*.

The goatee guy headed up the metal, spiral staircase. *She must have done some remodeling on this old house*. Everett heard laughter upstairs, so out of curiosity, he picked up the cage and followed the man.

"You mean you didn't even know your neighbor was Larkspur Wendell, the illustrator?"

Everett felt annoyed with his cheeky attitude. "Illustrator of what?"

The goatee guy stopped midway and turned around just to frown at him. "You know—*When Dragons Fly*, *In a Giddy Pickle*, or the *Electric Seeds* series?" The guy looked at him as if *he* were the creature in a cage.

Everett shook his head but wanted to pelt the guy with birdseed. *I should have had my coffee*.

The goatee guy shrugged his shoulders and continued up the stairs. "I tell you, she's one of a kind. I just love Lark."

Before either of them could say another word, they arrived at the top of the stairs. The French doors were open, and Everett could see Lark sitting on a stool at an art table. Her long, dark hair flowed around her slender shoulders. Even in overalls, she was no doubt a beauty, but even more than that, Lark had a distinct presence in the room. He could barely remember why he was so irritated.

Lark didn't see him as the two men stepped into the room. A female reporter chatted with her while some guy packed up his camera.

Lark turned around to him. Everett noticed the radiance in her eyes, akin to the sun coming up in the morning.

She jumped up and hugged him.

Everett brought his free hand up on her back for a pat.

"I just love Lark," the parrot repeated and then squawked.

Everyone burst into laughter except Everett.

"I'm so glad you're here. You brought Igor. By the way, he likes to repeat things." Lark wiggled her eyebrows. "So be careful what you say."

Everett frowned. "Well, I didn't. I mean—"

Lark looked at him as if they'd always been friends. "He's your housewarming gift. I had him delivered from Springdale. I thought since you were all alone, Igor could keep you company."

Chapter 4

A cough erupted from Everett's mouth. Just as he was about to explain himself, the female reporter lifted her chin as if to bring the conversation back to business.

"We have everything we need," the reporter said. "Thanks for your time, Ms. Wendell. You were marvelous." She lifted the lapel mike off Lark's overalls and shook her hand. "By the way, if I leave without an autograph for my daughter, I'll be in trouble tonight."

Lark gave each crew member a hand-signed piece of art and a hug good-bye. She stayed in the room with him, while the crew filed down the staircase. To avoid the Igor topic, he found himself simply glancing around, taking in the various aspects of the room. Light purple walls with a sign over the door that read, IMAGINE. Flower petals strewn on the floor. Electric guitar on a stand in the corner. Books and art magazines stacked here and there and a bowl full of jellybeans on the floor near a beanbag chair. "Aren't you going downstairs to lock your door?"

"No. We have very little crime here. In fact, sometimes I forget to lock up."

This woman is so naive. "You're being a bit. . .reckless," Everett said. "Don't you think?"

Lark walked over to the birdcage. "You don't like Igor, do you?"

Everett switched gears. "Why did you *really* buy me a talking parrot? You could have just brought me brownies. I like brownies." *Well, until I tasted Skelly's.*

"Why *not* buy a talking parrot?" Lark looked at Igor and smiled. "I saw him online, and he seemed like a gift you might enjoy. I really—"

"But how would you know that?" Everett rubbed his aching head. "You don't even know me. And I know it must have been very expensive."

"Don't you like pets?"

Everett shifted his weight. Keeping up with his neighbor's conversation was as exasperating as using a cup to empty a sinking boat. "Let's just say, pets don't agree with me."

Lark laughed. A bubbling kind of giggle that wasn't an altogether unpleasant sound.

"They don't agree with you?" Lark asked. "It's not like you're going to eat Igor for dinner."

"Igor for dinner." The bird shrieked and ruffled his feathers.

"I appreciate the thought, but I have no time for pets. I work long hours. He would be neglected, so I'd like *you* to have. . .Igor." Everett saw a little light go out of Lark's eyes. Something made him want to bring that light back, but he wasn't sure why. He might have to think on that one later. "I mean, it would be like turning my house into a resort for flying animals." *Guess I shouldn't have said that last part. Why is she staring at my clothes?* He looked down at his jeans, which were full of holes. And his feet were bare. *Not good.* He wondered how that happened. He never did that sort of thing. Well, at least the cold front hadn't made it through yet.

Lark opened the cage door. "Hi there, Igor. You're a sweetie."

"You're a sweetie," the bird said back to her.

Lark chuckled as she stroked his neck. The bird dipped his head next to her hand and closed its eyes.

While Lark appeared distracted, Everett took note that her office had no blinds or curtains at the huge window. Most people put up drapes and heavy shutters, but as an artist she must like to use the natural light.

He stepped over to her art table and looked at one of her watercolor paintings. The sheet of rough, white paper seemed to come to life with rabbits, foxes, and turtles all hiding among the ferns and tree trunks. The fanciful pictures were no less than what? Enchanting? He'd better not get caught using *that* word in public.

But the illustrations reminded him of an earlier time in his life when he used to read to children at one of the local hospitals in Fayetteville. Amazing. He used to actually volunteer his time, and he'd loved it. But that seemed like a lifetime ago, before life had taught him the lessons of unspeakable misfortune. "You didn't mention you were an artist."

"Well, you were busy herding your movers," Lark said. "And it seemed like they needed a little *coaching* as I recall."

She had more paint on her lavender overalls than on her paper. He saw her eyes searching his again. But what could she be looking for? "This current work here—is it to illustrate a new book?"

"No, I did it just for fun." Lark smiled down at the painting. "The idea came from a dream I had. So I thought I'd try to capture it."

"So you have pleasant dreams?" Everett asked.

"Almost always. Do you?"

He almost said no but then admonished himself for nearly sharing intimate details about his life. "It's rather hard to explain." Maybe he just needed to get back to work.

"I'm sorry about the gift," Lark said. "Sometimes I've been known to be a little too—spur-of-the-moment. It's one of my great weaknesses. But I assure you, God and I are working on it."

"Apology accepted." He offered her a wide smile since he was glad to be rid of Igor, but he wondered just how "spur-of-the-moment" she was and how many "weaknesses" she and God were working on. Suddenly he heard a series of clatters and bangs. "What's that racket?"

"Oh, it's Skelly. Our neighbor. He sometimes throws pots and pans at his brick wall."

"How peculiar. Why does he do that?" Everett wanted to see what was happening, but he knew Skelly's backyard wasn't visible from her window.

Lark stroked her hands along her arms. "Skelly lost his wife to cancer a few months ago. You know, when her hair fell out from the treatments, she wore a baseball cap. And wherever they went, Skelly always wore a baseball cap, too. Just so she wouldn't feel different or alone. Rose is in heaven now." Lark smiled at him with a faraway gaze. "I loved the way they loved each other." She shrugged. "So now he bakes everyone brownies just like his wife did, he prays a lot, and sometimes, when he misses her terribly, he finds it helpful to throw a few pots and pans against his brick wall. Why not, if it helps?"

"I'm sorry for Skelly. That must be hard." Everett paused, not really knowing how to respond to the man's sorrow, so he decided to change the subject. "But I still think you should lock your doors. I saw a hooligan-type last evening."

"Really?" Lark tied her long hair back with a clip and took a step closer to him.

"Yes. That riffraff on the bike. You know, the one who offered the *bee* a ride with no helmets." He raised an eyebrow and then rebuked himself for judging someone he barely knew.

Lark looked surprised. "That *riffraff*, who was kind enough to drive me to the church fall festival yesterday, happens to be Jeremy, our youth pastor."

Everett swallowed hard, but he felt like another retaliating remark building up. "Well, I hope he doesn't have a wife."

"Jeremy is single, and we go out from time to time. *And*, I might add, he's got a very successful teen ministry. Now don't you feel a little. . .silly?"

"I've never been *silly* in my life," Everett said.

"I'll bet you haven't, Mr. Holden." Her lips curled up at the edges.

"I'll bet you haven't," the bird squawked back at them.

"Oh, shut up," Everett said. *Oh man. Now I'm talking to animals. Time to go.* Everett looked away from Lark's bemused expression to stare out her workroom window. He noticed her office window was directly facing his own large office window. And the windows were only a few feet apart. A groan welled up inside him. "If you'll excuse me, I still have twenty-one boxes to unpack." He turned and moved toward the stairs.

Moments later, Everett offered his good-bye at the door. He knew the words came off rather strangled, but he felt more determined than ever to keep Lark at a safe distance. And he wasn't about to make this community his new family as Lark suggested. He repeated his mantra. "Passive resistance and neutrality."

⏤

What was it about this guy? Exasperating. Lonely. But so cute. Or maybe one of the things that captured her interest was his expression of subtle yearning.

She plunked down on her love seat, pulled a sprig of baby's breath from the vase, and stroked the tiny blossoms across her cheek. Lark suddenly thought of Jeremy. So dedicated and funny and genuine. In fact, he had so many good and godly qualities about him, she'd be crazy not to think of him in more serious terms. But she'd known since girlhood Mr. Lifetime would be poles apart from her. Like south meeting north and then trying to find a common parallel. She knew in her heart the Christian man she'd marry someday would not only garner her admiration and affection. . .but also leave her breathless.

She rested her feet on the coffee table. *Yes, an acorn has fallen,* Lark thought. *And Everett's neatly stacked pile is about to be scattered.*

Chapter 5

Lark stretched her arms out to a new morning. Sunday had gone well. Church had been good, but now Monday morning beckoned. The clock on the night table read 6:30 a.m. She never bothered with setting her alarm but instead let her natural body rhythms tell her when she'd had enough sleep. She flipped the light on and smiled at the bird in his cage. "Good morning, Igor."

Bits of his softness floated about the cage as he fluffed his feathers. "Good morning, Igor," the bird repeated.

Lark shoved her lavender comforter back, slid her wiggling toes into her slippers, and got up. She chatted softly to Igor as she checked his food and water supply. Still wearing her long, granny nightshirt, she padded up the spiral staircase, letting her hand slide along the cool metal railing up to her loft. No need for coffee since she let music rev her creative juices in the morning. Once in her studio, she flipped on her lights and her amplifier, strapped on her guitar, and prepared to rock. Was that classical music she heard coming from Everett's office? *Seems kind of loud.* She listened closely. *Wow! Vivaldi. Wind and brass. Cool.*

She didn't see Everett standing anywhere in his office so she decided to enhance the music with her own hard rock. *Oh yeah. Oboe Concerto in D Minor.* Lark positioned her fingers on the neck of the guitar and tapped out her own beat with her foot. *Almost time for my part.* Lark raised her guitar pick high in the air and lowered it on her strings, adding her own metal sound to the bright melody. She closed her eyes, swooning to the joining of two great musical styles. Crescendo. *Oh, there's that sweet spot on the guitar.*

The classical music stopped. Lark turned toward her window. Until now, she hadn't realized her large, bare office window faced Everett's large, bare office window just a few feet away. And when the lights were on, they could see each other perfectly.

Everett stood like a soldier in his suit with a no-nonsense stare. All in all, he looked pretty daunting. In fact, on the jovial scale, he was a minus fifty. But even so, he had an irresistible earnestness about him, too.

He held up a large piece of paper with a phone number on it. She let her guitar make a slow dying sound and placed the instrument on its stand. While still humming the melody, she pushed in all the right numbers on the phone.

One ring. Two rings. *Why is he waiting?*

He finally picked up the phone. "Hi. Everett Holden. Your neighbor."

Lark had to pucker her cheeks to keep from laughing. "Yes, I can see you. . . right in front of me. Good morning."

Everett cleared his throat so loudly Lark had to pull the phone away from her ear. "Please," he began. "Please don't tell me you get up every morning at six thirty to play your electric guitar."

Okay, I won't tell you. "I guess you want me to turn down my amp. It's just that I loved your Vivaldi, and I couldn't help but join in. It's so exhilarating." She shot him her sweetest smile and waited for his face to brighten. It didn't. "But I don't think it was any louder than your music." Lark tried to stay lighthearted.

Everett moved around the room, stacking manuals on his shelves, obviously multitasking. "But your music doesn't mix with my music."

Did he actually say that? Lark wondered what the magic words were to turn up the corners of his mouth. Maybe *spreadsheets* and *revenues.*

Then she noticed it. Tiny lacelike specs floating just outside the window. "Look. An early snow!" Still holding the telephone, Lark opened the window and stuck her head outside. Fresh, crisp air swirled around her. "Everett. Isn't this amazing? A snowfall never forecasted. Don't you just love things as unpredictable as the weather?"

Lark heard nothing from her telephone partner, so she looked back at Everett, who now wore a fixed and intent gaze. It reminded her of the glassy expression held by the stuffed, wild boar hanging in Skelly's den. She'd thought an impromptu celebration of the snow with some frothy cocoa would be fun. But Everett didn't appear to be in the mood for a festive beverage.

"Don't you like snow?" She heard his raspy breathing and wondered if smoke would puff from his nostrils at any moment. Rarely did she make anyone angry. Usually people left her presence with a hug and a kind word. The moment felt unfamiliar, yet strangely exhilarating, as if she were plummeting on a roller coaster ride.

"I like snow," Everett said. "In fact, I like a lot of things. But right now, I'm trying to work."

"Well then, have a nice day."

"Thank you," Everett said. "The same to you."

Was that a simper? He has a chink in his rock wall, Lark thought as she let a slow grin overtake her face. But then Everett dampened her optimism by parking himself down at his desk as immoveable and cold as a slab of granite. Oh well, hope still reigned. Even granite could be carved with the right tools.

Lark gave up on Everett for the time being as the snow claimed her attention. She had to be a part of it. She headed back downstairs, slipped on some moccasins and put on a coat over her long nightshirt. Once she'd flipped on the outdoor lights, she hurried out into her backyard.

The glorious white stuff fell more heavily now, floating all around her, engulfing her in a cocoon of softness. Suddenly she realized she'd never painted a winter scene. *I should memorize this moment.*

The pristine flurries had already lighted on the pines and decorated their boughs. *And what a unique quiet.* As if the snowy splendor commanded all the rest of nature to an awed silence.

The delicate feel of the flakes on her face reminded her of a feather tickling her cheek. Lark licked the melting snow from her lips. A gust caused the flakes to do a little tango. She raised her arms and danced with the flurries, dipping and swaying and singing. She knew God looked on, sharing her pleasure in His creation. An icy gust made her shiver, so she raced back inside, laughing the whole way up to her loft.

~≈~

Everett slammed his coffee mug down so hard a three-tiered bead of brown liquid rose in the air and then plopped back in his cup. Cold, bitter brew again. He made a mental note to throw out his coffee beans and buy some caffeine pills. His concoction always tasted like crude oil anyway.

He glanced over at Lark's office window. Her light was off, so she still must be out of her office. At least she'd finally gotten the good sense to come in from the cold. He'd seen her from his window, and she'd been outside twirling with her arms stretched wide. She looked stark raving mad. *Or maybe she's simply childlike.*

It reminded him of something he and his sister, Greta, had taken pleasure in when they were growing up. Sneaking out one night to play in the first snow of the winter. The moon had come out full that night, illuminated the snow, and made it glisten like stars. They'd pelted each other with snowballs. His sister had quite a hefty pitch as he recalled. Several times they'd doubled over laughing. He hadn't thought of that moment in years. But then he remembered they'd both caught colds, and his sister had been forced to the hospital when her fever and cough spiraled into pneumonia. He knew scientifically that their sickness had not actually come from being out in the weather, but in his mind he always associated the two.

He drank a glass of water, trying to get the acid taste out of his mouth. His sister had always been fun loving, yet so irresponsible. She'd always managed to convince him to go along with her schemes. But some of her ideas for amusement were reckless. In the end, her foolish behavior had been the undoing of their family.

Everett cleared his throat and wished he could clear his thoughts as easily. Yes, there had always been a price to pay for happiness. It had become his life's lesson—joy might come, but there would be the inevitable price to pay at the end.

He stared out at the falling snow and wanted to say, "Humbug." *Maybe I need some window blinds to help with the distractions. Mental note: Caffeine tablets. And wooden blinds.* Everett willed himself not to look out his window, but even as he made his private demand, he rewarded himself with one more glimpse. Hopefully, Lark wouldn't catch him gawking.

Abruptly her office lights flickered on, and she appeared at the window, giving him a wave. She had indeed caught him staring. Heat spread across his face while she slipped on that perennial, pesky, sunny smile of hers. With her hair pulled back in a ribbon, he could see the soft angles of her lovely face. Not thinking clearly, he picked up his coffee mug and then dropped it on his bare toe. The brew sloshed all over his pant leg. *Great.* He grabbed some tissues and tried to wipe up the mess, but he did more smearing than cleaning.

Mental note: Suit pants to the dry cleaners, caffeine tablets, and very *heavy wooden blinds.* Maybe he should hire someone to run his errands for him. That way he could get even more work done. Since he'd just gotten a raise from his biggest client, he felt an unwritten pressure to give more hours and produce more work. Kind of like a treadmill that management conveniently forgot to turn off.

But the additional labor was no real problem for him. He had almost no family left. No real friends. No obligations. Just the job. A clean and productive life.

Everett did a double click with his mouse and looked at his computer screen, which now displayed an electronic ledger. He stared at the cursor. It seemed to almost mock him with its incessant winking.

He looked down at his hands. His fingers were balled into fists so tightly he could feel his heartbeat in his hands. Probably from the wrath of paying an obscene amount of money for a home which turned out to have no privacy. He glanced back at Lark's window. This time she'd disappeared again. When did she ever get any work done? And surely illustrating didn't pay much.

What was the name of one of her books? In a Giddy Pickle? Okay, so now that he thought about it, he might have seen the book back in Fayetteville. Perhaps at a bookstore and on a special display at the grocery store. Okay, maybe she *was* slightly notable. But if she were *that* big, wouldn't she be working nonstop to keep up her position and lifestyle?

Everett heard some faint squealing noises next door, so he made a casual glance over to his neighbor's window. Lark and another woman were doing that girlfriend ritual thing of jumping up and down while hugging. He shook his head and groaned.

Chapter 6

W hat are you doing here? This is so great." Lark loved the idea of sharing a snowy morning with her best friend, Calli Dashwood.

"Well, you said you wanted me to surprise you sometime," Calli said.

Lark released her from their hug. "I'm so happy you're here. But what about the roads? Weren't they kind of slippery?"

"I drove carefully." Calli wagged a finger. "But did you know your door was not only left unlocked, it wasn't quite shut?"

"Oh dear." Lark realized it must have been left that way all night.

"I saw your car in the drive so I knew you were home," Calli said. "I rang the bell, but when you didn't come, I noticed the door."

"I guess I forgot. And I can't believe I didn't hear the bell. I'm so sorry." Lark folded her hands together in front of her. "Maybe I can make it up to you with breakfast burritos and lots of homemade salsa."

"Now you're talking." Calli took off her coat and pulled out a bag of candy from her pocket. "I brought you a present. Little Chocola' Rocks from Sweet Nothings."

"Is that the candy shop you're always talking about in Hot Springs?" Lark asked.

"Yeah. And the owner, Nori, is quite the entrepreneur. The next time we go to Hot Springs I think you'd both get a kick out of meeting each other."

"I'd love to." Lark accepted the beautifully decorated bag of sweets and put it on an easy-to-reach shelf, thinking they'd be great for munching while painting or reading or just about anything. "Thanks."

Lark noticed Calli's new casual look in jeans and tennis shoes. Her friend had her hair down in dainty curls, with a few tiny braids on the sides. She had always admired Calli's tall stature, her rich, cocoa brown complexion, and almond-shaped, brown eyes. She wondered if her friend wouldn't mind posing for her someday. She'd make a great model. Lark tuned back into the conversation as Calli chatted about all the ways *not* to make snow ice cream. They clomped down the stairs together, chuckling.

After breakfast and a few hours of much needed girl talk, they settled back into the loft. Calli sat in the purple beanbag chair to peruse Lark's newest picture book, *In a Giddy Pickle*. "This is so incredible. You know, Nissa is a great writer, but your illustrations make the book. And this cover. . .so whimsical and beautiful. Kids are going to love it. Congratulations."

Lark smiled. "Thanks."

"I guess you'll have some book signings again." Calli tried to get up from the chair and fell back down. They both laughed.

Lark reached out her hand to help her friend up. "My publisher has set up quite a few over the next several months. It should be fun meeting the kids and their parents. I hope you'll come to one of them."

"I always do," Calli said. "So has this new publisher hired you for another project? They should."

"Not yet. But it's okay." Lark fiddled with one of her camel hair brushes, making pats on her palm, pretending it was a butterfly. "I'm enjoying the break." Lark took a few mini packets of jellybeans out of her big bowl and tossed them to Calli.

"Ohh, yeah. Armed and dangerous." Calli popped a jellybean in her mouth. Then she strolled around Lark's studio and studied her paintings on the wall. "Your oils have gotten even better than the last time I was here. So much more depth and emotion. You are remarkable."

"Thank you." Lark fidgeted with her art supplies, moving her gesso and mineral spirits around from one spot to another. Watching her friend, Lark wondered why she felt so uncomfortable when people observed her artwork.

Calli milled around the other side of her studio and stopped to gaze at a still life of pears and yellow roses and then one of a Victorian village. "Now why is it you haven't shown these to anyone? There are so many terrific galleries here."

Lark shrugged. "I'm not sure."

"But that's what you told me last year. What's going on?"

"Guess I'm still not ready." Lark felt uncomfortable talking about her work beyond illustrating.

"Oh boy. I know that's not *this* ladybug talking," Calli said, doing a little lasso gesture with her finger. "You are indomitable, girl. Why? Because God is with you, and He's given you an amazing gift here that He expects you to share. And I don't just mean your illustrations." She raised an eyebrow. "Now do I hear an amen, sister?"

"Amen." Lark took her friend's hand and squeezed it. "Okay. I'll call one of the local galleries. . .sometime."

Calli tapped her finger on her cheek.

Lark laughed. "Okay. I will call. . .soon. I promise."

Calli took off her freshwater pearl bracelet and rolled it onto Lark's wrist.

"What are you doing? I can't accept this. It's your favorite. Isn't this the one you bought in one of the shops downtown?" Lark touched the bracelet, wondering if she should give it back. But she didn't want to hurt her friend.

"Yes, but I want you to have it," Calli said. "It looks good with your nightshirt."

They both chuckled.

"*And* I want it to be a symbol of the pledge you just made to me. A reminder. Okay?" Calli lowered her gaze as if to add an extra helping of serious.

Lark nodded. "You're the best."

"Yeah. That's what my customers keep telling me."

"You *are* the best Realtor in Springdale."

"Well, I guess I really like helping people find their dreams."

Lark held up the new bracelet on her wrist. "I can tell."

Calli glanced over at Everett's office window. "So I guess this is the new neighbor you were talking about. What was his name again? Everest Molden?"

Lark laughed. "You're close. Everett Holden."

"Wow, look at that," Calli said. "When he has his lights on, you can see everything he's doing. I mean, your windows are so big and close, it's like you're both in a fish bowl. His profile is certainly impressive. Uh-oh. He's glancing over at us."

They both waved at Everett.

Calli whispered, "But when he smiles, it looks more like he's lifting heavy furniture."

⤜⤚

Everett's office chair squawked in rebellion as he tilted it back. He stared at his knee. Looked like he'd picked up another tic. His foot bounced, making his leg continually jiggle. "Where did that come from? Maybe I'm being punished for something. And do other guys talk to themselves so much?" Of course, most men probably let off steam with their friends. But people just made life so tedious; he wondered if friendship was ever worth the bother. Everett pushed on his leg, forcing it to stop bouncing.

But on the other hand, the holidays were coming, and friends did come in handy to make things more festive. Christmas. Sure, he'd attend a client party or two and show up at a church activity, but for the last several years, the big day had been spent alone. He'd eaten foods he'd had catered and opened presents he'd given to himself. None of his life seemed dismal until now. Until he'd had a window view of the most maddening and fascinating woman he'd ever met. Larkspur. A woman who seemed to glow from the inside out. Kind of like a light bulb, only a lot brighter.

But what kind of strange air was he breathing in this neighborhood? *I don't even know the woman.* Then he remembered her holiday invitation. *Hmm. A thought: Eating over at her house would certainly save money.*

He stared back at his screen and the glaring numbers. He was always the bottom-line guy. Charts and spreadsheets and graphs had always been a part of his life, but now he wondered if they had consumed him. Some people had even come to fear him at meetings because of his stern reports. Everett whispered, "I've become the bad-news guy."

He looked up and noticed his sister's music box on the shelf. He lifted the memento down and rubbed his finger along its rough, carved surface. It was one of the last belongings of hers he'd kept. He tried to rotate the little crank, knowing it wouldn't turn. Greta had broken it from twisting it over and over until she'd wound it too tightly. The box seemed to reflect her life all too well.

He then saw the licorice chewing gum Lark had given him the day he'd moved in. The packet sat on his desk, daring him to try another piece. Finally, he rolled his eyes in exasperation and opened a stick. He studied the powdery grayness of it, thinking how ungumlike it looked and then stuffed it in his mouth. He chewed for a moment. Sweet. Unique. The flavor reminded him a little of molasses. Guess you'd either really love the stuff or really hate it. No middle ground. After another chew or two, Everett tossed the rest of the packet of gum in the wicker trash bin. He missed. Who cared? Time for action.

He snatched up his keys to his brand-new sedan with all the bells and whistles and headed out. Everett wasn't even sure where to go. Maybe he'd get a real cup of coffee downtown. And then later, he'd try to find the heaviest wooden blinds money could buy.

Chapter 7

After a shower and a few more hours of catching up with Calli, Lark's stomach began to growl.

"I heard that," Calli said. "Now did you mention some homemade cinnamon scones, or was I dreaming?"

Lark tugged on her friend's arm. "Come on. You weren't dreaming."

"I'm wearing elastic jeans so I can eat more than one."

They both laughed.

Just before they headed down the stairs again, Calli glanced over at a canvas sitting on an easel. "Now what is this one going to be?"

Lark paused before going downstairs. "I'm not totally sure. I've sketched in some of it. A garden with a woman sitting on a bench. But something is missing. The balance is off. It needs something. . .or someone."

Calli tapped her cheek. "Yeah. Maybe you're right." As she gazed out the window, her eyebrows creased, making angles on her perfect oval face. "Will you just look at that?"

Lark followed Calli's gaze into her neighbor's office. *Oh my.* She flipped off her lights and watched the play-by-play as a crimson-faced Everett trudged up a stepladder to fasten some monstrous, wooden blinds to his bare office window. He struggled with the blinds as if he were wrestling with an alligator. Without warning, Everett fell off the ladder.

Calli gasped.

"Should we call an ambulance?" Lark asked.

"Wait a sec," Calli said. "Maybe he's okay."

Everett stumbled to his feet again, amazingly unhurt.

Lark and Calli sighed with relief and then sputtered some pent-up giggles.

This time Everett made it up the ladder with the blinds, a rock hammer, and some nails the size of railroad spikes.

Lark noticed he didn't look all that chipper. She shoved her long hair behind her shoulders and cocked her head. "Go ahead, girlfriend. I know you're itching to say something about my neighbor."

"Owwee," Calli said. "I love all God's creatures, but who in the world installs wooden blinds in a three-piece suit and a button-down shirt?"

"Everett *is* kind of stiff," Lark said.

Calli folded her arms. "Honey, if he were any stiffer, I think we'd have to bury him."

Lark leaned against the window frame. "But I feel sorry for him."

"Uh-oh. I can see what's coming. Sure, you've got to love them in the Lord, but repeat after me, 'Everett Holden *is* a handsome man, but he is *not* a wounded animal.' He's not that skunk you nursed back to health when you were twelve."

Lark rolled her eyes at her friend. "It wasn't a skunk. It was a squirrel."

Calli put her hand up. "I'm just messing with you. I suppose God could have planted Everett over there for a reason. Should be interesting to find out what it is."

Lark wanted to discuss the lonely plight of her hermit professor, Dr. Norton, but the time didn't seem right, so she just sent up a prayer for her new neighbor instead.

❧

The next morning, Lark followed Calli out the back door to her car and then paused for a second to take in what was left of the breathtaking leaves. *I think the colors must get brighter every year. And they look especially pretty with a dusting of snow.* She finally pulled her gaze back to Calli. "I wish you could stay longer."

"Me, too. But I've got to show some houses to a couple this afternoon, so I'd better get going." Calli tossed her overnight bag in the backseat of her Mercedes.

"We had a really good time, didn't we?" Lark wondered if she'd ever get too old for slumber parties. She doubted it. There was nothing quite like staying up late eating a fresh batch of cookie dough while watching old black-and-white movies. But the best part was sharing the experience with her best friend.

"Yes, we surely did." Calli slid into her car.

Lark really liked her friend's power suit: tailor-fit, navy fabric, with a killer scarf. "Love that outfit."

"Thanks," Calli said. "Hey, come visit me. Okay? And I'll make you some homemade chicken and dumplings like my granny used to make. Best eating in Arkansas." She shut the door and started the engine.

"I know the roads are clear, but call me when you get in," Lark said. "Otherwise I'll worry about you."

Calli patted her hand on the car door. "Ladybug, I'm not going to worry you're worrying. Cause you've never been a worrier. Besides, the sun has spun gold this morning, making the leaves into jewels. And that'll keep me awake and singing the whole way. Thank you, Jesus." Calli turned on the heat. "You're turning into an ice cube out there. I'd better say bye." She waved and pulled out of the driveway.

Lark folded her arms around her middle and bounced to keep warm.

"Now don't you go and marry that next-door neighbor of yours while I'm gone. Do you hear?" Calli hollered back to her.

Lark put her fists on her hips to try to appear annoyed with her friend but gave up when she felt a big smile spread across her face. She then waved until Calli's car was out of sight. She glanced around at the spots of leftover snow, which had become like shimmering diamonds in the sun. All was so beautiful. *Yes, Everett would miss another dazzling day laboring in his grotto.* When she turned around, she noticed a sign hanging on his front door handle. *What is that?* She shivered but just had to have one quick peek.

She took a few steps toward Everett's house and peered up on the small porch area. Now Lark could read the sign clearly. Do Not Disturb. She couldn't believe it. Just as she tried to clamp her mouth shut from the reality of it, a van pulled up in front of his house. The name of the company was written across the van in purple and gold. Gourmet to Your Door. Cook No More. Everett was having his meals delivered? Wow. Hibernation to a new and scarier level. She wondered if he'd ever come back out for human contact. Oh well, he was a big boy. Not a squirrel. *Well, maybe a little squirrelly.*

Lark could smell wood smoke again. The scent made her think of cozy family gatherings around the fireplace, but since the cold wind was starting to seep through her sweatshirt and jeans, she scuttled back up the driveway and into the warmth of her kitchen. She immediately noticed her bowl of pomegranates on the counter. "Hmm." She grabbed a sketchbook out of her drawer.

Skelly had given her a bouquet of bougainvillea from his little hothouse, so she slid the vase of flowers behind the bowl and sat down on the kitchen stool. The petals had faded to an antique-looking peach and gave the fruit a nice backdrop. She added a tall bottle of olive oil to the scene. *Not quite right.* Less was more sometimes, but the balance looked off. A scene with an odd number of items always made a more pleasing picture though. To her, asymmetry was one of those mysteries of art. Lark glanced over at the sack of medjool dates she'd bought at the grocery store. *Okay, that might be interesting.* She added a handful to the scene. *Yes. Just right.*

Lark chewed on a date as she made some sweeping outlines of the objects with a charcoal pencil. Mmm. Medjool dates. They looked a little like roaches, but they were always so sweet and creamy.

She noticed some bad spots on a couple of the pomegranates. *Oh well.* She'd draw them as is, blemishes and all. It reflected life, didn't it? All things lovely still missed a vital connection to glory. In fact, wasn't art of every kind reaching for something more—hoping, dreaming of knowing that Someone who was greater than oneself? Too bad some people refused to consider the grace that could reconnect them to their Creator.

Lark continued her drawing, adding shading here and there. She held it up. *Not bad.* But soon her thoughts drifted back to Everett. Maybe he was reaching for something as well, but didn't know it. Perhaps in his case, he simply needed to be plugged back into life.

Lark fingered her earlobe, because somehow it made her think more clearly, and then out of the blue she got an idea. Just a little idea, but she thought it might have real potential. Just below her in a cabinet, she'd stored away a brand-new box of mothballs. She put away her sketchbook and reached for the box. She took some ribbon from a kitchen drawer and adorned the box with a silky bow and streamers. *Okay, pretty in an odd sort of way.*

Not bothering with a coat, Lark slipped out the front door and tiptoed over to Everett's house. No sign of the Gourmet to Your Door van, so all looked clear. She then crept up onto Everett's porch. The goofy sign still dangled from his door handle. Do Not Disturb. She set the box on his doorstep and rang the bell.

Perhaps the gift would come off a little startling, but she would certainly want someone to do the same for her if she'd become a workaholic recluse. Everett needed to take his life out of storage so as not to have the same tragic ending as her dear, old professor. Symbols were powerful tools, and the mothballs could be just the humorous and persuading gift to bring him to his senses. Lark hurried back to her porch, rubbed her arms to keep warm, and slid through her front door without looking back. *Everett will surely thank me someday.*

She completed her task and then plopped down on her beanbag chair for the next hour to get caught up on reading her new art magazines. Just as Lark finished absorbing one of her publications, the doorbell rang. She trotted downstairs and swung the door open, hoping it wasn't Everett ready to pelt her with mothballs. But no one stood on her porch. *Weird.* Just before she shut the door, she found an out-of-the-ordinary kind of object sitting on her welcome mat. *A gavel? Why is there a gavel on my welcome mat? It's from Everett.* She turned it around in her hand. Lark smiled even though she had no clue as to what it meant.

Once back in her loft, she continued to ponder its significance. She looked out her office window and stood in amazement. The blind on Everett's window had been removed. Yes, he must have figured out the mothball gift. He'd understood its meaning, and it had changed his life. Like an epiphany. A blissful, crocodile tear rolled down Lark's cheek. Life was so good.

She believed the gavel was indeed from Everett. He had apparently decided to give her a little funny present in return. *How sweet.* But now for the riddle. What could the gavel represent? Oh, she loved a good brainteaser. *Okay. Gavels are made of wood. Gavels are used in courtrooms.* The full meaning hit her as if she'd been smacked in the mouth by a giant, slushy snowball. What are gavels used for in a court of law? *To silence those who are out of order!*

Chapter 8

The computer screen glowed in front of Everett, keeping him connected to the pulse of life like an umbilical cord. The analogy felt strange and slightly worrisome to him, but some days it felt true.

Everett stared at the floor. The expensive blinds he'd purchased the day before had fallen in the weight of their own gloom and now sat in a strangled mess. He'd been glad when they'd come crashing to the floor and decided to leave them there to remind himself of what could come from decisions made in haste. He'd just have to learn to toss a wave to Lark in the morning and then focus on his work.

Everett glanced at the box of mothballs on his desk and broke out into another smile. He touched the soft ribbon tied on the box. After he'd heard the doorbell earlier, he'd brought the present inside and proceeded to waste an hour trying to figure out what the mothballs were for.

Then he got the meaning. The day of the Igor-gift episode, his jeans had been full of holes. And the mothballs were meant to be comedic in some way. Sounded ludicrous when he'd said it out loud, but he couldn't think of any other answer.

Back to the screen. Amazingly, in spite of all the interruptions from Lark, Everett had still caught up on his work. Of course, he'd worked half the night to accomplish his goals, but he'd been pleased to get a complimentary e-mail from one of his clients, praising him on a job well done.

So, in a flash of something he didn't fully comprehend, he allowed himself a moment of revelry to celebrate. He'd decided to place a gift on Lark's doorstep— an old gag gift from a party. He thought she'd appreciate the meaning. By giving her a gavel, he cleverly welcomed Lark to speak. In other words, she held the reins of speech now.

Is that the doorbell? Lark. He headed downstairs with the box of mothballs. Once at the door, he was surprised to see his principal client, Zeta, standing there on his porch. Her extra tall height loomed over his medium frame. Everett smoothed his blue tie and found his vocal cords. "Zeta? Hi. This is a surprise. A good...one." He wondered if he sounded wooden or anesthetized. He'd had little sleep and no client had ever come to his home before.

"Well, so here you are. Look at this place. I wouldn't have picked this enormous dollhouse as being quite your style. But it's impressive nevertheless." The angles on her face suddenly appeared sharper, and her dark eyes took on their usual narrowing glare. "In fact, maybe we're paying you too much."

Everett tried to laugh, but it came off like a choking cough.

"Well, aren't you going to invite me in?" Zeta stuck a loose strand of black hair into her felt hat.

"Would you like to come in?" Everett knew he sounded more like Igor than a highly paid accountant.

"Maybe. . .just for a moment." Zeta stepped inside, almost pushing him out of the way, and then looked around. "Hmm. Not too bad. But why do all members of the male species feel compelled to buy brown leather?"

What could he possibly say? Everett cleared his throat.

"I brought you the file we discussed." Zeta threw her cape over her shoulder, revealing a bloodred suit. Kind of a post-Dracula look. "You were so close by, I thought I'd drop it by on my way to lunch."

Zeta pulled another frown out of her hat, but he had no idea why. He wondered if he were simply out of practice at reading human emotions since he spent so much time alone. Locked away in his office, dealing mostly with e-mail, maybe he'd lost some people skills. Or perhaps Zeta just needed some lessons in manners. He cleared his throat.

"Do you need a lozenge or something?" Zeta set the file on his entry table.

"No. I'm fine." Just as he was about to ask if she'd like to sit down, the doorbell rang again. He felt some head pain creeping in.

Zeta raised an already arched eyebrow as she stared at the box of mothballs in his hand.

Everett opened the door. Lark stood in front of him looking radiant in a light purple sweater and white jeans as she clung to a rolled up newspaper. "Hi."

Lark smiled at Zeta and then held out the paper to Everett. "I believe someone left this paper on my doorstep. It must be yours." Lark licked her lips. "Have a good day."

Everett took the paper, but wondered why Lark wasn't her bubbly self.

Zeta tapped her foot. "Are you going to introduce me to your neighbor, Everett?"

Why not? What can I possibly lose? After he'd made the formal introductions, Zeta let out a yelp.

"Are you *the* Larkspur Wendell?" Zeta clasped her hand to her throat like a star-struck teen.

Lark hid her hands behind her back and glanced down. "That's me."

Everett noticed Lark's bashfulness. *A new look for her. Kind of cute.*

"I heard you lived here in Eureka Springs." Zeta pointed her red-painted fingernail high in the air with a flourish. "Everett, why didn't you tell me you had such an illustrious neighbor?" She leaned down to Lark. "My daughter has all of Nissa's books, but just between you and me, your illustrations empower them. My daughter has drifted off many a night while looking at those fanciful pictures. Especially the *Electric Seeds* series. We have them all."

"I'm so glad." Lark backed slowly to the door. "If you'd like, I could personally sign some books for your daughter. I always keep a supply at home to give away."

Everett met Lark's gaze, but she didn't smile at him. She stared at the box of mothballs with a forlorn kind of expression.

"Autographed books for my daughter! How wonderful!" Zeta clapped her fists together. "She'll love it. Oh, and I will, too."

"Well, I'll go and get them now. I'll be right back." Lark turned to leave and then whirled back around. "What's your daughter's name?"

"Amelia Stone. Thank you so much."

Lark hurried out the front door, while Zeta turned to Everett. "Well, aren't we full of surprises?"

Everett frowned. Even though Zeta was his most important client, he didn't like being talked to in the third person like a toddler. He set the box of mothballs on the entry table.

"So what's with the mothballs?" Zeta spoke in her usual brusque tone.

Everett swallowed his exasperation. "It's just a funny gift somebody gave me."

Zeta stood silent for a second, looked confused, and then burst into laughter. He'd never heard her laugh before. Guess he'd better count that as a blessing.

"How very clever," Zeta said. "I love it. Mothballs. Definition. A condition of being in storage. You know, you really are too much of a hermit here in your home office."

The conversation felt *way* too personal and more than annoying. Everett glanced in the entry mirror and noticed his face had reddened to a rich, tomato hue. Zeta's rudeness was more than he could stand sometimes, but he was determined to keep his cool. "Larkspur Wendell left the mothballs on my doorstep."

Zeta eyeballed him like Igor's assessing parrot gaze, and then she detonated with another round of laughter. Directed at him. Again. This brief meeting was racing downhill fast. And worst of all, he'd gotten the meaning of the mothball gift all wrong. Maybe it had been more of a putdown than a lighthearted gift between neighbors. His leg began to twitch all on its own again.

After a few more agonizing minutes, Lark tapped on his door and let herself in with a stack of books. She set them in Zeta's waiting arms. "Oh, thank you, Larkspur. May I call you Lark?"

"Yes, of course. I've personally autographed each one and added a little special note in the top one," Lark said.

Zeta's fingers clutched the pile of books as if she were afraid someone would take them from her. "You are a peach for doing this for my daughter."

Everett tuned out for a moment and then suddenly noticed the gavel in Lark's back pocket. She pulled it out and set it on the entry table with all the other assorted items.

Guess Lark didn't think the gift was witty after all. Then as she stared at him, her lovely, brown eyes softened. "Gavels are meant for silencing people. Aren't they?" Her voice sounded more hurt than angry.

Everett turned to Lark. "That's not what I—"

"Okay, I'm lost here," Zeta said. "I tell you what. You can finish this peculiarly stimulating conversation tonight. Everett, why don't you bring Lark with you to our company party? I read that Lark is single, and you have nothing important to do tonight."

"Company party?" Everett asked.

"You know," Zeta said with more than a hint of sarcasm. "Ozark Consulting?"

He'd totally forgotten. But then maybe he'd meant to forget it.

"You mean you hadn't planned on coming tonight at seven?" Zeta asked.

"I've been busy with the move, so I—"

Zeta touched her fingers under her chin in a dramatic gesture. "It's a stylish affair at the Majestic Hotel," she said to Lark. "I can already tell you'd love it. Then I'd get a chance to visit with you some more."

Is she arranging my dating life? He chose not to lash out at Zeta, but he had to admit his job and its handsome salary were being worn down by her edges.

Lark's expression continued to soften when she glanced at him. He thought the look might be one of pity. *Please, any emotion but that one. I may look like a toad next to my boss, but I still have my pride.*

Then Lark smiled at him, a warm and effervescent one. The kind he was growing very fond of. Something thawed between them like two blocks of ice left in the afternoon sun. Everett decided to set his aggravation with Zeta aside and just ask Lark to the party. "I have to admit it's a good idea. Lark, would you accompany me to the party this evening?"

Lark hesitated and then stared at him as if trying to read his expression. "Yes. I'd love to."

Zeta stomped her foot as if she were starting up some Irish dance. "Good. It's settled. I'm off. See you lovebirds tonight."

Everett rubbed the back of his neck.

"By the way, Lark, this is supposed to be our company Christmas party. Everett suggested we schedule it in early November on a Monday evening. Saves money," Zeta said.

Everett groaned inside as he walked Zeta to the front door. With one last salute to her, he shut the door.

"I guess I'd better get going, too." Lark made a few steps toward the front door.

"I wish you'd stay for a bit." Everett wondered what was going through her mind.

Lark turned back to him and smiled. "I like your boss."

Everett could feel his head pound just thinking about Zeta. "I'd better not say anything."

Lark looked concerned. "Is Zeta really that hard to work for?"

Everett wasn't sure how much to tell her. "Let's put it this way. Before she became my boss, I had more hair."

Lark chuckled.

She actually laughed again. A bubbly kind of noise. Not frenzied, but a pleasant sound of contentment. He couldn't even remember the last time he'd made anyone laugh so much. "Would you like to sit down?"

"I don't want to keep you from your work."

"Well, I put in some long hours last night, so I'm pretty much caught up for a little while."

"Okay, then. Maybe I'll stay for just for a minute." Lark eased onto the end of his brown leather couch. She picked up a small brass abacus and studied it.

Everett sat on the opposite side of the couch. They sat in silence for a moment, until he thought of how he wanted to apologize about the gavel. "I wanted to—"

"I'm truly sorry about the mothballs." Lark rubbed her earlobe. "I thought they would be an encouragement. You know, to get out of the house once in a while for some fresh air. I was concerned about you. But it *truly* was none of my business."

"Apology accepted." Everett rested his arm on the back of the couch and then realized he'd made himself too relaxed for what he needed to say. So he leaned forward. But now he couldn't see her. *Oh brother.* He gave up and just looked at her. "The gavel represented a way to welcome you to speak. In other words, 'you hold the reins of speech now.' I wasn't thinking of the other side of the meaning. A comedy of errors here, I guess, but I do apologize."

Lark sighed. " 'Errors like straws upon the surface flow: He who would search for pearls must dive below.' "

"Dryden?" Everett asked. *Or was it Shakespeare?*

"Wow. I'm impressed," Lark said. "I thought for sure you'd say Shakespeare. College literature class I presume?"

"Yeah. Forced at gunpoint by a sweet professor lady who loved English authors. Well, I say sweet. I think she really had a broom in the back."

Lark chuckled.

Oh, how he could drink up her laugher. *Drink?* Should he have offered her something to drink? He suddenly felt as clumsy as Frankenstein trying to learn social skills.

Lark scooted to the edge of the couch and rose. "Thank you for taking the time to let us dive below the straw for pearls."

"You're welcome." Everett got up from the couch. *Guess it's too late to offer beverages.*

Lark set the brass abacus back on the end table. "I admire people who are good with numbers. You were probably born counting your toes."

Everett chuckled, and he noticed how good it felt. "I saw one of your covers when you handed the books to Zeta. It was extraordinary. Were those pictures done in oils, too?"

"No. I do all my illustrations in watercolor. My oils are something I do more for me. By the way, I like your living room," Lark said.

"Thanks." She changed the subject, and he wondered why.

"With all the stone and wood, it makes me think of a vacation home."

"That's why I picked it." Had he been caught staring? Lark looked so beautiful today. Luminous dark hair and eyes that could wake a guy up in the morning better than any shot of espresso. Better than anything, in fact. He'd better not drift any further down that road. Dangerous territory. What had she said? Or had he been talking?

"So are you taking me to the company party to please Zeta?" Lark looked vulnerable as well as cute.

"No," Everett said. "I'm taking you to please myself." *Was that egotistical?*

"Sounds like an honest answer." Lark smiled as she walked to the door. "But I think Zeta railroaded you, so if you want to back out, here's your last chance."

"I don't want to back out," Everett said. "Relaxation tends to be at the bottom of my to-do list, but I really do want some fresh air. . .with you. Maybe you can teach me how to breathe again." Did those words actually come out of his mouth? Maybe there really was a romantic heart beating inside him.

Lark looked over at the corner of the living room where his mother's piano sat with the lid down. Then she smiled at him. "I guess I should go."

Everett opened the door for her, but he didn't want Lark to leave. He wanted to keep listening to whatever she had to say about anything. Her voice had a gentle ebb and flow to it like an ocean's tide. But duty called, especially since Zeta had brought the new files to add to his project.

"I'll pick you up at six thirty. Is that okay?" Everett asked.

"Yes." Lark stepped over the threshold, but when she turned back around, they were suddenly standing close.

"I look forward to this evening," Everett whispered.

Lark blushed when she looked at him.

The rosy color looked so good on her cheeks, he wanted to kiss the very spot he'd made warm by his words. In fact, what fragrance did she wear? Some expensive perfume, no doubt. "Okay." If he were being drugged by the scent, he knew he wouldn't put up a fight.

"Okay," Lark said.

Everett walked her home, which took all of two minutes, and then he settled into his office assimilating Zeta's file into his project like a good little accountant. Suddenly, he wondered if he could get by with a suit for the party or if he was expected to wear a tux. He couldn't even remember the last time he'd worn his tux. The goofy thing probably didn't even fit anymore. Did his sedan have enough gas? And what about flowers? Was he supposed to buy a corsage for Lark, or did that practice go out with the high school prom?

Everett looked over at Lark's office window. He couldn't see her because the sun's brightness had darkened the view inside. He tugged on the ribbon on the mothballs instead, hoping Lark was having just as much trouble concentrating as he was. *In fact, what could she be up to right this minute?*

Chapter 9

L ark went back to her sketchbook and then switched on her French language CD. "*Bon soir!*" she repeated after the teacher. She chuckled. *Who am I kidding?* She couldn't smother the anticipation she felt about the coming evening. Work suddenly felt like going through the motions, but she still tried to concentrate on her charcoal drawing. Half an hour later on the last bit of shading, the doorbell rang.

Everett? Hope he didn't change his mind. Lark flung the door open to find Jeremy standing before her looking ruggedly attractive in his ponytail and scruffy jeans. But then he always looked that way—like he'd just gotten back from bungee jumping in the Grand Canyon. "Welcome! *Soyez le bienvenu!*"

"Thank you. Guess you're working on those French language tapes again." Jeremy rubbed his chin, which seemed to have a perpetual five o'clock shadow.

Lark leaned against the doorframe. "Would you like to come in?"

"Thanks, but I'd better get going."

But you just arrived. Lark blinked hard. "You look sort of expectant."

"Boy, I hope not." Jeremy gave her a smirk.

"I mean, did I forget something?" A sparrow flew overhead looking jittery in the cold. Lark could certainly relate.

"The teen craft fair. Remember? You're the one in charge of signing people up for the pies. Since I have my bike, we can load your Hummer."

Lark's hand flew to her mouth. "Pies? Teen craft fair. I wish I could plead amnesia."

Jeremy frowned. "You're sweet, but you're not going to be able to charm your way out of this one."

"Oh dear. I'm in trouble, aren't I?" Lark asked. *I can't believe I forgot.*

"We've got a snag if you don't have thirty pies."

Lark smiled, wishing she could disappear. "I don't have any. . . I mean I didn't—"

"You didn't sign *anybody* up?" Jeremy's mouth popped open like he'd jumped off a cliff without the cord.

"No. But I can buy a lot of pies at the store. I have money. How many do we need?"

Jeremy scratched his head. "Well, I have to say, one of the reasons people

41

come is because they're looking forward to a thing called *homemade*."

"I'm so sorry. I don't think I can make thirty homemade pies by this evening."

"Not unless you're my grandmother." Jeremy wore his trademark half smile. "Okay, how about this. . .I *buy* the pies. Some good ones, and you'll owe me a dinner this week."

"You drive a hard bargain," Lark said. "Drive-through burgers, right?"

"Wrong. No junk food. I don't care where we go, but it's got to be expensive." Jeremy stuffed his hands in his pockets and cocked his head.

Lark noticed he had his usual stance when he was full of beans. "I'm being robbed here. Police!" She chuckled. "I'm truly sorry. I'm a mess about remembering things sometimes."

"Yes, you are." Jeremy shook his head. "I guess we'll need to get you some string to tie around one of your little fingers."

"Well, they'll probably want a rope for my neck when the parents find out those are fake homemade pies."

"No ropes, but there's still some tar and feathers in the church storeroom for me."

"Oh yeah? And what did *you* do?" Lark asked.

Jeremy shrugged. "I volunteered the teens to be servers at the Valentine's banquet. Without their permission."

"Ooww. You are in so much trouble," Lark said. "And who decided to have the teen craft fair so close to the fall festival?"

"Yeah, I know. Bad move. Bet I don't do that again next year." Jeremy shifted his weight back and forth. "And so what magnificent mischief have you been up to, little lady?"

"Oh, not a lot. Just trying to coax a hermit crab out of his shell."

"And have you succeeded?"

"Maybe," Lark said.

Jeremy put a hand up. "Well, I've learned never to ask details. So I'll pick you up tomorrow night for dinner. Six. Okay?"

"On the back of your bike?" She noticed his usual scent. Eau de motor oil.

Jeremy winked. "No, we can take your Hummer. Okay?"

Lark grinned and watched as Jeremy hopped on his motorbike, revved the engine, and rumbled off with no helmet. His habit of never wearing a helmet did seem kind of reckless, but it was hard to admonish Jeremy for irresponsibility when she had just forgotten all about the teen craft fair.

Pies. Hmm. She shut the door, vaguely recalling signing up. *I wonder what happened.* She glanced at the calendar on the side of her fridge. *Yikes.* She saw the bold words in the Tuesday slot. "Pies, craft fair, don't forget," was the note she'd scrawled to herself. *Maybe I need to get* my *life in order.*

Lark could hear the words *"How are you?"* coming from the kitchen CD player and then *"Comment ca va?" What a good question. How am I anyway?* She felt befuddled about her apparent unreliability and even more confused about her relationship with Jeremy.

The phone rang, and Lark startled. She glanced at the Caller ID as she picked up the phone. Calli was calling from her home in Springdale.

After a few pleasantries, Lark told her all about the day's events. "But I think it all ended well. Don't you?"

"Yeah. I guess so."

"I mean he invited me to the party this evening even though I sent over those mothballs. I still can't believe I did that." Lark groaned.

"I can't either. It's a good thing he didn't think you were crackers. What made you think of mothballs?"

"It was a spur of the moment kind of thing. You know—"

Calli made a comical huffing sound. "Before you had time to pray kind of thing?"

"Hey, are you spreading a little chastisement?" Lark sighed. "Oh well, I deserve it."

"No way, ladybug." Calli did a smacking thing with her lips. "Well, maybe a little."

Lark grinned. "Hey, what's with this ladybug stuff, anyway? Surely I'm not that flighty."

"I wondered when you'd finally ask me," Calli said. "This is a good story, so you'd better sit for this one."

Lark perched herself on a kitchen stool and waited for her friend to continue.

Calli took in a long breath. "Well, one time I was exiting off 540, and I saw this ladybug on my windshield. While I turned all my corners, it held on. No matter what happened, the sweet little thing stayed there fluttering its wings and clinging to dear life. When I got home, I held out my hand, and that ladybug climbed on my fingers and flew away as if it knew all along everything would be okay. With what you went through in your life, I guess it's kind of the way I see you."

"Thanks, Calli. It *is* a good story. Consider yourself hugged." A few tears pooled in Lark's eyes. "By the way, I sure wish you'd move to Eureka Springs."

Calli sniffled. "Find me a good man to marry there, and I guess I'd be forced to move." She blew her nose.

Lark wondered if her friend could be serious.

"Girl, now you know I'm kidding," Calli said.

"I wasn't sure." Lark stifled a laugh.

"You don't have to start setting me up with blind dates like some orthopedic queen."

Lark gasped. "I would never do that."

Calli laughed. "Well, I heard this pregnant pause, so I just thought maybe you were getting one of your little ideas."

"No, it's just indigestion from all the bean burritos we ate last night," Lark said.

After another round of laughs and some sweet good-byes, Lark busied herself by collecting acorns from the backyard. She found several dozen of the little nuts, which had been peeking their heads out of the snow. Lark gathered them up and stuffed them in the pocket of her lavender painting smock.

When she brought her treasures inside, she turned on the kettle for tea and gingerly placed her acorns in an earthenware bowl on the kitchen table. Some of the acorns were missing their little hats, but she thought those looked interesting, too, so she put them all together. After turning off the overhead light, she switched on a freestanding spotlight, which gave the acorns an oblique light of dramatic shadows. *Ahh. Perfect for sketching now.*

But her mind drifted again to the evening ahead. After all, Everett was escorting her to one of the most romantic places in town. She dropped three black currant teabags into her Victorian pot as she thought of the dress she'd wear—a floor-length emerald gown with color-coordinating evening bag and shoes. She laughed at her sudden attention to detail as if she were getting ready for her very first date.

Of course, crowds of people would be at the party. Perhaps even women who'd had a crush on Everett. *A speck of jealousy? This is so not me. Yeah, and I haven't been myself lately either. I guess attraction does that to people. Takes a perfectly sane, sanguine temperament and turns her into a paranoid melancholy. Snap out of it, Lark.* She poured hot water into her little pot, letting the heat relax her face. Maybe what she really needed was a few relaxing hours at a local spa. *A seaweed mask, some eucalyptus steam, and a massage. Oh yeah.*

The teacher on the French language tape said the next two words on her list, *roman* and *ami*, which meant romance and friend. Lark hurled an acorn at the CD player. Those two words were beginning to gnaw at her spirit whether in French or in English. They unfortunately represented the difference between Jeremy and Everett. And it broke her heart. After meeting Everett, she knew Jeremy would be just a good friend now. And no more.

Lark would always think of Jeremy as a great guy. They'd prayed together. Laughed a lot. And there'd even been a spark or two. But now she'd experienced the difference between intense fondness and what? Better not go there quite yet. Lark covered the pot with her mother's old, knitted cozy to keep in the heat.

While the tea steeped, she started her sketch of the acorns.

But with Everett, the attraction and the interest were growing by the hour, and she couldn't even transpose all her feelings into plain words. If all those mysteries *could* be examined, would one even want to know? Would people truly desire to dissect such a splendid gift from God? It would be like explaining the dynamics of a rainbow. Understanding every detail of its prismatic effects would not make a rainbow any more beautiful.

Lark poured her tea as she looked at her sketch. *Not bad so far. Perhaps better than the last one.* Maybe she could do a series of nature greeting cards using charcoal. Interesting thought. She did have a publisher some months ago who'd asked her to send some samples, but she'd never had the time.

She fiddled with the shading, smudging it, to give the picture more dimension. The steam curled up from her teacup. Black currant. Fragrant and fruity. She took a slow sip.

One renegade acorn suddenly fell away from the rest, so she placed it back with the cluster and then reflected on the day Everett had come to live on her street. She'd wondered how God would allow Everett Holden to change her life or how she would change his. It was happening, but not quite how she'd expected. She had a feeling now they'd be a bit more than friends.

Oh, phooey on the sketch. Her mind had gone to mush. She might as well shower and get ready for the evening. If she dressed early it would be as if she could make the evening come sooner. She chuckled at the silly thought.

Lark stood in her bedroom and studied her gown hanging by the closet. The breathtaking dress had a dark green, velvet bodice. Sheer silk of a paler hue flowed from the waist like a stream. She'd found the little gem on a clearance rack in Springdale, but it fit her figure as if it had been made for her. *How do you say* dreamy *in French?*

After Lark showered, she lifted and pinned her dark locks up in an elegant swirl. When she was in high school, her mother had taught her how to fix her hair for special dates. On those evenings, her mother brushed her long hair and hummed softly. It had felt so good and so comforting. What she wouldn't give for one of those moments to come again. *No, Lark, you're not going to let yourself cry.* She sniffled a bit. In the next breath, she hummed one of the songs her mother loved: "Go Tell It on the Mountain."

After a few more rounds of singing and lotions and primping and jewelry, she gazed into her full-length mirror at all her efforts. *Okay, not bad.* "Well, what do you think, Igor? Do I look pretty?"

"Pretty," Igor's one word was just enough.

"Thank you, Igor."

"Thank you, Igor."

Lark laughed and glanced at herself in the mirror again. Like Cinderella stepping into her coach, all was in readiness. She just hoped the evening would go better for her than it had for the fairytale heroine.

Well, now she could just sit down, twiddle her thumbs, and look over a coffee table book until Everett arrived. She eased down on the couch so as not to pull too hard on the bodice or crumple the silk. She flipped nonchalantly through a book on European castles. *Yes. Spectacular. It even comes with a moat.* Calli would certainly enjoy selling it. She'd say, "Your own unique security system." She thumped her finger on what was left of the castle's turret and then looked at the time. A little after six o'clock.

Moving right along. The castles of England. Okay. She looked more closely at the photo of a big, brooding castle on a hill. Lark slammed the book shut. She'd never been good at killing time. It was much too valuable to waste. She just wasn't used to getting ready for a date so early or fussing over anything.

In fact, so much of her career had come so easily, she'd let herself slide into a blithe approach to life. She wondered if the ease also allowed her to slip into foolhardiness when she wasn't paying attention.

But this evening's preparations had been anything but careless. She'd taken great pains in getting ready for what she hoped would be a perfect date with Everett. Like in a fairy tale, a classic evening they would never forget.

Chapter 10

The phone rang, making her jump. Again. *That's it. I'm going to turn down the volume on that thing.*

She decided not to rush to the phone but instead let the answering machine pick it up. But when she heard Skelly's panic-stricken voice, she jumped up from the couch and sped to the phone. In doing so, her left heel caught on the hem of her gown. She knew she could either let it rip or fall hard on her hands and face. In a split second decision, she righted herself, letting the silk rip. What an unhappy sound. Lark cringed.

By the time she'd gotten to the phone, Skelly had hung up. But she'd heard enough of the dilemma. Her beloved pet, Picasso, was out on the loose again, like a fugitive duck, nourishing Skelly's garden without his permission. Picasso was a true escape artist. She should have named him Houdini. Okay, so what could she do now?

Better assess the damage on my dress first. Not bad. Fortunately, she had some tiny safety pins to fix it with. As she reached into the kitchen junk drawer she got an idea. Just a little idea. But it had potential. *I could just lift up my gown, go out on my driveway, and call to Picasso. I'll bet I can get him to come back in with just a gentle reprimand.*

Since she'd once shamed Picasso back into his pen with a shake of her finger and a scowl, she felt confident of her plan. She swung open the front door, and sure enough, there was Picasso happily scurrying away from Skelly as he tried to coax him in the other direction.

Okay, I can do this. Lark raised her skirts and headed outside, scuttling like a crab in her high heels. No need for a coat. She'd only be out for a minute.

Even though it was already dark outside, the streetlights illuminated the whole area. Once she'd made it to the end of her driveway, she decided to try the soft approach first. "Picassooo. Sweeety. Come on in now. You've had your fun outing."

Picasso got one glance at Lark and headed toward Timbuktu. He quacked and waddled down the street so swiftly, he'd be out of sight before long. *And just when I'm about to have the date of my life. Oh well, it can't get any worse.*

"Oh, all dressed up," Skelly hollered. "Hate to get your pretty duds all messed up. I can chase after him."

Skelly's face appeared flushed as if he'd been trying to corral Picasso for some time.

"No, please don't. You know what the doctor said about your heart."

But in spite of her cautions to him, Skelly marched down the middle of the street, his elbows swinging as he called out Picasso's name.

Then she remembered a trick she'd used with her first pet duck. Yes. She needed the convincing boom of the megaphone she'd used in her college cheer-leading days. It was at least worth a try. She clattered on her heels back up to the house, found the megaphone on the bottom shelf of the entry closet, and clopped back down the driveway. Lark flipped the switch on the horn, and it squeaked to life. Suddenly like magic, she remembered the roar of the crowd from college—the students she'd revved up to a feverish pitch. The rush of winning. She wondered if she still had it in her. She lifted the megaphone to her mouth and announced, "Okay. Picasso. This is Lark speaking. Let's bring yourself on home now. You can do this, Picasso. Let's go. Let's go. Let's go!"

As if on some unexplainable cue, Picasso stopped in mid-waddle in the center of the street. He turned around, lowered his head, and began his descent from rapture. Skelly turned around, shrugging his shoulders at her. Then he laughed until his whole body quaked.

Hey. Kind of fun, but I hope Everett isn't watching. Probably wouldn't come off too romantic, all gussied up in velvet and rhinestones while hollering at a duck through a megaphone.

When Picasso toddled up to her, she reached down to stroke his neck. He felt as soft as her velvet. "Okay, little guy. Come on. I don't know how you got out of your cage again, but you have got to stop this. Your home is so nice and woodsy." Lark continued to murmur soft assurances as she lured him into the backyard. "It's full of your favorite treats. Isn't that right?" She reached inside the backdoor and flipped on all the backyard lights.

Picasso looked back at her with a darling expression. *Ducks are so cute.* She was such a sucker. But Picasso knew the fun ride was over. "Yes, sweetie. Time to go home." She closed the gate and secured it with extra heavy wire. There. Mission accomplished.

But somewhere in leading Picasso to the backyard, she'd forgotten to keep the flowing silk of her skirt draped over her arm. She hesitated, but knew she'd have to make an assessment. Slowly she moved her gaze downward. Some of the trim of her gown was splattered with muddy snow and white gooey duck drippings. "Picasso! You scalawag! You have ruined my first, and now probably my last, date with Everett."

As if knowing his guilt, Picasso began quacking anxiously around in his home.

"It's okay," Lark said. "Well, no, it isn't." She lowered her head, wondering how things could have gone so wrong so quickly.

The wind had picked up, and as always she had no coat on. She shivered as she trudged back toward the house. She could always put on another gown and shoes. But it wouldn't match her jewelry and eye shadow. *Get a grip, Lark. You've never cared about that sort of thing in your life. Guess I need to call Calli and have her slap me around to knock some sense into me. It's what friends are for after all.*

Okay. Focus. Another gown? *What time is it?* With lightning speed, she hurried into the kitchen and looked at the clock. Six twenty-nine. She had sixty seconds. *Oh dear.*

The doorbell rang. She popped in the powder room to look in the mirror. *Yikes.* She winced. Her hair looked like she'd been riding on the back of Jeremy's motorbike. For hours. She slogged to the door, opened it, and waited to hear how many creative excuses Everett could come up with as to why their date should be postponed. . .forever.

Chapter 11

Everett tried hard not to stare. But Lark stood there with her hair departing in several directions, none of which seemed to be the right ones. And her dress appeared soiled. A lone tear rolled down her cheek. He couldn't stand her distress a moment longer.

Within an instant, Everett came through the doorway and stood in front of her. He was close enough to feel Lark's breath on his face. *I barely know her. Would she want me to comfort her?* She didn't seem to object to his nearness, so he pulled out his handkerchief and wiped away her tears. Her skin felt so soft and her expression so appealing and feminine, he wanted to kiss her. But he didn't want to ruin the moment. "You must really love your duck," Everett said.

"You saw that?" Lark took a step back.

Everett slowly nodded.

"So what did you see, exactly?"

"Only what happened in your backyard. I heard you yell, 'Picasso! You scalawag!' And then something about him ruining your date with me."

Lark let out a tiny moan. "You could hear that?"

"Well, I was in my office, and I looked down when I heard a commotion." He smiled.

"Oh, well." Lark shrugged. "What can I say?"

"I would have come to your aid, but you already had him secured in his pen," Everett said. "Hey, you know, I thought I heard a megaphone earlier, too. Did you actually use one of those things to call him in?"

Lark nodded.

"I guess it worked." Everett noticed her blush again. He wouldn't want to take advantage of her in such a fragile moment, so he stepped back. "Would you still like to go to the party?"

Lark blew her nose into his handkerchief, sounding like a dainty foghorn. "If you don't mind me cleaning up and changing."

"Everyone's always late to these things." Everett hoped to make her feel at ease.

Lark sniffled. "I guess we could come in fashionably late then."

"Sounds good to me."

Lark started to hand him his handkerchief back and then stopped. "Guess I'd better wash this first." She hurried off into another part of the house. After a few seconds, she peeked back around the corner. "Please, make yourself at home."

Everett could feel his Blackberry in the pocket of his tux, even though he'd promised himself to keep it at home. *Must have picked it up without thinking.* Surely he could have disengaged himself from his world for a few hours. Guess not.

He glanced around the room at all the paintings. Lark had her signature at the bottom of many of them. Everett studied a wedding scene, which appeared to be set in the Ozark Mountains. A bride and her groom kissed in front of a quaint chapel with all the wedding party gazing on in delight. He was amazed at how much joy and laughter filled her paintings.

Then he took note of a still life of fruit. *Incredible!* It looked so visually accurate, it seemed as if he could reach in and remove one of the apples. Lark had an amazing talent. It made him think of his sister, Greta. He shook his head and moved on.

Lark had some prints of the masters on display as well as her own. He recognized the Mona Lisa. The woman certainly had an interesting expression. In fact, it reminded him just a bit of Larkspur's winsome smile.

The living room was also full of family photos. He walked over to the fireplace and picked up a framed photo off the mantle. In the picture Lark seemed to be in her late teens, and she stood between an older couple. Had to be her parents. She had her mother's eyes and her father's light, olive skin. Lark appeared cheery then as well. Maybe even more so. Her parents held her in a close hug as if she were a treasure. Anyone could tell they loved each other very much. He wondered if Lark's parents lived in Eureka Springs and if she visited with them a lot.

Everett looked at his watch. He thought it was a shame on one of his rare evenings out he'd be forced to share his date with a crowd of people, some of whom would be strangers. The minute they'd see the dazzling Lark, they'd be slinking over for introductions. And then Zeta would want to have her chunk of Lark's time.

Funny how life changes. Only a few days ago, he would have cooked up ways to avoid Lark and, well, all of humanity in general. But something felt different inside him. Something had willingly shifted, yet he also felt the uneasy kind of mental jostling that tends to drive a numbers-junkie toward the edge. But then maybe he'd forgotten that the view outside his precise perimeters was far more interesting. Without thinking, his hand went to his heart. He just hoped Lark came with a survival guide.

Everett puttered around a bookshelf, noting the dust on the shelves and the rows of children's books. He pulled a few books out until he found one Lark had illustrated. *In a Giddy Pickle. Intriguing title.* He studied the cover and then the drawings inside. There could be no doubt; she had a God-given talent.

Lark stepped out from her bedroom and sort of swished toward him in a long dress.

Everett's hand went right back to his heart. "Oh, wow."

Once in front of him, Lark grasped the sides of her dress and swirled around in a circle.

She is a vision as they say. A beautiful apparition in blue. He wasn't even sure he could describe the radiance of the color of her dress, so he just stared for a moment as he tried to think of what to say. "Your gown. It looks like the wings of a butterfly. You know the iridescent. . .dust stuff?" *Oh brother. Maybe I should have just used an old standby.* "You look beautiful," Everett said with all the sincerity he could surrender. It must have been the right words because a lovely smile started on Lark's lips and then lit up her whole face.

"And you look very handsome in your tux," Lark said.

"Thank you. I rarely use it." He held up Lark's book in his hands. "This is brilliant."

"Thanks." She bit her lower lip and said no more.

"Do you have a coat?"

"Yes. It would be nice to wear it for a change." Lark opened the hall closet, and she handed him a black, velvet cape. Once he'd wrapped the softness around her shoulders, he wanted to hold her close, but he kept telling himself timing was everything. He stepped away to safer ground and cleared his throat again. At this rate, his throat would be sore in ten minutes.

There would be a hug and maybe a kiss or two if all went well. He hoped it would. Not just for the kiss, but because he could already feel some kind of emotional free fall coming on by just looking into those gloriously impish, brown eyes of hers. He couldn't tell for sure what he felt, but if he had any hopes of a parachute nearby with the words *common sense* written on it, he was hopelessly out of luck.

With his hand guiding Lark at the small of her back, he walked her out to his new sedan.

"Thanks for having your car right here and all warmed up," Lark said. "That's nice."

Hmm. She noticed. As he tucked her and her frothy gown into the passenger side of his sedan, he noticed her perfume again. *What police squad would ever need tear gas? They could just hose the criminals down with this stuff, and every last one of them would be incapacitated. Should I say that? Naw.*

Everett scooted in under the wheel and settled into the leather seat. He gazed at her and smiled. She was such a pleasure to look at it was hard to stop himself from staring.

"I was noticing your CD selection," Lark said. "I love piano jazz. Maybe it's the kind of music you should take up if you start taking piano lessons."

"Piano lessons?" He shook his head. "I don't think so. I took a few when I was a kid. But I don't play."

Lark turned toward him. "But did you like it?"

Everett couldn't remember ever thinking about it. At least not for a long time. He'd locked those experiences away with his other family memories. "It was all right." He recalled his teacher, Mrs. Musgrove, bragging on how fast he'd caught on. "No, I guess it was more than just all right. My mind enjoyed figuring out the mystery of it." He laughed. "That's the way I saw all those black and white keys. Like a grand puzzle to be mastered. And when I did, people seemed to enjoy it."

Lark touched his arm. "So you took pleasure in it."

Everett thought again for a moment. "I did. But I guess my approach didn't have much bravura." He backed out onto Whispering Lane and headed toward downtown.

"Oh, but people who are good at math can also be wonderful musicians."

"I've heard that somewhere before." *Oh yeah. Mrs. Musgrove.* Everett flipped on his signal light. "So do you feel the same way about the guitar? Like it's a brainteaser?" He couldn't believe he was talking music. *Pretty artsy for a left-brain guy like me.*

"No, not really." Lark shook her head. "I thought it was a good way to communicate what I felt in here." She pointed to her heart.

Everett liked the way she expressed herself. "So do you like all kinds of music?" he asked as he maneuvered through the winding streets, still marveling at the way the homes hugged the sides of the cliffs.

"Yes," Lark said. "But mostly I love Christian rock."

"So I noticed." Everett grinned at her.

Lark's head went down in a cute act of contrition. "I'm sorry about that."

"Well, my music was just as loud," Everett said. "By the way, you have talent. Why didn't you pursue a music career?"

"I would have loved to, but I decided long ago there were only so many hours in a life. There just wasn't enough time to do everything well. Or even two things well enough to do them professionally."

"You're right about life having a limited number of hours." Perhaps it's why he guarded his time so cautiously. Or *rabidly* as he overheard someone say at a meeting once. "Thank you for sharing some of those hours with me." Everett saw Lark do the lighting up thing again, and it energized him. With other women, he'd never said anything charming, but then again, maybe he just hadn't been motivated. Until now. He slipped a CD into the player. Piano music swirled around them like a soft breeze. "I can tell you like art," Everett said. "I guess you chose well. How did you get started?"

"Well, I got an assignment right after I graduated from the University of Arkansas, and the book became so successful, I kept getting more and more work. They were all in watercolors, which I enjoy. And then I've also supplemented my income with a trust fund as well as some of my other investments. It's worked well. . .*so* far."

"What do you mean?" Everett asked.

"I don't have as much work as I used to, so I need to make some choices."

"Career choices?" He wanted to study her expression but felt he'd better keep his eyes on the road.

"Yes. I've been painting with oils for a long time now. That's my true passion. I nearly have enough pieces for a show. But I just need more time before I let someone see them. I mean someone from a gallery, that is. Change is always a little scary." Lark smiled but without her usual enthusiasm.

"That doesn't really sound like you." Did he know her well enough to say those kinds of things? "The oil paintings I saw in your office and living room are extraordinary." *Just as you are,* he wanted to add, but thought it might sound too cheesy. "I'm not an artist, but I think you should share your gift with the world."

Lark looked at him as if he'd said something shocking. "I can't believe what you just said. It's the same thing my best friend told me." She folded her hands in her lap. "I guess I should listen. It's true, I would be free to follow my own vision rather than follow someone's text. Although illustrating has been good work." She fingered her pearl bracelet.

Everett wondered if the pearls were a gift from her biker friend.

"I'd love to know all about your mom and dad," Lark said.

Everett could tell she wasn't just making obligatory date conversation, but he would have given up his whole CD collection if Lark hadn't asked that one question. He generally didn't go out with a woman more than once or twice, so it rarely came up.

"You don't have to talk about it." Lark licked her lips. "I understand."

Everett doubted Lark could identify with his situation, but he felt it was good of her to let it go. He mulled over Lark's question again while he listened quietly to the music. He had to admit, her question had been a sincere one, and he suddenly felt compelled to give her an answer. "My parents and sister died some years ago. Car accident. Icy roads." He switched the music off.

Silence filled the car. Everett knew why people shouldn't talk about such topics. What could be accomplished by dredging up misery? The pain needed to stay buried.

Lark reached out and touched his arm. "That's how I lost my parents, too."

"Really? What? I mean, did I hear you right?" Everett asked. *Oh brother.* He'd lost all his smooth conversational skills.

"My dad sold insurance here. He never made a fortune, but people loved him. And my mom and I were best friends. We always laughed a lot and sang songs together. Until a drunk driver snatched them away from me. The two great loves of my life gone instantly."

Everett swallowed hard. He'd had no idea. "I'm very sorry, Lark." Maybe she really did understand. At least about the loss.

"I miss them." Lark stared out the window.

Perhaps she expected his sad story in return. But if timing were everything, this wasn't it. In fact, he couldn't be certain the time would ever be right.

She smiled. "But I know where my parents are. So I try to do as they would do: Grieve a little and live at lot." Lark laughed. "Believe me, that is *so* my mother." She shook her head and smiled as if she were remembering them again.

Everett tried not to grimace. How could she be so glib about it? Or had she simply made peace with the circumstances? He breathed a sigh of relief when the hotel came into view.

"I've been to The Majestic a few times over the years," Lark said. "The hotel was built in 1887, but I think it's still so lovely. Just like the whole area. Did you know we're called Little Switzerland of America, and that we're—" She chuckled. "Sorry, I get carried away."

Everett pulled under the porte cochere. "No, I just think you love living here."

"I grew up in the Ozark Valley. It's truly my home." Lark touched the window as she gazed beyond the hotel.

He wondered how it felt to have such passion for a place.

A parking attendant suddenly appeared out of nowhere and rushed over to open Lark's door. When Everett got to her side, he offered his arm, feeling good he hadn't become a total thug over the years.

Lark circled her arm through his. "Thank you."

They strolled to the entrance as two doormen opened the massive, beveled-glass doors. Elegance seemed to usher them in as they stepped into the foyer. Expensive tapestries lined the walls, and silk rugs adorned marble floors. Everett felt himself nodding his approval.

Lark gazed upward. "I love chandeliers."

Everett thought maybe she was trying to drum up some small talk.

Lark's finger tapped her cheek. "Especially ones like this chandelier." She pointed upward. "It's an original Moiré, made of a rare, hand-cut and polished quartz, reminiscent of the rock crystal chandeliers of the sixteenth century."

Okay. Guess that wasn't small talk.

"Yes, very nice." Lark winked at him.

Or is she pulling my leg? He knew he was grinning like a schoolboy, but he couldn't stop himself. After checking their coats in, he steered Lark toward the banquet room where the party was being held. Everett glanced around, casing the situation. He could smell the usual party smells—people perfumed to the hilt as well as trays of steaming food at the buffet tables. Live jazz and bursts of laughter spilled around the room.

Company parties are always such circuses, Everett thought. One minute people were being pigheaded at departmental meetings and then suddenly jovial at company get-togethers. Guess he'd become a cynic at the ripe old age of thirty-five.

Okay, the big question: Who would run into them first? Oh boy, here comes Marge, the magpie. At least that was the nickname the other women at work used behind her back. But unfortunately Marge had earned it. She *never* stopped moving her mouth. Marge bounced up to them in her psychedelic dress. Somehow he felt sorry for her, but he hadn't a clue how to help her.

After the intros, Marge began her spiel. "I love your evening gown, Larkspur. Where did you buy it? Don't you just love it? It looks so perfect on you. Just like those fairy princess gowns we put on our dolls when we were little. You know, the ones with the billowy chiffon and all the little sparkles. Did you play with dolls, too, Lark?"

Everett felt a little bug-eyed, but Lark listened graciously to the voluminous questions. Eventually, his brain started absorbing the chatter as white noise. The ordeal took exactly eleven minutes.

When Marge was spent, Lark touched the woman's arm and said, "It's so nice to have someone ask me questions. Usually at parties people just talk about themselves."

Marge's chin did a shake. Was she about to rupture into tears of joy? He couldn't tell. "No one has ever said that to me before," she said with her hands gathered up to her heart. "Thank you. . .Lark."

They moved on through the crowd, leaving behind Lark's new friend for life—a woman named Marge. He just shook his head in amazement. *Oh no.* A man named Jamison Peabody moved toward them at an alarming rate. He was the guy at work who caused the fastest clearance of any break room. People ran from him like swimmers fled from jellyfish at the beach. It wasn't just the odors fermenting on Jamison's body, but the fact that he could literally corner people in thirty seconds flat. Give or take a few nanoseconds.

This is just great. Jamison lumbered over and stood right in front of them. In fact, so close, he'd burst their spatial bubble. Apparently, Jamison didn't realize his abdomen extended so far out they were close enough to do a three-way hug. Once they'd entered the point of no return, Everett made the appropriate introductions.

Jamison slimed Lark's hand with a kiss as he made a slight rap of his heels together and bow of his head.

Lark made no gestures of disgust but instead rose to the occasion and curtsied and smiled.

Jamison looked like he was going to pass out from elation. He added a few chortles, which made him nearly explode out of his cummerbund.

"What do you do at Ozark Consulting?" Lark asked.

Jamison began the tale of his brilliant skills, how he was the mastermind behind the company, the brain of the operation and true pulse of the company. In other words, he was a computer programmer. But Everett could tell from Lark's questions, she wasn't just nodding politely at Jamison, she was actually listening.

Everett squelched a yawn but caught a point or two of the dialogue. Jamison actually had some good ideas, but his social skills were so misplaced he'd never been able to relate his ideas to anyone of importance. Maybe he could mention Jamison at a meeting or two.

Everett moaned audibly when he saw the infamous Zeta bulldoze toward them through the crowd like a snowplow.

"There you both are," Zeta said. "With Jamison?"

"Hi. Good to see you," Lark said. "You know, Jamison was just telling us of his ideas to improve bandwidth on your corporate network. You must be very proud to have such talented people working here."

Zeta made all sorts of movements with her mouth. First a look of shock, followed by a glimmer of revulsion. After a brief sputter of confusion, she settled on what all big shots liked to land on. Awareness. "Of course, Jamison is very good. I always keep alert of new talent." Jamison then shook hands with Zeta, said something miraculously quick-witted, and walked away a new man.

Life was full of surprises. At least it was while standing near Lark. Maybe Everett really needed to just buy a ticket and watch from the stands. But for now, his mouth felt like paper. The rough parchment kind. "Would you like something to drink?"

"Root beer, please." Lark smiled. "Lots of ice."

"Oh, icy root beer sounds *so* yummy," Zeta said. "But I'm afraid I'm dieting. Definition: eating flavored air."

Zeta released one of her laughs, and Everett willed himself not to cringe. In fact, he decided to take the high road and smile at her.

"Nothing for me." Zeta shot Everett a cagey look.

"Okay." He noticed when Zeta opened her mouth, her bright red lipstick stuck to her canine teeth. He decided not to take that one any further in his mind.

Everett tromped away, deliberately straightening his shoulders. *Great. I get the evil eye for the kind act of offering a cool beverage.* That's Zeta. The woman who had made his professional life *miserable.* Definition: to be made exceedingly uncomfortable. Kind of like trying to hug a porcupine.

Somebody he knew said, "Hey. How's it going?" Everett was about to tell him, but the guy just kept on trucking toward the food tables. Oh, well. What did he expect when he hadn't spent any real time chewing the fat with these people before?

When Everett had finally made it through the drink line, he stood there for a moment observing Lark from a distance. A few days before he wouldn't have thought to leave a fellow human being alone with Zeta, but somehow he knew all would be well. Lark could handle herself better than he could. She seemed like some elfin creature from those animated movies he watched as a kid. Lovely. Mischievous. Magical. Maybe he was good at romantic feelings when he had something to work with.

Uh-oh. Why did Zeta look so ecstatic, and why was Lark hugging her again? Zeta appeared to be crying. What in the world was happening over there? Should he barge in, or let the scene play itself out?

Everett took a sip of his cold sparkling water. He wished he could pour it over his head instead. He hadn't realized until now how exhausted he felt from worrying about losing his biggest client as well as his big salary. "The more one gains, the more one has to lose," his father used to say. And he certainly had a lot to lose.

But no matter the status of his coffers, he'd had about enough of Zeta. Surely he could express his views without getting fired. Some way to keep her from reducing him to a sniveling fool. He strode toward them as his hot hands gripped the cold glasses. Warning bells went off in his head. The pile of bills at home needing to be paid came into his mind's eye. *You're a Christian. Don't say anything rash. Nothing you'll regret.*

The second Everett arrived in their midst, Zeta threw her arms around him. His arms rose in the air to keep the drinks from spilling. The expression on his face must have looked peculiar. He would give a sizable chunk of his income to know exactly what Lark had done.

"I guess I'd better explain," Zeta said as she disengaged. "I've wanted to quit my job for ages. I already had my resignation written, but I just wasn't quite ready to mail it. All month I've had confirmation after confirmation. And now Lark has just given me yet another one. It's finally time to leave this miserable job and live my dream. So I quit." Zeta revved up her machine-gunfire laugh again, and Everett thought it was the most inspiring and lyrical sound he'd ever heard.

Chapter 12

Amidst the shock of it all, Everett lost the motor control in his fingers. The drinks fell out of his hands and crashed to the floor, sending wetness and shards of glass everywhere.

Suddenly, men in crisp, white outfits came to his aid. They seemed to emerge right out of the mirrored walls and within seconds had whisked away all debris with a broom, dustpan, and mop.

Zeta took in a deep breath. "Well, I guess my announcement comes as a bit of a surprise to *some* people." She laughed, only this time she sounded more ladylike. "My vision has always been to open a day spa, but I always got sidetracked with making money instead of doing what I was born to do. I've saved a fortune, and now it's time to take a chance. To live!" Her voice had escalated to the point of drawing a small crowd.

Everett shook Zeta's hand and wished her the best. He'd no idea she hated her job, but it must have explained her unpleasant attitude.

"And so now I must take my leave." Zeta's hands went up in a flourish as she made a theatrical exit out the doors like an aging actress on her last curtain call.

Everett felt grateful he had nothing else in his hands to drop. He stood in stunned silence along with Lark and a few of his coworkers. They mumbled words of surprise and relief. He tapped his face.

Lark took told of Everett's hands. "Are you okay? You look a little pale."

He looked at Lark but wondered if he was really focusing. Who was this woman? The night suddenly had a *Twilight Zone* kind of feel to it. Really good, but really weird. What a strange marvel had appeared in his life.

"I had no idea Zeta would do what she did," Lark said. "One minute I was telling her what a good time I had at one of our spas, and the next moment, she was crying. I hope you're not upset with me."

Everett opened his mouth to talk, but nothing came out. He felt overcome with gratitude. He hadn't lost his biggest client, only Zeta.

"Maybe we need some fresh air," Lark said.

Sounded good. Everett hurried back for their coats and then escorted her right through the French doors and out into the garden. It was time to give Lark a big kiss or a large amount of cash. Whichever she'd prefer. He kept them walking until they were alone. The full moon dazzled the night sky, the fountain burbled and splashed, and he couldn't remember the last time he'd felt so good. "Who *are* you?" Everett laughed.

"I am Larkspur Camellia Wendell." She seemed to enjoy his odd question. "My mother loved flowers."

"I guess so." He stepped closer to her. "It's a *beautiful* name." He needed to come up with a new word besides *beautiful*. *Mental note: Buy thesaurus.*

"Thank you. I like your name, too. And your parents and grandparents must have liked it, too, since you are the third. Did everyone end up calling you Junior?"

"No. They tried. But I put a stop to it. Too infantile."

"I agree," Lark said. "So are you wanting to name your son Everett Holden IV?"

"No. It wouldn't even be a good name for a dog, let alone a kid." He'd never understood the need for male family members to have the same name. It reminded him of dogs marking their territory. It was a ludicrous custom.

"So. . .do you like. . .kids?" Lark fingered her earring.

Everett thought for a moment. A long moment. Slowly, he nodded. "Yeah. I like kids. Always thought maybe I'd want a couple someday."

"Yeah. Me, too," Lark said. "I'm curious about something else. Did you have a dog growing up?"

"Boy, and I thought *I* had all the questions." Everett smiled. "Yeah. I had a dog when I was a kid. But I've never had one as an adult." He put his hands in his coat pockets. "They require a lot of attention."

"And that's why Igor is living with me instead of you?"

Everett nodded. "I'm sorry. I don't have a lot of time for a pet."

"Well then, what makes you think you'd have time for a child?" Lark teased.

Oh, doesn't she have all the piercing questions? Everett took in a breath of air. "It's a matter of priorities, I guess. Pets aren't a priority for me. Children would be." He suddenly wondered how committed he was to those words. She seemed bent on having him think through his whole life-agenda in one evening.

Lark gave him a smile. "Since you're busy, I'm so glad you had time to talk to me."

"Well, I guess I hoped there'd be a bit more than just talk." *Did those words actually come out of my mouth?*

Lark's mouth came open in surprise. "Are you flirting with me, Mr. Holden?"

Everett wondered if his timing was off. "Maybe a little."

"Maybe you'd better tell me about your objectives so I can decide if I approve." Lark pretended to straighten his bowtie.

He decided to throw caution to the wind and just say it out loud. "Well, I'd like to kiss the palm of your hand." *Did that come off nerdy or appealing?*

"That's honest." Lark fluttered her eyelashes. "Permission granted."

Everett reached for her hands and held them for a moment. Warm and soft. The way he imagined them. He brought one of her hands to his lips, slowly turned it over, and did just as he'd promised. When he looked back at Lark's face, she had a contented expression. "I guess I didn't answer your question from before. I'm not upset with you about Zeta. I won't lose Ozark Consulting as a client just because she's leaving."

"I guess you don't seem too upset." Lark grinned.

Everett stared at her lips. "In fact, you seemed to fix my life tonight. As well as Zeta's. How do you do that?"

Lark stepped back as if trying to regain her composure. "I'm just being me. It's what my mother always said. 'Just be yourself, Lark. Love people, and most of the time, they will love you back.'"

"And has it been true?" Everett asked.

"Not always. But enough."

Everett watched Lark as she moved her cape aside to touch the petals of a rather delicate-looking flower that had survived the freeze. Some of the fabric on her dress billowed outside her velvet cape. The gauzy material stirred around her in a breeze, making her look more like a fantasy than anything real. He thought she must have lived a pretty sheltered life. But he didn't want to spoil a really good moment, so he let it go.

"What will happen now?" Lark asked. "Do you know who your new contact at Ozark Consulting will be?"

"Well, I guess Bard Langley would be up next for Zeta's job. And that would be a good thing because we've always gotten along well."

"I'm glad for you."

Yes. I'm very glad for myself, too. He had this sudden urge to buy something for Lark. A boat or a house. . .or a diamond ring. *Come on, old boy. Not ready for that one yet.* But he *was* ready for a kiss. And this time not the palm of her hand. Without wasting another minute, Everett traced a finger down her cheek. He then leaned over and brushed his lips across her face.

Lark's eyes drifted shut as he moved his mouth over hers. His heart rate sped up as if he were sprinting. *That's never happened before.* In spite of the cooling air, Everett broke out into a sweat. *Am I having a heart attack? Mental note: Better make an appointment for an EKG.* But whatever was happening, he didn't want to let go of Lark. He held her close as she lifted her arms around his neck. Her breathing changed tempo, and he wondered if she were experiencing the same sort of alarm bells.

Then a floating sensation washed over him as if he'd been set adrift in a small boat. Well, floating felt better than a heart attack. From somewhere in his head an old mantra came back to taunt him. *Passive resistance and neutrality. I can't believe those were my earlier words concerning this dazzling woman in my arms.* Whatever resistance he had left was asked to leave.

When the kiss ended, Lark looked dazed, almost breathless. "That was the most wonderful kiss I've ever had," she said.

Everett felt pleasantly startled. He wondered if people on first dates were supposed to reveal their private thoughts. "Really?" he asked, without thinking.

"Electrifying." Lark looked down as if she were suddenly a little embarrassed.

"You mean like touching a light socket?" He grinned.

Lark laughed. "No."

"Yeah, well I had this fast heartbeat thing going," Everett said. "And it certainly doesn't seem cold out here anymore."

"Well, it wouldn't kill you if we kissed again, would it?"

"I guess there's one way to find out." He leaned in for a bit more of the sweet stuff.

When Everett released her, Lark looked at him as if she were trying to read his thoughts. Without either of them saying a word, they both sat down on a nearby bench. She looked up at the moon.

Everett followed her gaze.

"It's so lovely. What do *you* see, Mr. Holden?"

"Well, I suppose there are seas, craters. . .scars." Everett wondered what she meant. "You know, moon parts."

"Close your eyes," Lark said.

Everett hesitated and then complied with her request. The sounds around him changed. He could hear her breathing. Soft. Steady. Then he felt the tiniest kiss on each eyelid. *As delicate as a breeze. That felt pretty good.* He opened his eyes again as she sat back down.

"What else do you see, Mr. Holden?"

Everett looked up at the moon and then followed its radiance to her face. "You glow from the reflection. You look like a guardian angel."

"You do, too." Lark kissed his cheek and smiled.

A gust of cold air whistled through the pines. "Let's go back inside." After another brief kiss, they headed toward the party.

Once inside, Everett noticed people were staring at them. *Has something else happened? Or could it be because Lark looks so—new word—spectacular in that blue dress?*

"Are you hungry?"

"Very," Lark said.

"All right. Let's go for it."

"While you're waiting in line, do you mind if I check my lipstick? I think it's been mussed a little." She grinned.

"It looks perfect, but I'll be right here in line."

The moment Lark left his presence, Sylvester Markus, the owner of Ozark Consulting, barreled over to him. Sylvester leaned in to talk quietly. "Well, I guess you heard about Zeta. A day spa." There was an awkward moment, and then a blubbering bout of laughter. "You've been a first-rate contractor, my boy, and so I wanted to talk to you about becoming an employee here. You could take over Zeta's position, and it would mean a hefty raise. So I'd like to see you in my office tomorrow morning," he said. "What do you say?"

"All right." Everett tried not to overreact, but he gave the man plenty of affirmative answers even though he had to dodge his spit as they continued to talk.

After Sylvester walked away, Everett's mind reeled with the news. Hadn't he secretly hoped to have a more permanent position there? He glanced around, eager to spot Lark, to tell her about the offer. Suddenly, Everett heard a slapping noise. One of those loud, cracking ones like in the movies when a woman slaps a man. *Surely not.* But rumors were that Sylvester's hands could be a bit nomadic with the female personnel.

A few people gasped. The small crowd parted. Everett stared at the sight. Lark appeared flushed as a mortified Sylvester put his fingers up to the red handprint on his face.

Lark strode over to Everett, looking upset. He placed a reassuring arm around her as he frowned his disapproval at the very man who appeared to control a big part of his professional life. Sylvester. What a terrible turn of events.

He wanted to raise his voice at Sylvester, but unfortunately, people were waiting for that very reaction. The party atmosphere and music died out. He could hear their murmurings, and they wanted blood. Or at least a scene of some kind. But there wasn't going to be an ugly spectacle. Just a promise.

Everett raised his head. "I will not be coming to your office tomorrow to talk about a job or a raise," he said to Sylvester. "In fact, if this is the kind of sordid behavior promoted at Ozark Consulting, consider our contract terminated."

Chapter 13

Lark gasped. "No," she whispered.

Everett offered her his arm. She hesitated and then finally circled her arm through his. *Why would Everett do this?* Granted, the man who pinched her was obviously a womanizer and deserved to be punished, but not like this. And did Everett say something about declining a job and a raise? How could this be happening?

Lark could barely contain herself. She wanted to put everything back the way it was. Right now.

She walked arm in arm with Everett through the crowd and watched it part like the Red Sea. Their stride toward the main doors didn't let up, but she could hear voices in the crowd. "Way to go," some guy hollered. And then a woman's quiet voice not far from them said, "Thank you, Everett." The only negative comment along the gauntlet was an almost whisper, "You'll be sorry tomorrow." Or maybe it was the voice screaming in her head. Her heart sank. She'd dreamed the evening would always be remembered. How brutally true that wish would turn out to be.

Once outside in the foyer, Lark pulled away from Everett. "I've kept quiet because I didn't want to embarrass you, but you can't do this. I won't let you."

Everett led her to a secluded alcove that was surrounded by tall palms. "It's already done. There's no turning back." He folded his arms. "And I don't regret it. Granted, I didn't really plan on losing my biggest client tonight, but Sylvester has been harassing women for a while now. Someone had to speak up."

"But you said something about a job there and a raise. Did Sylvester offer you Zeta's job?"

"It doesn't matter now. It's the right thing to do."

Lark noticed a flicker of something in his eyes. Could it be doubt? Regret? Who knew? She couldn't fully discern his heart. But she did know it was the most heroic thing any man had ever done for her. "I shouldn't have slapped him. Maybe I could have just growled at him or said something fierce."

Everett laughed. "I don't think you have a fierce bone in your body."

"Well, I guess I have a fierce slap," Lark said. "It's just my mother always taught me to defend myself if a man ever tried to take advantage of me."

"Remind me to be careful," Everett said lightly.

"You've lost so much. Would you please be serious?" *Those are some pretty curious words coming out of my mouth.* People had been lecturing her on that same subject for years.

"Lark." Everett sat down on one of the overstuffed couches and looked up at her. "I don't want you to—"

"I am so sorry." Lark felt a panic surge through her—an emotion she wasn't used to.

"No." He shook his head. "I should be apologizing to you for bringing you to a party where—"

"Honestly, I had no idea that man owned the whole company." Lark glanced around to see if they could be heard. A group of people stopped near them and then walked on by.

Everett took hold of Lark's hand. "You're not hearing me. It doesn't matter who Sylvester is in the company. He has no right to manhandle my lady friend or any woman. Am I right?"

Lark sat down next to him. "What will you do now?"

"Well." Everett released her hand and locked his fingers together. "Look for some more clients through my network." He looked back at her. "And. . .pray. It's time I took my faith seriously again." Everett let out a long breath of air. "Come on. Let's get out of here. I'm still hungry. Are you?"

Lark nodded, but what she really wanted was to help Everett. To hear him work out his frustration from the evening—to talk about his future plans if he chose to share them with her. And she needed to make sure all was well between them. It mattered to her. Now for some reason, it mattered more than ever.

Chapter 14

Lark woke up the next morning with a pounding headache, a pain she rarely suffered. She rolled over in bed like a sack of potatoes. The sun streamed in through the shutters in bright sprays, but her disposition felt far from sunny. The big clock read nine. She'd never slept so late in her life. But today felt different. If the day had a taste, it would be soured milk.

Her foul mood certainly couldn't be blamed on Everett, but on herself alone. The rest of the evening had gone very well. He'd taken her to a fine restaurant and treated her like a princess. They'd stayed out until midnight talking and laughing. She discovered him to be a Christian man of excellent character. And in her mind, a hero, too. The fear of him becoming a permanent recluse seemed almost absurd now. But a dark shadow still circled over them like a vulture waiting for disaster. Waiting for Everett to notice his date had ruined his life. And why? Because she sometimes tended to act impetuously and foolishly and. . .surely something else. Oh, yeah. Irresponsibly.

Lark turned over and groaned. What must she look like wallowing in child-ish self-pity? Her mother would say, "Have a cup of Earl Grey and then reach out to somebody who needs your help."

Suddenly her last thought triggered another memory—a nugget of wisdom from her mother on the subject of love. When Lark was young and confused about beaus, her mother would say, "You know, honey, you'll know when you're falling in love. You'll feel so many new emotions all at once, it'll feel like love is putting you together and tearing you apart all at once. You'll know. I promise."

Oh no. It couldn't be. Could it? And she hadn't even known Everett for a full week. How could it happen so fast? What should she do now? "Mother."

Igor hopped in his cage and squawked, "Moth–er."

"Ohhh." She rolled over and groaned again. What had Everett called her? His lady friend. It sounded so old-fashioned, she wasn't sure what it meant. So was she his friend or his lady? Big distinction.

She opened one eye since the other one was plastered on the pillow. Even her ultra-soft, Egyptian cotton sheets couldn't smooth out her mood. And then it hit her. She could paint, play her guitar, eat ice cream, talk to God, and call Calli—a few things that could get her out of her slump. But maybe God wouldn't appreciate the order she'd put them in. *Maybe I'll try the last three first.*

Lark crawled out of bed as she sent up her usual praise, confession, and requisition to heaven. Then she wrapped herself up in her chenille robe and dragged herself into the kitchen for some serious comfort food—mocha ice cream with dark chocolate chunks and caramel swirls. It had been suitably named, Mocha Madness, and it would always be her favorite. She grabbed the portable phone, pressed Calli's number in, and slumped down on the floor with a ladle and a fresh pint of Mocha Madness.

"Calli Dashwood speaking."

"Hi, Calli. Do you have a minute? It's me." *It's so nice to be able to just say, "It's me." Now that's a comfortable friendship.*

"What's up? You sound kind of. . .I don't know. . .different. How did it go with your neighbor, the mothballs, and the party?"

"Long story. Got a few weeks?"

"Well, my commode just overflowed, my housekeeper just quit, and I've got two closings in half an hour, so can you lay it on me in five minutes?"

"I'll take it." Lark proceeded to quickly unload all her story to Calli. The party. The kiss. The now infamous slap. Everett's heroism. The whole enchilada. When she finished her tale of woe she stuffed a shovel of ice cream into her mouth while Calli absorbed the shock.

"Oh my," Calli finally said. "Oh my, my, my, my."

"Got any other advice?" Lark asked, talking with her mouth full and tapping the ladle against the carton.

"I don't know," Calli said. "I'll have to pray about this one."

"What if Everett had to move away?" Lark suddenly realized how telling those words were.

"I think something else is going on here."

Silence.

"So *that's* it," Calli said. "You're falling in love with him. Well, all I can say is you must have really loosened up this guy or he's got you under some sort of spell."

"I think a little of both." Lark took another bite. Buttery caramel and mocha flavors sort of caressed her mouth. *Oh yeah.* Lark belched and then hiccupped.

"What in the world? Larkspur Wendell, are you under the influence of Mocha Madness?" Calli said. "Put that ladle down. You know if you eat ice cream all day, the dairy is going to make your neck glands swell up like a chipmunk. I won't let you do this to yourself."

"Okay. I won't eat another bite." Lark set the carton down on the end table.

Calli sighed. "You know, Jeremy might take this pretty hard. I know you guys have just been going out as friends, but I think he might feel more than that."

Yikes. Jeremy. I owe him supper. "Oh, Calli. I have a date with Jeremy tonight. Sort of. Another long story. What am I going to do?"

"Lord," Calli prayed, "I lift up my sister, Lark. Bathe her in wisdom and let peace and victory be hers in the name of Jesus. Amen."

"Amen, sister." Lark smiled.

"Call me later," Calli said. "I love you, sister-gal."

"Love you, too. And thanks."

The moment Lark hung up, she heard a rapping on her front door like a woodpecker. She tightened her heavy robe and then took a look at herself in the entry mirror. *Wow. Major damage.* She gazed through the peephole. Her neighbor, Skelly, stood on her porch looking upset. *Picasso? It's impossible. He couldn't have gotten out again.*

Lark opened the door. "Skelly? Is everything okay?"

"I don't think so." He was dressed in an old, wrinkled shirt, and he wasn't wearing a coat or a smile.

"What is it?" Lark reached out to touch his sleeve.

"Well, today is my wedding anniversary. First one since Rose died. And I don't know whether to grieve or celebrate. Do you have any Earl Grey?" Mist filled his eyes.

Lark hugged Skelly. "Come on in. I have a huge supply of Earl Grey. And my kitchen is always open."

Skelly walked in, looking a little older than he had the week before. He didn't stand as straight, and he appeared thinner. He looked like he needed a little more than tea. He needed some real food, but she knew he wouldn't accept anything unless she ate, too. So while Skelly settled in with her newspaper at the kitchen counter, she snuck out her frying pan from below the stove and a carton of eggs from the fridge. "I haven't eaten yet, so will you have some eggs with me?"

An anxious frown crossed Skelly's face. "Well, as long as you're having some." Lark decided to whip up some of her best scrambled eggs. Once they were almost folded to perfection, she lowered the bread in the toaster.

Skelly insisted on helping, so she let him make the tea. He and Rose must have drunk a lot of the beverage because he seemed to know what he was doing. Lark set out some muffins from the local bakery and some pear slices, hoping Skelly would eat. When they'd sat down, Lark prayed out loud over their food and thanked God for the many good years of marriage Skelly had known with Rose. And she prayed the Lord would hold him close as he mourned his great loss. "Amen." *What a baby prayer,* Lark thought. Why couldn't she pray those steeple-raising prayers like Calli did? When her dear friend sent up words to heaven they seemed to move mountains and truly encourage the saints.

"Thank you," Skelly said. "That was a mighty good prayer."

"You're welcome." *Well, maybe God can use baby prayers, too.*

"This looks good." Skelly took a sip of his tea. "Rose was a fine cook, too, and I liked helping her. In fact, we took some cooking classes together. But preparing food for myself just isn't any fun. In fact, not much of anything is fun without Rose."

Skelly paused with a wistful expression and then took a bite of the scrambled eggs. "I know your secret, Missy. You folded real whipping cream into the eggs. Rich and creamy. They're good." He ate some more of his eggs and toast. But when he reached for a pear his arms dropped to his side. "I can't pretend anymore."

Lark touched Skelly's arm but said nothing. He felt so thin she wondered if he'd been eating at all.

"Things really aren't going well," he went on to say. "I've been having panic attacks in the night when I wake up without Rose by my side. I've never had anything like that in my whole life. I didn't even know what had happened to me until the doctor told me what it was. People tell me it's okay to grieve. But I don't want to. I just want my Rose back." Then Skelly was overwhelmed with heaving sobs. His hands covered his face as if he were embarrassed. One of his tears fell on her hand.

Lark knelt down beside Skelly. She really didn't know what to do, so she begged God to help her say the right words. Just as she'd finished her silent prayer, her mind went blank. Tears came instead as she just wept with Skelly. He patted her head, and they cried until the eggs had gone cold.

After they'd both cleaned up their faces, Lark prayed silently for a way to help Skelly. Then gradually she got an idea. Just a little idea, but she felt it was an inspired thought this time.

Lark picked up her acoustic guitar from a stand she kept in the laundry room and said, "You know, I've been working on a love song for about five years. It never had a title, but now I know why. The song should be called 'Rose.'"

Skelly put his fingers to his lips as if to stop a fresh flood of tears. "Will you play it for me?"

Without another word, Lark set the guitar on her leg. She felt the cool smoothness of the wood against her hand and then reached up to gently pick out her song of love. She'd never known where the tune had come from or why the lyrics had meant so much to her, but now it seemed as if all of the words and all of the notes had come together all these five years for this one moment in time. It was for Skelly. To celebrate his love. And to heal his heart. She finished her gentle picking as she sang the chorus one last time:

> "Sing now our love song,
> That's echoed through the years,
> Words so sweet and clear.
> I loved you, Rose,
> And I love you still."

The name Rose fit so perfectly tucked inside the chorus, Lark smiled. God's mercies had a way of making little miracles like that happen. Just when life's mosaic appeared to be no more than misfit pieces, then the Almighty offered a hint of heaven. A glimpse of the magnum opus. A foretaste of knowledge that all worked together for good and each life had a reason for being.

This moment matters to God. She must have said the words out loud, because Skelly nodded. It *all* mattered. Skelly's tears. Everett's courage and loss. Her own uncertainties about the future. Something warm returned to her heart, bringing back the glow. Her mother's words had rung true. "A little Earl Grey and somebody else's needs." Lark set her guitar back on its stand and prayed she, too, could know a lifetime of love like Skelly and Rose. Instantly Everett's face came to mind. She patted Skelly's hand. "Are you all right?"

"No. . .but I feel *better.*" Skelly said. "Thank you for the song. It was perfect for this day. If Rose could have heard it, I know she'd feel the same way. Are you really going to name it after her?"

"Yes." And then Lark got another idea, but she wasn't sure if it felt inspired or was budding up from enthusiasm.

"I have a question for you. It's a big one." Lark sat back down. "And you can say no if you want to."

Skelly nodded. "Fair enough. What is it?"

"Could I pay you to be my chef tonight? I have promised Jeremy a nice meal. I owe it to him because. . .well it's kind of a long story. In fact, my life seems to be full of long stories lately. But I wondered if you would enjoy doing that? You can fix anything you like."

Skelly clapped his hands together. "I'll even *serve* it to you both. It'll be fun, and it'll get me out of the house for a change."

"But since this is a special day for you, maybe we should be serving you," Lark said.

"But I enjoy the cooking more than the eating. And I don't want you to pay me, just the money to buy the food. Is it a deal?"

"Okay, it's a deal."

Skelly started to say something then shushed himself.

"What were you going to say?" Lark asked.

"Oh, nothing. None of my beeswax." Skelly shuffled his feet. "Well, you know, I like Jeremy. He's a good youth minister, but he's not your type."

"And so who exactly is my type?" Lark tapped her finger on her arm in pretend irritation.

Skelly grinned. "Well, our new neighbor might be your type if he's a nice Christian boy. Which I think he is."

"And why do you say he's my type?" She couldn't imagine Skelly paying so much attention to her romantic interests.

"Everett is kind of a simple guy. Intelligent, but simple. He's like the beginnings of a compost heap. You know, leaves and dirt. And you're like all the other goodies that get thrown in it to make it good."

"You mean like egg shells and animal dung?" Lark asked, trying not to chuckle at his off-beat example.

"Okay, so the analogy breaks down a little." Skelly's face brightened. "You are so funny. And see? That's part of the goody getting thrown in. Don't you see it?"

"I get what you're saying. But what is Jeremy then? Is he the dung or the dirt?" Lark asked, laughing.

Skelly chuckled so hard it made his body jiggle.

Lark felt for the handkerchief in the pocket of her robe. The one Everett had given her to dry her eyes when she'd ruined her gown. She pulled it out just enough to see the initials, E. M. H. She suddenly wondered what the *M* stood for. *Milhouse. No way. Milroy. Is that a name? Milton. Too old. Millard. Sounded like a duck. Montague. Too Shakespearean. Montgomery. Maybe.* Lark came to herself and realized Skelly must have caught her drifting by the smile on his face. Thankfully he was too polite to mention her lapse or the handkerchief she clutched tenderly but possessively. "So you're sure I won't marry Jeremy?" Lark asked to get the conversation going again.

"You won't, my dear friend, because that is all Jeremy will ever be. A dear friend. Like me. But he will discover friendship is a good thing, too." Then he put his hand in the air. "Well, I am so outta here as you young people like to say." He headed to the front door. "Seriously, I'll be here with groceries at four thirty. Sharp. Oh, and I kind of busted up my pots and pans, so do you mind if I borrow yours?"

"I don't mind at all." Lark handed Skelly two fifty-dollar bills. He waved them in the air and headed down her front walkway. He still looked tired, but at least he had a little more spring in his step.

As soon as Lark shut the door, she wondered what Everett was up to. Would he be busy making phone calls? She hated to bother him because it'd been her fault he needed to spend the next few weeks pounding the streets for clients. Knowing she'd had a hand in truly messing up his professional life made her nearly ill, but every time the reality tried to bring her down, she gave it back to the Lord to deal with.

Once she'd showered and dressed in her favorite pink velvet overalls, she settled back in her office. Lark sat down and pretended to work at her art table. She hated to just stand up and gawk and pound on the glass, so she turned her swivel chair ever so slowly as she glanced into Everett's office window.

What? Lark rose so hastily, the chair zoomed out from under her, making her tumble to the floor. After scrambling to her feet, she blinked her eyelids to make the scene in Everett's office disappear. But it refused to go away.

Chapter 15

woman. An attractive blond stood next to Everett in his office. In fact, the woman had positioned herself so closely to him, even the thinnest résumé wouldn't fit between them. Guess it wasn't a job interview.

Should she open the window and toss something to get their attention? Like a sofa? But did she have the right to stop Everett? Her last thought gave her pause. She and Everett weren't engaged. They hadn't made any verbal commitments. Yet there seemed to be such an amazing bond between them. Such a hope for greater things to come. Soon.

Lark stared at them again. She couldn't see perfectly, but since his lights were on and the day was cloudy, she could see well enough. Everett seemed to take the woman by the shoulders and gently move her away. He glanced out his window and looked in her direction. Lark stepped away from her window. Since her lights were off, perhaps he hadn't seen her glaring at them.

Suddenly Everett's lights flickered off, and both of them disappeared into another part of the house. Lark felt like a sleazy private eye, and the emotion did not suit her. She also felt a bit hoodwinked. Who was this woman?

Lark had never been one to carry on over a man. But Everett had changed her heart. He had changed everything. And apparently her heart had soared before she'd had time to engage her thinking parts.

The phone rang. She and Everett had exchanged numbers, so she knew it could be him. *What am I supposed to do now?* In her mind, he would always have the heart of a hero, but weren't champions sometimes terribly flawed? The phone kept ringing. Could it be Everett was capable of goodness as well as deception? Or had she overreacted? Just as she reached to pick up the phone, it stopped its beseeching noise. The caller ID let her know Everett had indeed called.

Lark went to sit in a place where life's puzzles seemed to unravel. Her tire swing. Flying-freedom-on-a-rope her mom always called it. She pushed off and then pumped her legs to fly higher and higher. At least as high as one could go in a tire swing. But despite its limitations, laughter always came, no matter what mood she was in. How could one not feel lighter while swinging free? Surely there would be tire swings in heaven.

As she peered up, she noticed the light playing hide and seek among the branches. She stopped her swinging and held her hand up to the glimmer, pretending the topaz-colored leaves were jewels on her fingers.

Lark slowed her pace and breathed in deeply of the brisk, fresh air. The snow had nearly gone, but there were still patches of the icy remains hiding from the sun. Picasso was in a jolly mood. He munched on something in the grass and then paddled around in his small pond. A duck's life looked so easy. Why couldn't her life be so simple? *A good place to sleep and eat and someone to love you.* Oh, there was that word again. Love. It seemed to stir up either euphoria or anarchy.

Lark turned her swing in circles until the rope made a cracking noise and would go no tighter. She lifted her feet and spun in faster and faster circles until she felt dizzy. She couldn't help but look up at Everett's office window when she made one of her last passes. She stopped herself when she saw something in his office window. It read: PLEASE CALL ME NOW!

Okay. How funny. So why didn't Everett just come to her front door? It's not like he'd build up any kind of sweat hiking over those twenty feet. Of course, it would help if she were in the house to answer the front door. Phooey. This was crazy. She needed to do something. Or maybe take a nap or watch a few minutes of the home shopping channel. No, not that last one. It would make her feel too pathetic.

Just as she rose from the swing, warm strong hands closed over hers. Most women would probably shriek about then or ready themselves for a karate chop. But even though she hadn't known the feel of Everett's hands long, she knew. It was him.

Lark turned around and looked up into Everett's eyes. Kind. Absorbing. Anxious. Yes, and he *should* be a little anxious, she thought, as she came to her senses. "How did you get back here?" She felt a little spirited all of sudden.

Everett released her. "Well, I opened the latch on your gate and walked through."

Why did his matter-of-fact statement make her want to laugh? "You are on private property." She stepped out of her swing.

"Oh, is that right?" He grinned. "I suppose my lack of an invitation has something to do with the view from your office window a few minutes ago?"

Lark folded her arms. Then she realized how ridiculous she looked as a spurned woman, tapping her foot and huffing.

"Don't you ever wear a coat?" Everett whipped off his tweed jacket and placed it around her shoulders.

She waited for a plausible counter from him, although having him closer to her made her forget a bit of what she felt anxious to know. *Closer* was the trigger word. Like a mousetrap on her finger. Yes, indeed. He'd been much *closer* to someone else just minutes ago. And she had long, platinum blond hair. *Oh, how cliché.*

"Apparently, the incident at the party last night caused quite a disturbance in the company. I haven't been doing much today except answering the phone and talking to women who've been harassed by Sylvester in the past. They've even come by to get advice. To sue or not to sue. I told them they'd need to pray about it and then seek the counsel of an attorney."

"Is that what you were doing in your office a few minutes ago? Praying with that woman?" Lark asked with a slight edge to her voice.

Everett's eyes widened. "And did you not see the part where I physically moved her away from me?"

"Yes. . .I. . .did." Lark felt a tremor of guilt. Well, maybe the tremor was really a six-pointer on the Richter scale.

"Madeline and I went out for coffee a few months ago. I wanted her opinion on something at work. I thought she and I might be friends since I didn't have any. But it appears to have backfired on me. She wanted more. But I was always honest with her. And as far as today, she said she dropped by to discuss Sylvester's harassment at work, but her real agenda surfaced pretty quickly. I'm sorry you saw it happen. But I have nothing to hide from you."

Oh dear. Lark saw the sincerity in his eyes. She wanted nothing more than to embrace him and start the falling in love process all over again. But the speeding locomotive had already left the station and all of the emotional jostling would be part of the ride. There was no going back now. "Look, I hope you'll understand me when I say. . .I think I'm feeling something here," Lark said. "I've never acted this way before. I've got some new. . .*sentiments* I'm dealing with when I'm around you." *Yeah,* sentiments *was a good and safe word.* "And I—"

Everett took her in his arms and quieted her with a kiss.

Yes, that's a very good way to deal with my new sentiments. She sweetened the moment by returning his kiss with enthusiasm as her arms wrapped around him. When the fervor between them both heightened, Everett gently pulled away.

"Woman, you've got quite a kiss there." He let out some air and raked his hair back with his fingers.

Everett's hair suddenly stuck up a bit, looking kind of spiky. It looked so cute, in fact, she wanted to muss it up some more.

"I think we'd better cool off for a second." Indeed he appeared to have broken out in a perspiring glow.

They both grinned at each other.

The air seemed filled with sounds again. A car honked. A jet flew overhead. Funny, how during the act of kissing, one became insulated from the world. "Do you need your coat back?" Lark asked.

Everett laughed. "Are you kidding?"

Was he actually trying to catch his breath? Being thirty-five years old, surely he'd kissed a woman before. Or maybe Everett felt some new *sentiments*, too. "Why didn't you have any friends?" Lark asked.

"There are a couple of reasons." Everett looked down at his loafers. "But when you're a slave to your job, it's one of the hazards."

Lark wondered what the other reason was for not having friends. He didn't say.

Everett lifted her chin to look at him. "Please go out with me tomorrow night."

"Will you feed me?"

Everett grinned. "Yes."

"Then I accept."

He felt the velvet strap on her overalls. "Everything you wear is so soft. Do you plan that every morning to be so appealing, or does it just come naturally?"

Lark gave him a one-shouldered shrug. She picked up an acorn and set it in his open palm. "Tell me, what do you see?"

To her surprise Everett held the acorn up between two fingers and studied it. "Well, from an accountant's perspective, I see potential. . .for growth."

"Potential is good," Lark whispered.

Everett put the acorn in his pocket and then lifted her hand to point to the tree above them. "And what do you see up there?"

"This big, old oak?" Lark thought for a moment as she gazed up into the branches and falling leaves. "I see a filter of light. A marker of time. And for birds, it's their birth, home, and first flight."

"Very perceptive. There's a painting in there somewhere." Everett released her hand. "But I suppose there is a scene to paint everywhere."

Lark suddenly wondered if he always planned to live in Eureka Springs. She knew her moving pains would be acute if she ever had to live anywhere else. "Don't you just love it here?"

Everett glanced over at his house across the fence. "Yes, I like my house."

"No. . .I mean Eureka Springs."

He smiled as if he knew what she was really asking. "You're here. So I wouldn't want to live anywhere else."

Lark breathed a sigh of relief.

Everett leaned over and gave Lark a slow, lingering kiss.

Okay, that felt very pleasant. She almost lost her footing.

"I'll pick you up at six. . .tomorrow evening." Everett squeezed her arm. "Casual. Okay?"

"I'll be ready," Lark said. Casual talk from a suit guy. Amazing. And he wore a green turtleneck instead of a button-down shirt. As he turned to leave, she remembered a question that had been tickling her curiosity. "Everett? May I ask what your middle name is?"

He looked back at her and groaned. "That information is given out on a need-to-know basis only."

"That bad?" Lark winced.

"Moss. It's Moss. You know—"

Lark tried to be polite and not chuckle. "You mean like the—"

"Yeah. Like the fuzzy, green stuff you tromp underfoot."

She laughed.

"But my mother liked it because Moss is a form of Moses, which means 'saved.' So maybe that redeems the name a bit."

"I believe it does." She found herself captivated by his golden brown eyes. Without thinking, she reached up to his face. Her hand was midway in the air when she heard Everett's cell phone come alive like a monster-sized beetle.

He frowned down at the phone, took it off his belt clip, and opened it to look at the screen. "It's somebody returning my call. I'm sorry, but I need to talk to him."

"Please, go. Take the call." Lark shooed him away sweetly. Everett mouthed the words, "I'll call you later." He answered the phone as he strode toward her gate. He'd forgotten his coat, but he didn't seem to even notice. She tugged it around herself, wanting to relive the warmth of his arms. She breathed in his scent. *Mmm. His cologne is spicy but sweet. Nice.*

As Everett closed the gate, she remembered his words about the woman in his office. *"But I was always honest with her."* How honorable. Had she been that straightforward with Jeremy? She hadn't led him on, but she really hadn't been clear about how she felt. This very evening, she vowed to make her feelings understood, even if it meant Jeremy would be disappointed. Lark had never liked confrontation, but if she expected to build a relationship with Everett then she would need to speak the truth to Jeremy.

<hr>

When six thirty had come, Lark still hadn't quite figured out what she'd say to Jeremy. Skelly had been busy peeling and sautéing and baking in her kitchen to prepare his specialty—baked salmon with garlic mashed potatoes. *Sounds good. Too bad she might not have much of an appetite.*

Lark decided not to dress romantically for the evening since what she had to say might not seem too festive. She took one last glance at her suit and then headed into the kitchen. Delicious scents filled the house. She picked up a sprig of rosemary and took a sniff.

"You look nice," Skelly said. "Kind of like you're headed to a business meeting instead of a date, though."

Lark noticed Skelly's hairnet and forced herself not to chuckle. *Guess he was concerned about fallout. What had he said? Oh yeah. I look businessy.* "Excuse me? And who said I shouldn't marry Jeremy?" Lark teased.

The doorbell rang. "Saved by the bell." Skelly busily retied his apron and adjusted his hairnet.

Lark sent up a quick prayer of supplication as she walked to the door and opened it.

"Hi. You look. . .nice." Jeremy raised an eyebrow.

"So do you." Once the compliment had come out of her mouth, she hoped it wasn't a lie. Jeremy wore a wildly-colored western shirt, so eye-popping in fact, it could replace caffeine. *Funny, I've never seen him dress that way before.*

Jeremy scratched his head. "You look very. . .professional. Like you're about to close some kind of deal."

She gulped the air. *What did he say?* Maybe he could see the word *closure* in her eyes. "Thank you."

"Are you ready to go?" Jeremy asked. "I parked my bike off to the side of your garage door. That way you can back out your Hummer."

"Well, I've had a change of plans." Lark splayed her fingers in the air and faked a smile. *I must look like a cartoon character.* "Our own Skelly from church is a gifted cook, and well, you know Skelly, don't you?"

The two men waved to each other from a distance. "Hey. How you doing?" Jeremy said.

"Good to see you," Skelly hollered back.

"And he's going to fix us our dinner," Jeremy said as if he'd come up with the idea.

"Do you mind?" Lark asked.

A pleased kind of smile crossed Jeremy's face. "It's a good move."

How could she not love this guy? So easy to please. But who knew the mysteries of love? One couldn't break the rules. *Even if I knew what they were.*

After Jeremy stepped inside, Lark took his leather jacket as Skelly strode over to shake his hand.

"Something sure smells good." Jeremy said. "Hey, you know we're in need of a cook at the church. We could sure use you. There's even a small salary."

"Really?" Skelly fiddled with his apron. "But maybe you better see how you like my cooking before you offer me a job."

Skelly had set up the dining room table with candles, a white tablecloth, and her best china, but the candles were left noticeably unlit. Maybe he was trying to send her a subtle reminder.

Jeremy seated himself and then looked up at Lark. He chuckled and then rushed around to pull out Lark's chair for her. "My momma would beat me with a sharp stick if she saw what I just did. Sorry."

"No problem." Lark noticed Jeremy didn't smell like motor oil. *Much better.*

Skelly brought in the first course. *Vichyssoise.* After a prayer from Jeremy, Lark took a sip of the potato soup. *Yumm. Creamy. Thick. Satisfying.*

Jeremy slurped up a spoonful and then set the spoon down with a loud *clank.*

"Don't you like the soup?" Lark whispered.

Jeremy glanced behind him. "I don't want to hurt Skelly's feelings, but the soup is cold."

Okay, so what should she say? If she told Jeremy vichyssoise is normally served cold, it might hurt his feelings. If she sent the soup back for heating, it might upset Skelly. *Are there prayers for this, God, or am I on my own with this one?*

"Uh-oh. I've made kind of a boo-boo, haven't I?" Jeremy asked. "Is it supposed to be cold?"

Lark nodded and thanked God for giving Jeremy the heads-up, but she wondered why he was acting so peculiarly. He'd never been overly sophisticated, but he'd always been well-mannered. And he was missing that smirk she liked so much.

Jeremy gulped a few more spoonfuls and then squirmed in his chair. "Listen, before Skelly comes back in, I just have something I need to tell you." He tapped his spoon against his bowl as if he were doing a countdown before a launch of some kind. Then he stopped and looked at her. "I think you are one of the sweetest gals God ever made. Purdy as all get out."

When did he start saying hick words like purdy? Lark looked at him, thinking the real Jeremy must have been sucked up by aliens.

"And talented. And nice," Jeremy went on to say. "And kind. And purdy. Oh, I think I already said—"

"Jeremy, are you trying to tell me something?" *Oh, wow. I never saw it coming. Jeremy just wants to be friends, too. And here I thought I had the corner on miscommunications.*

Jeremy took in so many short, fast breaths she thought he might hyperventilate. He fiddled with his napkin but looked at her intently. "I think we. . .you and I are best suited as—"

Skelly slipped in looking sheepish as he served the plates of baked salmon, sautéed veggies, and garlic mashed potatoes.

Jeremy's soliloquy halted.

Was Skelly coming in to eavesdrop? "This looks so good. I can't believe what you're *doing.*" Lark gave Skelly the evil eye and then grinned. *Boy, Skelly certainly got jaunty all of a sudden. Like a buoy in a gale.*

"Thank you. I hope it all goes down well for you." Skelly's hangdog expression changed to an all-knowing smile. "*Bon appetit!*" Then he disappeared.

Lark offered the silver basket of hot rolls to Jeremy, praying he would continue his speech. *Was Skelly actually listening in around the corner?*

Jeremy reached for a roll and began eating it. With a huge hunk of bread tumbling in his mouth, and while breaking every rule of etiquette imaginable, Jeremy said, "I think, Lark, we should just be good—"

The doorbell rang, making Jeremy nearly choke on his roll. Skelly must have been shocked, too, because he dropped a metal pan on the kitchen floor. Lark just groaned.

Chapter 16

"I am so sorry," Lark said. "I can't believe this."

"Neither can I." Jeremy let out a puff of air from his cheeks.

"It'll just take a moment. Please go ahead and eat." Lark placed her napkin next to her plate. "Be right back." She trudged to the front door and looked in the peep hole. *Oh dear. Everett. How could this be?* Her date with him wasn't until the next evening. *Wasn't it?* It had never crossed her mind Everett would happen over on this scene because she wasn't having a real date. She was busy tidying up her life. Wrapping up some loose ends so she could focus on Everett. She looked again. He wore casual attire and carried a big load of groceries with a loaf of French bread sticking out of his bag.

Lark made the executive decision to open the door and calmly explain everything. When the bell rang again, she yanked open the door. "Everett." Did she say his name too brightly? "Weren't you going to pick me up tomorrow evening?"

"Yes," Everett said. "But I just got back from the grocery store, and I bought too much food. So I thought I'd try being spontaneous for once and surprise you by fixing you dinner."

"You did. You did surprise me." *Okay, I guess that settles it. The hounds of Murphy's Law have finally caught up with me. And to think I've been an optimist all these years. What a waste of time.*

"Well? I make a mean macaroni and cheese. And I thaw the best cheesecake you've ever tasted. Have you eaten already? Lark. . .you're looking a little pasty. Are you okay?"

Hello. My name is Desperation. Lark finally opened her mouth to introduce everyone, but from observing the sudden downcast look on Everett's face, he must have already seen Jeremy sitting at the dining room table.

Everett turned around with his load of groceries and walked back down the path. The look of dejection in his eyes was enough to slay the coldest heart.

Lark wanted to shout something like, "There is a reasonable explanation for this," but she knew the words would come off hollow and soap operalike. Especially since she'd just made wild accusations against him which were false. Everett wouldn't be listening to anyone right now anyway. He looked too upset. Lark just watched him go and prayed God would give her a chance to unjumble the new mess she'd just made. Well, if falling in love indeed contained euphoria and anarchy, somehow she could guess which vat she'd just been dropped into.

It sounded as if Skelly tried to start some music on her stereo because he'd accidentally hit the French language CD instead. The teacher said, "Good-bye," and then, *"Au revoir!" How apropos.*

Slowly Lark plodded back to the dining table as if she had bricks attached to her shoes. Then she sat down in her chair with a thump. Apparently Jeremy hadn't missed her too much. He was busy constructing a little Tower of Babel with his mashed potatoes.

"Please go ahead," Lark said. "Unless we have a tornado or some volcanic activity, I think you'll be able to finish your sentence now."

Jeremy chuckled.

Out of the blue, Spanish guitar music wafted in through the dining room speakers. *Good. Music will soften the uncomfortable edges of the moment.*

"I know we've been dating on and off for a few weeks now," Jeremy said. "But I just felt I needed to tell you. . .I see us as good friends more than anything else. I'm so sorry."

Lark freed a lungful of air, hoping she didn't sound too obvious. "Thanks for saying it first. I was about to tell you the same thing, but it's hard."

"Boy, you got that right. Like chewing on glass." Jeremy looked so thankful he reached across the table and squeezed her hand.

Funny, how she felt very little when Jeremy touched her. No stirring wonder. No electrifying euphoria. Just a soothing kind of brotherly comfort. But she still had a question gnawing at her. "Do you mind if I ask why were you acting like a redneck Neanderthal earlier?"

Jeremy laughed and took a long sip of water. "I don't know. I got this crazy idea if I acted like a jerk, maybe I wouldn't hurt your feelings that way. You know, maybe you'd be glad to be rid of me. But it just made me feel like a fool. Guess I forgot the words, 'And the truth will set you free.' It's what I always tell the teens when I counsel them on dating." He shook his head. "Lark, I'm embarrassed by what I did. It was—"

"I know you did it with the best of intentions," she said with an earnest smile. "And I will always be glad to be your friend, Jeremy."

"Good move, Lark. For making an idiot look good."

Lark sighed. She watched as Jeremy rolled up his sleeves and dove into his meal with startling gusto. While he dug deeply into his salmon, Lark leaned over for a peek in the kitchen. She saw Skelly doing a little celebration jig with her broom. *Amazing.* Well, at least all appeared well with two gentlemen in her life.

❧

Lark was obviously still dating the biker. Everett slammed the front door, making the window glass rattle. The door had already been shut, but he had a sudden need to open it and slam it again. In fact, he'd done more door slamming in the last week than he'd done in his entire life.

He appeared to have been right all those years. Spontaneity wasn't all it was cracked up to be. People caused pain. Numbers didn't. What could be plainer or easier to grasp? He just needed to get back to the basics. Work. But even his job had taken a nosedive. How could his tightly woven way of life come unraveled so quickly? Everything had been going so well—a sterling example, in fact, of the good old American work ethic paying off. Until, of course, he'd moved next door to Larkspur. Now he'd lost his biggest client. *And a big chunk of my income.*

The reality of it hit him full force. Maybe the time had come to have a serious talk with God. So easy to give advice to other people about the power of prayer, but now when the going got tough, what was he really made of spiritually?

But perhaps all of the problems could have been avoided if Lark hadn't brought over my newspaper. Then Zeta wouldn't have invited her to the company Christmas party, which means Sylvester wouldn't have had the chance to be disgusting. But playing with the endless scenarios felt useless. Somebody had to stand up to the lout eventually. He just hoped God would reward him for doing the right thing.

But in spite of everything, Everett longed for the delight of Lark again. He shook his head. When had he ever needed *delight* before? He'd banned the word from his daily schedule years ago.

Delight. He opened a dictionary he kept in a kitchen drawer and read the exact meaning. *Something that brings enjoyment. Hey, I can get enjoyment out of my combat simulation game and a double espresso.* And then he noticed the word *joy* listed next. He had to admit *that* emotion was harder to come by.

Everett slapped the dictionary shut and started putting his groceries away in the refrigerator. Milk. Juice. Bread. The essentials. But then he dug out other items from the bag he'd never purchased before. Caramel cheesecake. Vegetarian sushi. Maple-covered walnuts. All because he thought the items would please Lark.

But what nagged Everett the most was the guilty expression Lark had while he stood there with questions all over his face. And right after Lark had pelted him with queries of the same nature. She must be going out with a number of different men at the same time with equal earnestness. Or perhaps she was just dating that one youth minister with the rebel hair and kamikaze jacket. But his intellect told him to let go of Lark. *Now.*

Everett opened the freezer door and let the air cool his face. But who was he kidding? He wasn't about to let go of Lark that easily. Just because some beefy guy kept showing up with a ponytail and a macho vehicle as if he'd just driven off the set of a "B" movie? He'd simply wait for the biker to exit, and then he'd fire a few questions at Lark. Perhaps he could utilize some of the same queries she'd bombarded him with earlier.

Everett closed the freezer door and sat down at the kitchen table to look over his list of contacts. Concentration would be difficult if he checked his watch every five minutes, but what else could he do? After he'd heard the rumbling of the bike next door, he waited another half hour.

Hoping Lark was finally alone, Everett changed into a green shirt and khakis and stomped over to her front door. As he reached up, the door magically opened. She stood there smiling at him guilt-free. "I thought you'd never come."

"Well, I'm not coming in until I've had my say." He had practiced his spiel, and he felt determined to get it out.

"Okay," Lark said.

"I don't know the rules of dating very well, but I'm just going to say it straight out." He took in a little extra oxygen for support. "Yesterday evening felt unique. Memorable. I'm not talking about what happened with Ozark Consulting. I'm talking about us. Anyway, I'm not going to be dating anyone else. I thought you felt the same way. I'm hoping we can see where our. . .as you called them. . .our 'sentiments' are leading us. Do we have an understanding here? Are we clear?" Everett wondered if his words were coming off too robotic.

"Yes, sir. We're clear, captain, sir." She saluted and tugged on his coat, laughing. *Guess that answered my question.* Everett frowned.

"Now will you please come in out of the cold?" Lark asked. "I promise what I have to say will make all things well between us."

"Is anybody here?" Everett looked over her shoulder. He couldn't believe in a matter of a few days he had gotten so possessive.

"No. Jeremy left about half an hour ago, and my neighbor, Skelly, left about five minutes ago. Please come sit down."

Everett managed to settle himself in the cushy, lavender sofa. Froufrou pillows surrounded him threatening to cut off his circulation, so he removed a few. Then he stretched out both his arms across the back of the sofa. He stared at Lark, waiting for her story.

Lark sat on the love seat across from him. "Jeremy and I have been dating on and off for some weeks now. Mostly just going out as friends." She licked her lips. "Everyone in the church thought we would get married. They said we were a matching set. But I'm not totally sure what they meant." She fluffed one of the pillows.

Everett thought Lark appeared uneasy. He noticed she would either lick her lips or massage her earlobe when she felt uncomfortable. But he really wasn't in the mood to deviate from the subject. *Cut to the chase, Lark.* "And were the people in the church right?"

"No, they weren't." She fidgeted in her seat. "Since a certain man moved next door to me, I discovered I didn't want a matching set. Maybe in dishes, but not in marriage."

Everett rested his elbows on his knees. "And if I hadn't moved here, would you have married him?" He wasn't sure he really wanted to hear the answer.

"I think of him more as a friend. And besides, this evening, just as I was about to tell Jeremy how I felt, he said it first."

"You mean he dumped *you*?" Everett leaned back.

Lark furrowed her brows. "Well, I don't really think of it that way. I've gained a friend."

Everett laughed then realized how rude it seemed. "I'm sorry, Lark. I'm laughing from relief. I just spent some unpleasant hours next door concerned you were enjoying yourself too much over here. Well, you know what I mean."

Lark sighed. "I do. . .know what you mean."

"I don't know how to say the things I feel. I'm not even sure *what* I feel. It's as though I've known you for a long time."

"I feel the same, Mr. Holden," Lark said. "Kind of makes me want to sit next to you with some cocoa and a cozy fire."

Everett patted the cushion. "I think that can be arranged on this big, purple couch."

Lark got a match and lit some cinnamon candles on the coffee table. "Actually, the couch is lavender with violet flowers." She winked at him and headed into the kitchen.

He followed her and then watched as she brought out some cocoa packets from her pantry. "Need help?"

"Why don't you pick out some mugs up there." Lark pointed to one of the cabinet doors. "All I have is the instant kind of cocoa. Do you mind?"

"My untrained taste buds wouldn't know the difference." Everett picked out two mugs. One had a Michelangelo painting on it and the other had comic book characters. *Funny combo.*

She grinned at his selection of mugs as she poured in the whole milk.

"I like your casual clothes," Lark said. "You look nice in green."

"Thanks. And I've never seen you in a suit before. It's a great look, but then I'm beginning to think everything is a great look on you."

"Even a soiled evening gown?"

Everett nodded. "Even that." He leaned against the counter. "So is lavender your favorite color?"

"Yes." Lark popped the mugs into the microwave. "Lavender represents a coolness and a warmth at the same time. A calming pleasure to the eyes and a warming to the heart. At least it's how *I* feel about the color."

Everett had never thought much about colors. But when he wasn't wearing a suit, he tended to buy green shirts. Now he suddenly wondered why. Maybe it was because his middle name was Moss. "I want to remember what you said. It's important."

"Why?" She poured the cocoa packets into the hot milk.

Everett's hand covered hers as she stirred the cocoa. "Because you make me believe in life again," he whispered in her ear.

Lark looked a bit loopy all of a sudden.

"*And* you're the only person who's ever been able to knock me off the pedestal I put myself on."

She pulled back in surprise. "I didn't expect you to say that."

"Another danger of being a workaholic. In fact, my life had become a monotone, one-dimensional, black-and-white kind of existence. I don't really want to live that way anymore."

Lark reached up to touch his face. "I'm glad."

He touched her hand. *Lark is all of the wonderful opposites of my life. She's the depth, the variety, and the color I didn't even know I needed.* But he did. *Such romantic thoughts from a bean counter.*

When the cocoa had been heaped with marshmallows, Everett turned on the gas fireplace while Lark flipped on a Bach CD. They sat on the couch together, sipping on their beverages.

Harp music swirled around them. His arm settled around her easily as she nuzzled her head in the curve of his arm. It was as if they'd cuddled that way for years. Scented with roses, she felt soft and warm. *So this is what marriage will be like.* Suddenly the computer-espresso life appeared unfulfilling and trivial in comparison.

Lark set her mug on the coffee table. "I love the feel of your crisp, starched shirt. I'd love to have one of those."

Now who could have guessed those words would come out of her mouth next? Then Lark gave him a heavy-lidded look. It felt like the right time for a really great kiss, but he needed to know one more thing. "Lark?" He set his mug down.

"Hmm?"

"What is it you like so much about a starched guy like me?"

She grinned. "You do have a reticence about you—that's true—but there's also such a sweetness just under the surface," Lark said. "Even in this short time together, I can tell. You are like my favorite dessert."

"And what is your favorite dessert?" Everett asked.

"S'mores. You see, you have this crusty graham cracker on the outside, but inside I can tell there is all this sugary, creamy, marshmallow-and-chocolate middle oozing out all over the place."

"Oh, really," Everett said, enthralled by her amusing depiction.

Lark pulled out a lavender rose from a bouquet sitting on the coffee table. Her big, brown eyes looked up into his. "And I know right here," she placed her hand on her heart, "something special is happening between us. And I want to keep my heart open. I don't want to miss God's blessing."

Everett kissed the tip of her nose. No one had ever called him a blessing before. He didn't feel worthy of such high praise, but he liked the way she said it.

She lifted the rose to his cheek.

He took a whiff. *No scent.*

"You were trying to find the fragrance. These roses don't have any. But they bring pleasures in other ways."

"Oh?" Everett asked.

She stroked the petals along his cheek. "They are a piece of His creation and bring us beauty and wonder."

"Just like you." Everett couldn't imagine anything more wonderful than the woman who sat next to him. His words must have been appreciated, because Lark smiled at him, looking sweeter than s'mores. Everett gently swept her long brown locks over her shoulders so he could see all of her lovely face. Then he lowered his head to kiss her. *What a sensation! Floating again.* He'd kissed women before, but mostly to thank them for a nice evening. His contact with Lark fell into a category all by itself. He felt ready to tell her more of the things in his heart when suddenly his cell phone came to life.

Lark looked down at the buzzing interruption but didn't seem upset.

He glanced at the screen. The call appeared to be from Chet Riley, someone he knew at Ozark Consulting. "Maybe I'd better get this. I'm sorry."

Lark nodded, so he stood to take the call.

"Everett here." He mostly listened as Chet gave him the latest news. "Sounds great." Astonished and relieved with the promise of employment, Everett thanked Chet and said good-bye.

"What it is?" Lark asked. "You look dazed."

"I guess I am." He sat down. "Apparently, there's been an unexpected event. Sylvester is finally selling the company to Chet Riley. He's a good Christian man. I've known Chet a long time, and he wants me to replace Zeta as soon as the ink dries."

Lark threw her arms around him and kissed him. "Thank God. I've been praying for you."

"I prayed for a job, too, but I had no idea how it would work out." Everett shook his head. "I'm not sure why Sylvester sold out just now. Maybe it was the threat of reprisal from all the women he'd harassed. But I'm really glad he's gone. And everyone has you to thank for that."

"No. *You* were their hero last night. And mine, too." Lark snuggled her hand under his, and he squeezed it.

After a couple more tender kisses, they both promised each other to celebrate the next day. Since the weatherman guaranteed sun, Lark suggested an edgier form of entertainment—hiking at Beaver Lake. Everett surprised himself by agreeing. Since he'd never been a big outdoorsy guy, he just hoped he'd live to tell about it.

The following day, after hours of jam-packed spontaneous adventure, Everett not only survived the hiking, he thought he could take on just about anything. *Canoeing. Mountain biking. Motorized paragliding. Well, maybe not that last one. But the day has proven to be quite illuminating. And fun. Such a foreign word before Lark.* Even though he'd nearly tumbled down the side of a ravine once or twice, he felt a satisfaction that exceeded any previously known pleasures. In other words, he experienced joy with Lark. So simple and real, he couldn't stop himself from wanting more.

What a day! Everett tossed his keys on the counter and put away his coat as well as his brand-new Rollerblades in the hall closet. He smiled at the framed photo of Lark he'd asked her for. *Wouldn't do having her picture in the office. I wouldn't get a thing done staring at it, and besides, I have the real thing just a glance away.*

Everett set the picture on the coffee table and headed upstairs to his computer. It had been awhile since he connected with his other self. The feeling would be like going back to work after a long vacation, except usually he didn't take long vacations. He usually just worked. A lot. But now he felt rested and optimistic. Something that gave him a genuine smile.

As he sprang to the top step, the doorbell rang. *Couldn't be Lark. She's at a French cooking class. Maybe it's Chet.*

Everett trotted back down the stairs and opened the door. Someone with long hair, a beard, and shabby clothes stood on his porch. Someone who looked very familiar. His brain did a quick gathering of information. "Marty? Is that you?" Everett leaned closer to him. "What are you doing here?"

Marty held out his hands. "Coming to see my only brother."

Everett could barely get his mouth to move. "Where have you been all this time?"

"Doing a road trip to Hawaii." Marty slapped his leg. "That's a little joke. Hey, aren't you glad to see me?"

Everett jerked his brain back to the present. "Sure."

Marty grabbed him with gusto. Everett lifted his hand for his usual pat but gave his brother a hug instead.

"Do I get an invite inside?"

"Sure." Everett opened the door and let him in. He went through the motions of leading Marty to the living room as well as adding a few pleasantries, but he really felt numb. Along with that bothersome tingly sensation. Everett tapped his face. The past came crashing back in a wave of grief. All that he'd kept at bay for three years. His elderly parents. The responsibility. The foolish decision. The accident. The funeral. "Why did you really come?" Everett heard himself say out loud.

Marty seemed to study him. "Hey, man, I haven't seen or talked to you since the funeral, so I thought it was time. You know."

"Yeah. You're right. It's been a long time. It is good to see you," Everett said. So much had passed between them, though, he just wasn't sure when he'd be ready to reunite the last of his family. But at least now he knew what had become of his brother. "Do you want something to eat?"

"I'm always hungry," Marty said. "Thanks."

"Okay." Everett noticed his brother still wore the same aftershave. The same one he always splashed on in his teen years. In fact, it had been their dad's favorite. "I've got some frozen entrees." Everett closed up his laptop on the coffee table and headed into the kitchen.

"Sounds good." Marty picked up the photo of Lark off the coffee table. "Wooow! Who's this?"

Everett didn't even need to glance back to figure out whom his brother was talking about. *Lark.* He wished Marty hadn't seen the photograph, but there was no time to hide it now. Maybe he could come up with a safe answer. "She's a woman I'm spending some time with." That sounded pretty lame when he knew he felt more than that.

"You're serious about her, aren't you? I know you wouldn't say that unless you had some serious feelings for her." Marty set the photo down.

How could Marty know me so well? They hadn't spent much time together since he'd left for college. He looked back at Marty. "Her name is Larkspur. And yes, I care about her." *Changing the subject would be good about now.* "So do you have a girlfriend?"

A ripple of pain crossed Marty's face. "I did have a girlfriend, but she's gone now. Left me for a rich guy."

"I'm sorry. You've had a rough time these last few years since. . .well, you know."

"You can say it," Marty said without a hint of anger. "Since mom and dad and Greta died in the car accident. You're right. I haven't been doing so well. But I'm doing better now."

"And why is that?" Everett asked.

"Because I'm here with you, Ev."

Everett smiled, remembering a happier time when they were kids and Marty would always call him Ev. Seemed kind of strange to hear the nickname now. Haunting echoes of the past.

"Have you seen the house?" Marty asked.

For a moment, Everett wasn't sure what his brother meant. Then he realized Marty was referring to their old home in Fayetteville. He shook his head. "No. I haven't been back since—well, you know—since it sold." *Excellent time for another new topic.* "So where are you living now?" Everett asked.

Marty laughed. "That's the good part. I'm living with you now, Ev."

Chapter 17

Lark came in from her French cooking class with a monstrous appetite. All the foods she and her classmates had prepared were donated to a soup kitchen, so her stomach felt ready for some serious eating. She stood there with the fridge open. *Mmm.* "Let's see." *Whipped yogurt. No. Like eating flavored air. Grapefruit.* "Way too sour." *Ohh. Leftover quiche.* She reached down to the bottom shelf to pull out the pie dish. "Oh yeah. Just right."

She wondered if Everett would be eating yet another one of his frozen entrees. He claimed they were gourmet, but how many of those things could a person eat? She imagined a block of frozen gravy slowly defrosting. Not a pretty sight. Maybe she could just slip over there and give him a slice of her quiche. He would love it. It was her best. Swiss cheese and crab. Before she could talk herself out of it, Lark covered the glass pie dish with plastic wrap. "Well, this is one night, Mr. Holden, you're not going to eat from a cardboard box."

Not bothering with a coat again, Lark ran up to Everett's house and tapped on his door. She hopped around trying to stay warm. A hairy sort of man who looked like Everett answered the door. *Who is this?*

"Woow. The gorgeous phantom from the photo. I'm Marty. Everett's younger brother. And you must be the woman he's falling in love with. Looks like my brother has very good taste."

Lark noticed Everett coming up right behind his brother. "That'll do, Marty." Everett playfully slapped him on the back.

Marty held out his hand to Lark, but she pulled him into a hug as she balanced the quiche with her other hand. "I'm so glad to meet you. I had no idea Everett had a brother. This is so wonderful."

"I can tell you're good for my brother." Marty opened the door wider. "And not just because you're a good cook." He winked. "Looks like you brought provisions. Real food."

Lark held up her offering. "I had some leftover quiche."

Marty took a whiff. "I don't smell anything, but you've got my stamp of approval."

"Thanks," Lark said. "I thought I'd bring it over since Everett always eats out of a box."

"Come on in," Marty said. "We can all break bread together."

Lark looked at Everett as she came inside. He smiled and escorted her into the kitchen, but Everett didn't appear happy about the situation. *How sad.* She would love to have had a sister or brother, but she'd been an only child. Perhaps a rift had come between them.

She glanced at them both again, intrigued with the comparison. Even though they looked a lot alike, their speech was poles apart as well as their clothes. Marty wore a dirty T-shirt and jeans while his brother looked as neat as a package of unopened napkins. She wondered if Marty had fallen on hard times or if he just lived a very laid-back lifestyle.

Everett heated up the quiche and found a bag of herbal greens while she and Marty brought out the dishes and flatware.

"How long do you get to stay?" Lark asked.

Marty chuckled. "Funny you should ask. I'd just told Ev I'd come here to live with him, but it was just a little joke. I'm passing through on my way to stay with a buddy who lives up in Missouri. But I love it here. These hills are full of poetry. You just have to be listening. That's all. Makes me want to pull out my guitar and cook up a song." He pretended to strum the prongs on the fork he held. "Composing and playing is like being airborne without a plane."

"I know just what you mean. I play the guitar as well." Lark was amazed Everett had never mentioned any of it.

"Really?" Marty folded the last napkin and set the fork on it. "After we're finished eating maybe we could jam awhile."

Did a tiny groan come out of Everett? *Surely not.* Marty didn't seem to notice. She'd give Everett the benefit of the doubt. "Sounds good," Lark said. "I'd like that. I don't get to play with anyone very often."

"Is that what you do?" Marty asked. "Play professionally?"

"No. I illustrate children's books." Lark cut the quiche into slices. She couldn't help but notice that Marty had set the table as if he'd taken a home economics class.

Marty slipped his thumbs through his belt loops. "Just like my sister, Greta. She was an artist, too, before she died. Boy, she'd love everything about this town. The galleries, the music, the hills and woods."

"Sounds like you love it, too." Lark offered Marty a thoughtful smile. "I don't think I knew your sister was an artist."

"Yeah," Marty said. "She sure had a lot of promise."

Lark noticed Everett's expression seemed more like irritation than sorrow.

"So what book do you have out now?" Marty asked.

"My latest is *In a Giddy Pickle.*"

"Sounds cool," Marty said. "I'd love to see it sometime."

When they'd all sat down for the meal, Everett skipped the prayer, so Marty jumped in and said a quick one. Short, but with so much heart about his brother, the words brought mist to Lark's eyes.

Before Marty took a bite, he took the gum out of his mouth and set it on his plate. Everett looked at him but didn't say anything.

Marty shrugged. "Been trying to quit smoking."

"I've heard quitting is hard." Lark smiled at Marty. "Does chewing gum help?"

"Sometimes." Once Marty took a slice of the quiche and then a bite, he moaned. "All right. Now, Lark, this is a supremo quiche."

"Thanks."

"It *is* very good," Everett said.

Lark touched Everett's hand. "Thank you." Funny about the two brothers. They were indeed different, yet there were similarities as well. Their hazel eyes and build appeared identical, but sometimes they also had the same pensive look. People might read the expression as arrogant, but to her it appeared more like they were lost in thought at times.

"Are you coming back for Christmas?" Lark asked Marty.

"No," Marty said in a forlorn kind of way. "I don't think so." His eyes brightened as he made a drum roll on the table with his fingers. "Now I know who you are, Larkspur. *In a Giddy Pickle.* Yeah. I saw your book at the grocery store. They had this fancy stand for it. So how does it feel to be famous?"

Lark chuckled. "I've never thought of it that way. I love to paint, and kids seem to like what I do."

" 'The meek will inherit the land.' " Marty scrunched up his mouth. "Ev, if you don't propose to this woman, I will."

Lark looked back and forth at them, grinning. Everett stared at her with such a sad longing in his eyes she wanted to get right up and kiss it away. What could have made him suddenly so quiet and unhappy? Then she got an idea. Just a little one. Perhaps from God. Or maybe the idea really came from Sunday school when she was a girl. "I think we should play a game," she said.

Everett groaned again. Noticeably. "Sorry."

"Okay. I know it sounds corny, but what would it hurt?" Lark asked.

Marty turned to Everett. "You used to love games when we were kids. Greta and I used to call you the game meister. You were always the one we came to when we were bored spitless. Remember?"

"Yeah. I do," Everett said. "Okay. Let's try your game. What do we have to do?"

Lark took a sip of water. "Well, we each go in a circle a couple of times and just say something we like about the other person. I know—"

"Since there are no winners or losers, technically, it's not a game." Everett raised an eyebrow.

"We'll all be winners with this one, and it might be entertaining," Lark said.

Marty gestured with his hands. "Sure, why not?"

"All right," Everett said. "I'm not going to be made the Scrooge here, so let's go."

"Okay. I'll start." Lark folded her hands in her lap and straightened in her chair. "I like the way Everett is firmly committed to things. Never wavering. And witty, even if he doesn't think so."

"Thank you," Everett said to Lark.

She looked back at him. "Your turn."

Everett held a forkful of salad in front of his mouth. "Okay. Marty's pretty decent on the guitar. Could have done it professionally, in fact."

"Thanks, man." Marty gave his brother a good-natured slug on the shoulder. "Never heard you say that before." He rested back in his chair. "Okay. Let's see. I like the way Lark sees things other people would totally miss."

Everett tilted his head at Marty. "You only met Lark thirty minutes ago. How could you possibly know something like that?"

"I don't know," Marty said. "Just a feeling."

Lark noticed Everett had a look of total confusion. Like he was in a dark room feeling around for the light switch. "Do you want to go another round? Or am I making you guys feel like you're in kindergarten?" Lark asked.

"It's kind of different," Marty said. "But it's not a bad kind of different. Okay, I'll start." He looked intently at his brother. "I like the way Ev sticks to things. He always reaches his goals. He's somebody any employer would want. All the right stuff."

Everett looked pleased. "Sounds like I'm hired."

Marty and Lark laughed.

Everett cleared his throat. "I like the way Lark smiles. She lights up the room. And she lights up people's lives." He opened his mouth to say more and then closed it.

"Thank you," Lark said. "Okay. My turn." She took in a deep breath. "I like the way Marty loves his brother. I would give anything for a brother or a sister."

"Well, if Ev marries you, you'll have me." Marty chuckled.

Everett stuffed a hunk of quiche in his mouth. He smiled at Marty, but it didn't seem like an expression of benevolence.

Oh dear. "Could you really have played professionally, Marty?" Lark asked, hoping to soften the pressure on Everett.

"Yep." Marty rubbed his chin and stared across the room as if he were traveling back somewhere in time. "A group called the Living Legend. I tried out when they lost one of their guitar players. I made it in, but. . .I never got to play."

"I've heard of Living Legend," Lark said. "They play some good Christian rock. Do you mind if I ask what happened?"

Marty glanced at Everett, who had his lips in a hard line. "Bad stuff happened," Marty finally said. He waited for a moment and then went on. "Our parents and our sister, Greta, died. Car crash on some icy roads going toward Springfield, Missouri." He choked back some emotion. "I was the only survivor of the wreck."

"Everett mentioned the accident. I'm so sorry." Lark knew Everett didn't like to talk about the accident, so she let it go. She noticed the scar on Marty's cheek. Must have been from the crash. "So what do you do now, Marty?" Lark asked, hoping to diffuse the building tension between the brothers.

"I don't do much." Marty took a sip of his iced tea and then dropped in a few sugar cubes. "I kind of bum around mostly. Odd jobs. Friends help me out when I get in a bind." He took another sip and then added some more cubes. "Guess I'm kind of a drifter." He kept clinking his spoon around in his glass until Everett glared at him. He put his teaspoon down. "Seen a lot of this country but don't really have much to show for it."

"You *could* get a job. You could stay in one place," Everett said. "It's a choice."

Marty wiped his mouth on his napkin. "My choices sort of crashed along with the car that day of the accident." He wiped his mouth again.

"I'm sorry, but that's just a cop-out." Everett threw down his napkin on the table.

Lark thought the two brothers might want her to leave. The moment felt more like a private family conversation. She sighed inside. The rift between them ran more deeply than she'd first imagined. "Should I go?"

No one responded. She felt invisible as they seemed transported back in time.

"It's not just about the accident, Ev. It's about you," Marty said.

Everett folded his arms. "How could it be about me?"

Marty paused as if weighing his words. "Because you never forgave me. You blame Greta and me for the accident," he said gently. "You always have."

"When did I ever say that to you?" Everett asked, raising his voice a notch.

"You didn't have to." Marty shook his head. "The blame was in your eyes. It was the day of the funeral. And it still is."

"Well, why did you take mom and dad out when you both knew the roads were icy? There was no emergency. You didn't have to take them clear to Missouri that day. You and Greta were always so reckless. Always had to push everything to the limit. Spontaneity was always paramount to responsibility." Everett rose.

Marty lowered his head. "We didn't know the roads were icy, Ev."

Everett straightened his shoulders. "But couldn't you have turned around when you saw the roads were getting dangerous?"

"The roads had been okay. But there was just that one bad patch." Marty touched his fingers to his forehead. "*One* spot. There's no way we could have known, Ev."

Everett dabbed at the perspiration on his face with his napkin. "But why did you always have to take mom and dad with you? Why?"

"Greta and I brought them along because we loved hanging out with them. And they loved coming along." Marty stood up and paced the floor. "Look, I've never mentioned this because I don't like putting you down, but somebody had to spend time with them and take them places. You didn't. You were always in a work mode."

"Working to pay off some of their hospital debts." Everett sat back down. "Somebody had to have a job. You and Greta were too busy living the artist's life to work a *real* job."

Everett glanced at her with regret in his eyes, but she still wanted to disappear. His last comment felt personal. Kind of stung her heart like a wasp with a double load of poison. Lark reminded herself that both brothers were wrestling with the past, finally bringing up long-suppressed emotions that needed to be addressed. She'd just gotten caught in a little crossfire, but she hoped it wouldn't injure their growing relationship. She placed her hand on Everett's shoulder, but he edged away. *Oh God, please show me what to do.* Maybe it really was time to leave.

Everett traced his finger across his brow, looking drained.

"Please. I need to hear you say it," Marty said. "We can smooth so much rough road between us if you can just forgive me."

Everett looked at Marty and sighed. "If I say it, I want to mean it. And I'm just not ready. I'm sorry."

Lark bit her lip. *What an awkward silence.* Heart wrenching, in fact. When her parents had died in the crash, all the blame had gone to the drunk driver. Perhaps that fact had made the grief easier. Then she realized both Everett and Marty hadn't known such a strange comfort. They'd become paralyzed from a lack of closure. Each had reacted to the tragedy in a different, yet parallel way. Both had tried to escape into a hermit's life—one at home within the refuge of his computer and the other as a loner who couldn't attach himself to any one place.

Marty grabbed his coat off the back of the chair. "Listen. I've got some stuff to do. I won't be spending the night. I'll drop by tomorrow morning to say good-bye. Then I'll be off to Missouri." He looked at Lark. "Sorry about all this. Pretty heavy stuff. But I was glad to meet you, Lark." He reached over to shake her hand. "And I hope you won't hold this against us. Everett is a good guy. We just have some issues to work out."

Lark shook his hand. "It's okay. And I was glad to meet you, too, Marty. I hope someday we can play some music together."

"Me, too. Thanks." He shot Everett and Lark the peace sign. "See ya."

Everett started to rise, but Marty held up his hand. "I'll let myself out."

"Do you want to take the quiche with you?" Lark asked.

"No." Marty shook his head. "Thanks. Lost my appetite."

Lark felt a bout of righteous indignation coming on. Or maybe just pure fear that Everett was entering dangerous ground. That he was closing off all those he loved just as her professor had years before. She gave Everett a look of disapproval with an imploring kind of smile attached as if to say, "Stop your brother and forgive him."

Everett seemed to ignore her pleading gaze, took out his wallet, and handed his brother a one-hundred dollar bill.

Marty just set the money back down on the table. "I didn't come for that, Ev."

"I know." Everett put the bill back in his wallet. "You don't really have to go."

"I don't think you understand." With those last words, Marty ambled to the door and left into the cold night.

If Lark thought the silence felt disheartening before, once Marty shut the door, a cheerless kind of gloom settled in around them in spite of the love she tried to offer him. There was *that* word again, but she couldn't turn back. Even if Everett shunned her now, she knew where she stood. Love could be a one-sided choice if it had to be, because no one could stop a person from feeling it. But caring for Everett made it even harder to watch him self-destruct from a lack of forgiveness. He'd been so hurtful to his brother and so irrational, she wanted to shake him. What could she say?

"I'm sorry you had to witness our dirty laundry," Everett said. "You can understand now why I didn't want to talk about it the other night."

Lark looked at him, wanting so badly to help him.

"Look, I know what you're thinking, and I don't need to talk this through." Everett shoved his food aside. "You're bursting to say something. Please, go ahead."

"I've gone through this," she said. "Not quite the same, as you know, but similar circumstances. I was forced to forgive someone."

Lark looked at Everett; his eyes were full of pain. She waited for him to speak, but he just gripped the table as if he couldn't let go.

"I didn't have to blame myself or any of my relatives for my parents' accident. That was the easy part." Lark moved her plate away. She'd lost her appetite as well. "But I allowed the offender to write me from prison. He asked for forgiveness. I didn't want to do it. I fought it for about six months. And then I couldn't stand it any longer. Every single day I chose not to forgive him, I hurt inside. It kept extending the grieving period as it ate away at my spirit. So I asked God to help me."

"And He did it?" Everett asked. "Just like that?"

Lark shook her head. "No. I had to do it over and over until I really meant it, but God seemed to honor even my simple efforts to do the right thing."

"The right thing," Everett repeated. "You don't know the whole story. My brother and sister had a pattern of this behavior." He folded his arms. "My sister Greta was an artist like you, but she had a penchant for all things outlandish. And sometimes her tastes leaned toward the reckless. She took my parents hiking down in west Texas, and my father nearly died of heat exhaustion. I warned her, but she refused to take advice from her older brother. She was determined to do things her way even if it could hurt someone."

Everett stared off toward the front door. "My brother and sister were always alike. So wild and passionate about everything. They couldn't just *smell* the air before a rain. They had to go up in a plane during a thunderstorm and experience the source of the rain. So Greta could paint the rain with more realism and Marty could compose words about storms with more passion. How exasperatingly maniacal." He let his balled-up hand fall on the table, making a loud *thud*. "It's like I knew it would all end this way somehow, but no one would listen. No one. Now is that easy to forgive and flippantly dismiss?"

Lark looked at him intently. "Just because a person forgives someone doesn't mean it's done easily or flippantly. It's an act of courage." She paused and then felt an urge to continue. "And. . .the icy road Marty talked about. It sounds like he and Greta just didn't know. I mean, was the accident really their fault?"

Everett shook his head. "I'm sure you're trying to help me, but I'm just going to have to work this one out alone." He rose in his chair.

Lark took the cue and started cleaning up.

He took her hand. "No. I don't want you to do that. I'll get it."

Somehow his look pierced her heart. Everett was closing her out. She could sense it in every word and action. "Okay." Lark looked up into his handsome but sad eyes. "Is everything okay. . .you know. . .between us?" Her hands shook as she reached over to finger his collar. "I mean, I know I'm kind of spontaneous. And, well, artsy. But I hope you'll see it in your heart to—" She couldn't go on with her appeal since she felt close to tears. Lark licked her lips and fought to keep her chin from trembling.

Everett touched her hair. "I just need some time to work through this."

Is that true? Or are you trying to say good-bye? Lark put her hand over her mouth to steady her emotions. "Okay."

He kissed her cheek. "Why don't you pray for me? I'm sure I can use it."

"I will." As he walked her to the door, Lark looked around. She hadn't paid much attention before, but his house looked so empty. "You know, we haven't known each other long," Lark said. "But, well, I know this is putting my feelings sort of out there. But I think I'm—"

Everett gently placed his finger over her lips. "Are you sure you want to say this?"

Lark nodded. "I'm sure, even though I guess what I'm about to say will come off too impulsive, but it's what I want to say, so I'm just going to say it."

"I wish you would." Everett almost smiled.

"I think I'm falling. . .you know. . .sort of in love with you," she said. "Can't help it. It just happened, so I wanted to mention it to you." Lark could feel her words coming faster and faster like stones tumbling down a steep hill. *Oh, what a silly goose I've become.* "So, while you're working things through over here, at least you'll know how I feel over there." Lark kissed her forefinger and then touched it to his cheek. She hurried back to her house, not wanting Everett to see the tears that were beginning to flow.

Chapter 18

I'm a mess. I'm an absolute mess. Calli wouldn't even recognize me. Lark shut the door behind her and leaned against it for support. Even as a girl, she'd never been one for bouts of tears like some of her friends. With her sunny temperament, she'd always discovered lots of things to be fascinated with rather than moping for hours. But this wasn't a breakup from a schoolgirl crush. This felt like some serious peril to her heart. Or had Everett meant what he said? That he just needed some time.

Maybe I shouldn't have told Everett how I felt. But couldn't he see it in her eyes anyway? A dull ache trickled through her. *Not good. Okay, options. Paint, play guitar, Mocha Madness, pray, or call Calli. Or I could sip some Earl Grey tea and think of the needs of someone else.* Those were all good things, but first maybe she'd just treat herself to another round of tears.

Then she remembered what Calli had said—that God might have planted Everett next door for a reason. But what if the real purpose was to help Everett in some other way? What if the falling-in-love part wasn't destiny? *Wait a minute. Do I believe in destiny?* She groaned, wondering how her mother would respond. Maybe she'd say, "You know, honey, maybe you can't see the whole picture. Maybe God is working things out, and you just can't see it."

Okay, time for some prayer. Lark slipped on her gray sweats and knelt by her bed like she did when she was a girl. She surrounded herself with boxes of tissues like a fortress and began, "Please help me."

"Please help me," Igor repeated in his cage.

Lark slumped onto the bed. "Can't pray in *my* bedroom."

"My bedroom," Igor squawked.

Yes, I guess it is your bedroom. She smiled and shook her head at Igor. She decided to pray silently, and this time, mean it. *Please show me the way, and if Everett is meant only to be my good friend, then give me the courage to face it.* Then she thought of the severed relationship between the two brothers and prayed for a miracle of forgiveness and healing. Her own lack of responsibility and impulsiveness came to mind, so she asked for maturity in all areas of her life. She stayed on her knees until a peace washed over her like a warm bubble bath. *Maybe talking to God has more to do with sincerity and trust than the perfect words.*

Lark picked up the bedroom phone. Now for a good talk with her best friend.

Calli's phone rang a couple of times, and then she answered. "Hey, girl. I was just thinking about you for some reason. Sent up a prayer, too. What's going on?"

"My emotions have been jumbled like they've had a few rounds in a blender," Lark said. "But I'm better now."

"Somehow I know this has to do with that neighbor of yours. You're either going to have to move or marry him."

"You don't know how true that is." Lark related the latest as Calli made noises of astonishment. "But I've given it to God," she finally added.

"It's all you can do," Calli said. "But I still think Everett needs to be slapped upside the head for good measure."

They both laughed.

"Wait a minute," Lark said. "I hear a funny noise in Everett's backyard. Hold on." Lark ran up to the loft with the portable phone to have a look. "You will never believe this. You know how Skelly throws pots and pans sometimes?"

"Yeah."

"Well, Everett thought it was so goofy. But I can see him doing it. He's got his backyard lights on, and he's out in the cold heaving pots against his brick wall."

"Oowwee. He must be in a bad way about his brother," Calli said. "And, you know, maybe he's wrestling with his feelings for you, too. Anger and love mingle in the same stream sometimes. I'll pray for him. But I've gotta go, ladybug. My doorbell is buzzing, and I have a date with one of the finest Christian gentlemen in Arkansas. We're doing my favorite thing."

"Let's see. Japanese cuisine where this samurai guy whacks up your steak in midair?"

"You got it."

Lark chuckled. "You go for it, girl, and then tell me all the finer points later. Bye." She hung up. *Well, that wasn't as satisfying as I thought it would be.* Usually Calli had more time to talk, but then she had a life, too. Calli certainly couldn't be expected to be on call 24/7 just to listen to all her latest romantic catastrophes.

She couldn't help but wonder when one of them married someday if their friendship would change significantly. She would certainly miss their closeness. Their sisterhood. But even so, she hoped Calli had the most beautiful evening of her life.

Lark sighed and then stared down at the man who held her heart. Everett. *How did it happen?* Yes, somehow while she was busy helping Mr. New Guy out of his shell, he'd become Mr. Lifetime. She'd been minding her own business when love simply took her by surprise. Well, that wasn't totally accurate. She had indeed meddled in his life, but the surprise part was true. He had left her breathless. *And isn't that what I've longed for?*

Lark just hoped Everett was down there having a few good thoughts about her. Unfortunately, he had another pan in his hand, ready for a launch. *What could he be thinking?*

~⮽~

Everett rose from his deck chair and threw a saucepan even harder than the first one. *What a little minx.* Ever since he'd moved next door to Larkspur, every component of his life had been negatively altered. None of the past miseries with Marty would have been dredged up had it not been for her childish game. He would have made the best of his time with his brother, and then Marty would have been on his way to Missouri in the morning.

Everett shivered even though he'd put on a heavy coat. He felt for his Blackberry, but it wasn't in his pocket. He'd always kept his Blackberry with him wherever he went, but at the moment he couldn't even remember where he'd left it. *My life is getting seriously out of control.*

Why did Skelly throw pots anyway? Seemed more insane than helpful. And it would eventually loosen up the mortar on his brick wall. He noticed all the dead mums around him, grunted, and trudged back inside. He felt so many intense emotions it frightened him.

Everett's head reeled with a headache. Where was his bottle of medicine? *Mental note: Buy five-year supply of painkillers. Or just move away from Larkspur. Same effect.*

He couldn't find the medicine in any of the usual spots, so as a substitute, he sat in front of his computer. *Long time, no see, old friend. It's great to be back in the pilot seat.* He didn't bother looking over at Lark's office window. He refused to succumb to the temptation this time, and instead gazed into his real world. *Ah, yes.* The soft glow of the screen was like a reassuring friend. And he'd have a good, steady job soon. Maybe with some discipline he could make the rest of his life just as it had been.

Everett flipped on his stereo. *Liebestraum* by Franz Liszt was playing. *Hmm. Not very invigorating to get the juices flowing.* He changed CDs to Mozart's *Allegro. Now, that's a little more like it.*

But every time Everett stared at the screen for more than a minute, those big, brown, impish eyes of Lark's seemed to be staring back at him. Full of sweetness. Then he summoned up a more recent expression of hers. At dinner with Marty, her glow hadn't been so loving. In fact, her look at him had been reproving, or at the least, pleading.

He leaned back in his chair, making it moan. Even his chair seemed against him. Could Lark have been right? Had he been too tenacious with his views, and had his lack of forgiveness eaten away at his spirit? Granted, Marty and Greta had always relished in proving they were covered with some kind of invincible powder, and he'd always been more than willing to take up the role of the nay-saying, older brother, but all of that aside, had the accident truly been their fault? One unfore-seen patch of ice causing them to career into a ravine. *Maybe the same thing would have happened if I had been driving. But then how could it have happened with me? As Marty said, I never took Mom and Dad anywhere.* Had it been true? Had he been so busy trying to impress his parents with hard work that he'd forgotten to just be their son?

He flipped off his music. Oddly, he only listened to the classical music to stimulate his mind for higher productivity, not because he had a passion for it. He felt like a fraud.

Back to his headache and what felt like the beating of a bass drum inside his skull. Everett yanked open one of the top drawers on his desk, thinking he might have stuck his medicine inside. *No medicine. Great.* Instead he saw some crumpled documents inside. He rummaged through the pile. *Hmm. Old insurance paperwork. Funeral expenses for Mom, Dad, and Greta. The brake job on my last car.* Brakes. *Why does that word always stick in my head?* In fact, for the last several years, every time he heard that word, it was as if he were searching in his mind for a lost piece of a puzzle.

Brakes? My car. My family's funerals. Mom and Dad's car. My responsibility. That's right. Once his parents had gotten elderly, Greta and Marty had watched over their house, but it had been his job to take care of his parents' car. Had he forgotten about some car repairs? *Brakes!* That was it. He was supposed to have had their brakes worked on. Had he been too busy? Why had he blocked it from his memory. . .until now? Out of convenience? Hidden guilt?

Everett squeezed the temples of his forehead. He'd let his parents down, but more than that, perhaps the brakes were the real problem when the car went out of control. His body jolted back in the chair. A dead nerve seemed to twitch back to life. *What's happening to me? Maybe now I'm feeling the stinging guilt Marty has suffered for years.*

Everett took out a handkerchief from his back pocket and wiped his fore-head. He put his hand to his stomach. All of a sudden he felt quite ill. He raced to the bathroom just in time to throw up in the toilet. Was it bad quiche? Maybe Lark was interfering with his stomach now. He already knew the answer as he leaned over for another heaving wave of nausea. *The food isn't the problem. It's your life.*

He allowed dozens of thoughts to drift in and out of his consciousness. His life had become just like his parents' car. Careering off into an abyss. He'd missed so much. A relationship with his brother. The volunteer work he'd given up. Friendships he'd walked away from. He flushed the commode and wiped off his face.

And why had he insisted on closing up his heart all these years—the coldness masquerading as a good work ethic. To punish his brother? To destroy himself?

Or had he conjured up some magical thinking? He wondered if subconsciously he'd kept emotionally vacant in case that could keep life from zapping him again. And did his noxious mixture of emotions include anger toward God? So many questions.

Once his stomach settled, he knew what he had to do. Since he was already on his knees, he decided to stay there. *God, where do I even begin with this prayer? How can You forgive me for what I've done to Marty? I guess people don't have to be artsy to be irresponsible. Obsession with my career has accomplished that very well.*

Everett continued his prayer, asking for forgiveness and guidance. Then he rose feeling different. He knew the cold, dispassionate cement he'd built around his heart was crumbling down. *Okay. I guess I've got a job to do, and this time it won't be at my computer.* The relationship with his brother had suffered too long with a festering wound. The time had come for healing.

Just as he headed to the bathroom for a shower, the doorbell rang. *Lark? Marty?* He hurried to the door. When he opened it, he found a woman standing on the porch looking anxious.

"May I help you?" Everett asked.

"I'm your neighbor, Melba Sanders. Next door to Lark."

"I'm Everett Holden." He noticed the older lady had a pleasant smile and held a plant of some kind.

Melba reached out her hand to him. "Pleased to meet you."

Everett shook her hand. "Same here. Would you like to come in?"

"Oh no, thank you. I just brought over this little ivy plant here to welcome you. I wanted to bring it last week, but I had a run-in with my gout."

"I'm sorry to hear it." Everett accepted the houseplant, which sat in a small, wicker basket. "Thanks for the plant."

"Oh, you're welcome. I would have baked you a cake instead, but I'm a terrible cook," Melba said with a pleasant chuckle. "Yes indeed. One of my floppy cakes is no way to meet and greet a new neighbor, I always say." She tilted her head as she took in a deep breath. "But I also stopped by to tell you Sam Wentworth, next door to me, is in the hospital with a broken wrist. Sam should be fine in no time, but I just wanted you to know. We all keep up with each other around here."

Everett thought maybe he should help in some way. "Should I go and see Sam. . .in the hospital?"

"Oh, no need to go right now. Lark is there. But it's nice of you to ask. You know, you're going to fit in really well here, Everett. Yes indeed."

Once Melba had gone, her words still clung to him. *"No need to go. Lark is there."* If there were ever a problem or a need, Lark would always be there because she was the kindest, most generous human being he'd ever known. Not to mention a woman with the sweetest kisses.

Now that Lark had gone to the hospital for a visit, the neighborhood did seem quiet. *Too quiet.* He missed her electric guitar adding her own wild additions to his classical music—two very distinct genres of music, yet they meshed in some strange and wonderful way. *Just like we do.*

Everett fell on his bed, exhausted from an overload of feelings. He gazed at the moonlike ceiling. He'd thought of himself as such a rock, but Lark had managed to tenderly smash his indomitable mind-set with her dainty, velvet mallet. One week in the shadow of those intense eyes and he was toast. Worthless to do anything but love her.

The fact remained, Lark would always be an artist-type with a grin brimming with impetuosity—a real loose cannon with some zany added to the fuse. But Lark was also the dearest woman he'd ever met. *The only question that could possibly remain is—should I marry her?*

Everett drifted in and out of sleep all night. In the morning, he awakened sweaty and tangled in his bedding as if he were Scrooge waking up from a horrific night of time travel. As his dreams gained clarity in his mind, Everett realized he'd indeed been like Scrooge—stingy with his money *and* with his feelings.

In one of his nightmares, he'd seen his epitaph: *Here lies Everett Moss Holden III, a miserly bean counter, survived by no one.* He'd tried to run, but as in most night terrors, it became impossible to even move a muscle. He'd thought, *No. I don't want to grow old alone. I want to give more—love more. Well, at least all my nightmares finally have some good use.* He knew now his life needed some modifications.

Everett rose from his bed and sat down at the kitchen table to write out his apology to Marty. When he'd finished pouring out his thoughts onto the paper, he tore up the letter and decided to talk to his brother straight from the heart. He gazed into the living room at the piano. *Who knows? Maybe a dose of forgiveness and some music will ease my nightmares and headaches.*

He took a stroll to the coffee table to pick up Lark's photo. He smiled as his hand went to his heart. Everett vowed that after he made all things right with his brother, he would take care of some business next door, as well. Maybe he'd even utilize a little spontaneity again. "Okay, Larkspur Wendell, prepare to be dazzled."

Chapter 19

Lark woke up thinking about Everett, and she wondered how a creative God planned on working out all the messy details of their lives.

She smacked her lips. "Oww." Her mouth felt like a litter of dust bunnies had played all night in there. And had she aged ten years overnight? How in the world had she made it past age thirty without needing coffee in the morning? Suddenly she wanted some. *A large amount. Right now.*

After two large mugs of French roast and a visit to her tire swing, Lark made her way up to her studio loft. She was eager to squeeze some fresh oils onto her pallet and load her camel hair brush with paint, but she knew the sketch on her canvas still lacked something she couldn't quite grasp. The balance still looked off, and there was no intrigue. No joie de vivre. But maybe God would give her the inspiration she needed today.

As she stared at her canvas, Lark detected a movement out of the corner of her eye. She looked down into her neighbor's backyard. Everett appeared to be putting up a birdfeeder. He dropped the huge thing on his toe and then hopped around in pain as seed spilled everywhere in his backyard. Lark gasped, wanting to help him. Everett patiently refilled the container, hung it up on the tree limb, and then sprinted back down the steep hill to his house. *Why is he running? What is he up to?*

Lark looked back at her work. Maybe she just needed some sugar reinforcement. *Jellybeans. Yes.* Lark glanced into her big glass bowl. *Empty!*

Okay. Calm. There was plenty of backup licorice in the desk drawer. She pulled out two sticks and let them hang out of her mouth as she chewed. Before long, she had both pieces consumed. *Mmm.* Creativity flowed more easily on a sugar high.

Did I hear the doorbell? Everett? Lark dropped her pencil in the jar and trotted down her spiral staircase to open the door.

"Skelly. How are you?" Lark tried not to show her disappointment.

He had a funny expression as he touched his lips. "Uhh. You've got—well, your lips and mouth area sort of look gray. Are you okay?"

Lark thought for a moment and laughed. "I've been on a licorice binge."

"Oh." Skelly grinned. "I don't have time to come in, but I had some news. Jeremy made me a formal offer to be the chef at the church. It's not a lot of money, but I think I would like it. What do you think?"

"Yes, it's perfect. What a God-gift." Lark hugged Skelly, noticing he'd put on some fresh clothes and he had a faint smile on his lips.

"And the Valentine's banquet is coming up, and I'd like you to play that song you entitled 'Rose,'" Skelly said. "Would you?"

"I'm a little rusty," Lark said. "Maybe you can sing harmony with me."

"You bet." A shadow passed over his face. "You know, I think my taking this job would please Rose. I thought maybe she'd be upset with me if I sort of just wasted away down here. Maybe she'd want me to do something more useful than just throwing pots and pans."

Lark smiled. "I think Rose would be very proud of you. Just as I am."

"You gave me the courage to do this. I guess what I really came over to say this morning was...thank you." Skelly wiped his eyes.

They hugged again, and then Skelly hurried down the stone walk but this time with purpose in his step. *What a difference a week can make.*

Skelly mentioned the word courage. In fact, that word had been popping up a lot lately. Lark glanced up and noticed the bracelet Calli had given her. It sat on the entry table as a reminder of her pledge. How odd to push Everett toward bravery, and yet she didn't have the guts to follow through with her promise to Calli. She slipped the delicate pearls on her wrist. Such lustrous beads from the stress and strain of humble creatures. Something so lovely coming from so much pain. Life was just that way sometimes. For Everett and for her and for everyone.

Well, she certainly couldn't force Everett to fall in love with her. She could only apologize for her rambunctious spirit, love him, and pray for him. In the meantime, she would follow the path the Lord had made clear. What had Calli said? *"Your art is a gift from God, and He expects you to share it."*

Lark nodded as she headed toward the kitchen. After all, how could she encourage others to follow their dreams when she kept hers at a safe distance? She wondered how she'd allowed such a large facet of her life to become so weak and cowardly. Was it from being an only child? Too pampered growing up? Or had she known too much success too soon, and now she secretly required all life-journeys to be easy?

Whatever the reason, the time had come. Lark pulled out the kitchen drawer that contained the small directory of galleries—a list she'd been avoiding for a long time. *Today, I will follow through with my future, even if it doesn't include Everett.*

Her last thought gave her some real heartache, but she knew she would keep her pledge no matter what happened. Lark blew out a puff of air. She reached for a backup package of licorice from the pantry and stuck two more twists in her mouth. *On the other hand,* she thought, *maybe when Everett put up the birdhouse, it was a sign of change.*

The doorbell rang again. *Everett?* This time a shy-looking stranger stood on her porch. He stuttered a bit and then handed her a huge bouquet of lavender roses. She thanked him with a tip and a hug. He looked at her funny, blushed profusely, and scuttled back to his van. Lark opened the card. It read,

> *I am a lone vase, and you are the bright flowers that fill it.*
>
> > *Affectionately,*
> > *Everett*

> *P.S. All is well between Marty and me now, thanks to God and a little neighbor lady I know.*

Guess it's my turn to cry. Lark kissed the card as she blinked away the tears. She looked up at the Almighty and thanked Him for helping Everett. If he had ever been on the same road as her old professor, Dr. Norton, he certainly wasn't now.

Then Lark got an idea, but this time she knew it wouldn't muddle anyone's life, another step to being more responsible in all areas of her life. She finally realized what had been missing on the canvas in her studio. The young woman had been alone in her garden. She'd been content and had even donned a faint smile on her lips, but the path to the garden had also been empty. If Lark sketched in a gardener coming up the path toward the young woman with his hands full of lavender roses, people would be moved. Well, at least Lark knew she would be stirred by the scene. *Yes. Two people, poles apart, coming together for a lifetime. Loving each other even when everything seemed against them.*

Lark put the roses in a vase and trotted up the stairs to her loft. Once she'd sketched in the gardener, it would complete her vision for the painting. And she prayed it would be her finest.

Just as she reached for her pencil, the doorbell rang again. This time about ten times in a row. *I'm coming. I'm coming. Couldn't be Everett. He would never ride the doorbell like that.* A deliveryman the size of a grizzly bear, spewing some pretty creative adjectives, handed her a big box with a lavender bow.

She accepted the gift and handed the man a tip, but he continued to stand there as if he were waiting for something else. Surely he didn't want to know what was in the box.

Isn't this supposed to be a private moment? Oh well. Maybe he was friendless and never got any presents. So Lark decided to rip open the box in front of him. She never could open boxes with dignity and patience. In fact, she felt like some squealing was in order when she tore back the tissue paper and gazed at the gift inside—a starched, white shirt all folded up neatly. She pulled the shirt out of the box and laughed. *Everett actually remembered what I said.*

"Must be a private joke of some kind," the man said.

"Yeah. It is." She pulled out the card and read it out loud. "I was never good at giving gifts to women. Until now. You inspire me! Yours, Everett."

The big guy nodded. "That's real nice."

Did he actually sniffle?

"Well, have a good day," the man said, giving her the same strange look as the other delivery guy. He lumbered off the porch and back into his flow of delivering objects of importance from one life to another. Lark recognized his lonesomeness and breathed a prayer for him.

Immediately on shutting the door, Lark put the shirt on over her sweats. *Nice. Crisp and fresh.* Then she reminded herself not to paint in it.

The doorbell rang again. *Boy, maybe I should just prop the door open with my shoe.*

This time the delivery guy was a teenaged girl from one of the local grocery stores. "Hi. Are you a"—she stopped to look at the clipboard—"a Larkspur Camellia Wendell?"

"That's me."

"This is for you then." The girl handed her the box. "We don't usually do deliveries, but I offered to come. I already know what it is. I made up the box a few minutes ago."

The young woman looked desperate to tell her what she knew. "Okay," Lark said. "So what's inside the box?"

"S'mores. Can you believe it?" The young woman went at her gum like a cow chewing in fast motion. "I mean, guys used to call the flower shops and have flowers delivered, you know what I mean? Now they call the grocer for cheap candy, marshmallows, and graham crackers. I mean, hello? How cheapo is that?"

"I think it's perfect." Lark handed the teenager a tip.

The young woman motioned to her mouth. "Well, I sure hope you love this guy is all I have to say." The girl's grin showed almost all her teeth. She walked off, still chatting. "Men. It's like they don't get it. They're from Pluto. Or is it Mars?"

Okay, that was a semi-weird encounter. In spite of the cold weather, Lark left the door open this time. Just in case Everett showed up as her next surprise. She opened the box with one tearing sweep. Sure enough, inside the box were all the makings for s'mores as well as a few packages of cocoa. She read the card that came along with the gourmet s'mores.

Please invite me to your church. I'll bet you'll get a different answer this time.

He'd signed it, *Love, Everett.*

Lark did a little jig. Guess she had a few things to share with Calli. But when Lark pulled the goodies out of the box, two folders fell out. She opened them. *Oh my, my, my. Two airline tickets to Paris? I can't believe it. No wonder the delivery girl was grinning from ear to ear when she walked away.*

At that thought, the man of her dreams, who also happened to be the boy next door, came striding up the walk wearing a tux. When Everett arrived at the front door, he wrapped his arms around her and kissed her before she could even let out a single thank you. And among kisses, it had to be a ten. What Lark would really call a crying-in-your-popcorn, chick-flick kind of kiss, intended to make all the females in the audience cry a river. "You are so *my* guy. I guess this means you forgave me for all my impetuous meddling. My silly games."

Everett pulled away for a moment. "Well, what happened with my brother was long overdue."

"But I am sorry."

"You are forgiven." Everett picked her up and kissed her. "So did I get it right? The romantic thing?" he asked with a bashful grin.

"Oh, you got it *very* right."

Everett tugged on the tail of her starched shirt. "I like your shirt."

"Me, too." Lark cocked her head at him. "Hey, you must have been taking a crash course in romance lessons."

"Not really. I think it was all there. Just didn't want to waste it on all the wrong women." Everett grinned.

"But Paris?" Lark shook her head. "*Très bon!*"

"Well, since you're learning the language and all." He shrugged and grinned.

Mist stung Lark's eyes. "I've never been to Paris before, but I've always wanted to go." She let out a big breath of air.

"And of course, there is the Louvre in Paris," Everett said. "I thought you might have a bit of interest there."

"Interest? The paintings! The sculpture!" Lark bit her lower lip. "I've dreamed of going there ever since I was a little girl. I suppose that's why I've been learning the language. But I'm not sure why I've never gone."

Everett pulled her to him. "Because you were waiting to see it all with me."

"Yes. I suppose that's it, and I just never knew it, until now. I can't think of anyone I'd rather share Leonardo's *Mona Lisa* with than you." Lark absorbed all the love of the moment. In fact, she felt certain this very scene would wind up in a painting someday. "Thank you so much." Lark kissed him again, just to make sure the moment was real. "By the way, you look very fine in your tux. Are you wearing it for any particular reason?"

"I wanted to ask you out tonight. . .only I wanted to do it in style since I'm taking you to the Whitestone Bistro on Beaver Lake."

"Really?" Everyone in the area knew Whitestone was *the* restaurant for serious romance.

Everett looked down at her lips and grinned. "Your lips are extra sweet, but they are the color of my tux."

Color of his tux? His tux was gray. Lark pulled back in horror. She glanced in the mirror. She'd forgotten that her lips were tinged dark gray from eating licorice sticks. Lark laughed. "And you still *kissed* me? So that explains why the delivery people kept looking at me funny."

Everett threw his head back in laughter.

Lark liked the way he looked down into her eyes with such tender love. "I got your note about Marty."

Everett shared all the revelations of the night. Then Lark's heart soared with joy when he told her of his apologies to his brother and their reconciliation. "I'm so happy for you both." She squeezed his hand.

"Oh," Everett said. "And I discovered some essentials."

"And what are those?" Lark kissed him on the chin.

"Well, the important stuff can't be found in the hard drive of a computer, but right here." He lifted her hand up to his heart. "Do you want to know what else I see?"

Lark nodded. "Yes, I do."

"I see you and what you are to me," Everett said. "My joie de vivre. . .my sweetness of life."

Okay, now is that romantic or what? Lark swallowed a giggle.

Everett gently caressed her lips with another kiss.

She wiggled her eyebrows. "Oh, this is way better than a chick flick."

Lark suddenly remembered the little acorn drama in her backyard when she'd first met Everett. She knew God would somehow allow their lives to bounce off each other, touch each other, and change each other. But whether acorns or humans, she knew the conclusion would always remain the same. Life was pure adventure.

Epilogue

Lark was pleased to discover that Whitestone Bistro had all the romantic delights everyone had boasted of. She enjoyed many more evenings there with Everett as well as sunny afternoons hiking and heart-to-heart talks about their faith and their future as they strolled the downtown shops along with the tourists.

Then one morning Lark took another joyride on her tire swing. When she slowed to a stop, warm hands covered hers. She turned around to see Everett standing over her. He held a small, velvet box in his fingers.

Lark put her hand to her mouth. "Is that for me?"

"It is," Everett said. "Unless you think Picasso might like it more."

She laughed as she accepted the gift. *I can't believe this is finally happening to me. Let the earth know that on this glorious Arkansas day, Larkspur Wendell will say "Yes" to Everett Holden.* She slowly raised the lid. The hinges made a little crackling sound before the box snapped all the way open. Lark gasped. Sitting cozily in the black velvet rested the most eye-popping, marquise diamond ring she'd ever seen.

Tears welled up in Lark's eyes as she looked at the ring and then back at her Everett. "You leave me breathless."

He touched her cheek and wiped away the tear. "I hope that is a good thing."

"It is. . .a *very* good thing." Lark ran her fingers over his arm as she looked into his golden-brown eyes.

Everett knelt down on one knee in front of her. "I guess I've been waiting for you all my life, and here you were. Right here." He took in a breath and smiled. "Larkspur, will you be my one and only? I've never known anyone like—"

Lark hopped out of her swing and kissed Everett with fervor. She hadn't formally said yes, but Everett seemed pleased with her response. Even Picasso waddled around in his pen with more gusto.

Over the next few weeks, Lark and Everett planned a simple, but elegant wedding. The ceremony would take place in a chapel nestled on a hill not far from the famous *Christ of the Ozarks* statue. They also chose the church for the magnificent scenes in the stained glass windows, which they hoped would remind all in attendance of the greatest love gift of all.

On the big day, Skelly proudly escorted Lark down the aisle to give her away. When Lark arrived at the altar, the pastor asked, "Who gives this woman in marriage?"

Skelly sniffed a bit. "I do."

Lark squeezed Skelly's trembling fingers as he lifted her hand toward the man she adored. She met Everett's gaze. He looked so handsome and loving she thought her heart might burst from joy. *Oh, Mom and Dad, I wish you were here.*

Later at the reception, Lark lifted her bouquet to an eager crowd of single women. She aimed the flowers at her dearest friend and maid of honor. Calli caught the flowers intended for her with one hand. Lark also pleasantly took note that several of the single ladies seemed to be clustered around Everett's brother and best man, Marty.

When the day's festivities had come to a close, Lark and Everett dashed through a rain of pelting rice and into a white, stretch limo waiting for them by the chapel. The next morning they caught an early flight to Paris. First class.

Their honeymoon in Paris was full of delights with leisurely walks down the Champs Elysées, visits to the Louvre, lunches at the local bistros, and the services provided by their hotel, including the sign Lark enjoyed hanging on the door that read, PLEASE DO NOT DISTURB.

THE LOVE
SONG

Dedication

To Irene Powers (Aunt Reny Beanie), your joy and whimsical outlook has sweetened every life it's touched, especially mine.

Much gratitude goes to Pat Durham for her help in understanding the life of an image coach. Appreciation goes to Chris Colter for answering my questions about paramedics. And a big thank-you goes to Robin Miller, Joanne Brokaw, and my daughter, Hillary, for their enthusiastic help.

Anita Higman

To my Lord and Savior, Jesus Christ—my Shepherd. I can hear You singing Your "love song" over me, even now.

Janice A. Thompson

Chapter 1

I don't belong here. Clair stared at the crowd inside the banquet room as she clutched her dress like a lost child.

Just beyond the gilded doors, laughter rose up through the party like soda bubbles. She wondered what clever remark had been said to amuse the guests, but unless she ventured inside, she would never know. *Three steps. That's all it takes.*

Clair stared down at her simple evening gown with a sigh. A dreary and familiar pain washed over her. Even if she dared enter, she would be invisible. But then maybe going unseen was easiest after all.

Perhaps she shouldn't have agreed to come. Oh, how she wished Ima had been feeling better. Ima liked parties. Clair didn't want to disappoint her employer, but she didn't know how to face such a large gathering of what she called "the beautifuls." Maybe she could just slip out of the River Walk Hotel and make her apologies to Ima in the morning. She took in a deep breath and, with regret, turned to leave.

A man, one of "the beautifuls," emerged from the music and laughter. He breezed by her, and then spun back around. "Are you leaving? The party is just getting started."

Clair glanced up at him, startled, then stared down at her shoes. "Are you talking. . .to me?"

"Well, I'm certain you're the only one sharing the foyer with me," he said.

She ventured a look up at the stranger. The man appeared to be in his midthirties, and his hazel eyes flashed with gold, reminding her of the brooch Ima had given her for Christmas. In fact, he shined so handsomely before her, she thought he must be a phantom. He winked. Clair could feel the flush of heat rising in her face at the sudden attention.

"Did you just arrive?" he asked with perfect diction.

Clair only nodded, and then scolded herself for not speaking.

"Then why would you want to leave? If you don't mind my asking."

"I. . .don't belong here." She admonished herself for being so bold with a stranger.

He strolled toward her. "Anyone invited here tonight *belongs* here. Come on now, you don't want to leave without meeting the author. Leslie Mandel has an uncanny sense of humor." He smoothed his tie. "And the guests are having a wonderful time. I think you will enjoy yourself, too, if you give it a chance. Please say you'll stay."

The stranger's words, as well as the soothing music, began to woo her. Her resistance faded. "Who are you?" she asked in a whisper. *Oh no.* Had she breeched another societal convention of some kind? Too quiet, and then too blunt? Her unfamiliarity with social graces always seemed to be her undoing, which was one of the many reasons she enjoyed spending most of her days tucked away in Ima's Bookshop, like a forgotten volume of a book no one cared to read. It was easy. Quiet. Certainly less stressful than mainstream life.

The handsome gentleman laughed in a rich bass voice. "Who am I? Good philosophical question. I've been asking myself that for years and have only recently found my answer inside the pages of the greatest book of all time." He placed his palms together. "Where are my manners? Sorry, I didn't introduce myself. I'm Glenn Yves, image coach." He bowed slightly.

"I'm Clair. . .O'Neal." *Am I supposed to reach out my hand first?* In introductions, her hands sometimes flailed around like the tail on a kite. Not knowing for sure about proper etiquette, she decided to twiddle her fingers behind her back.

"So glad to meet you, Ms. O'Neal," he said. "I'd love to introduce you to the author. This party launches her latest book, but she's also one of my former clients. Leslie Mandel is one of Little Rock's finest."

Clair thought of an excuse to get away, but she could only manage to stutter unintelligibly.

Glenn held out his arm to her as if she were his date. "May I escort you inside?"

Too late to run. She remembered her promise to Ima to represent the bookshop at the party. She would do it for Ima. Somehow. She whispered a prayer for help.

Glenn looked into her eyes, waiting for her response.

Clair finally accepted his arm. Glenn then whisked her into the magical land of "the beautifuls." As they walked, she ventured a glance up at his face. He stood tall, with shoulders straight, head held high. She took in the aroma of his cologne. No doubt expensive, because of the way it made her head go giddy.

Clair tried not to gape at all the pretty decorations. Thousands of twinkling lights illuminated the room like winking fairies. Three guitar players sat strumming classical music on a small stage. Not far away sat a huge ice sculpture in the center of a buffet table.

A couple of the guests offered up polite nods as she and Glenn walked through the crowd. In spite of this, Clair felt a little unnerved. Were they looking at her dress? She knew her secondhand gown didn't measure up to the others in the room, but it was the nicest thing she owned, and the soft brown color went with her hair. *Didn't it?* She glanced at herself in a wall mirror. Her shoulders slumped even more as she looked at herself. *Too thin, too pale, too awkward. I look as feminine as a cigar. Why does this man even want to talk to me?*

Glenn looked down at her and treated her to another stunning smile.

Clair felt dizzy, as though she were riding on an out-of-control merry-go-round. Her heart skipped a beat as she broke out in perspiration. She reached out to a nearby table to steady herself.

"You're trembling. Don't be afraid of these people. I'm sure they have fears, too. They've just learned to hide them better," Glenn whispered, and then he grinned. "The gentleman over there in the cowboy hat is Edsel Armstrong, Leslie's publicist, and the woman talking to him is Larkspur Wendell Holden. She's an artist from Eureka Springs and newly married. She'll have a show in the summer at one of the galleries here."

Clair sighed inside, trying to keep up. "I think—"

"First, let me introduce you to Leslie." Glenn swept Clair into the presence of a tall, elegant woman adorned in a brocade dress of steel blue. The author stood self-assured and theatrical looking next to a glitzy book cover, which sat on a large easel.

"Leslie"—Glenn kissed the author's flushed cheek—"I have someone I'd like you to meet. This is the beautiful Clair O'Neal. Clair, this is the illustrious Leslie Mandel."

Clair looked back and forth at them, not knowing how to reply. His choice of the word *beautiful* floored her. The irony stared her in the face. Why would he say such a thing?

"I love your name." Leslie's hand made a flourishing wave. "It sounds like an Irish actress in one of my novels. Guileless, yet. . .perceptive somehow."

While Glenn and Leslie cooed softly together like two pigeons, Clair suddenly felt as exposed and as foolish looking as a plucked chicken. She knew what Leslie's words meant, but she wasn't sure what to say. Clair rubbed her wrist against the back of her dress, and then bunched up a ball of the material in her sweaty palm. *Silly me.* She wished she could simply crawl away unnoticed like a worm back into the earth. It would be far less torturous than the current hyperventilating folly. "Your novel," Clair finally managed, "*The Saffron Veil. . .*"

"Yes?" Leslie leaned in toward Clair with renewed interest, tapping her ruby-painted nails against her mandarin collar.

"It's selling well at our bookshop," Clair said.

Leslie bobbed her head like a puppy waiting for more treats. "Please, tell me more."

"Your novel. . ." Clair swallowed hard. "It's. . .allegorical. . .tracing the prideful journey and the descent of civilizations that chose to follow false gods." She breathed deeply to gain control of her fear.

Glenn and Leslie stared at her for a moment.

What had come out of her mouth? *It must have been garbled,* Clair thought in growing panic.

"Well." Leslie gave Clair a slow, assessing nod. "I'm impressed. Some of my biggest fans failed to make that connection."

Clair sighed. She needn't die of humiliation just yet.

Glenn's fingers brushed Leslie's hand. "Clair, did you know that Leslie's *Dream Born* has just made the *New York Times* Best Seller list?"

"Yes, and I'm so happy for you." Clair nodded in Leslie's direction, then continued to watch as both Leslie and Glenn exchanged an occasional light touch or expressive glance. No man had ever behaved in such a comfortable manner around Clair. She wondered how it would feel to be pretty and charming. Surely such a man could make her feel that way. Embarrassed, Clair forced herself back to reality and tried to pay attention.

"Actually, that's another reason my publicist put this little festivity together," Leslie said. "Promotion. . .*and* celebration. By the way, which bookstore do you work at, Clair?"

"Ima's Bookshop. It's—"

"Oh yes. I know the one. It's in the River Market District just down the street from my brother's guitar shop. I did a book signing there in my early days. I remember Ima well."

"She's grown rather frail lately. I'm—"

"Sorry to hear it." Leslie glanced over at a small cluster of people who were chuckling. "Tell her I said hello."

"If you ladies will excuse me." Glenn touched Leslie's arm. "I see someone I need to share some hearsay with." He leaned over to Clair and whispered, "Will you be all right? I'll be back in a few minutes."

Clair nodded so quickly, she felt like her head might jar itself off her neck.

Glenn smiled at her and walked over to a small swarm of "the beautifuls." She could hear him speaking to someone in what sounded like French.

Clair realized she was alone with Leslie, and she had no more ideas for chitchat. Alarm rose in her chest, making a tight circle around her heart. *Why is Leslie staring at me? What should I say?*

Several people closed in on Leslie, so Clair backed away like a turtle into its shell. She glanced around in hopes of an escape. The main doors were too far away now for comfort. She felt her throat constricting as a parched sensation seized her.

Clair spotted a silver punch bowl across the room. Surely she could risk walking across a wide, open space for a cool drink. She took a few steps forward. No one seemed to notice her activities now that she'd moved outside of Glenn's circle.

All at once the music stopped. A man tapped his glass in front of the microphone, trying to get everyone's attention.

Maybe she could just finish her journey across the room while all eyes were on the emcee. Clair stepped out again with a hesitant stride, but midway across the marble floor, something slippery made contact with her shoes. *Water?*

The world became unstable as Clair's feet slid out from underneath her. Her hands grabbed the air, and she landed with an inelegant *thump* on her backside in the middle of the room. The bottom half of her dress twisted around her legs as her evening bag slid away. Just when she'd taken in the horror of the moment, a spotlight clicked on overhead, bathing her in a shaft of light.

Quiet laughter trickled through the room.

Clair certainly didn't feel invisible now. She struggled to get to her feet, but the heel of her shoe caught on the hem of her dress. The small awakening of hope she'd felt earlier now fluttered away like an injured bird.

No tears, Clair. No tears.

Chapter 2

To Clair's relief, the glaring spotlight swiveled to Leslie. The burst of applause and the refocused attention gave her a reprieve from her shame.

She looked up to discover a man with kindness in his eyes. He gently released the offending hem from her shoe and, with one sweep, lifted her off the floor.

Clair appreciated his gallantry, but knowing he'd seen her pitiful state made her shy away. In spite of her timidity, she noticed the stranger wore an endearing smile.

"That was quite a fall. Are you okay?" The stranger's breath felt warm and was scented with cinnamon.

Clair wanted to rub her sore posterior, but she didn't. "I'll be all right."

The stranger glanced down at the floor, crouched down, and then swiped up the spill of water with some napkins. He caught the attention of one of the waiters, frowned at him, and then tossed the balled-up napkins over to him.

"Thank you," Clair said. On closer inspection, she noticed her rescuer was an athletic sort of man in his early thirties. His brown hair appeared sun lightened, and he had a faint, but noticeable, five o'clock shadow. She glanced down at his feet, trying not to stare. He wore tennis shoes with his trousers. She recalled what Ima always said about humans coming in all sorts of astonishing designs. It appeared to be true.

"By the way. . ." The stranger's face went blank. "I'm. . .I'm Hudson Mandel. I sort of forgot who I was for a second." He laughed.

"Clair. . .O'Neal." *Does he have the same last name as the author?* Ima had mentioned Leslie Mandel was single, so perhaps he was her brother.

"Glad to meet you."

Without taking time to fret about it, Clair reached out her hand to him. The warmth and security of his touch made her want to hold on. But as she released his hand, she could tell he'd been the one to linger a bit longer. "I don't usually go to. . .parties."

He tugged on his collar as if it were a noose. "I know the feeling." He lowered his voice. "They're impossible to navigate sometimes. It's easier to be up on stage than to do this mingling thing." He grinned. "A pack of wild boars might be less grueling."

Clair felt something unfamiliar rising out of her—laughter. Something she'd forgotten how to do. She covered her mouth. The moment would hold enough joy for her to live on for a long time.

"You have a nice laugh. . .musical." Hudson had a hint of a smile. "You could put lyrics to it."

Did he actually mean such admiring praise or was he just being gregarious? "Thank you." Clair noticed Hudson appeared to be the same age as Glenn, and just as handsome, yet he seemed different—less intimidating.

Hudson pulled a package of gum out of his pocket and extended it in her direction. "Would you like a piece? Helps you to deal with the crowds. . .you know, to exchange profound and witty remarks that mean absolutely nothing. I'm sure you. . .well. . .uh. . ." He chuckled as his face flushed. "I guess I need some." He took a piece and popped it into his mouth with a smile.

"I think you're doing fine." Clair removed a stick of gum from the packet, thinking how much calmer she felt standing next to Hudson. She noticed he was the same height as she was—not tall and not short, but somewhere in between. His eyes were far from average, though—luminous, coffee-colored, and memorable. "Thank you for the gum."

Hudson pressed his lips together. Then he folded his arms and looked at the floor.

His obvious uneasiness warmed Clair all over. She felt an immediate kinship with him and delighted in every second, since she knew the perfect moment would end soon.

"By the way"—Hudson gestured toward the small stage—"those are my students up there."

She glanced over at them, amazed. "You teach guitar?"

"Well, I own the River Front Guitar Shop, and I have the honor of volunteer tutoring some disadvantaged, but very dedicated, teens."

I know that shop. Clair realized Hudson was indeed Leslie's brother, since she'd mentioned his guitar shop was down the street from Ima's Bookshop. In fact, Clair had walked by his storefront countless times. She doubted anything would come of their acquaintance but still tucked the knowledge of it away in her heart. "Your students are very good." Her shoulders relaxed.

"Yes, they are. I'm proud of them."

"Classical." Clair shook her head, relishing the delicate and moving strains. "So beautiful."

"Oh yes." He looked back at her. "Beautiful," he repeated in a whisper.

How he loves his students. Clair admired his dedication.

"Do you play?" Hudson asked.

"No, not at all. But I would love to. Vocal music has always been an important part of my life, but playing an instrument has eluded me—at least so far." She surprised herself, answering so quickly and candidly. Though she loved to sing, she'd never spent much time thinking about playing the guitar until this very moment. The idea settled in, and a wave of contentment washed over her.

"Come by the shop, then. I would love to teach you."

Clair couldn't think of anything more delightful; she only wished she had the money for such a wonderful endeavor. "To be able to share your gift of music—nothing could be finer." Why was it so easy to talk to him?

"I couldn't agree more." Hudson wore a dreamy sort of expression as he hummed a tune.

The melody sounded familiar to Clair—a song from her youth—entrancing and bittersweet.

Hudson rubbed his chin, looking bemused as if he were trying to think of something else to say.

Clair thought she should help him out. "I work down the street from you. At—"

Suddenly, a burly man in hippie attire bolted over to them. He looked as out of place as Clair felt. "Hey, I thought that was you," the fellow said to Hudson. "Do you remember me? I'm your old college roommate, Nathan Taylor." He gave Hudson a scrunching hug.

Their manly embrace looked painful to Clair, but she was far from familiar with male customs. She decided to give the two friends some time to themselves, so she backed away.

As Clair headed in the direction of the punch bowl, her muse about Hudson intensified. A twinge of pain came over her, along with exhilaration. How could it be? She'd never felt so wistful and yet so consciously alive—so forlorn and yet astonished. *Have I just met the desire of my heart? Dear Lord, I wish, oh how I wish. . .*

When she arrived at the punch table, Clair accepted a cup of the foamy pink drink. "Thank you." She took a sip then turned back to indulge in one more secret glimpse of the man who occupied her thoughts. She nearly dropped her cup as Hudson emerged from the crowd and marched right toward her.

Chapter 3

Hudson strode up to Clair, hoping he didn't look too red-faced. "Hello again."

"Hi." Clair's face lit up.

He offered up a shrug. "You were welcome to stay and visit back there."

"I didn't want to interrupt. . .your reunion."

Hudson was relieved she didn't seem upset in the least. "Turned out, he wasn't my roommate. He had me confused with somebody else."

"Really?" She fiddled with her empty cup.

Now that Clair was standing in front of him, he was speechless. He pointed at her cup. "Is that stuff good?" *Oh brother. That was deep.*

"Yes, it's some kind of pink minty foam."

He grinned at her. "Sounds awful."

Clair laughed. "Not really."

"I'll give it a try." Hudson picked up a full cup off the table and drank it straight down. *Oh. Wow.* He tried hard not to make the revolting expression his taste buds demanded. The stuff tasted like nausea medicine. What was his sister thinking?

Clair pointed to her lip and smiled. "You have a little pink mustache." She offered Hudson a napkin.

For a second their hands touched in midair. If he'd known how to make the moment last longer, he would have made it happen. *I'll drink three more cups if she'll keep handing me napkins.* In fact, he knew he'd be willing to drink every drop in the bowl just to be near her. And he wasn't even sure why.

Clair held her cup over to the server, and the man refilled it up to the brim. Clair gave Hudson a shy smile as she sipped off a bit of the foam.

Now Clair had a cute little mustache, so he handed her a napkin from the table. Inside the haze of Hudson's romantic inclinations for Clair, he heard a woman's voice calling his name. He turned and realization set in. *It's Nona.*

"I'm sorry," he whispered to Clair. "I really wish I could stay longer, but I need to go." He let out a lingering sigh. "I gave someone a ride this evening. Nona. She's a friend of a friend who wanted to meet Leslie. *And* I promised her I'd introduce her around at the party."

Clair glanced over in Nona's direction. "That was very kind of you."

Hudson wished he hadn't been so kind. He'd like to get to know Clair better and take her out for coffee later. But duty called.

Clair set her cup down and looked at him. "I understand."

I think she really does. Hudson turned to go, and then stopped. *I don't want to walk away. I'll never see her again.* "Where did you say you worked?" He backed away from Clair without taking his eyes off her.

"Ima's Bookshop."

"I know the one. Just down the street from me." He smiled. "Maybe we could. . ." *No, don't say it. Not yet.* "Take care."

"I will." Clair's gaze shifted to the ground.

"Later then." He paused one more time to take in her sweet face, and then headed over to the bouncing and waving Nona.

❧

Clair's shoulder's sagged as she watched Hudson maneuver through the cluster of guests. Why did her heart ache as he disappeared through the crowd? Had she thought, even for a moment, he might have been working up the courage to ask her out on a date? Would she have said yes?

She felt foolish standing there pining away, so she switched her attention to an exit she hadn't noticed before. With renewed vigor and swift steps, she made her way through the double doors, past the main entry hall, and outside into the cool night air.

To catch her breath, Clair stopped for a moment and leaned against an iron railing. People all dressed up in shimmering gowns and tuxedos glided by her and into the hotel. *Guess I'm a plain sparrow fluttering among a flock of doves.* She chuckled.

Clair filled her lungs with the late March air. A fresh breeze sweetened the night, feeling like silk against her skin. She suddenly thought of everyone gawking at her while she was sprawled across the floor. *It will be enough disgrace to last me for years.* She sighed.

But Hudson and his kind spirit would linger in her mind much longer than the embarrassment. She opened her hand to look at the gum he'd given her. She unwrapped it leisurely, rolled it up into a wad, and stuffed it in her mouth. Juicy. Spicy. Sweet. Hudson was right. Chewing the gum did calm her.

Clair noticed a couple getting into a black limousine, but she knew she couldn't even afford a taxi. The hike home was several blocks, but she was used to walking, though not necessarily under the shadows of the evening.

So, Clair glanced back once more, and then headed down the sidewalk, wishing all the while she could afford to fix her car. As she crossed the street at the first available stoplight, she prayed the Lord would protect her every step of the way. Then she focused on the sidewalk, doing all she could to avoid the eyes of passersby.

After a few minutes, the darkness felt like a heavy wool blanket, closing in around her. A shiver ran down Clair's spine as the night's shadows seemed to swallow her whole. She quoted a familiar scripture, seeking God's protective hand as she inched her way along. " 'Even though I walk through the valley of the shadow of death, I will fear no evil. . .'" Somehow just whispering the words from the psalm brought comfort.

Suddenly, from out of the cover of night, a white stretch limo cruised up next to her. Clair's heart quickened, and she kept watch on the vehicle as she picked up her pace.

One of the heavily tinted windows rolled down, revealing a man in a suit.

Clair couldn't see his face. She strode away from the limo. Her heels clatter-clomped on the concrete as if to keep time with her racing heartbeat.

"Don't be afraid. Glenn to your rescue here."

She stopped, relieved to hear a voice she recognized. As she turned and caught a glimpse of Glenn's face, Clair's fears dissipated. "But why are you following me?"

Glenn leaned outside the window. "I must confess I came looking for you because I was worried."

"Ah." *He must've seen my fall.*

"You disappeared like Houdini." He flashed a rehearsed pout.

"Sorry. I guess I should have said good-bye."

"But I thought you were having a good time."

She shrugged and glanced around, slightly unnerved by the sound of approaching footsteps. "A little."

"I want to drive you home. I feel responsible somehow."

"Why?" Clair wasn't sure what to think of his attentions. People, especially men, rarely even noticed her.

"I don't know," Glenn said. "Maybe because I talked you into something you didn't really want to do."

Clair started walking again, slowly. "I. . .can't let you take me home." Through the shadows, a couple of men passed her by. She tried to remain focused on the sidewalk, tried not to be afraid. *"Even though I walk through the valley of the shadow. . ."*

"And can you please tell me why?" Glenn gestured with his hand.

The limo crept along with her as she walked. "Because I don't know you. . . very well."

"Oh." Glenn chuckled. "That makes sense. But I promise you I'm a fine Christian man." He leaned back inside. "Drew, my man, tell this young lady what a great Christian guy I am."

The front window rolled down. The chauffeur tipped his hat back. "Good evening, miss."

"Hi."

"I've known Glenn a long time," Drew said. "He's a good guy. Cheap as a used toothpick sometimes, but—"

"Marvelous." Glenn frowned. "Thanks."

"You're welcome, sir," Drew replied with a grin.

Glenn peered out the window, donning a beseeching look.

He's trying to soften me up. "I'm not sure."

Off in the distance, a man stepped out of the shadows and leaned against a light pole. He took a long drink from something hidden inside a paper bag then glanced Clair's way. A shiver ran down her spine as the stranger staggered toward her.

She gasped and turned toward the limo. "Yes please. Help!"

Chapter 4

The limo lurched to a halt. Drew jumped out and opened the back door for Clair.

She scooted inside the car and gripped her hands on the seat. "Please lock the—"

The moment he slipped back inside, all the doors locked soundly.

Clair let out a breath of air. *Safe.* After she'd calmed down, she told them her address.

The stranger, just outside their window, spewed obscenities at them. He reminded Clair of a mangy dog she'd befriended once on the playground at school, but all she could safely do now was send up a prayer for him and one of thanksgiving that she hadn't been hurt.

In spite of her relief, Clair stayed near the door handle. Even though Glenn had a consoling smile and she felt grateful for his help, he still seemed an imposing figure.

Once the car shifted back into gear and they pulled away, Glenn turned to her. "If you get any closer to that door handle, you'll make Drew think you're about to jump ship." Drew laughed, and Glenn added, "I promise. . .you have nothing to be afraid of in here."

Clair nodded then glanced back toward the street as the man disappeared from view.

"Looked like a scary guy," Glenn observed. "I don't even want to think about what could have happened to you back there."

He seemed concerned. She stopped chewing her gum and shifted it to the inside of her cheek as she explained. "My car—it needs a new transmission. That's why I was walking."

Glenn lowered his voice. "Well, taking a cab is always an option."

How much should she reveal about her financial situation? Glenn would soon see her modest home, so he might as well know all of it. "I needed the money for my. . .electric bill next month."

"I shouldn't be pressuring answers out of you. I apologize." Glenn appeared perplexed. He drummed his fingers on a book sitting between them.

Clair glanced down to discover a leather-bound Bible. She relaxed and let go of some of her fears. *"For you are with me; your rod and your staff, they comfort me."*

She glanced around, taking note of the limo's interior—the creamy leather, the romantic lighting, and the soft swirling jazz. So luxurious. Like a miniature palace on wheels. So unlike the surroundings she'd grown used to. She gave her gum a few more chews, but it'd become tasteless and stiff. When she thought Glenn wouldn't notice, she slipped the little round ball back into its wrapper.

Glenn held out his hand in front of her.

Oh dear. He'd noticed the gum. Had she been smacking? Clair could feel her eyes widen and her skin color all the way down to her toes. She gingerly placed the wrapped gum into his palm. "Thank you," she whispered.

"My pleasure." He disposed of it then flipped open a leather-covered lid. Inside were sodas and sparkling water on ice. "Would you like something to drink?"

Clair shook her head.

"I'm curious about your job." Glenn took a Perrier from the cooler. "You said you work at Ima's Bookshop in the River Market District?"

"Yes. I work for Ima Langston. She owns the bookshop. I stock the shelves and help with the paperwork."

"And is that what you want to do with your life?" He poured his drink into a glass.

Clair ventured a glance in his direction. His double-breasted suit framed an elegant build, and his silky dark curls softened his extravagant exterior. "Ima is. . . good to me. So it would be unkind if I left her now. She needs me."

"But if you could do anything, what would it be?" He took a sip of his beverage.

She twisted her wrist against her leg. A babyish habit, but somehow it gave her comfort when life got too exhausting. Or when questions got too probing. "I suppose I want to. . .own a bookstore someday. I guess. But that would mean I'd have to deal more with. . .customers and employees. It's a people kind of business, but I'm a. . ."

"You're a what?" Glenn's tone came off gentle but concerned.

"It's not easy for me to talk about." A stillness settled around them. The quiet seemed to last an eternity to Clair.

A few moments later, Drew pulled up in front of her house.

"Thank you. . .for bringing me home." Clair felt self-conscious about the shabbiness of her small home—the peeling gray paint and the broken sidewalk that led up to the front porch. But she certainly couldn't change anything now. *If only I'd had enough money to plant some tulips.*

"Yes, of course." Glenn's expression changed from buoyancy to pensiveness as he looked beyond her toward the little house. His window motored down halfway and then he gripped the glass. "It was my pleasure." He stared at her home in silence then turned to take in the rest of the street.

Was he shocked at the ramshackle cheerlessness of it? Or was he not feeling well?

Glenn turned back to her with the oddest look on his face, one she couldn't interpret. Then he reached to take her hand, wide-eyed. "Clair, before you go. . ."

"Yes?"

"I. . .I feel a prompting from the Lord to help you."

"Help me?" Clair felt more confused than ever.

Glenn looked just beyond her face. A flicker of something distant and forlorn passed through his expression. "I remember a time when I could barely speak in front of anyone, let alone a crowd. I was the kid at the back of the room, petrified of my own shadow."

Glenn seemed to wait for her reaction. What could she say? Confidence and charisma seemed to mark his every move and word. He spoke so well, he could surely command a room full of people with a mere wave of his hand. It was difficult for her to imagine him as a quiet, frightened boy. "You seem. . .fearless." She felt her cheeks warm.

"Cocky is a better word," Drew called from the driver's seat.

Glenn chortled. "Thanks, old buddy. You're killing me here." He pushed a button. Drew rolled his eyes and grinned as the glass enclosed them in a cocoon of privacy.

"Many years ago, someone offered me some help and I took it. I was then able to pull myself up from some pretty rough circumstances." He smoothed his tie. "Now I teach people how to present themselves in their business and private worlds."

Clair squeezed her hands so tightly she could feel her heartbeat in her fingers. "But I can't afford your help." Surely he could tell that by looking at her home.

"Please let me explain. This man, Walter Sullivan, gave me the leg up with one condition. He wanted me to pass the help on to someone else once I'd succeeded in my profession. I'm embarrassed to say I'd totally forgotten my promise to Walter, until I saw you tonight."

Clair put her hand to her cheek. "I've always been. . .shy. But I guess I didn't realize how pitiful I looked."

"No. Not at all." Glenn turned toward her and smiled. "You, Clair O'Neal, are a gift from heaven this earth has yet to open."

She met his gaze. His hazel eyes appeared so startling and inquisitive, she looked away. *Why would he say such a thing? He doesn't even know me.*

Glenn cleared his throat. "I didn't mention it earlier, but I did see you fall."

Clair cringed. "I was afraid of that."

"Yes. I almost made it to you in time, but I saw Leslie's brother, Hudson, come to your aid." Glenn turned away. "Then later, I couldn't find you."

"You saw me fall. . .and you *still* want to help me?"

"I'm certain I do." Glenn reached out his hand but then drew it back. "But not as a client. As a friend." He appeared to study her expression. "Please understand me. I mean this offer within a totally professional context. But I want to handle it as Walter did—as a friend. I know you don't know me. And all this must seem strange to you"—he turned once more to glance at her house—"but I can assure you I've never been more serious in my life."

Clair looked at her hands, intertwined like a knotted rope. "I want to be. . . less bashful? It makes me feel so. . ."

"Caged and helpless?" Glenn finished.

"Yes. Sometimes." She turned away to the window again, embarrassed to be speaking of such intimate matters with a person she'd just met. Then again, perhaps the Lord had sent Glenn Yves to her as a gift—to push her beyond the insecurities that had held her bound for so many years, to rid her of the unspoken doubts and fears.

"I believe I can help."

Oh Lord, I'm ready, if this is Your timing. I've walked this road for so long.

Clair's palms perspired again. Could she truly find a way out of the lonely place she'd known since childhood? It seemed impossible, but maybe the words of her stepfather had been untrue. Perhaps she wasn't a misfit. She suddenly imagined herself doing some of the things she'd dreamed of—waiting on customers at the bookshop, joining the women's group at church, and maybe even helping needy kids.

Clair had no idea how the Lord might use Glenn to bring about such miracles, but saying no to such a generous offer seemed unwise. She summoned her courage to look at him. Compassion filled his eyes, yet something else lingered in his smile. A glimmer she couldn't read. No matter how kind he appeared, she would keep her caution within reach.

"Yes," Clair said softly, "I guess you'll be Dr. Frankenstein, and I will be your monster."

Chapter 5

Glenn threw his head back and laughed.

Clair was pleased to make him laugh, but in spite of the sudden camaraderie, she felt grateful all had been made clear. Glenn would simply be fulfilling a promise. Besides, the thought of any romantic interest with him was beyond silly. Even if he could help her with her timidity, she would still be one of "the invisibles," and he, one of "the beautifuls." Clair felt her face getting warm just knowing what she'd say next. "Will you be able to help me stop. . . blushing?"

"Now why would I want to do that?" Glenn rested back on the soft leather seat. "It's an endearing quality. People rarely blush anymore. Most people have seen and heard too much, I suppose."

"But it makes me feel. . .like a child."

"No, you're just unassuming and meek. And if this book is true"—he rested his hand on the Bible—"the meek do not go unblessed."

"True," she whispered.

He glanced at her house once more then turned back, giving her a warm smile. "I do believe we were meant to meet tonight, Clair. Surely the Lord had a hand in this."

"Do you think?"

"I do." He kissed the back of her hand and whispered, "But it is late, and I don't want to keep you."

"Thank you so much for the ride. And. . .for your offer to help me."

"You're welcome." He released her hand. "Good night, Clair. We'll wait until you're snugly inside before we go. And in the next week or so, I'll drop by your bookshop." He smiled at her.

"Good-bye." Like a coach's door in a fairytale, Clair's door magically opened.

Drew stood near, uniformed and dignified, but he smiled, tipping his hat at her. "Take care."

She thanked him and then took long strides up the path. As she approached her front door, she remembered leaving her evening bag in the hotel. *Oh no! How could I have done that?* Clair reproached herself and reached under the planter for the extra key, trying to recall the contents of her thrift store purse. A house key, a peppermint, Ima's business card, a plastic comb. . . Whoever discovered the bag would certainly be unimpressed. But what else would the person find? Ah yes. Her driver's license. Surely that would help in the recovery process.

Clair turned back around to the street, noticing that Glenn and Drew still waited in the limo. She raised her hand in a wave and then slipped through the front door. Clair made her way through her musty house with the glow from a clear moon. Except for the eternal ticking of a wall clock, she noted what a cave-like space welcomed her home. Eager to see, she flicked the switch.

Light flooded her small abode.

As she turned, Clair caught her reflection in a wall mirror—thick eyebrows, forlorn brown eyes, and shoulder-length, mousy dark hair that hadn't had a real beauty shop cut in five years. And yet just this evening, Glenn had referred to her as beautiful. *Hmm.* She leaned in a bit closer, looking for some sort of hidden treasure. She would have to remember to look up *beautiful* in the dictionary. Surely the meaning had been updated to read, "Plain as a mayonnaise sandwich."

The wall clock came to life. Eight chimes. *I'm probably the only twenty-first-century female who ever left a party before nine o'clock. Oh well. There are worse things to be known for.*

Clair gave up on her image and headed to the kitchen. She looked around at the existence she'd created for herself, which was now illuminated by the harsh florescent lights. Clumps of flowers, dried from her backyard, hung upside down over the sink, faded and lifeless. The rest of the kitchen was almost bare except for a table and chairs. *Not too appealing.* Clair wondered if Glenn could help her be a bit more light and merry. *How lovely that would be.*

Just before bed, Clair settled into her worn but comfortable chair with a cup of chamomile tea and a novel. Dear Ima allowed her to read any of the books in the shop as long as she didn't bend the pages, but even the latest hot-off-the-press Christian novel couldn't keep her thoughts from whirling off, playing the night's events over and over in her mind. Especially the moments with Hudson. What a wonderful addition he had been to an otherwise nerve-wracking night. His eyes, filled with kindness. The sound of his voice bringing comfort. The touch of his hand as he reached to help her.

Yes, the Lord had surely sent Hudson at just the right time. She sighed as she pondered it all. So much to take in. Years had gone by in her life with less activity than she'd known in one brief evening. Clearly, the Lord was at work. There was no denying it.

And what about Glenn? She wouldn't lay aside the idea that his offer of help might be linked to the stirring hand of God also. Could it be it wasn't too late for something wonderful to happen in her life?

Clair bit her lower lip, forcing herself not to cry. There had been too much sorrow in her childhood, more than any little girl deserved. But now hope had come near—a brand-new emotion. And that hope gave her courage to believe the impossible.

Yes, surely the Lord had orchestrated this evening's events—in preparation for something more, perhaps? *"He restores my soul."* The psalm continued to run through her mind, bringing assurance and a sense of overwhelming peace.

Clair set the book down on her lap and began to sing a familiar worship song, a joy she'd known in solitude for as long as she could remember. Like a reassuring hug, she let the words soothe and encourage her.

Bedtime arrived, but sleep did not come easily for Clair. She stared out into the moonlit night, thinking and praying.

After a restless sleep, Clair rose later than usual. She hurried to get dressed, anxious to see if Ima was feeling better. She put on her best wool slacks and pullover sweater and began her walk to the bookshop.

In spite of the budding trees and smell of spring, the weather had turned frosty overnight. The chilling breeze seeped through her coat, so Clair snuggled her hands down into her pockets and walked more briskly toward the river.

For a brief moment, the street emptied of cars and an unearthly quiet settled over her spirit. Music—a familiar friend—began to play in her head, first as if from far away and then louder and clearer. As Clair strode along the sidewalk, she sang the tune softly to herself. *Ah yes.* Sweet and stirring, like a fragrant zephyr. The song was a favorite from her past and the very same melody Hudson had hummed at the party.

Looking both ways, she trotted across the street toward the bookshop. Clair had always admired Ima's storefront. The redbrick facade and the antique sign made the shop quaint and appealing. The benches and black lampposts along the avenue also gave the area a charming look. A streetcar suddenly rolled by on its tracks, and Clair couldn't help but smile as she noted the smiling tourists inside. She loved all of the old-fashioned elements of her fair city. They brought a familiar comfort. If only she had been born in a different era, a time when quiet, reserved women were the norm instead of an anomaly. Yes, she would surely have made a fine character in a nineteenth-century tale.

Thinking of books reminded Clair to stop dreaming and check on Ima. She pulled out her key, opened the door, and listened to the familiar jangle of the bell. How she had grown to love the sound. It meant she'd entered the kind and comforting world of Ima and her treasures.

Clair closed the door. "Ima." She glanced down at the chair where Ima always tossed her purse. There it sat, reassuring her that all was well. Clair breathed in the smell of peppermint. Her employer liked to keep lots of potpourri around the shop in little terra-cotta bowls. The soothing fragrance along with the soft chairs and oak shelves made the Christian bookshop cozy and inviting. Ima had wanted the store to be like home, and the customers loved it.

The metal bell above the door jangled again. Clair turned to discover Hudson Mandel standing in the doorway. She could hardly believe it. Her heart pounded faster at the sight of him, and she couldn't seem to hide the smile that rose up.

"Hi," he said.

Clair smiled and tried to still her thumping heart. "Hello."

"Something smells good." Hudson cleared his throat. "Well, I. . .uh. . .came by to give you this." He eased her evening bag from his coat pocket and set it down on the counter as if it were an heirloom.

She slipped her coat off. "Thank you." Clair felt a little dismayed, wishing the purse hadn't been the reason he'd dropped by.

Their eyes met. Clair realized it hadn't been something she'd made up in her mind. Hudson really *did* have the warmest, darkest brown eyes she'd ever seen.

After staring at each other for an immeasurable amount of time, Clair moved her gaze to a row of empty shelves. Her thoughts shifted to the changes Ima wanted to make in the bookshop. *Ima?* She still hadn't heard her employer make any noises in the back room. "I'm sorry. But I need to check on Ima. She hasn't been feeling well lately."

"Don't let me keep you. But I don't mind waiting." He removed his coat. "I wanted to ask you something."

Ask me something? Clair blushed. "I'll only be a moment." She made her way toward the back room, stepping around boxes stacked in the hallway. She glanced toward the ladies' room. Open and lights off. "Ima? Are you okay?" When Clair heard no answer, she felt a quickening of her heart. She hurried to the tiny kitchen, panic engulfing her as she saw Ima, pale and lifeless on the floor.

"No!" Clair grabbed onto the doorframe to steady herself. She wanted to scream, but only a sob escaped. Her head went dizzy. Clair willed herself to stay conscious as she knelt next to Ima and placed her finger on the side of her neck. No pulse. "Ima, can you hear me?" Should she try to do CPR or call 911? Clair heard a ringing in her ears, and she felt like she was moving through a tunnel. *I cannot pass out! Lord, please help me.*

Hudson burst into the room. "Clair, what happened?" Without waiting for an answer, he rushed to Ima's side.

Chapter 6

C all 911!" Hudson tilted Ima's head back and put his ear to the woman's mouth to listen and feel for her breath. Nothing. He pressed his finger to her neck. No pulse. *Oh God, help this woman.*

Clair stood frozen, the color draining from her face.

"We need to call 911!"

"Yes." Clair staggered to her feet and grabbed the phone on the wall.

Hudson stared at Ima. No breathing. No pulse. He knew he'd have to do CPR. Was it ten compressions or fifteen? *Quick, think, man.* He started the compressions. "One. Two. Three." He continued to count to fifteen. He blew into Ima's mouth two times, hoping he was right.

Clair knelt down opposite Hudson, still clutching the phone. "They're coming," she said, "but they've asked me to stay on the line. D–do you feel any heartbeat?"

Hudson felt for a pulse again and watched Ima's chest for movement. Nothing.

"She has to be okay," Clair whispered. "She has to be. Oh please, dear God. . ."

Ima remained unresponsive, and her skin felt cool like marble. Unnaturally cool. Hudson feared she'd already gone. He kept up the CPR. After a moment, he glanced up. Clair's eyes had that faraway look again. "You okay?"

"Yes." She continued to grip the phone.

"Count with me."

Clair's mouth eased open, but no words came out.

"Are you with me?"

She caught his gaze and nodded.

"Come on," Hudson said. "Five, six, seven, eight, nine. . ."

Clair began counting along with him.

After a few more minutes, Hudson could hear the sirens. "They're here."

"I'll go." Clair passed on the information to the person on the other end of the phone line, then ended the call. She scrambled up off the floor and ran out of the room.

The wail of the sirens grew louder until Hudson heard voices at the front of the store. Immediately paramedics surrounded him. He stepped away from Ima. "She's not breathing, and I can't find a heartbeat."

Clair's eyes rolled back as she slumped against the wall.

Hudson caught her before she fell to the floor. He swept her up in his arms and took her from the room.

"Do you need some help?" one of the paramedics yelled to him.

"She's fainted, but I think she'll be okay." Hudson noticed the store's tiny back office, just a few feet from where he now stood, and began to move in that direction. *A couch.* With care, he eased Clair down onto the cushions.

He snatched some paper towels from the bathroom and ran some cold water. He glanced through the door.

One paramedic pulled out what looked like defibrillator paddles.

Once back at Clair's side, Hudson brushed her hair away from her face and dabbed the damp towels on her forehead and began to pray. The morning certainly hadn't gone as planned, but somehow he knew he was in the right place. Surely the Lord had led him here so that Clair wouldn't have to face this alone.

Just then, she let out a puff of air and released a faint moan.

He took hold of her hand. "Clair?"

Her eyes fluttered open.

Hudson smiled. *Thank You, Lord.* He squeezed her hand, noticing how fragile it felt and yet how warm.

"What happened?" Clair took in a deep breath.

"You're okay. You just fainted."

"Ima." She looked over his shoulder with wide eyes. "I've got to help her. Is she okay now?"

"I think they're about to put her on the gurney. She'll be on her way soon."

"I want to go with her." Clair clasped the sleeve of his coat.

She had the most earnest look on her face, he wanted to take her into his arms and tell her all would be well. But he knew he couldn't make that promise, and noting Clair's shyness, a hug would more likely shock her than comfort her. "I doubt they'll let us go with them, but I'm sure we can follow the ambulance."

"You don't have to take me. I'll call a taxi."

"I'm glad to do it."

"It's the second time," Clair whispered.

"Second time for what?"

"I keep falling," she said. "And you keep picking me up."

He smiled at her.

"I'm all right now." She rubbed her head as she rose to a sitting position.

Hudson helped her off the couch and then held her until she was steady on her feet.

They made their way back into the store, watching as the paramedics lifted Ima's body onto a stretcher and wheeled it out the front door. All the while,

Clair stood in silence, her face pale.

Once the ambulance pulled away, Hudson again offered to drive her to the hospital. She agreed this time then locked up the store and hurried with him to his pickup truck.

A chilling wind whipped their clothes as Hudson opened the door for her and helped her inside. He glanced upward, noting the clouds and the approaching storm. He ran to the driver's side, scooted in under the wheel, and followed the flashing lights and sirens down the freeway.

Hudson caught a glimpse of Clair as he turned the corner. She sat still and lovely like a pale rose. *Is she afraid for Ima or afraid of me?* They'd only just met the evening before, so it was possible she didn't fully trust him yet. But he couldn't have felt more different. Somehow, he not only trusted her, he felt an immediate connection.

Then the thought of her soft sweater against his skin came to mind. *I need to keep my wits.* Hudson gave the steering wheel a white-knuckled grip to concentrate on his driving. "You okay?"

Clair nodded as she stared down at her hands, which were folded together like a little nest.

Perhaps she was already grieving for her employer, thinking as he did that Ima had already passed away. He wanted to console Clair but wasn't sure how. He'd always been better expressing emotion through his lyrics than his lips. *Wish I could fix that someday.*

Minutes later, they pulled into the emergency parking at St. John Medical Center. Once they were inside, a nurse asked them to sit in the waiting room. They made their way through the starkly lit room, amidst the smell of disinfectant and the throng of people.

Clair finally chose a string of empty molded seats in the corner by the snack machines. Hudson slid in next to her. The chairs felt hard and unforgiving, so he leaned forward with his elbows on his knees. He made another appeal to the Almighty to spare Ima, but he knew her life would have to be left in His hands.

Clair rose and paced back and forth, her arms hugging her waist. She hummed ever so faintly.

The minutes drifted on and on as they waited for news of Ima. Hudson shifted to find a more comfortable position. *What a miserable little seat.* He rubbed his hands along the legs of his jeans and noticed a stack of magazines. The entire heap, though, appeared to be for women. *Great.* After he'd flipped through and read all he could stand on menopause and fashion tips, he slipped the magazine back into its pile for some other lucky guy to digest.

He glanced over at Clair. She stood near the soda machine with her eyes closed. He couldn't tell if she was praying or just resting her eyes. He realized she might want something to drink, so he pulled out his wallet.

A man strode up to them wearing a white jacket and a grave smile—a smile that surely revealed the truth of Ima's fate. He introduced himself as Dr. Milburn.

"I'm sorry to have to tell you this. . ." he started. His gaze shifted down to the ground, then back up again, as he spoke in a low voice, "Your friend. . .I'm afraid she didn't make it."

Clair shook her head, and a look of disbelief came over her.

The doctor gave her a sympathetic look as he explained. "She died of heart failure."

Clair's trembling hand covered her mouth. She blinked a few times, but no tears filled her eyes.

Hudson ached to reach out to her but felt he should wait for a sign that his comfort might be needed. No sign came, so he just stood near her.

Moments later, they were whisked off into the administrative office. Clair answered all their questions, giving them information about Ima's sister in Pine Bluff.

After Clair viewed Ima's body once more, Hudson waited for her just outside the door. When she came out, he gently placed his hand on her back and steered her through the clusters of people who waited with their own heartbreaks and hopes.

When they reached the foyer, Clair said, "I'll call for a taxi. Thank you. . .for everything. You've been so kind. How can I ever—"

"Please let me drive you home or back to the store." He studied her expression. Her large brown eyes took him in yet still kept him at a distance.

Clair glanced away. "Why are you helping me?"

"Well, you're a fellow human being, and you need help." That was all true. But why couldn't he be bold enough to say the rest? *Probably because she'd think I was certifiable.*

Truth was he liked her, even though they'd barely met. In fact, Clair seemed to be just like the woman he'd written about in one of his songs—a young woman who was a little misplaced in the world, yet so full of goodness. He'd never known a woman like Clair could really exist beyond his own imagination. *But she's standing right in front of me.* He thought of her anguish again. *I better not push.* He knew grief had to be a personal journey.

Clair's gaze slowly met his. "Okay." She nodded. "You may drive me back to the bookshop."

Hudson felt so pleased with her answer he wanted to embrace her. *Not good. I just need to calm down.*

Later as he drove Clair back to the store, Hudson considered grief and all its revelations. A person's disposition certainly seemed easier to discern while under fire. Based on all he had seen thus far, Clair had a strong and steady faith. Hudson recalled his own response to his uncle's sudden heart attack, and how he'd allowed his mind to become coated with a dark layer of doubts about God. Fortunately, over time, he'd been able to rise above the uncertainties, but it wasn't easy.

He wondered what Clair's haunts—the word he always used for the things that bugged people—were. Their weakest links. Everyone had them. Even Christians.

Once Hudson had Clair safely back at the shop, he caught himself gazing at her just as he had that very morning. Fortunately, the color had come back to her face, but the sadness in her eyes tore at his heart.

He glanced around the bookshelves so he wouldn't be caught gawking at her. He hadn't noticed before, but many of the bookshelves were empty, and stacks of boxes sat near the counter. It looked like they were about to restock. On the wall just above Clair's head were all kinds of hats—a fedora, a derby, a sombrero, and even a green beanie cap with a little red propeller on top.

Hudson coughed since he couldn't think of anything to say. Should he ask her out for coffee at the shop down the street? Would she consider him the worst kind of jerk under the circumstances, or would she welcome the company? *In a second or two, you'll have to either say something or leave. Just open your mouth.*

Chapter 7

Instinct told Hudson the moment wasn't right to ask her for what she might consider a date, even though he longed to help Clair deal with her grief. "I guess I'll go. Let me know if you need anything."

"Okay." Clair seemed to look at everything in the store but him.

Hudson shuffled his feet, thinking he must look more like a squirming child than a man. "If you need anything at all. . ." *Anything. I'm here.*

She nodded.

He opened the door of the shop and turned once more to Clair. If the bookshop were to close now, he might never see her again. The very idea tore at his heart. "I'd certainly like to take you out for some coffee."

Clair suddenly looked surprised. Maybe shocked was a better word.

"I would like to, but under the circumstances, I'd better not," Clair said. "But thank you."

Hudson's mouth flew open. *I was mumbling out loud again? Oh brother.* "What did I say. . .exactly?"

Clair blushed. "You said you'd like to take me out for some coffee."

"I have this habit of just saying what's in my head. Sorry." Hudson wondered what else he'd said. Should he offer to go with her to Ima's funeral? Maybe he'd better leave before she knew he was a total fool. "Bye. Be careful now."

"Bye."

Without humiliating himself further, Hudson waved and eased out the door. He could have kicked himself for putting his needs first. *What was I thinking?*

Walking back toward his shop, he reached another impasse in his mind. If he wanted to ask Clair out on a date, he'd have to dredge up his persuasive skills again.

But then there was also the issue of Tara Williamson. His family and Tara's folks had indeed known each other since the origin of dirt, but even with the manipulative efforts of her family and his sister, he and Tara had only dated a little on and off. Mostly as friends. In spite of all the facts, when it came to Tara and matrimony, he still felt the pressure.

A car honked, jerking Hudson from his thoughts. He stuffed his hands in the pockets of his coat. Even with his long-sleeved shirt and heavy coat, the air still felt cold to him. Maybe he'd have a hot cup of coffee anyway. *Darrell can handle the guitar shop for a bit. I need some time to think.* A steaming mug of coffee sounded good, even if he had to drink it alone.

☙

A couple of weeks later, Clair stood in front of Ima's Bookshop, key in hand. She hesitated to enter, focusing instead on the truth of her new situation. *How can it be that I now own this bookshop?* Just as she slipped the key in the lock, she heard a voice calling her name.

Glenn Yves, in all his dazzling glory, strode up to her. With his black suit and lofty frame, all he lacked was a sword and horse. He reminded her of the daring heroes in medieval novels who slew dragons. But then again, she never went out. She had no point of reference concerning men. *Perhaps I embellish them in my mind.*

Glenn touched her arm as if she were his dearest friend. "How are you, Clair?"

His sudden closeness made her catch her breath. But he didn't laugh at her childishness. He just looked at her with those startling hazel eyes of his. Clair stared down at his hand, which was still in contact with her arm. She had yet to get used to people touching her.

He removed his hand but not his gaze. "You've lost some of your rosy glow. Are you all right?"

"I'm just. . .surprised to see you."

"I know it's been awhile, but I've come to honor my promise. How about lunch at the River Grill? We can begin our quest."

"I'm sorry." Clair wished she could say yes. "It just that. . .I can't afford to eat there."

Glenn waved his hand. "No, no. I'm buying."

"But I can't accept—"

"You haven't changed your mind about my offer." He leaned down to catch her gaze. "Have you?"

Clair clutched her purse in her hands, twisting the top back and forth, trying to rev up some courage. She'd need his help now more than ever. If she were to run the bookshop, learning to deal with customers would be vital. She had no real excuse to suddenly change her mind, except for barely knowing this man whose intense look almost swallowed her whole. "But I never expected our sessions to include lunch."

"I usually meet my clients at my office, but I thought a casual atmosphere might be more to your liking." He gestured with open palms. "Less intimidating."

Clair stared down at her threadbare dress and worn-out shoes with dismay. "I'm not really dressed for—"

He shook his head. "It doesn't matter. All of that will be taken care of. . .

later." He gave her an encouraging smile. "So, what do you say? Will you let me change your world?"

Clair let out a long breath of air, wondering what he meant. She knew almost any small improvement in her life would be welcome, but she still couldn't figure out why such a savvy and sophisticated man would be interested in helping her. Then she remembered Glenn's promise to Walter Sullivan, who'd reached out to help him years before. *He will surely tire of me, but in the meantime I may learn something that could help me run the bookshop. I will do it for Ima.* "Okay. Change your world. I mean. . .*my* world." Clair reddened at her blunder.

"Who knows, Ms. O'Neal," Glenn said. "You may very well change *my* world. Yes indeed." He flashed his straight white teeth at her—like ivories on a grand piano.

Clair smiled back at him, covering her mouth with her hand. She hadn't liked her smile since grade school. Too peculiar—it didn't fit her face.

"It's really nice out today. Want to take a walk?" He took her elbow, and they glided forward. "By the way, you have a wonderful smile. No need to cover it up."

Oh dear. Clair strolled with him down the sidewalk. *I'm slumping again. Straighten up, Clair!*

Glenn cleared his throat. "The first piece of advice I have for you is to raise your head and pull back your shoulders. Stand tall. Think tall. You can practice as we walk. You're much too beautiful to droop like a faded flower."

He notices everything. Clair could feel her face getting warm as she drew herself up straight. But why had he called her beautiful? Was he making fun? She did her best to straighten her shoulders and raise her head as they walked toward the River Grill, but she felt self-conscious and embarrassed with her new posture, as if she were putting on airs.

Without warning, Clair tripped on a piece of uneven sidewalk. In her effort to catch herself, her hands slapped against the concrete.

"Clair!" Glenn took hold of her arms and lifted her up. "Are you all right?"

She nodded, feeling the wasp-like sting on her palms and feeling more like a fool than she ever had before. If that were possible. *Oh God, please help me. I'm a walking disaster.*

After taking a handkerchief from his pants pocket, Glenn gently wiped the dirt off her hands. In that one moment, he was indeed the hero, and he had just slain a thousand dragons for her. Clair straightened again and tried to smile. "I'm afraid I—"

"People trip all the time. I once tripped going up on stage to give a speech on 'Why Image Makes All the Difference.'"

"Really?"

"Does it get much worse than that?" He grinned.

"Did people laugh?" She couldn't imagine such a thing happening to one of "the beautifuls."

"Well, some of the people did. And then I laughed, which sort of gave permission for other people to chuckle. It certainly made a good icebreaker."

As Clair listened, she noticed two women batting their eyes at Glenn while they strolled by. Clair supposed that sort of thing happened to him often.

"I ended up using the accident as a teaching tool in my speech." He held the handkerchief out to her. "You may keep it."

"No. I—"

"Please, I insist."

Clair finally reached out and accepted his gift. The material felt expensive and sumptuous and was monogrammed with the gold initials G. Y. "Thank you." She eased the handkerchief into an inner pocket of her purse where she kept all objects of importance. She couldn't help but ponder Glenn's upbeat attitude. *If I'm around him long enough, will it rub off on me?*

Clair felt the sharp tingle from a pebble in her shoe. Why hadn't she felt that before? Humiliated enough for one day, she decided to just absorb the pain as they walked.

Moments later, after passing two souvenir shops, a bakery, a T-shirt shop, and a café, they were suddenly breezing by the River Front Guitar Shop. Clair turned her head for a glimpse through the window. She didn't expect to see Hudson, but she looked anyway. Funny how she'd strolled past that guitar store many times and had no idea who worked inside. *Hudson.* Would he ever come by the bookshop again?

After a few more strides, Clair could smell the mouth-watering scents wafting out the front door of the Arkansas River Grill. Relief. At least there'd be no more falling accidents.

When they stepped inside, the maitre d' promptly escorted them to an intimate table overlooking the Arkansas River. Sunlight played on the water, making rhinestone shimmers across the water. The table, decorated with white linen, floating candles, and a spray of orchids, appeared romantic in every way. *Like something out of a movie. But this certainly isn't a date, and it's not exactly casual. At least, not from what I can gather.*

A waiter removed Clair's napkin, fluffed it, and then snapped it in a theatrical gesture. He bent low, positioning the white cloth on her lap with precision.

"You prepare a table before me. . ." She bit her lower lip, trying not to allow a nervous giggle to slip out.

Then their very efficient waiter handed them their menus and mentioned the specials of the day.

Clair glanced around, absorbing the loveliness of the restaurant. Her gaze stopped on a startling sight. She could barely believe her eyes. Hudson sat on the other side of the restaurant. He was with someone—someone fair-haired with straight shoulders and a confident air.

Clair wanted to hide behind something, but the menu wasn't big enough. Hudson deserved to be with a woman who could actually open her mouth and talk. And talk she most certainly did. In fact, Hudson's date appeared to be so blessed with copious amounts of talk and giggles that she drew the attention of the other patrons.

Then the woman's sudden burst of laughter drew Glenn's attention. He glanced across the room. "I don't know that chatty woman in black, but I do recognize the man with the blazer and...ahem...tennis shoes." He winced. "It's Leslie Mandel's brother, Hudson. Remember, you met him at the party."

"Yes."

Clair was glad Glenn wasn't looking at her, since a rush of heat had spread across her face. She touched the velvety petals of the orchid blossoms in an attempt to take her mind off who was sitting across the room.

"Well, looks like Hudson's got quite a live wire there." Glenn seemed amused. "Her shoes may be alligator, but her cackle is genuine hyena."

Clair wanted to laugh but held it in. Could a woman so beautiful actually have a flaw? Such an idea had never entered her mind before.

All of a sudden, Clair saw that Hudson noticed her from across the room. He waved, but his eyes were filled with surprise and confusion. She felt so discombobulated, all she could muster was a smile. She would need to turn her chair a bit more to the window to keep her mind on the matters at hand. Hudson was clearly with someone else anyway. Clair realized now she'd been childish to have gotten her hopes up concerning him, but then maybe Hudson wondered what she was doing here...with Glenn. *I hope he doesn't think we're dating.* She turned her attention back to the menu.

Glenn fingered his watch. He was wearing a wristwatch that looked just like the gold Rolex Clair had seen in a magazine ad. She'd never known anyone who could afford such luxury. She tried not to stare.

After they'd considered the menu and asked the waiter a few questions, Glenn ordered a filet mignon to be cooked rare, and Clair ordered the chicken cordon bleu since it appeared to be the least expensive thing on the menu.

When the waiter left, Clair eased back in her chair, gazing out at the Arkansas River, at the bluish-green colors and the smooth cool surface. The *toot* of a steamboat could be heard in the distance. She could picture it now, filled with tourists. A sailboat glided along the water, looking tranquil.

"I love strolling on the river trail." Clair let her mind play with happier times. "And I love all the bridges here. Most of all, I love the old-fashioned trolleys and the horse-drawn carriages." In truth, the remnants of days gone by seemed to suit her personality, though she wondered why she'd let herself ramble on about it in such a way.

"I especially love the older bridges. They have a lot of character." Glenn's words poured out as rich and smooth as a malted milk shake. "I'd love to hear what's been happening in your life."

Clair turned her attention back to his question. "Well, I. . .uh. . .Ima passed away."

"Oh no. So suddenly?"

"She'd been unwell for some time. Ima was a friend to me. My only friend." Clair wished she hadn't mentioned the last part. It sounded too bleak.

"I'm sorry," Glenn said. "When did she die?"

"The morning after the party. . .of heart failure."

Glenn touched her hand.

Remembering bits of the funeral, she sighed inside. The meager flowers, the solemn service, and the desperate expression on the face of Ima's sister—so forlorn and lost. The same way Clair felt inside.

"What will you do if the bookshop closes?" He released her hand.

"I. . .she. . .left the business to me. . .in her will."

"Now *that* is something." Glenn took a sip of his water.

She smiled, not wanting to tell him how much it grieved her to own the shop, how undeserving she felt to receive such a generous gift. She took a long drink of her water, wishing she could wash the thoughts away.

"I assume you'll keep it open, then."

"Yes, I plan to. And hopefully our customers will continue to frequent the shop. Ima always said people spend money on the things they truly love."

"And she loved books."

"Like they were her friends." Clair smiled. "Ima had plans to expand the bookstore."

As the conversation continued, Clair thought of Hudson again and glanced his way. *Oh my.* He'd risen from his chair and was walking toward her. She suddenly couldn't breathe.

Hudson approached her table. But when she looked at him, he halted mid-stride and stared at her with the most beseeching expression she'd ever seen. Everything around them—the talk and the clatter—all seemed suspended. Clair felt alone with Hudson just for a second as their gaze intensified. Then he veered toward an alcove of restrooms, and the moment dissolved as he went on his way. A rush of sound filled her ears again. What could it mean? Did he feel the same way she did? *If only Hudson would give me another chance, I would say yes!*

"Ima's plan could be a smart business move." Glenn's brows came together. "But what do *you* want?"

I need to stay focused. Clair quickly brought her mind back to the conversation. *Let's see. Glenn asked me about the shop.* "Ima had already ordered some of the new books and gifts." She drew in a deep breath and tried to continue. "But. . ."

"Yes?"

"It's not easy for me." Clair sighed. "I have to deal with customers. Greet them. And I will need to hire some part-time help. I'm afraid I'll either say the wrong things. . .or nothing at all. . .or too much. Just like right now." She looked down at her hands, trying not to think about the look on Hudson's face.

"That's why I'm here. To make the way smoother for you. But, if you don't mind my asking, how did someone so smart and lovely as yourself decide she wasn't smart and lovely? You must have had a rough road growing up." His eyes were filled with compassion—just as they had been that night in the limousine, when he had seen her house for the first time.

Clair wondered how he could have known about her childhood. *He's very perceptive.* She decided to keep revelations of her past to a minimum. "My stepfather was a hardworking man but poor as a church mouse, as they say. I think it must have been a burden for him. . .to raise me." She twisted a chunk of her hair around her finger.

Glenn shifted in his chair. "I shouldn't have asked you such a personal question. I apologize." He cleared his throat and looked at her. "I have faith in you, Clair O'Neal. In spite of your hesitations, I think once we do some tweaking, you'll make quite the businesswoman."

"I'm wood," Clair mumbled to herself.

"What did you say?"

Clair blushed. "I'm sorry. I don't mean to be impolite. It's just that I've always been like a block of wood. . .with people." *Does Hudson see me that way, too?* "I'm not sure how I can be fixed."

"You can make a work of art out of a chunk of wood. You just need the right tools. As an image coach, I have those tools."

Change. Clair picked up her water goblet to diffuse a growing uneasiness in the pit of her stomach, but her hand shook so much she had to set it back down. She breathed a prayer and summoned all her courage. Then she looked straight into the eyes of the man who claimed he could help her conquer her fears and set her on a new path. "Well then, Mr. Yves,"—she forced her shoulders back—"how shall we begin?"

Chapter 8

Glenn seemed pleasantly surprised with her response. "Well, first you mentioned saying the wrong things to customers. You can always slow down a bit. Think about what you're going to say and then say it distinctly. There's no rush. Smile when you speak. Look directly into people's eyes when you're talking to them."

"Okay." Clair made an effort to keep her gaze from constantly darting away.

"Very good." Glenn smiled. "And during conversations, some people aren't listening. My grandmother always called these folks prairie dogs. They stay down in their holes, not paying attention. Then they pop up their little heads when it's their turn to talk. They'll usually have a surprised look on their faces, because they haven't a clue as to what was said." He raised an eyebrow. "Even though you don't always look at me, I believe you are listening. People will think you're a good conversationalist simply because you pay attention to what they're saying. And that's all I'm going to cover on listening, since I think it's your strong suit."

"It is?" Clair couldn't believe she'd impressed Glenn. She bit her lower lip, wondering why she suddenly felt so warm and prickly.

"But about that chewing on your lower lip... You're making little pink marks underneath your lips. So, you'll want to retrain yourself not to indulge in that habit."

Clair nodded quickly, wanting to please him. "You're right. I'll try to stop."

"Good girl." Glenn cleared his throat. "Now, about confidence around people. Like at the party the other evening. If you're in a crowded room, the best thing to do is search for someone who looks more afraid than you do. Make it your goal to make that person feel better. . .more comfortable. Then you've helped two people at the same time. And you might even make a new friend."

"Is that what you were doing?" Clair almost bit her lip but chose to lick it instead.

"What do you mean?"

"The night of the party. You made me feel more at ease. Were you afraid of something, too?" The second the words came out, she regretted them. Every time she loosened up with people, nonsense poured out of her mouth.

"You *do* listen." Glenn shook his finger and grinned. "You want to know if I was uneasy. Well, like I said, everyone has his or her moment. That night, just

149

before I saw you, I'd gotten off the phone with a client who'd just lost her mother to pneumonia. I saw you and thought I could cheer us both up."

"I understand."

Glenn looked at her with an earnest gaze. "Yes, I know you do."

Thunder crackled in the distance. Oddly, the sky seemed clear and the sun still shone brightly. When Clair looked back at him, she noticed something else in Glenn's expression. Something knowing—and yet searching. *What is he looking for?*

"Life is full of surprises. And sometimes, they take us by storm." He grinned.

Was he being philosophical, or should she ask him what he meant? Since she'd spent little time visiting with people, the protocol eluded her. She shivered, wishing she'd brought a sweater to the restaurant.

And she still felt that irritating pebble in her shoe. With her feet, she tried to turn her shoe over to empty it as inconspicuously as possible, but suddenly the shoe flipped away, just out of reach. Clair glanced under the table, hoping Glenn hadn't noticed.

To Clair's horror, Glenn rose from his chair and then lowered himself next to her. "I'm so sorry." She bit her lower lip.

"I see you've lost your slipper." He retrieved the stray shoe and, taking hold of her ankle, added, "Let's just see if it fits." He gingerly slipped the shoe back on her foot and smiled. "There you go."

Right away Clair thought about the run in her hose from her fall and the hole in her shoe. *How embarrassing.* But how could she ever forget his compassion? Never. She managed a bashful thank-you.

"You're very welcome." He looked up at her.

She saw that knowing smile again. *Who is this man?* And wasn't he going way beyond the duties of an image coach?

A woman with long auburn hair stepped over to their table. "Glenn, what are you doing crawling around on the floor?" she asked. "That move wasn't in your coaching manual!" Her laughter sounded almost musical—like water rolling over river rocks. Clair liked her right away.

Glenn stood and smiled as he spoke her name. "Katherine. You look lovely."

Clair had to agree. The woman's jade-colored outfit suited her in every way, and her hair and makeup added to the overall effect.

"Thank you." The woman kissed him, leaving a scarlet imprint on his cheek. She turned to Clair with a warm and inviting smile. "And who do we have here?"

Glenn seated himself. "Katherine, this is Clair O'Neal. Clair, this is Katherine Burke, a former client of mine."

"Good to meet you." Katherine extended her hand.

"I'm glad to meet you, too." Clair lifted her trembling hand, and the elegant woman gave it a warm shake. She appeared to be the very epitome of gracefulness and charm. Clearly, her time under Glenn's tutelage had paid off. Clair sighed. Oh, if only *she* could come off as polished and refined. Was such a thing really possible?

Katherine nodded in her direction and responded as if reading her thoughts. "Meeting Glenn was truly one of the best things that ever happened to me."

Glenn's eyes glistened, but a slight look of embarrassment crossed his face.

"I confess I didn't give him much to work with. . ." Katherine added with a look of chagrin. "At first, anyway."

"Of course you did," he argued. Glenn turned to Clair. "Katherine has a natural love for life—and for people. I just needed to draw that out. And she's a wonderful Christian woman, so that made our working relationship even more pleasant. We had a number of things in common. Still do."

Katherine nodded. "I always say the Lord sent Glenn to me at just the right time. My career was just taking off, and I needed a little encouragement to step out into the public eye. I was always such a shy little thing."

Shy? Clair could hardly imagine it. Why, this woman was anything but. Katherine exuded confidence. It showed in her smile. Her sparkling eyes. Her hands, which didn't appear to tremble in the slightest as she reached up with one to brush an imaginary speck of dust from her jacket.

Katherine turned as a gentleman in a tailored suit approached from behind her. "I'm sorry, but I must go now. Work awaits. . ."

"Katherine, it was a pleasure, as always." Glenn stood to his feet.

Clair couldn't help but wonder if he did this for all women as they came and went from tables.

Katherine took his hand once more. "It was wonderful seeing you again, Glenn. And I enjoyed meeting you, Clair." The refined woman nodded in their direction.

Clair returned the gesture with a smile.

As Katherine turned on her heel, thunder rolled outside and then swelled into a deep booming rumble that rattled the window by their table.

"She always did like a sensational exit," Glenn said with a laugh as he took his seat once again.

Clair couldn't help but sigh. "She seems so. . .ideal."

He laughed. "She's come a long way from the nervous, withdrawn girl I used to know." He paused for a moment then looked Clair in the eye. "I can polish the outside," he explained, "but sincerity and kindness come from the inside. It's already a part of you, Clair. That's something of the heart. Something of *real* value. And something I can never teach."

Before Clair could stop herself, she reached out and touched Glenn's hand. Then, with a fingertip, she pointed at his cheek to remind him of the lipstick imprint Katherine had left behind. He chuckled and wiped it away.

The waiter made an appearance with their salads and a loaf of hot bread.

"Looks good." Glenn said. "Thanks, Ty."

Clair stared back and forth from her food to her flatware, sighing at the sticky situation before her. Which fork should she use for the salad? She never could seem to remember.

Glenn picked up the smaller fork and stuck it into some salad leaves.

She followed his lead and began to munch on her spinach salad, which was garnished with walnuts, mandarin oranges, and a delicate dressing. She ate slowly, letting the flavors linger on her tongue as she listened carefully to Glenn's speech on confidence and poise.

Clair asked questions, and he answered them patiently. Finally, he mentioned other essentials, such as hair, makeup, and dress. She could feel herself wanting to bite her lip, but she straightened her shoulders instead. *How can I tell him I have no money for such indulgences?* "I don't have the—"

"Please." Glenn raised his hand. "I already know what you're trying to say. But when I made this offer to you, I immediately made an appointment for you at Armando's Spa and Boutique. The services have already been paid for."

"Oh, but I can't. I couldn't expect—"

"I insist. There's no reason to tell an angel how beautiful she is without giving her the wings to fly." Glenn lit up with another smile.

Clair's thoughts flew, at once, to Katherine Burke. The beautiful woman had taken Glenn's teaching to heart and the payoff was obvious. If Clair went along with his plan, would she one day have Katherine's confidence and grace?

On the other hand, was accepting such a generous gift from someone she barely knew appropriate? Would there be unsuitable expectations? She almost laughed at the thought. No one could possibly be interested in her in an amorous way. She wasn't the sort to date, and men seemed to pick up on that. Didn't they?

"Walter Sullivan did the same for me," Glenn went on to say. "He even paid to have my teeth straightened. I certainly wasn't born with these pearlies."

"Do you mind if I ask why he did so much?"

"Because he'd been very successful, and he wanted to do something that had nothing to do with making more money. He was a rare individual and one of the people in my life whom I truly respected."

Clair nodded at Glenn and decided to take one final look over at Hudson's table. Amazingly, the woman with him was still talking, and Hudson was still listening. His shoulders sagged as badly as her living room couch.

Should she be happy about that? *Oh dear. Has Glenn said something, and I wasn't listening again?* Clair placed her hand over her mouth in dismay. "What did you say? I am so sorry."

"What's the matter?" He reached his hand out to her.

Clair blushed. "I've been such a prairie dog."

Glenn threw his head back in laughter.

After eating more luscious food than Clair had ever eaten in her life and after listening to more suggestions and advice than she'd ever thought existed, she was deposited back at her shop with a very agreeable good-bye. She waved and then watched until Glenn disappeared down the street.

Suddenly the appointment he'd made for her at Armando's Spa and Boutique came to mind. She'd certainly keep the appointment, but not without some anxiety. What would the technicians think of her? Would they feel she was a dusty moth trying to be a butterfly? There'd be rooms full of pretty women, all perfumed and groomed, and there'd she be—Miss Ragamuffin, the name her stepfather had always called her.

Wiping the straggly hairs from her face, she reached over to the light switch. *But if I am to run this bookstore, I don't want to look shabby.* She glanced around at the boxes, which had arrived just prior to Ima's death. They contained the latest in Bibles, books, gifts, and CDs. She sighed as she realized they would all have to be unpacked and shelved—without Ima's assistance. Clair knew the basics of running a small bookstore, of course, but the whole expansion process seemed overwhelming. Ima had wanted to change the name of the store, but she'd never told her what it would be.

There was so much to think about—so much to plan. She'd need to redo the sign outside, order new floor displays, restock the shelves, and so forth. And then there was publicity and the hiring of part-time help. *Oh my.*

Clair felt the rumbling ache of defiance within her stomach. Even though eating expensive food had been delightful, she wasn't accustomed to ingesting rich sauces and desserts. Her stomach felt as if there were some kind of skirmish going on inside. She just hoped she could keep the food down. She sat on a stool near the cash register, rubbing her stomach and missing her employer—the woman who'd been her only friend.

She noticed a slip of paper Ima had posted on the bulletin board. The note reminded her to "walk in joy and eat more soy." *Dear, sweet, funny Ima. If only I'd arrived at the shop earlier that morning, Ima might have survived.* She could have called for help at the first sign of trouble. *How can I possibly deserve this shop?*

She sighed, recalling the reading of the will. Afterward, Ima's sister, LaVerne, had insisted Clair take the business, wanting to honor her sister's request. What a dilemma. Mist filled her eyes. *No tears, Clair. No tears.*

Some of Ima's words came back to her. *"If you don't have a plan, then plan for a headache."* Clair smiled at the remembrance and thought how sad it would be to let Ima's dream die. But Clair could live the dream for her.

She would need to get organized. Clair rummaged around in a top drawer behind the counter and found a large pad of paper for scribbling down notes. Preparing for a grand reopening would require a lot of work, but hard work had never been a problem.

And money? Hmm. There was still enough cash in the business account to make the switch. But what about dealing with the public? A recluse would now be forced into the "people business." Clair shook her head at the virtual impossibility of the notion. Glenn wasn't around, so she treated herself to a good lip-chewing session. Then his words came to mind. "Once we do some tweaking, you'll make quite the businesswoman." *How can he have more confidence in me than I do?*

Clair started to hum one of her favorite hymns, and soon ideas for the new store began to flow. She took copious notes on every aspect of the reopening. She stayed so busy in fact, she thought of Hudson only every fifteen minutes.

The bell over the front door jangled.

Hudson stood in the doorway clutching two cups and looking striking in his sapphire-colored shirt and denims. Steam rose from the two cups in soft, friendly curls. "How about some coffee?"

He came back. He really came back! Clair's tummy ache vanished.

Chapter 9

Hudson loved the way Clair smiled. *I think she's happy to see me.*

Clair rose from her chair, straightened her shoulders, and looked him straight in the eye. "Yes. I'd like some."

He walked over to hand her a cup. "You look different. Good, I mean." His voice had the tiniest stutter. *Oh brother.* He could sing on live television, face huge crowds, but he couldn't give Clair the simplest compliment. She did look slightly different, though—more self-assured or rested or something. Why didn't *she* seem nervous? *And why won't my lips work? It's like having a big wad of peanut butter in my mouth.*

"Thank you." Clair took a sip of her coffee. "It's good."

"You're welcome." Okay. What to say now. "I should have made a list."

"What kind of list?"

Hudson chuckled. "Sorry. You caught me mumbling out loud again." He balled up his hand. "I might as well cough it up. I wanted to talk to you about some things, but I lost them in my head." He felt the calluses on the ends of his fingers from playing the guitar, and it reminded him that all things worthwhile required work.

"I feel that way all the time," Clair said.

"You do?" He took a mouthful of his drink. *Mmm. Maybe hot caffeine will come to my rescue.* Hudson beat his brain until he thought of a subject. "How was Ima's funeral?"

Clair paused, looking lost in thought. She finally said, "It was joyful because of where Ima is, but sad because I miss her so much."

"I wish. . .I'd gone." Hudson shuffled his feet, guzzled some more brew, and set the cup on the counter. "Sorry, I'm not usually this tense."

"And *I'm* not usually this relaxed." Clair's hand went to her mouth.

For some reason, she appeared astonished at what she'd just said. Hudson thought she looked cute. They both stared at each other and then chuckled.

"I'm glad you feel that way around me. It's probably good for me to flub up once in a while. Keeps me humble." He grinned. "Otherwise my sister tells me I get too self-absorbed."

"I can't imagine that." Clair offered him a stool. "Would you like to sit down?"

Hudson felt restless. "No thanks." His mind refused to let go of one fact—they'd both been dining with someone else at the same restaurant. The very day he'd chosen to ask Clair out. *Not the best turn of events.* He decided to turn his focus to the half-empty shelves. "What will happen to the shop now?"

She licked her lips. "Ima gave me the bookshop. . .in her will."

"Really?" Hudson marveled at the news. He'd never heard of an employee receiving such a generous gift. "She must have loved you like a daughter."

"She never said so, but I knew it in the things she did. She was a very precious woman." Clair took a slow sip from her cup. "Ima was going to expand the shop, adding a larger area for music and gifts. That's why the inventory on the shelves is so low right now, to make room for the changes."

"So, you're going to follow through with her plan?"

"Yes."

"It's a good idea. I think it'll do well here." Hudson wondered why she'd answered so briefly and why her voice sounded like all the air had gone out.

Clair set her cup down as her face lit up. "I don't have a name for the new store. Any ideas?"

"Let's see. . ." Hudson looked upward as he did a little brainstorming in his head. "Hmm. Okay, maybe. Nah. Don't think so. Let's see. . .heaven, harps, angels, river, gold. . ." He picked up his coffee to give his hands something to twiddle with. He was so used to creating while holding his guitar, he felt awkward without his companion to help him think. "I don't know. How about something like Rivers of Gold Christian Bookshop?"

Clair's eyes widened. "I like it very much. How did you think of it?"

"I'm not sure." He smiled. "But I'm glad you like it."

"Ima would approve." She made some notes on a pad of paper. "Thank you."

You are so welcome. "Do you need any more help?"

"I might later."

"If you ever need me, I'm right down the street. Well, you know that." Hudson stuffed his hands into the pockets of his jeans. He considered Clair's expression. *Does she wonder who I was with at the River Grill? Maybe I should tell her straight out—that the woman won a lunch with me in a charity auction. And what's the deal with Glenn Yves? Is Clair dating him?* He had no idea how to bring up a topic as prickly as cacti, but maybe he could just hover over the subject. "I was surprised to see you at the River Grill today. I've never seen you there before."

"I've never been there before."

"Well, that must be why. . .I've never seen you there before." *I'm just going in circles here. Maybe I'd better just cut to the chase.* "I'm playing at the Silver Moon Café tomorrow evening. It's a restaurant, and they have performers who. . .perform." *Oh brother.* "Would you like to go with me?"

"Yes." Clair's hand flew up to her mouth. "Yes, I would. Yes."

"All righty then." Hudson smiled, feeling confident she really wanted to go with him. Suddenly he was in the mood for his coffee again. Lots of coffee. He reached for his beverage as his enthusiasm radiated through his fingers, causing a squeezing action on his grip. He couldn't stop the gush as he watched the coffee make a slow motion kind of rise and fall all over his very favorite shirt.

Chapter 10

Saturday morning, Clair rose early to ready herself for her big day at Armando's Spa. She scrubbed herself extra clean in the shower and dressed in some of her best clothes—a brown pantsuit from a local garage sale.

After fiddling with her hair for an hour in an effort to make it look fashionable, she gave up, letting the strands droop around her shoulders. *Oh well. I guess they can't shoot me for being ugly.* A little giggle escaped her lips, making her face light up. *I don't look quite so dull when I smile.*

When she'd primped as much as she knew how, Clair locked her front door and headed down the sidewalk. Since she still couldn't afford to fix her car, she left the house early so she'd have time for the twelve-block hike to Armando's.

After a breeze had whipped her hair to shreds, and her feet throbbed in her too-small shoes, she spotted the spa across the street. Her anxiety swelled as she dipped from the pot of fears that'd been accumulating since Glenn had told her about the makeover.

Every part of Clair wanted to turn around and walk back home, but Glenn had been so generous, she couldn't disappoint him. *And maybe I should make the most of the gift since tonight is my very first date.* At that moment, Clair let something seep into her life—anticipation. A foreign word to her trembling heart. *Hudson.* She'd be on a real date and one she'd cherish forever. *I guess Hudson really wasn't dating that woman at the River Grill.*

Clair gathered up some gumption and marched over to the spa like a woman on a mission. She paused at the big double doors in front, which were painted a cobalt blue and lacquered to a mirror finish, then bit down hard on her lower lip and reached for the handle. *Maybe a smile would help.*

The moment she entered the posh surroundings of Armando's, a woman in an elegant white dress and with silver hair, glided toward her as if she were floating on a hovercraft. "Oh, *soyez le bienvenu*! Welcome! You must be Clair."

Clair nodded briskly. "Hi." The sounds of falling water and classical music flowed around her.

"Well, mademoiselle, I'm Destinee Armando, and we've been waiting for you." The woman stared at Clair, looking at both sides of her profile. "Hmm. Mr. Yves was correct. You have fabulous bone structure. Oh, we have lots to work with. But such tragic eyes."

Clair just listened, not really knowing what to say. Did she really look tragic? She brightened her smile.

"Mr. Yves has taken care of everything. You are just here to enjoy the delights." Her hands swept upward, her long, manicured nails highlighted by the gesture. "Are we ready?"

"Yes." She tried not to stare at Destinee, who was unquestionably beautiful with her flawless makeup, chic hairstyle, and impeccable clothes. Clair felt so out of her league, the urge to hide became overwhelming. She spotted a closet door, and it looked tempting. *Come on now. You're being silly.*

Destinee led her into a small room full of pastel-colored lockers. "You may undress in here and then slip on one of those fluffy robes. Would you like champagne or sparkling water?"

Clair folded her hands in front of her. "Water, please."

"Very well. Come out when you are ready." Then like a petal on a stream, she drifted off.

Clair slipped out of her clothes and into the lush blue robe. She opened the door and peeked out. *Am I supposed to wait here?* Trying to shed some of her shyness, she crept out into the main room. She could get a better look at the décor now. *Oh my.* A quaint Italian motif with a cascading fountain in the middle—she'd never seen anything like it.

Suddenly, a group of women, in various stages of beautification, swooped through like a flock of blue herons. She pulled herself out of their way as she tightened her robe. No one even noticed her.

Just when Clair thought about scurrying back to the locker room, Destinee appeared out of nowhere. She handed Clair a crystal goblet of sparkling water with a slice of lime and then escorted her through a hallway and into a small room lit only by candles. A massage bed sat in the middle of the room. Piano music and the scent of lavender drifted through the air. The familiar psalm ran through Clair's head once again. *"He makes me lie down in green pastures."* What a delicious present this day was turning out to be.

Then something—or rather, *someone*—caught her eye. A buxom woman with broad shoulders and muscular arms stood before her like a Viking. All she lacked was the helmet with horns.

The bulky woman slapped her enormous hands together. "*Gut.*"

The sight tickled Clair's funny bone. *Is this comical?* Her sense of humor had been sequestered for so many years, she wasn't certain.

"This is Helga, your massage therapist," Destinee said. "By the time she's done with you, you'll be so relaxed, your bones won't even feel attached to your body!"

Clair swallowed hard.

"Fraulein," Helga said, smacking the massage table. "Are ve ready?"

Destinee lifted the glass of water out of Clair's suspended hand and then left the room, doing that floating thing again.

Twenty minutes later, after Clair had been rubbed, pounded, and kneaded like bread dough, she started to unwind a little.

"Gut," Helga barked.

By now Clair realized the woman merely sounded gruff. In fact, Helga seemed determined to make sure she'd be pleased with the results. Clair almost laughed at herself for being so anxious over such a simple thing as a massage, but she'd grown up with so little physical contact, the sensations felt peculiar to her. After a while though, Clair started to enjoy herself.

What would Ima think if she could see her now? She'd probably say, "Make the most of it, kid. It's supposed to be fun!"

Thirty minutes later, Helga removed the cucumber pads from Clair's eyes and directed her to another room on the other side of the facility. Clair was so relaxed she could barely walk. Still, she could hardly wait to see what exciting adventures lay ahead.

Next on the day's agenda were a body polish, an herbal wrap, and a European facial. Then on to the hair designer for a haircut, subtle highlights, and a deep condition. In between all the pamperings, the attendants offered Clair sumptuous goodies. As she tasted the orchid tea and the scones, she tried to memorize every flavor and every sensation of the day, since she knew such luxuries would never come again.

After lunch, Clair had both a manicure and a pedicure, which included massages with peppermint balm and dips in warm paraffin. Then a new batch of technicians took over, reshaping her heavy eyebrows and giving her a rather laborious application of makeup. When they were finished, the staff gave her several gift bags of makeup and hair care products to take home. Clair's mind staggered with the idea that Glenn had paid for such extravagances.

Just when Clair thought everyone had finished, someone escorted her into the adjoining boutique with the promise of finding the perfect outfits to enhance her coloring and figure. She'd never considered such a concept before, since the only things she'd ever purchased were garage sale items and leftovers on clearance tables. Still, before all was said and done, she had selected nearly a dozen new ensembles to hang in her closet. Oh, how drab those old clothes would look now draped alongside these new, fashionable ones.

When Clair's day at the spa was finally complete and she'd been dressed in blue silk finery, Destinee led her to a full-length gilded mirror.

Clair saw herself and stepped back. Then slowly, she leaned in closer. *Could this really be me?* She touched her face and hair and new silky dress.

"Well, mademoiselle, what do you think?" Destinee placed her hands on her hips and raised her chin. "You are the masterpiece, and we are the artists. We are *très bon*. No?"

Out of the blue, the employees as well as the other clients broke into applause. Even stoic Helga seemed misty-eyed as she looked at her and hollered, "*Schön.*" Clair assumed that was something good.

Feeling a little embarrassed with the sudden attention, Clair wanted to hide or at least twirl her finger in her hair, but with a prayer and some grit, she let go of her timidity and grinned with excitement. The day had turned out light years beyond anything she'd imagined. "I don't know what to say." She felt herself choking up as she tried to express her gratitude. *"My cup overflows."* "I think all of you are. . .magnifique!" *Where in the world did that come from? I guess the mouse has finally squeaked!*

Destinee nodded, looking pleased with her response. In the midst of another agreeable uproar, a male figure emerged from the patrons and staff. Glenn stood a few yards away, sporting a tweed jacket and a generous smile. He was like her fairy godfather suddenly appearing to make sure the magic had worked. It had. Clair's fingers reached up to her lips to keep her emotions in check. *No tears, Clair. This is a happy time.*

Glenn took a few steps toward her, his gaze never leaving her. She felt a rush of gratitude and wanted to thank him with a kiss but stopped herself since she thought it might be improper.

"Miss Clair O'Neal. . .you look drop-dead gorgeous." Glenn raised an eyebrow.

A sigh rippled through the crowd. Destinee nodded, and Helga clapped her hands.

Clair could feel herself flushing a deep crimson, but she didn't mind this time, since the words and the moment had brought so much pleasure to Glenn. But as she boldly gazed into his eyes, something else lingered in his expression— something new to her. *Could it be attraction? For me?* She dismissed the musings as she straightened her shoulders, gathered her hands to her heart, and mouthed the words, "Thank you so much."

Chapter 11

Hudson knocked on Clair's front door for the second time. Had he written down the right address? A truck rumbled by, leaving a wake of noise and blue smoke. *Maybe Clair changed her mind.*

No, thankfully the door opened, and a woman who looked like Clair emerged from the house. "Clair?" He tried not to stare, but he felt utterly helpless not to. The woman had the same soft brown eyes like a doe and delicate smile as Clair, but something had happened to the rest of her. Her hair, clothes, and well, everything else about her looked transformed. She'd been a lovely woman before, but now she appeared dazzling in her blue dress. *I'm staring like an ape. Okay, I'm going to look at the ground now.*

"Hi," Clair said.

Good, same voice. "You look. . .radiant." Hudson wondered if he should ask her what happened or if that would be rude.

Clair put her hand over her mouth, looking a little worried. "I went to a spa."

"Well, you sure got your money's worth." *Oh brother. I'm sounding like a country bumpkin now.* "You look incredible. I mean, well, you always looked pretty." *Oh man.* "But now, even more so."

A shining smile lit up her countenance. "Thank you."

"Are you ready?" He looked at her elegant attire and then at his jeans and black shirt. Maybe he should have dressed up a little more.

Clair locked her door and rushed down the path ahead of him.

Why is she in such a hurry to get away? Was she self-conscious about her house? It didn't matter a bit to him where she lived. Hudson caught up with her, and with his hand gently against her back, ushered her to his pickup. Once he had her safely tucked inside, he trotted around to the driver's side, relieved his vehicle was clean for a change.

Once they'd arrived at the Silver Moon Café, Hudson got Clair settled in his favorite spot, walked up the stairs to the stage, and waited for Big George Cummings, the owner, to introduce him. He looked around, still trying to absorb the newly renovated interior of the café—brick walls, black ceiling, and a larger stage area. *Nice.*

Big George appeared from the other side of the stage, grabbed the microphone, and gave his usual animated spiel like a grizzly bear on espresso.

THE LOVE SONG

While the audience applauded, Hudson strode toward the spotlight. He lifted his guitar from its stand and made himself comfortable on a stool. He gazed out over the audience and offered a grin, then cleared this throat. "Good evening. I'm Hudson Mandel."

The crowd applauded again, and he glanced down at Clair. He felt another tug. Would she think him too forward to sing the song he'd written for her? *Is it too soon?*

When the inspiration hit, he'd barely been able to write the words down fast enough. They'd come from a place in his heart that had never been touched before.

A baby let out a squall in the back, reminding him he was on stage, so he turned his attention to his music.

"I wrote this song for someone special. I call it 'Clair.' Hope you like it." Hudson started to pick out his tune while singing along. When he came to the chorus, he sang:

> *"Ever since I saw your face*
> *I have never been the same,*
> *I lose a piece of my heart*
> *Every time I say your name."*

When Hudson wrapped up his song, a startling silence permeated the room, and then the stillness was replaced with booming applause. He'd avoided Clair's eyes during the song, but he couldn't wait any longer to see her reaction, so he gazed down at her. She appeared as luminous as she looked confused. *I'll take that as encouragement.*

Hudson played a few more tunes and then decided to take a short break. He walked up to Clair's table and slid into the chair next to her. The glow from the incandescent light above created a halo effect around her head.

"The audience loved you," she said.

"But did *you* love me?"

"Yes." She clasped her hands together, smiling. "Very much."

He knew Clair's words referred to only his performance, but he wondered if she could ever feel more.

"Your folk songs are rich and original and affecting." She drew back as if surprised by her own words and then she touched his hand. "I *love* your music."

Clair obviously had no idea of the impact of her compliments or of the soft touch of her hand. Hudson wanted to kiss her mouth this minute, but he would be a patient man. "You're my favorite critic so far."

Clair laughed.

She seemed wonderfully different. Still Clair, but more open with her thoughts. He couldn't fathom the psyche of a woman, but he wondered if the trip to the spa had given her more confidence. Or perhaps she simply felt more comfortable being around him. Whatever it was, he liked it. "I hope you didn't mind. . .about the song."

"Mind?"

"The song, 'Clair.' I wrote it. . .you know. . .for you." Why did he get so tongue-tied around her?

"I wasn't sure." She fiddled with her napkin.

"You're the only Clair I know."

"Thank you." Her head dipped down. "I feel honored." When she looked up, her eyes were misty.

"You're welcome." Hudson gave her hand a squeeze. "Are you hungry? Maybe we should order something before I go back on stage." He gave a signal to one of the waiters.

Otto, a portly man who dropped more plates than a Greek dancer, barreled over to them. "Here we are," he said as he handed them their menus. When Otto saw Clair, his jowls shimmied a bit. Then after he took their beverage requests, he stood transfixed, gaping at her.

"Otto." Hudson cleared his throat to release the poor man from his trance. "Thank you."

"Sorry." Otto shrugged his shoulders and grinned. "I'll be back in a minute with your drinks."

Clair didn't even seem to notice Otto's ogling. In fact, when she looked up from the menu, she had a faraway gaze. Hudson leaned toward her. "I would love to know what you're thinking."

"Actually. . .today is my birthday." She licked her lips. "And your song was by far the finest present I've ever gotten."

"Thank you. But really, *today* is your birthday?"

She brightened. "I'm thirty-one years old."

"We're the same age." Hudson grinned.

"Really?"

"How did you overlook your birthday? Didn't the cards from relatives and friends tip you off?"

"My relatives are all gone." Clair set her menu down and sighed. "And Ima was my only real friend." She chuckled. "It sounds so Charles Dickens-ish when I say it out loud."

Hudson reached to touch her hand, at once feeling her pain. He hadn't known the extent of Clair's solitude. He wanted to know more but didn't want to come off too pushy.

Before he could think of a comment, Otto arrived, this time a little more restrained. He brought their drinks, took their orders, and then shambled off toward the kitchen.

Hudson looked back at Clair. "So, what did your parents do for your birthday when you were little?"

"I never knew my father, and my mother died when I was very young." Clair's shoulders slumped. "And my stepfather. . .well. . .he saw no need to celebrate birthdays."

Hudson saw the sadness in her eyes. His heart went out to Clair—to the little girl who'd been ignored growing up. He couldn't imagine such behavior in his family, since his birthday, as well as his sister's, had always been a colossal affair. He hesitated inquiring further into her past, but he had to put his mind at ease with one more question. "Your stepfather. . .did he treat you well otherwise?"

"He was never the same after my mother passed away." Clair folded her arms around her middle. "He didn't like to spend time with me, even when he had the opportunity. I always got the feeling he felt he'd been stuck with me. I guess he just didn't know what to do with a daughter."

Hudson drew in a deep breath and held his tongue.

"I had my own way of coping." Clair's gaze shifted downward. "I worked hard around the house—did my chores, kept things clean. I guess I thought he would notice me that way, but after a while I just felt kind of invisible. . .at least to him. And I always felt like that at school, too. I wasn't what you would call a social child. Never really found a group to fit in with."

Hudson found it hard to believe anyone could overlook Clair but didn't interrupt her story.

"I got it in my mind that people didn't like to be around me," she continued, "especially my stepfather, so I steered clear of him. There was a little room up in the attic. . .my mother had used it for storage. Some of her things were still there after she died. It might seem strange, but I felt close to her when I went into that space. I guess I just started using it as a sanctuary, of sorts."

"Understandable." *But horribly sad.*

Clair's eyes filled with tears. "I have to admit, half the time I'd go up those stairs to get away from my stepfather, and half the time I sat up there, wishing he would call out to me, ask me to come down and watch TV or play a game with him." She used her fingertip to brush the moisture from her lashes. "Sorry. It's still a little hard to talk about."

Hudson gathered Clair's hands into his. "I'm sorry."

Clair paused for a minute as if she were collecting her thoughts. "Sometimes I would sit up there till evening, just to see if he would notice I was missing. I'd rummage through the boxes of my mother's things and imagine what life would have been like, if she'd lived. I'd dress up in her clothes and pretend to be beautiful."

You are beautiful.

"As the light shifted in the room I imagined monsters in the shadows." She smiled. "I think all kids do that, even in their bedrooms. But I had no one to run to when I got scared. No one to hold me."

I would have held you.

She tilted her head, looking as withdrawn as she had the first day he'd met her. With all the clinking and chattering around them, he suddenly wished they were in a more private place. "You don't have to talk about this, if you don't want to." Hudson squeezed her hand as he wondered what kind of a man would neglect a child in such a way.

"It's okay." She took a slow sip of her root beer. "I wasn't afraid. Just lonesome. I spent a lot of time looking out the window. I think I grew up watching life more than living it. But I learned how to entertain myself. . .by singing." Her eyes lit up a little. "It's amazing what a child can do, when left to her own devices. Music became very important to me during my alone time. I think it was God's way of ministering to me—and me, to Him."

"So, that little room became a prayer closet?" he asked.

She shrugged. "I wouldn't have known to call it that then, though I certainly sensed God's presence in there." Her eyes brightened. "And I don't want to make it sound like I had no interaction with other children. I made a couple of friends over the years, and there was this one little boy. . .one summer. He somehow managed to rig a pulley from his tree house over to my window. And he sent me little bunches of flowers and funny notes." Clair's hand went to her cheek. "We never met in person, and he didn't sign his name, so I never knew who he was, or. . ." Her voice faded. "In one of his notes, he said he loved me, that he was coming back to rescue me someday."

"I wish that boy had been me."

A forlorn look came over her. "He and his family moved away at the end of the same summer, but I kept all of his little notes. In fact, I took special care of the last one. It's buried in a box, somewhere among my mother's things in the attic. I never saw the boy again, but I've always remembered his kindness. It brought some light during a dark time. . .like a bright warm sun coming up just for me." Suddenly, she looked embarrassed. "I'm sorry. I didn't mean to go on and on about myself."

"No, it's fine." Hudson gazed into her eyes, wishing she were in his arms. "It's your day, after all." He sighed. "If only I'd known the secret to your heart, I would've written you a letter, too." He gave her a wink. "Especially on a day like today."

Clair's cheeks glowed pink.

Without warning, Otto exploded over to their table, interrupting the perfect moment. But to Otto's credit, he lowered the heaping plates in front of them without a single mishap. When two of the other waiters applauded at his flawless service, Otto rolled his eyes. "Where's the faith?"

Hudson turned around to discover Tara Williamson rushing his way.

"Where in the world have you been?" Tara gave Hudson a possessive hug and a kiss on the cheek. "I haven't seen you in ages." Her voice had a flirtatious edge to it. "And Hudson, you look fantastic in black. I think you forgot just how great. . .that color can be." She tucked a long, dark curl behind her ear.

"Thanks." Hudson flinched a bit as he took note of her slinky black dress then turned to Clair. "I'd like you to meet Tara Williamson. Tara, this is Clair O'Neal."

Tara made a fist with her hand and held it to her stomach. "Of course, the song, 'Clair.' It was for you."

"I'm glad to meet you." Clair held her hand out to Tara.

"Same here." Instead of shaking her hand, Tara waved to her parents.

Stanley and Joan Williamson rushed over, dressed to the hilt and gushing all the way. After the introductions, the attention turned back to Hudson.

"Well, Maestro," Stanley said. "Your performance gets better every time we hear you."

"You were wonderful, dear." Joan straightened Hudson's collar. "By the way, when are you coming over for dinner again? We miss you. *Tara* misses you."

"Mother, really." Tara shook her head but looked intently at Hudson.

"Thanks for the invitation." Hudson groaned inside, thinking Joan's comment sounded like a sour note in an otherwise harmonious evening. He glanced at Clair, hoping she hadn't heard the remark, but he couldn't quite read her expression.

"Well, don't make yourself so scarce," Stanley said to Hudson. "And I hope you've had some time to think about my offer. It's still good." He slapped Hudson on the back.

"Sometime we want to show you the photos from the trip we all took to Switzerland." Joan patted Hudson's arm. "Okay?"

"I might drop by sometime," Hudson said, trying to be polite. "Thanks."

"Well, good to see you, son." Stanley looked over at Clair. "And nice to meet you, Blair."

"Her name is *Clair*, Daddy. Hudson wrote a song for her. Remember?"

"Oh yes. Sorry, Clair." Stanley smacked his hands together. "We'd better get rolling. We're headed to some chick flick, which I love as much as heartburn, but the women outvoted me." He winked.

After a gush of good-byes and an exit by the Williamson family, Hudson sat back down. He could see the bemused smile on Clair's face. "I'm sorry about that. They mean well. But they've got me all wrong. You see, they've always wanted me to marry their daughter. They're always scheming, which is why he mentioned an offer. They have this plan. I'll marry Tara, we'll sing together, and we'll live happily ever after."

"Oh?" Clair chewed on her lower lip. "Is it a plan you'd consider?"

"No." Hudson hoped to make himself very clear. "I will *never* marry Tara."

"Okay." Clair met his eyes. "Do you mind if I ask. . .what the offer was?" She folded her hands in her lap. "I'm sorry. I shouldn't have asked."

"I will tell you." Hudson covered her hands with his. "Stanley has more money than he knows what to do with. So, he's always said if I marry Tara, he'll buy the Silver Moon Café and give it to me as a wedding present. But I could never accept his offer. It's ridiculous. I don't love her. I've always liked Tara and her parents. They treat me like family. But you can't be forced to love someone, even if it appears to be a good idea for everyone involved. It's too medieval to think that way. It's not the nature of love."

"I don't know much about love." Clair's shoulders relaxed. "But I think it might feel a little like flannel pj's."

"That's right. Like a warm, soft. . .embrace." He leaned over, wanting to kiss her cheek before he headed up on stage, but out of the corner of his eye, he noticed yet another person coming toward their table. Next time, he would have to remember to take Clair on a date away from the crowd, a place where they could sit and talk quietly—just the two of them.

Clair's expression lit up as Glenn Yves approached.

Great. Hudson took a good look at the fellow. Sure, he was tall, wore an Italian suit. And yes, Glenn was probably considered handsome by some females, but why did he look at Clair as if he had some claim on her? Hudson tried not to narrow his eyes, but he certainly wanted to. "Glenn, how are you?"

"Great." Glenn smiled as he gazed at Clair. "I just wanted to say hello to Clair. Hope you don't mind."

After handshakes and small talk, Hudson was glad to see Glenn move on. He glanced at his watch. His break was over, so he took a couple of bites of his sirloin steak soup then stood to make his way back toward the stage.

"You hardly touched your food," Clair noted.

"Doesn't matter. I'll be up on stage gazing down at you. Plenty of sustenance. . . like a seven-course meal."

He watched a warm smile spread across her face—a smile he could bask in for a lifetime. *God help me. My heart is no longer mine. How did this happen?* He gave her a wink and strode up to the stage.

As he glanced back, he noticed Glenn stationing himself at a table near Clair. In spite of his rising annoyance, there wasn't much he could do about it. He'd have to put his relationship with Clair in God's hands, even though it wouldn't be easy. He certainly couldn't force her to fall in love with him any more than the Williamsons could force him to marry Tara.

After the spotlight illuminated Hudson, he said into the microphone, "I've always loved living here in Little Rock. . .the city by the river."

A few people let out a whoop of approval, making Hudson grin. "This is a little song I wrote while sailing down the Arkansas River. I hope you feel the same way." He began his song and strummed his way to the chorus. This time he gazed into Clair's lovely eyes as he sang:

> *"Whenever I lose myself*
> *The river can find me.*
> *Whenever my life is bound,*
> *The river sets me free."*

Just as Hudson wound up his tune, he noticed Clair's gaze shift to Glenn, who leaned in toward her. *What is he up to?*

Glenn began to chat with her intimately—like two-peas-in-a-pod intimately. A few seconds later, he was laughing at something she'd said.

Clair suddenly knocked over her glass of water, and Otto, who hadn't broken a plate all evening, came to her rescue, knocking over two trays of food in the process.

Glenn got up, but Otto continued his comedy of errors by inadvertently hitting him with his elbow. Glenn stepped backward, losing his footing, and took quite a tumble to the floor, with his feet actually rising above his head like in a cartoon.

Hudson wasn't a genius when it came to the subtleties of love, but he knew one thing for certain—he wasn't the only one falling head over heels for Clair.

Chapter 12

Later, after Hudson brought her home, Clair closed her front door, scolding herself for the fiasco at the café. What in the world had gone wrong? Why was she so clumsy and silly?

In spite of her ongoing censures, Clair readied herself for bed and gave herself the luxury of bringing up a few of the brighter moments of the evening. In particular, the way Hudson sang to her, and then later brought a cake out from the kitchen to celebrate her birthday. His gaze had been full of tenderness and affection.

And then there was the way Glenn seemed to hang on her every word. Hudson may have been perturbed with Glenn's presence, but she couldn't be sure. Perhaps these were merely the pathetic imaginings of a desperate woman. *God, even if there is more to their feelings, do I deserve their attentions? Both Hudson and Glenn belong to "the beautifuls." Who am I?* A question she'd been trying to answer her whole life.

She slipped on her old nightgown, the one she'd worn so much it had become like velvet against her skin. Ima—and her sweet ways—came to mind. *She used to call me* beloved. And hadn't Hudson used that very word in his song about her?

Clair gazed in the mirror, studying herself. "You are beloved," she whispered and smiled. *Hmm. It sounds unfamiliar, but welcome. Very welcome.*

After scooting underneath the covers, she let go of all the bittersweetness of the evening and began to sail away into a deep sleep.

Many hours later, she woke up to the sound of her alarm clock. She yawned and stretched, knowing she should get out of bed but wanting to linger a few minutes before dressing for church.

Clair spent a few blissful moments coming awake then reached for her Bible. As was so often the case, she turned to the book of Psalms, reading aloud the verse that gave her the courage to face this season of her life. " 'The Lord is my shepherd, I shall not be in want. He makes me lie down in green pastures, he leads me beside quiet waters.' "

Her thoughts shifted to the banks of the Arkansas River. She closed her eyes and pictured the Lord taking her by the hand and leading her to the very edge of the water, to sit in peaceful solitude and enjoy the view. Her heart swelled at the thought of it. God—the Maker of the Universe—wanted to spend time with her. To draw her to a quiet, intimate place. To call her His *beloved*, just as Ima had done. To wash away the pain from the past in the mighty rivers of His love.

"God, my Father. . ." She started to whisper a prayer but stumbled across the word *Father*. Visions of her stepfather came to mind right away, but she pressed them back and forged ahead. Clair poured out her heart to the Lord, thanking Him for all of the marvelous changes in her life over the past several days. She prayed for His guidance regarding the bookstore, and for His will concerning her new friendships.

Afterward, she felt the strangest sensation—as if the Lord had swept into the room and lifted her into His arms. For the first time in a long while, she truly felt as if she could conquer all of the demons of the past. She pondered these things as she showered and dressed for church. And she continued to think about them as she went into the kitchen to grab a bite to eat before heading out.

Her reflections were interrupted by a rap on the front door. Clair set down her muffin and hurried toward the door. Through the peephole, she could see an elderly woman dressed in raggedy clothes. Clair opened the door. "Yes?"

"I'm Harriet Plow. You the O'Neal girl?" The woman clutched an enormous handbag, which looked like hunks of faded tapestry sewn together to make a satchel.

"Yes, I am."

"Used to live next door to you. Right over there." She pointed her bony finger to the tan house with green shutters. "Glad I found you. Thought you'd be gone by now—moved on from this forsaken place." The woman released a wheezing kind of chortle.

As Clair considered Mrs. Plow's features and voice, memories trickled back. "Yeah, I do remember." Clair opened the door wider. "I could make tea."

"Won't trouble you for any fancy drinks. But I could sure use a place to take a load off. My dogs are howling."

Clair led the woman through the door, noticing she hadn't had a bath in ages. *I wonder why she's here.* Perhaps she needed some kind of help. The older woman eased herself down on an armchair while Clair sat across from her.

"You grew up to be a real beauty." Mrs. Plow's sharp black eyes seemed to assess Clair. "Just like your ma." The old woman rubbed the hairs on her chin as if she were stroking a cat.

"Thank you." Clair still wasn't used to all the attention, but she was glad to hear someone speak of her mother.

Mrs. Plow glanced around the room. "Only been in this house a handful of times. Do you remember me looking after you when you had the chicken pox? Course, you were a young'un then. Mighty little. Oh, you was such a skinny little thing then. Made me wonder if your stepdad was taking proper care of you."

More childhood scenes came back to Clair—when she'd watched the comings and goings of Mrs. Plow from the attic window. The many times she'd hung out her laundry on the line and when she'd fed table scraps to a stray dog. And a few times when the older woman had waved at her and smiled. "Thank you for taking care of me when I was sick."

"Fiddlesticks." Mrs. Plow hunched over and grimaced. "I didn't come for no dainty gratitudes. Truth is. . .I didn't pay enough attention to you growing up. Should've done a whole lot more." She rubbed her gnarled hands together. "God told me to come back here and say something." She pointed her crooked finger in the air, looking upward. "I'll get to it."

Was Mrs. Plow talking to God or was she deranged? Clair waited for the woman to go on.

"Not sure what I'm supposed to say." Mrs. Plow pounded her fist into her palm. "He just said I needed to come."

They both sat in silence for a while, until Mrs. Plow started to chuckle. Then she looked at Clair. "Guess I shoulda got a clearer report before I found you."

Mrs. Plow sniggered so much, Clair started to laugh along with her. What an odd morning this was turning out to be.

Finally Mrs. Plow's laugh turned into a rasp and then a cough. "I'm getting kinda dry. Feels like my mouth is full of chicken feathers. Maybe I *will* have some tea."

Clair headed to the kitchen, where she got down her favorite teapot from the upper cupboard and a box of Darjeeling from the pantry. Mrs. Plow poked her head around the corner, making Clair jump.

"Didn't mean to scare you." The woman's smile showed a few missing teeth.

"It's all right. You're welcome to sit at the table."

"I know this is bad manners, but you got any food to go with the tea?" Mrs. Plow clutched her big handbag as she sat down.

Clair's heart went out to the woman. Even though Mrs. Plow had asked the question with a touch of humor, she looked hungry. Clair opened the refrigerator and pulled out some cheese and grapes. In the pantry, she located another muffin, along with some peanut butter.

When Clair had laid out their little feast, the older woman said grace and then began to take a few poised nibbles. Soon though, Mrs. Plow ate with gusto. After she'd gulped down several helpings of everything, the woman finally looked up from her plate. "I hadn't eaten in a while. Thank you, missy." She started to laugh again.

Clair joined in, grateful to have helped the woman.

Mrs. Plow glanced upward and said, "Okay, okay. I'll tell her, Lord. But I don't know what good it'll do her now. Be like stirring up the dregs and making everything dirty again." The old woman gave a wave toward heaven, clasped Clair's hand, and then paused.

"You can tell me. It's okay." Clair twisted the material on her shirt with her free hand, wondering what the woman was getting at.

Mrs. Plow pulled back, sighing. "After your ma passed on, your stepdaddy hurt so bad I think he blamed you for her death." She raised a wrinkled hand. "Don't you worry yourself, now. It was just his grief talking. You done nothing wrong."

Clair stared at the bare wall, trying to remember her stepfather's accusation, but no memory of it came to her. And yet she'd felt the friendless atmosphere that had permeated the house.

"You lived with him far too long, to my way of thinking."

"Eighteen. My stepfather died of an aneurysm when I was eighteen." The words escaped her lips in a whisper.

"I'm glad you got this house. It was your ma's home before he came. Not his. He didn't own nothing." Mrs. Plow's mouth twisted into a scowl.

Clair wondered what memories Mrs. Plow had of her mother. *Lord, help her to remember—about my mother.*

Mrs. Plow poured cream in her cup from the tiny pitcher then gulped the tea down, leaning her head way back to get the last drop. "Ahh, haven't had nothing that tasty in a long time," she said into the teacup. Then she looked back at Clair. "Your ma, oh, she was a good one. She knew the Lord, and she'd do anything for you." She patted Clair's hand. "I can see you got her kind spirit."

"Thank you." Clair took a sip of her tea. Mrs. Plow's words were sweeter than the little muffins set before them. *I remember now. My mother used to sing to me. She had the prettiest voice.* Clair remembered her smile—a lovely face leaning down to kiss her good night. And then her mother was gone. Forever.

"I'll just say it straight out." Mrs. Plow fidgeted in her chair, playing with the soiled lace on her sleeves. "I ain't never been one for regrets. Never been in my nature. But I am sorry about something."

"What do you mean?"

"I know what your stepdaddy did to you, how he ignored you. Saw it firsthand a time or two. He wasn't quite right in the head after your mama passed, God rest her soul. And he couldn't see beyond his own pain. That's true enough but was no excuse." Mrs. Plow's eyes fluttered as her shoulders sagged. "I know you spent a lot of time up in that little room with your mama's things."

Clair drew back, saying nothing. She wasn't sure if she wanted Mrs. Plow to continue. Until the recent conversation with Hudson, her past concerning her stepfather and the loneliness of the attic had been cloaked away in some dark corner of her mind. *Because when you name a thing. . .it truly exists. Then you have to deal with it.*

"First, I thought maybe you was just playing up there and peeking out the window like children do." Mrs. Plow grasped the tiny pitcher and drank the rest of the cream straight down. She wiped her mouth on her sleeve as she puckered her brows. "But you was up there too much, and you didn't look merry like the other kids. Then I heard a neighbor talking. Old Harvey Medville. He was over at your house, visiting, and he heard you up there, singing. So I know it was true. And I been blaming myself all these years for your loneliness. I shoulda stepped in and wrapped my arms around you, kissed away your tears."

"But it wasn't your fault or Mr. Medville's." Clair chewed on her lower lip.

The woman shook her head. "When a neighbor knows. . .and does nothing about it, well then, it's just the same as if they done it."

"But I don't blame you." Clair touched the woman's sleeve. "It's okay."

"Your stepdaddy could have put you in foster care." Mrs. Plow got a stern glint in her eye. "Or I coulda come over here and beat the living tar out of that man. Reminded him he had a daughter to care for."

The woman shook her head as her glare softened. "But I didn't, and I'm here to say, I knew a little of what you suffered. I never wanted you thinking his meanness was some fault of yours. You was such a fine child, sweet as jelly."

"He made sure I had the basic necessities," Clair said softly. "Food, clothing, a place to sleep at night. He just never knew how to give me the other things— love, affection. . ." Pain shot through Clair—one she'd never known. She'd always wondered if anyone had discovered her dismal plight. Now she knew for sure, and the sensations felt numbing and thorny at the same time. Was it anger that pierced her heart or merely a resignation that life didn't always offer justice? She knew some women might need counseling for having journeyed through such a pitiful youth, and yet she'd never felt compelled to see a therapist. Perhaps she'd been in denial or she'd pushed the past back into the attic like dead flowers pressed into a book.

"Basic necessities," Mrs. Plow huffed, balling up her fingers into a knotty fist, "wasn't enough." She let her fist thunder down on the table. "Not for an innocent child."

"I made it through okay." Clair gave her a sympathetic smile. "There wasn't anything you could have done."

Mrs. Plow pulled out a wad of tissues from the box on the table and blew her nose with vigor. She made a droning sound with her mouth and then patted Clair's cheek. "You have your mother's eyes. Just like the seraphim." She slipped the box of tissues into her enormous satchel and rose from her chair as if she'd left something heavy behind. "Well, I said my piece." She pointed to the food on Clair's plate.

"You gonna eat those sweets?"

"No. Please take them."

Mrs. Plow opened her satchel wide and dumped the little plate of food into her bag. "I can't stay," she said with a sigh.

Clair's heart twisted within her at the thought of Mrs. Plow's leaving. "Will you come see me again? You're welcome anytime."

"Of course."

"Well, feel free. And, if you get the chance, come by and see me at work sometime. I run the little Christian bookstore in the River Market District. It's called Ima's."

"I'll do that, sweetie." Mrs. Plow limped to the front door.

Clair offered to pay for a taxi, but Mrs. Plow wouldn't hear of it. So, after hugging the older woman, Clair slipped a ten dollar bill in her pocket without her noticing—quite a sacrifice, considering her own current financial plight. But how could she do less? Mrs. Plow lumbered off down the sidewalk, looking tired but content.

Clair glanced at her watch and groaned. Somehow the time had gotten away from her. The church service was half over by now. No point in going today. She drew in a deep breath, pondering all that had happened this morning and feeling God's presence all around her. *"He guides me in paths of righteousness. . ."* The familiar words from her Bible reading urged Clair onward, motivated her to do something she'd never before had the courage to do.

Clair suddenly had an intense desire to see the attic—a place she'd avoided for years. Whether the need came out of curiosity or for closure, she didn't know, but maybe now, because of Mrs. Plow's words, the place would ring with truth instead of falsehood. And maybe one more sight of it would allow her to confront the soiled memories of her past and set them free.

She made her way through the same hallway she'd known all her life, but her heartbeat quickened as she carried herself up the dim and narrow staircase. With a trembling hand, she turned the doorknob and let the door swing open wide. She stumbled her way to the center of the room and pulled the chain above her head. Light filled the middle of the room, but shadows remained in every corner like murky vapors. A bare bulb swung from its chain as if the light itself had been hanged. *How did I endure this tomb-like place?*

Taking in a lungful of air, Clair looked around at the world she recognized all too well. *The attic.* The space smelled of mold and stale air, and except for a few old cartons of junk, the room appeared empty. She could almost hear a child singing—her own voice—but it was only memories haunting the air.

Clair sat down on a rope rug next to the dormer window where she'd spent hours at a time—watching, thinking, dreaming, singing, praying, and hoping someday to find a world beyond the gloomy walls and the lonesomeness it had brought her.

Her eyes misted over and, before she could convince herself to stop, a gush of tears came. She'd always found a reason not to cry, but this time no logic convinced her otherwise. The reality came to her full force—her stepfather hadn't wanted her or loved her. *Oh God, why did my mother have to die? What was the purpose in sending her to heaven so young? I needed her. My life would have been so different. I would have known love.*

Minutes seemed to flow into an unhurried stream as bits of the past came to her one by one. Clair wept softly. She leaned into the pain, knowing she could no longer drive it back. After her face felt washed clean with tears, she drew in a deep breath and turned her attention to the window.

A squirrel scampered over to the neighbor's sycamore tree and gazed upward. Then a precious little girl, dressed in violet overalls, tried catching the little animal. The squirrel scurried up the tree, making the child giggle.

Out of the blue, the little girl looked up at the dormer window, squinted, and then waved up at her as if she were a longtime friend. Clair rested her open palm against the warm glass and smiled. Amazingly, the child seemed to be the mirror image of herself when she'd been the same age. *Who is she?* The girl then skipped up the sidewalk as if she hadn't a care in the world. Perhaps that's how her heart felt now—just a little lighter. Clair stole one more glance, but the child had vanished.

What could this mean? Clair rested her head against the wall and wondered why she'd stayed in the same house all these years. Obligation? A sense of connectedness with the past, no matter how bleak? Or did she have a perverse need to continue her stepfather's tradition of neglect, thinking she somehow deserved it? Clair cringed at the thought.

Another one of Ima's sayings floated around in her head. *"God gives us opportunities. He opens doors, but we have to decide to walk through them."* She could almost hear Ima speaking to her. *"Well, what are you going to do now, girly?"*

Clair bowed her head and prayed for courage and wisdom. After a few minutes, she rose from the floor, and with determination, walked down the stairs as if she were being delivered into a new world.

Chapter 13

Clair knew where the telephone directory was, and she intended to use it. Ima had always talked about a Realtor friend of hers who had a reputation of being quite good. She scanned the yellow pages and found the familiar name—Elaine Kowalski.

After dog-earring the page, Clair closed the telephone book, and the words of the psalm flooded over her. *"He restores my soul. He guides me in paths of righteousness for his name's sake."* Her awareness became more illuminated by the minute. The Lord—her Shepherd—had stirred her world, and she felt roused to action. Exhilaration coursed through her. *What shall I do next?*

She threw open all the kitchen windows—ones that had never been opened—and let the breeze blow through. She took in the fragrant air and accepted an unfolding truth. Even though she'd avoided the attic since her youth, she still hadn't escaped its hold on her. She knew now her spirit had been trapped up there all those years, pining away for permission to live. And to love.

She felt the mending touch all the way to her soul. Something shattered had been made whole. The trust and love once snatched away by human hands was divinely restored. God had used a unique and quirky woman named Harriet Plow to make it come to pass. All of heaven rejoiced with her, and she could almost hear the angels singing. She'd never been more ready to step into the light.

❧

Early Monday morning, Clair signed a listing agreement with Elaine Kowalski and watched with pleasure as she placed a realty sign on her front lawn. Then Clair busied herself cleaning the house from top to bottom. Once she had her small abode spick-and-span, she looked around satisfied. *Hmm. Ancient and small, but clean.*

Knowing she had lots of work to do at the bookshop for the grand opening, Clair headed toward the bathroom to clean up. She carefully applied some of her new makeup and then slipped on a black-and-white pantsuit that Destinee had called chic.

An hour later when she arrived at the bookshop, she suddenly took note of the drab walls. Why hadn't she noticed the dull paint before—the color of rusty ship bottoms? *Hmm. Fresh paint would give the store a whole new look. Maybe a rich green would be nice—airy, soothing, and woodsy looking.* Just as she assessed the floors, a young woman with multi-colored, spiky hair pushed her way through the shop door with a large package.

"We're not open," Clair said. "At least not yet."

"Here for a delivery." The young woman smacked her gum between words. "Ms. . . .O'Neal."

"Thank you. You can just put the box on the counter."

The girl set the box down and then paused to chew her gum, blowing a mammoth bubble.

Clair handed the girl a tip and smiled. "I used to enjoy blowing bubbles, too. But I never got one as big as yours."

The girl handed Clair a couple of pieces of bubblegum and sauntered back outside.

Clair watched her go, feeling pleased with herself that she could talk so easily with a stranger. She popped a piece of the gum in her mouth and opened the newly delivered box. A smaller gift, wrapped in peach paper and a chiffon bow, sat nestled inside. *How lovely.* She wondered if Hudson had sent it.

Just as she lifted the gift out of the box and eased off the delicate bow, she heard the bell on the shop door again.

Hudson stood in the doorway. "Hi."

"Hello." Clair didn't hold back her joy. "Please come in."

"I realize you're busy getting ready—"

"It's okay. Really." She thought Hudson looked wonderful in his corduroys and his red-checked shirt. His boyish smile seemed to be in delightful contrast to his five-o'clock shadow.

Surprise also covered his handsome face. "You look more dazzling every time I see you," Hudson said. "This time it's in your eyes. How do you do that?"

Clair shrugged her shoulders. "Thank you." She held up the gift. "I got your present." *Oh dear.* In her enthusiasm, she might have goofed. *What if it's from someone else?*

Hudson walked closer to her. "I didn't send anything, but please, don't let me stop you." He stuffed his hands in his back pockets. "Let's see what it is."

Under the peach wrapping paper and folds of tissue sat an elegant bottle of perfume with a French name she couldn't pronounce. She knew little about such luxuries, but she could tell it was expensive—Rolex expensive.

"Looks like someone you know has excellent taste." Hudson's smile looked a little askew.

Clair opened the attached card. It simply read, *Glenn.* "It's from Glenn."

"Glenn Yves." Hudson lost his smile. All of it.

Should I explain or will it make things worse? "Glenn has taken me under his wing as my image coach. Years ago, someone helped him, and so he promised to help someone else in return." She swallowed hard. "*I'm* that person."

"Pretty generous of him." Hudson shifted his weight. "How did he choose you. . .if you don't mind my asking."

He had no hint of sarcasm in his voice, and yet Clair hoped he didn't think less of her for accepting the offer. She searched her mind for the right words. "I think I must have looked pitiful that night at the party."

"I didn't think you did." Hudson ran his finger along the counter. "I thought you looked. . .amazing."

Amazing? She would tuck that word away for later. "Thank you."

"Maybe he's really wanting to. . .you know. . .date you." He looked away. "Although I certainly can't blame him."

"Glenn sees me as a debt he must pay." Clair laced her hands together. "But I am grateful for his help." She realized she'd been smacking her gum, so she hid it in the side of her mouth.

"You could never be just an obligation. . .to anyone."

She saw the sweetest expression of concern in his eyes. "I will be careful." What a wonderful feeling, to have someone worried about her.

"Good." Hudson didn't look persuaded by her promise. "I also think you're somewhat naive where men are concerned." He rubbed his chin.

She could feel the familiar heat come to her face. "Maybe you could tell me what I need to know about them."

Hudson coughed and blinked.

Did I surprise him? Is that considered flirting? The sensation appeared to be enjoyable, yet disconcerting since she had no earthly idea how he would react to it. "Please."

Hudson's expression was a mix of bafflement and amusement. "Well, some men. . ." He turned away. "Not me, of course, but some men have expectations when they buy expensive gifts for a woman." He turned back to her with quiet intensity.

"Glenn is a fine Christian man." She crossed her arms and then uncrossed them. "In order to run this shop, I'll have to work with customers. He's helping me get over my shyness."

"Yes, I'll bet he is." He shook his head. "Oh boy. This really isn't my business." He raked his fingers through his hair. "But. . ." He pulled a guitar pick out of his pocket and passed it back and forth between his hands. "The reason I came. . . I wanted to invite you to go hiking with me. It's one of my favorite things. . .well, that and the Razorbacks." He grinned.

"Hiking?"

"Do you like to hike?" He had hope in his eyes.

"Yes. No. I mean, I've never been a hiker, but I would like to try."

"Well then." His face brightened. "One of my favorite places is Petit Jean State Park. I think you'll like it. So. . .how about Saturday?"

"Okay. Yes." *Am I smiling too much?*

Hudson beamed. "I'll pick you up at seven so we can get an early start. Just wear some comfortable clothes and sneakers. Okay?"

Clair nodded, wondering why she'd never hiked before. The thought of it sounded pleasant enough, especially with Hudson alongside her.

"By the way, how's the store coming along?" He leaned on the counter.

"I'm going to repaint." Clair pointed to one of the walls. "A woodsy green, maybe with a book border at the top. What do you think?"

Hudson nodded. "I'd love to help you."

Clair found it hard to accept help since she'd always done everything for herself. "Well, I uh—"

"I mean it. I'm not like other people who just say things like that to be polite." He smiled then gestured toward the bottle. "Aren't you going to try on some of the perfume?"

"Oh. . .I guess." She removed the lid off the chunky bottle and dabbed a little of the pale amber liquid on her wrist. She took a long whiff of the scent. *Ohh my. Paradise in a bottle.* In a moment of boldness, she raised her wrist to him.

Hudson closed the short distance between them and leaned over her arm with a playful smile. He took in a deep breath. "Very nice. Maybe it *is* worth the money." He continued to hold her arm.

The combination of the stirring aroma and Hudson's warm touch made Clair's head go a little light. Suddenly embarrassed by her boldness, she eased away from him and held out a piece of bubblegum instead.

He accepted the gum with a grin, unwrapped it, and slipped it into his mouth. "Thanks. Well, I guess I should be going. Got to get back to my shop. I have a new hire, and she's like this cleaning lady on steroids. If she tries to organize my office, I'll never find anything again." He sauntered to the front door and then looked back at her. "Be careful now."

Clair gave him a little wave and wished she could have offered him coffee. She made a mental note to buy beans and filters.

"Let me know when you're ready to paint. I'll be happy to pick up a paint bucket and some brushes. Anything you need."

"Thanks. That would be great." Clair's hand went to her heart. *What an attentive and caring man.*

"You're welcome." Hudson seemed pleased.

"Okay." Clair watched him through the window as he strode in the direction of his guitar shop, chewing his bubblegum with great enthusiasm. Out of the blue, Glenn appeared, walking right by Hudson. They exchanged polite nods as Glenn reached for the handle on the shop door. The last sight of Hudson was a frown directed at Glenn.

Oh dear.

Chapter 14

Glenn came through the door with his usual flair, once again wearing a gleaming smile and tailored garments, which made the most of his physique. "Hello."

"Hi." Clair reminded herself to thank him for his generous gift.

He glanced out the window. "Hudson stopped by, I see." His comment came out heavily, as if it were burdened with questions.

She nodded.

"Ah." Glenn frowned, smoothing his tie. "Looks like I'm better at what I do than I want to be."

Clair wasn't sure what he meant, so she just let the comment go.

"If Hudson wants to make it big in the music business, he needs to buy some new clothes." Glenn crossed his arms.

Clair did her best not to respond.

"I'm going to break my own social rules here and ask you something impolite." Glenn cleared his throat. "Are you dating that guy?"

What should I say? "We're going hiking."

"Hiking?" Glenn said the word as if it were vulgar. "Why hike when there are spas and fitness centers? Besides, you aren't the type."

"Thank you for the perfume. I've never had anything so. . ." *I shouldn't say expensive.* "Anything so elegant. But you shouldn't have spent so—"

"My mentor was generous with me, and I intend to be generous as well."

Clair noticed a yearning kind of expression in his eyes. *Perhaps he's ill.*

He moved toward her. "By the way, I came by to take you to lunch. . .if you're free. Today we'll be discussing proper attire. Also, we'll talk about how to deal with the media."

"Media?" Clair tried not to look panicky.

"Well, I'm sure you'll want to announce your opening. Set up some book signings. Talk it up with the media." He made a gesture with his hands. "You know, create some buzz."

She took in a deep breath and made a point to look at Glenn. "Okay."

"By the way, your black-and-white outfit is a good choice."

Clair smiled. "It's all because of your kindness."

"I disagree." He arched an eyebrow. "A rose is still a rose even when it hasn't bloomed yet."

She wanted to say something clever back, but her mind became a blank sheet of paper. She chewed on her lower lip, but then remembering Glenn's instruction, she stopped herself.

"Listen, I have a client to visit with for a few minutes, but I could meet you at the Harbor Inn Café at noon." Glenn glanced at his watch. "Will that work for you?"

"Yes."

"See you then." He maneuvered his way through the standing bookshelves and tables and then slipped out the door.

Clair still couldn't get over the fact that a man as remarkable and refined as Glenn Yves had decided to mentor her. She picked up a broom nearby and began to sweep the floor as she thought about all the recent events in her life. She wondered how she'd ever get her shop opened with all the sudden attention. *But I enjoy being cared for.* In fact, she wondered what would happen if all the benevolence toward her suddenly stopped. Would the loneliness feel worse than it had before?

Ima had always said, *"You can't depend on other people for your happiness. Just make sure things are right between you and God and then the other joys will come."* Clair thought her friend's words sounded like good advice, so she dismissed any more melancholy thoughts.

Just as Clair had swept up a sizable pile of dirt, the door opened again. A woman exploded into the shop, looking annoyed and in a hurry. *It's Leslie, the author, from the party—Hudson's sister!* Clair dropped her broom. "Hi. It's nice to—"

"It's Clair, right?"

"Yes. I'm—"

Leslie fiddled with her earring until she grimaced. "You don't look like the same woman I met at my party. You've had your hair done or something."

"Yes. I went to a spa, and—"

"I've stopped by to see about doing a book signing." Leslie made a dramatic gesture with her hand, nearly knocking over a display ornament.

"O–oh?" Clair stammered. "Well, we're undergoing renovations right now. Besides, Ima's the one who always takes care of book signings and she's—"

"Yes, I heard about that. So sorry. But I thought perhaps holding a book signing would help increase your business. When you're ready, of course."

What a kind gesture. Clair fumbled around, looking for the calendar. As she located it, Leslie continued to talk.

"I, um, saw you with my brother at the Silver Moon Café the other evening."

"Yes." Clair couldn't help but smile. "I had a wonderful time."

"Seemed a little odd, that's all." Leslie shrugged.

"Oh?" Clair looked over at Leslie, trying to make sense of her meaning.

"Well..." Leslie fidgeted with her hair. "Hudson has been involved with Tara for so long now, it's just...different to see him take an interest in someone else."

Clair lowered her gaze to the pile of dirt, clutching the calendar in her hands. "But I—"

"I know you can understand the love a sister has for her brother. I simply want what's best for Hudson." Leslie strolled around a table of books.

"Oh?" Leslie's perfume seemed to fill the entire store. Clair pinched her nose to keep from sneezing.

Leslie's green eyes took on a more intense hue. "Tara's a great girl. A good friend. And it's been a lot of fun to watch her relationship with Hudson blossom like it has."

I'm breathing too fast. Clair's head went wobbly. "But what if Hudson doesn't care for her...in that way?" She'd blurted out the question before she'd thought of the ramifications of such a bold query.

Leslie gazed at her fingernails and then looked back at Clair. "Men rarely know what they really want. At least, that's been my experience." She adjusted the collar on her blouse.

"But he wrote a song for me." The moment Clair spoke the words she wished she'd kept them to herself.

"Yes." Leslie set her purse down on a shelf and ambled about the store as if she were looking for something. "I heard the song. There's no doubt it's beautiful." She shrugged and smiled. "But that's what songwriters do—write songs when they're moved. I'm sure you've inspired him, but you see, he's touched and stirred by everything around him." She held up a novel. "He's an artist. It's what we do—use the things around us for our work."

Clair closed her mouth and released her hold on the calendar, setting it on the table. Leslie hadn't come here today to talk about a book signing. Not even close. A sickening feeling churned in Clair's stomach. What happened? Could the beginning now be the end? *No tears, Clair. No tears.*

All the recent hopes and joys were disappearing like Cinderella's coach—midnight had clearly come. The girl who had always been known as nobody would now make her quiet exit. She chewed on her lower lip until she flinched in pain.

Leslie set the novel back on the shelf with a thump and then glared at the bottle on the counter. "Oh, don't you love that brand of perfume? I have the very same bottle! Glenn Yves sent it to me. You met him at my party, I think."

"Y–yes."

Leslie fingered the bottle with a dreamy look in her eyes then glanced at her watch. "I should probably be going. I've got an appointment." She took a few steps toward the door then looked back with a whimsical smile. "I'll, um, call you about that book signing. We'll work out the details."

Sure we will.

As soon as Leslie left, Clair shut the door and made sure the closed sign was in place. Then she wilted into a nearby chair, deep in thought. Would she really be forced to stop going out with Hudson? Life had not only become too fast, it'd also become peopled and problematic. How had she gotten into such a dilemma? All because she'd agreed to replace Ima at a party.

A banging on the shop window jolted her back to reality. A stranger had stopped in front of the shop and had apparently pounded on the glass. The woman stared in at her as if she were an animal in a cage. Surely the lady could read the sign on the door.

Clair slumped to the floor. *Oh dear God, what am I doing?* Did she even have the temperament for running a store? Would she really be able to handle all the challenging customer demands? *And is dating this difficult for everyone else?*

Clair pulled herself from the floor and shut off the lights. Without intending to, she knocked over a chair. The deed felt unexpectedly good, so then one by one, she knocked all the decorative hats off the walls. Then she stared at the bare spaces. *What am I doing?* She'd never been aggressive or destructive in her life.

Then the realization hit her full force. *I care about him. I have feelings for Hudson.* Just hearing Leslie's comments about Tara caused a gripping pain in her chest. Was she right? Would Hudson be better off with someone as polished and refined as Tara? Surely Leslie thought so.

Clair lowered herself to the floor again and scooted under the ledge of the counter. She rested her chin on her knees in the quiet darkness of the shop. As she sat there and prayed, her stomach growled. *Hunger. Food. Lunch. Glenn. Oh no.* She'd forgotten to meet Glenn at the Harbor Inn Café. What would he think of her?

Moments later, the bell jingled over the front door. Who could that be? Clair decided to stay put. *Maybe it's Leslie returning to tell me all the men in Little Rock are off limits.* Her last thought surprised her. She'd rarely ever entertained sarcasm, and that was definitely sarcastic!

"Clair? Where are you?"

It's Glenn's voice. "I'm down here." She started to scramble to her feet.

Glenn peeked around some shelving. "There you are. No. Don't get up. I'll come down to you."

"But your suit. It'll get all—"

"Stay put." He took off his jacket and tossed it on the counter. Then he sat down on the floor next to her.

Amazingly, he didn't even ask why she was sitting on the floor. "I'm so sorry I forgot about lunch," she said.

He seemed to study her expression. "When you were late, I decided to come and find you."

They sat for a while without speaking. For the first time, Clair felt truly comfortable with Glenn. He seemed so out of character to just be sitting on the floor with her, staring into space like he had nothing better to do.

"May I be honest?" Glenn asked.

"Yes."

"You have some joy in your eyes since I met you at the party, but I think you're still living as if you don't really matter."

Clair looked away. "It takes time to rewrite a book."

"I'm going to ask you something personal, okay?" Glenn draped his arms over his knees.

"Go ahead."

"What are you most afraid of—above all else?"

Had she ever really thought about the subject from that angle? "Well. . .I wouldn't want to pass through this world without ever touching another life. I wouldn't want my shyness to keep me so incapacitated that I couldn't live the life I was meant to live."

He shook his head and smiled. "You know exactly what you want, and you know what's holding you back. Most people don't have a clue."

Clair wondered why she couldn't have been more articulate with Leslie.

Glenn smoothed his gold tie. "Clair. I like your name."

"I always thought it sounded old-fashioned." She suddenly noticed his scent—the heady smell of a life lived sumptuously. She realized some women would give anything to live such a life and to live it with him.

"No. Your name has a pure and gentle sound. . .like rain." His voice trailed off as he lowered his gaze to her lips. The shop door opened, making the bell jangle hysterically again. "She's closed," Glenn hollered to the intruder.

The rhythmic clomping of high heels grabbed Clair's attention. Maybe she'd need to make her closed sign bigger.

The woman, whoever she was, kept clomping until she stood in front of them. Leslie Mandel stared down at them with her hands on her hips.

Clair's heart skipped a beat.

Glenn looked up with surprise. "What are you doing here?"

"I forgot my purse." Leslie snatched up her bag from behind a stack of books. She stared at them with huge eyes as if she were watching a horror movie.

"Well, well, well. Glenn, I wondered where you've been. Guess this answers that question."

Glenn shrugged as he said, "Clair and I are just sitting here talking."

"Right." Leslie stormed out the door, slamming it so hard the glass shuddered in the window.

"Hmm. Not good." Glenn groaned. "As you know, Leslie is a past client of mine." He leaned his fist against his chin. "I've never led her to believe we were anything more than friends."

Clair touched the sleeve of his jacket. "She cares for you."

"I suppose." He shook his head. "I never meant to hurt her."

"I'm sure you didn't."

Glenn let out a lungful of air. "Tell me, Clair. If you were in my situation, what would *you* do to put a closure to this?"

As the irony of what Glenn asked became clear, the moment turned to agony. She would soon be faced with the same situation, since she had no intention of allowing herself to cause a rift in Hudson's relationship with his sister. *Not ever.* Family was essential to life, and she would sacrifice her own happiness for it.

After a long pause, Clair said, "I think I would tell her as tenderly as possible."

Chapter 15

Hudson and Clair strolled out of the lodge at Petit Jean State Park and headed down the path, which led to a ridge overlooking the Arkansas River Valley. Hudson drank in the sight—the sky mingled with the hills in layer upon layer of azure blue. *Nice.*

"I've always loved Arkansas," Clair said. "It's so beautiful." She took a few steps closer to the edge. "But I had no idea this was here."

"I've been here many times." Hudson pointed straight ahead. "Right over there is Mount Nebo. There're some pretty interesting legends and history here." He took in a deep breath of fresh air. "I really think early spring is the best time of year. Life is sort of hatching out. . .lots of promise."

He glanced over at Clair. On the drive to the park, she'd seemed pleased to be with him, but he noticed in spite of her more outgoing manner, some kind of anxiety lingered in her countenance. In fact, during the week, he'd wondered why she hadn't taken him up on his offer to help her paint the bookshop. "I'm glad the weather warmed back up for us." He smiled. "And I'm glad you dressed in sneakers and jeans. You'll be glad you did. It's a two-mile hike."

Clair grinned back at him. "You're scaring me. Is the hike down to the falls strenuous?"

"You'll do just fine. I promise."

As they descended the rock stairs, Hudson held her hand to steady her. A soothing warmth pulsed through his fingers.

Clair hopped down a step or two ahead of him.

He watched her, pleased she seemed to be enjoying herself. With the exception of a few tourists, they had the place to themselves. He suddenly remembered a brief mention of rain in the day's forecast. *Maybe the threat of a rainstorm kept the visitors at bay.*

She stopped suddenly. "I hear a waterfall."

"It's right down there." Hudson pointed to the left. "This is just a small one. But one time I wrote a song sitting right over there."

"Really?" Clair climbed over the rocks to the little falls and sat down on a boulder. She remained quiet for a moment and then said, "I value your passion for composing music. I mean, to make something beautiful that has never existed before. . .to have it manifest itself from your creative mind must be. . .unspeakable rapture."

"Unspeakable rapture?" He couldn't help but smile at her word choices. Everything about Clair warmed his heart, right down to her vocabulary.

She lowered her fingers into the clear, rushing water. "Do you suppose that's how God felt when He made all of this?"

"Maybe." He sat down next to her. "I don't know for certain. I'm not God. Although I know a couple of people in the music business who *think* they are."

Clair chuckled.

Hudson wished he hadn't devalued an awesome moment by making a joke of it, but his mind couldn't seem to stay on course. He just wanted to take Clair into his arms and explain how he really felt. He restrained himself again, knowing the moment wasn't right.

"You know, I don't really create something from nothing," he said. "I have life to inspire me." Should he give her a glimpse into his heart? "And I have *you* to inspire me." He noticed a flash of pain shadow her face. *What could be troubling her?*

Hudson rose, gazing at the view. Like ancient monuments, the bluffs and hills never seemed to change with time. He glanced back at Clair, wondering if through the years he'd ever passed her on the streets of Little Rock, not knowing who she was—not knowing she'd be the one to change his life. After a moment or two longer, Hudson said, "Tell me when you're ready to move on."

"I am." She dusted herself off and headed back to the main trail.

He followed her, pondering her silence.

After a while, they reached the bottom of Cedar Creek Canyon and then hiked along the water's edge. Hudson took in the sounds—the burbling noises of the creek and the occasional chirp of a small bird. Even though the ground was coated with brown leaves, tufts of green grass sprang up here and there and the trees flourished with new green buds. Glancing upward, he could see a jagged outcrop of charcoal sandstone against a velvet blue sky. He'd grown to love the canyon and the way it helped him relinquish the day and lose himself in the natural world.

Clair stopped to look at a moss-covered log. "You know, you have a very gifted voice."

That was certainly unexpected. "Thank you." *One compliment from her is better than a hundred pieces of flattery.*

"Have you always loved music?" Clair brushed her hand against the tiny yellow flowers peeking out from the leaves.

"Yeah. Even when I was a little guy, my parents said I always tried to make musical instruments out of junk. You know. . .buckets were drums and seeds in empty toilet paper rolls were maracas. That sort of thing. Believe me, our house was pretty noisy when I was growing up."

Clair chuckled.

"But I've always liked the way music changes people—makes them pause to think about something else. Something that lifts them up above the roar. . .to hear again." Hudson stuffed his hands in his pockets. "Sorry. I'm rambling."

"No, not at all. I think life would be unbearable without music. It. . .ushers us into the presence of God."

He watched as her face lit up with a fervor that surprised him. *She really does understand.*

When the path narrowed a bit, Hudson let her walk ahead of him. After a while, he could hear the thundering waters.

When Cedar Falls came into view, they stood still, taking in the beauty of it. The water fell nearly a hundred feet over a shelf of weathered rock. Mist formed at the base of the falls, creating a rainbow effect.

"It's wonderful. Can we get closer?"

Hudson pointed to the left. "Why don't we climb over there and sit under the overhang?"

They maneuvered around the uneven terrain. Hudson wiped off one of the powdery boulders and they sat down.

"This is a perfect spot." She clasped her hands together.

He gazed at her and then looked up at the falls. The waters crashed down before them and collected in a small lake, as if nature had given it a respite, before moving on again through the canyon.

Clair turned toward him. "I was just wondering. . .about your shop. Do you enjoy running a business?"

He didn't need to think long on that question. "Not really. But I do enjoy teaching the kids. . .watching their excitement. . .seeing their progress. Owning a business is a ton of work. And because of the shop, I don't have much time to perform."

"Do you want to perform full-time someday?"

"Sure. But right now, I need the income from both. I would like my songs to reach more people, but it takes promotion, which in turn takes a lot of cash. I guess you could say the music is the beauty and the promotion is the beast."

Clair didn't respond but just seemed to listen quietly. Hudson decided to continue. "And there're other pressures. My sister, Leslie, has always been an overachiever. She got published at twenty, which is very young. She was always a go-getter through high school, too. Cheerleader, president of the student council, prom queen, you name it."

Clair appeared to consider what he'd said. "Weren't you prom king?"

Hudson laughed. "No way. I had thick-rimmed glasses, acne, and a severe case of the chubbies."

She shook her head. "I can't imagine that."

"It's true. And I think I always compared myself to Leslie, strange as that seems." He shook his head. "Maybe it's just her excessive interest in my life, my business."

"What do you mean?" Clair's expression grew more curious.

Hudson shrugged. "She's always wanted to remake me. Fix my hair, dress me, pair me up with just the right girl—that kind of thing."

"Ah."

"I think she believes I'm meant for bigger things in the music business than teaching a few guitar lessons and singing in a café. I don't have any record deals, so sometimes I feel like I've let her down."

Clair looked as if she might say something but then didn't.

"I think it's why some of my songs tend to run a little on the melancholy side. I guess you could say there are things from my childhood that still haunt me." He gave her a warm smile. "So, even though I have no idea of the kind of isolation you had growing up, I knew how it felt to be on the outside looking in. Hey, that'd be a good song title, wouldn't it? 'The Outside Looking In.'"

"Yes, it is good."

Hudson picked up a rock chip and skipped it across the water.

"I feel some pressure, too. . .about the store," Clair said, breaking the silence between them. "But I don't want to disappoint Ima."

"I know you loved Ima, but she wouldn't want you to run the store if that wasn't what you were created to do. Would she?"

Clair looked at him. "I'm not sure, but I don't think so."

Oh, how he loved those brown eyes full of sweetness. Hudson handed her a flat stone to toss.

She pulled back and threw the stone, making it light upon the water like a dragonfly.

"That was a good one." Hudson sat down on a rock near her.

"Since no one is here, would you sing to me?" Clair asked. "Only if you want to. But I love to hear you sing."

"Okay." Hudson took in a deep breath and began to sing the first verse of "Amazing Grace." After he'd finished, he stopped and said, "Do you know the last verse?"

"Yes."

"Will you sing it with me?"

Clair shook her head. "No. I don't think so."

"But we're alone—just you and me and God. It'll be okay." Hudson began singing the last verse and then Clair joined him. At first she faltered and sang so softly he could barely hear her. And then something astonishing happened.

She straightened her shoulders and sang more loudly. Really sang. Her voice rose up, sweet and clear as it echoed through the canyon. In fact, her voice sounded so extraordinary he almost stopped singing. Had she had lessons growing up? Where had she learned to sing like that? He felt awestruck and tried not to stare at her.

When they'd released the last word of "Amazing Grace" up to the heavens, he felt exhilarated. And something else. The very air around them seemed charged with expectancy. Hudson paused to compose his words. "Where. . .did you learn to sing so beautifully?" He stood up and touched her arm.

Clair lowered her head. "I. . .well. . .as I mentioned, I sang in the attic. I sang every song I heard on the radio. And sometimes I would make up my own songs."

Hudson wasn't sure what to do next. He hadn't heard a voice like hers since. . .well, he couldn't really remember when he'd heard such an exquisite and unique voice. "Has anyone ever told you that you have a remarkable gift?"

"No."

"You mean you've never sung for anyone?"

"No. Only when I'm alone." Clair looked away. "Or at church. But there, I'm just one voice among hundreds. No one would single me out, and you would certainly never catch me singing solo."

"But why?" Hudson couldn't fathom a voice like hers left undiscovered.

She sat down on a nearby rock and gave him a puzzled smile. "I'm not sure anymore."

"I'm sorry for badgering you with so many questions. It's just. . .well. . .God has given you such an extraordinary talent." He took in a deep breath, still trying to absorb what he'd heard.

"Thank you." Clair brought her shoulder up to her cheek in a shy shrug.

"I really enjoyed singing with you just now." Hudson sat down next to her.

"I liked it, too." Even as Clair shared those encouraging words, her eyes seemed to be expressing two conflicting messages—joy and sorrow.

There were so many things he still wanted to ask her, and yet the moment seemed to be leading them elsewhere. "Clair?"

"Yes?"

Surely she didn't think they were just friends. "I would like to. . ." Like the leaves aloft around them, Hudson's voice floated away on the breeze.

"What were you going to say?"

"You've got to know."

She shook her head.

Clair seemed so innocent in so many ways—so honest and uncomplicated—he found it impossible not to adore her. He reached over to her and swept a lock of hair over her slender shoulder. She didn't pull away. Good sign. *If I kiss her would she run?* Probably not. Would she slap him? Never. But he might see disappointment in her lovely face, and that response he couldn't take.

In spite of Hudson's reservations, he took hold of her hand and, while cradling it, lowered his head and tenderly kissed the palm of her hand.

Clair's eyelids fluttered shut.

He took her reaction for a positive sign. Not wanting to waste another second, he lifted her chin and leaned over to kiss her.

Chapter 16

Hudson traced Clair's cheek with his fingertip, gazing at her lovingly. Did she have mist in her eyes? "What are you thinking?"

"About your kiss." She smiled as she folded her hands in her lap.

"And what exactly were you pondering about that kiss?" He covered her hands with his.

Clair's expression became wistful. "I was thanking God my very first kiss was with you."

Did she really say *first* kiss? *But Clair is thirty-one years old.* Suddenly feeling protective, he rose up and pulled her into his arms. "How can that be possible?"

Clair reddened. "I'm afraid it's true."

"Then. . .I feel honored."

She relaxed in his arms and rested her head on his shoulder.

How could a woman like Clair go unnoticed for so long? The idea could not be understood.

Hudson continued to hold Clair, enjoying the closeness and her steady breathing. So constant and gentle—qualities he hadn't seen an abundance of in the music business. Then a vision came to him—one of her singing with him on stage. *Should I ask her? What would she say?* "I know this might seem sudden, but would you ever consider singing with me at the Silver Moon? I already know people would love your voice."

"Oh, I don't know." She drew away from him and sat down, gripping the rock underneath her as if it could fly away.

Clair's gaze seemed so far away, he wondered if he'd ever be invited into her world. Hudson stared back out at the waters cascading over the top of the chasm and thought of his own wild fears of performing. "The first time I got up on stage I actually passed out." He chuckled. "They had to drag me off the stage like a side of beef."

A grin eased across her face. "I don't believe you."

"Yep. Made a total fool of myself. And then the second time I performed, I threw up. And I'd just had an enormous lunch. I won't go into the details, but that incident was even more humiliating because I was awake to see the audience's reaction."

Clair's hand went to her mouth. "What was it—the audience's reaction?"

"Mostly horror." He laughed.

"Then why did you continue?"

"Because making music is what I was created to do. And I knew I wouldn't be content until I fulfilled the desire of my heart." He shuffled his feet and grinned. "And I guess some in my family won't be content until I get a record deal."

A hint of sadness came back to Clair's eyes, but Hudson decided to put his concerns on hold. He picked up a rock near his shoe and considered the sheets of shale all layered together into one stone. *Time put this rock together, and time will take it apart.* He didn't like where his thoughts were roaming, so he looked back at Clair, smiling at her and absorbing the miracle of her. He took hold of her hand and brought it to his lips.

"You know. . .I think you are a fine man." Clair gently removed her hand from his grasp.

Hudson liked hearing the compliment but wondered why Clair pulled away. He handed the gray stone to her, hoping to lighten the mood. Her hands appeared to be shaking. "You're trembling. Are you cold?"

Clair slowly shook her head. "How can I say this to you?"

"This sounds more like an ending than a beginning. What's wrong?"

She lowered her gaze. The rock slipped from her hand and clattered against the other stones.

"What is this?" When Clair said no more, Hudson realized she didn't want to pursue a relationship or even continue the conversation. "Was it because I asked you to sing?"

"No. Don't ask me why." Clair turned away. "Please."

"But your kiss. I thought you—" He stopped when Clair shook her head. Swallowing back the lump in his throat, he asked, "W–were you kissing me good-bye?" As if someone had punched him, he felt the air empty from his lungs.

She nodded.

His mind reeled with the truth. *God help me. What did I do? Why is she rejecting me?* Disappointment and confusion tore through him.

Thunder rumbled around them. A blue-black horizon crowned with boiling white clouds loomed near. *How could the storm have crept up so quickly?* Streaks of lightning, blinding and jagged, exploded all around them. He refocused his attention from the inner tempest churning inside him to the approaching storm. "We'd better go now before it pours."

They alternated walking swiftly and jogging through the canyon. It seemed like an eternity before they made it up to the park building and then safely into his pickup. The moment they shut the doors, the rain came down in heavy sheets.

"Quite a storm. I'll get you home." Hudson looked over at her, so very near him yet so far away. "I don't want this to be good-bye." Hudson tried to keep the desperation out of his voice, but he felt the raw emotion in each word. "If we could just. . ." His voice faded away.

Clair's face appeared full of compassion as she reached over and kissed him on the cheek.

Or was it pity? What could have gone wrong? For a few moments he'd seen love in her eyes. He rebuked himself for asking her to sing with him at the café. Had he frightened her or was there something else at play? A man named Glenn Yves? He pulled out of the parking lot, wounded and distressed, but determined to find out what or who had turned her away from his love.

Chapter 17

Monday morning, Clair dragged herself into the shop, feeling worn out and disheartened. Over the weekend, a family had made a low offer on her house. She'd told Elaine to accept it, since the home was old and in need of repairs.

But her home meant little to her compared to her feelings for Hudson. She'd removed herself from his life. Even though the closure seemed to be the right thing to do for his career, it didn't feel right in her heart.

In her years spent alone, she'd learned how to close herself off to pain. But now, only weeks after she'd crept out of her shell, the world had crushed her newly exposed feelings. And never had her singing felt so meaningful as in those few moments with Hudson.

What am I to do? I have no mother to talk to. And I don't feel right about talking to Glenn about it. The situation would be awkward, but she wasn't sure why since Glenn was only a mentor and friend.

Clair plopped down on a stool behind the counter and stared at her to-do list for the store's grand opening. First, she needed to get her car repaired so she'd be able to run all the necessary errands. Although she hated to take money from the bookstore funds, she also knew there was no other way to accomplish her goals. As she decided which car repair place might give her the best deal, a woman entered the shop.

"Yoo-hoo," she called out.

"I'm closed. . .for now."

"Oh, honey, I know." The woman stepped inside. A red feather on top of a purple hat waggled above the bookracks as she made her way toward Clair.

"May I help you?"

The effervescent fifty-something stopped near the counter. She had skin the color of cocoa, dancing black eyes, and a smile as warm as hotcakes off the griddle. "I don't know if you remember me, but I attended Ima Langston's funeral. She was a dear friend of mine."

"Yes, I do remember you now."

"I'm Mabel Sugar." She laughed. "My momma had a fine sense of humor, didn't she?"

Clair chuckled with her. "You had the lovely spray of lavender flowers. I know Ima would have liked them. It was her favorite color." Clair strode over to Mabel and reached out her hand. "I'm Clair O'Neal."

Mabel shook Clair's hand with enthusiasm. "It's mighty fine to meet you." Mabel crisscrossed her hands over her heart. "I'm here. . . Well. . .the good Lord and I have an offer for you."

"Offer?"

"For the shop. I know you own the shop now. Ima's sister told me. And well, I would love to make you an offer to buy your shop."

"But the shop isn't for sale."

"Let me just say this, and then I'll go." Mabel took off her purple hat and patted it against her leg. "When I was growing up my momma read to me all the time on our front porch swing. She always said the bookstore held its head higher than the candy shop, because cultivating the mind and feeding the soul were superior to nourishing my cavities."

They both chuckled.

"Your mother sounds very wise," Clair said.

"Oh yes, she was." Mabel became somber. "And I always listened to my momma. I've saved some money, and now I hope to buy a bookstore right here in Little Rock. It's where I grew up. I love this city. We have the friendliest people in the world here. So this is where I'll have my store." She looked around. "I knew Ima's intentions. In fact, I'm the one who gave her the idea for renovating the store. I just wondered, honey, if this isn't your dream, then I would love to make it mine."

"You want to buy the business from me?" Clair repeated the words to let the news settle in.

"My offer would be more than fair." Mabel fiddled with the clasp on her purse. "The good Lord has been bighearted with me, so I can afford to be generous. If you have a few moments, I would like to speak with you about the particulars."

"Yes, I have the time."

Clair was thankful she had brought a coffeemaker to the shop as over a fresh-brewed cup, Mabel made her more-than-generous offer. She couldn't help but wonder if this was more confirmation that she really wasn't meant to continue with the shop.

"I'll leave you now." Mabel put her hat back on. "Give you some time to ruminate, as momma always said."

"I will. . .think about it. Seriously." Clair shook Mabel's hand again. "Thank you for coming."

"You are so welcome. Here's my card." Mabel handed Clair a handsome-looking business card with gold lettering. It read, "Mabel Sugar, Realtor," and gave her contact information.

Clair wondered how it would feel to change midcourse to follow a lifelong dream.

"Just pray about it, honey." Mabel ambled to the front door. "God will show you the way." She walked out the door, her talk turning into singing. " 'And lead us to the Promised Land.'"

Clair wilted into a soft chair. Life was speeding along like a locomotive. She'd most likely lost Hudson's companionship forever, she'd soon have to move out of her house, and now Ima's friend had forced her to question whether she was ever meant to run a bookstore. Panic rose inside her.

⤎⤏

Many hours and prayers later, Clair ran some much-needed errands for the shop. By late afternoon, she drove home with her newly repaired car, which was something she hadn't been able to do in some time. *Oh, the luxury of a working vehicle.*

The moment Clair shut her front door, her stomach growled. Instead of rummaging around in her fridge for something to eat, she found herself showering and dressing for the evening. She picked a dress from her new wardrobe—a simple but elegant black dress.

Some part of her wanted to go back to the way things were weeks earlier; hiding would certainly be easier. But Clair knew those days could never be again. Her life had finally moved on from the attic. And yet, she felt more alone than ever. Had she made a terrible mistake saying good-bye to Hudson?

There's one way to find out. He's playing at the Silver Moon Café. Tonight.

Chapter 18

Hudson lifted his guitar from his stand and settled down under the spotlights at the Silver Moon Café. "Good evening. I'm Hudson Mandel."

After waiting for the usual applause, he gazed out over the heavy crowd. The house lights were still high enough to see some of the people. Tara Williamson and her family were in the middle, beaming and clapping as always. But when he scanned the left side, he caught a glimpse of his sister, Leslie, talking to someone—someone who looked just like Clair. In fact, when she turned a bit, he could tell the woman was indeed Clair.

Hudson felt so startled to see her he nearly forgot where he was. "Clair," he accidentally said out loud. Some girls from the audience yelled, "We love you, Hudson," which shocked him back to reality. He decided since he'd said her name, he would sing her song. "This first one. . .is for someone very special."

Perspiration beaded up on his forehead, and his heartbeat picked up its rhythm. Hudson hadn't felt so unnerved since he'd first started performing. *Breathe.* He hugged the guitar and positioned his hands. The song began softly as a hush swept over the audience. He knew he had them, but he really hoped he had the attention of the woman he'd written the song for.

When Hudson finished, he thanked everyone and gave his signature salute, but all that occupied his thoughts were Clair's presence and the possibility that she'd changed her mind. He certainly hoped so as he scanned the audience, looking for her again. He spotted Clair by the exit, walking out with someone. *Glenn Yves.*

Hmm. Maybe his sister knew something about it, since he'd seen her talking to Clair earlier. He hurried down the steps and sat down next to Leslie. "I noticed you were talking to Clair."

Leslie cocked her head at her brother. "Well, hi to you, too."

"Sorry. It's just. . .well. . .Clair left suddenly with Glenn."

A twinge of something dark passed over Leslie's face. "Well, a girl has a right to leave with anyone she chooses. They can't *all* worship you."

"Come on, Leslie. You were talking to her. What did you say?"

Leslie shook her head and tugged on the corner of his shirt. "You really need to let me help you shop for some new clothes." She turned her attention to the sautéed vegetables on her plate.

"*What* did you say to Clair?"

"Are you insinuating I ran her off?"

"Not necessarily. Did you?"

Leslie looked annoyed. "I met her when she came to my party. I just told her how surprised I was to see her."

Hudson leaned toward her. "That's all?" He raised an eyebrow, thinking she looked a little guilty of something.

Leslie took a sip of water and then stared at him over her glass. "You really do care for her?"

Perhaps I should just tell her. "I want to marry her."

"Don't say it so loudly." Leslie cupped her hand near her mouth. "Tara's right over there. She can hear you."

Hudson rose. "I really don't care who hears it. I would have said it from the stage if I thought it would have made Clair stay."

"Well, maybe you should let her go. It wasn't meant to be, Huddy."

He let out a slow breath to calm his frustration. "I'm a grown man now." He splayed his fingers on the table, leaning toward her. "And please stop calling me Huddy."

"But it's so cute."

"I'd like to put childish things away. . .if you don't mind." Hudson gave her his most sober look.

"Okay." Leslie held up her hands wildly in mock surrender. "I get the message."

Hudson slowly nodded. "Very good." He gave his sister a quick hug and headed back to the stage.

Knowing Clair had left with Glenn weighed heavily on his spirit. *She must have meant her good-bye.* But he knew two questions would burn in his mind all evening. *Why had she come alone, and then why did she leave with Glenn?* Or had something else happened, and he just didn't have all the facts?

❧

Early the next morning, Clair slowly unlocked the bookshop door and wondered why such a simple task seemed so tiring. But the previous evening had been quite an emotional ride.

On a whim she'd wanted to watch Hudson perform—to make certain she hadn't made the worst mistake of her life by driving him away. But Leslie had been there, too, and she'd acted very surprised to see her. Her greeting hadn't been the happy kind of surprise like most people experience among friends but a dismayed kind of surprise—a response that made Clair want to run and hide and never bother anyone again.

Clair tried smoothing the crinkle in her new suit. *Does it really matter?* Mist filled her eyes as she felt a twinge of envy—envy for the fierce kind of love that made family members protect one another. She'd never known such devotion intimately, but she knew she'd cherish the sentiment if it ever came her way.

How could she blame Leslie for shielding her dear brother from the likes of a nobody like her—someone who had no money and no connections. *No sense in lamenting my past. It does no good. Haven't you learned that yet?*

Clair released a long, moaning sigh, thinking of Glenn and how he'd come to her rescue at the Silver Moon. How did he always know when she needed help?

Clair shoved her hair out of her eyes. She secured the door as she thought about Mabel Sugar's offer to buy the shop. *But what would I do then? Where would I work?*

Suddenly, a familiar face appeared in the window—her old neighbor, Mrs. Plow. Clair unlocked the door and let her in.

"Hi there, missy. How are ya?" The old woman lumbered in, dressed in a lively colored poncho. "You like my getup?"

"Yes. You look like a rainbow." Clair also noticed Mrs. Plow had taken a bath.

The older woman grinned, showing her missing teeth. "Things ain't always as they seem, missy." She ambled around the shop like she already knew where everything was. "You glad to see me?"

"Yes, of course." Clair smiled. "Would you like to sit down? You look a little tired."

"Fiddlesticks." Mrs. Plow fingered a pink ceramic angel bell, which sat on top of a box of gift items. "Oh my. Looky here at this purdy thing." She shook it, causing it to make a tiny tickling sound. Then she rested the angel against her cheek. "Works on this old heart like a tonic." She did a little jig as if she were young again.

"Would you like to have it?"

"Ohh, ain't you sweet. I always knowed you were like your ma." Mrs. Plow clasped the angel in her hand and it disappeared under her poncho. "Course, you was always a sweet one." She smiled and a reminiscent look came over her. "Truth be told, I loved all the children in the neighborhood, even the ornery ones who got into my flowers, like that Glenny boy. But you was always my favorite."

Glenny?

"Yes'm, you was my favorite, for sure." The old woman limped over to Clair, reached up, and cradled her face in her gnarled hands. "Well, I best be saying my good-byes."

"Thank you for coming by."

The old woman sashayed toward the door. "I hear tell that Glenny Yves boy grew up right fine. Just goes to show you." The bell above the door jingled, and Mrs. Plow disappeared like the angel bell.

Clair gasped. What did she mean, Glenny Yves? A roar filled Clair's ears. *Glenn Yves is the boy I watched from the attic—the boy with flowers and letters and a promise to set me free.*

The room began to spin as she slumped to the floor unconscious.

Chapter 19

Clair drifted in and out of awareness. Someone's warm breath tickled her face. Had she been asleep at the bookshop? Had someone just kissed her? But who?

"Home," she heard herself say from a long distance. A familiar voice spoke to her, but it, too, sounded far away. Muffled somehow. Was Jesus calling her? *Am I dead?* She felt suspended in the air. "Hudson?" she whispered to anyone who could hear.

"It's Glenn. I've been worried about you. I almost called 911. I can still call for help."

Clair rubbed her forehead. "No." Her eyes focused, and then she realized Glenn was leaning over her. "I'll be all right. I just fainted. It's always been a weakness of mine." She felt silly causing such a fuss, although she did feel safe.

He looked into her eyes but said nothing.

"I'm all right now." She smiled.

Glenn didn't budge. "I think you should go to a doctor about this. Promise me you will, or I will take you to the emergency room."

"Okay."

He helped her up and into a soft chair.

Promise. She remembered that word from somewhere. The reality of Mrs. Plow's words came back to her. Glenn had promised to return to her when he'd grown up.

"Mrs. Plow was just here." She looked up into his eyes. "She told me. . ." Clair stopped cold, unsure of how much to reveal. Would it be best to let Glenn take the lead?

"Ah." Surprise lit up Glenn's face. "So. . .you know. . .who I am?"

Clair nodded but couldn't manage to say anything. Not yet.

"The ever-present Mrs. Plow. She used to shoo me out of her garden." He chuckled as he pulled up a chair next to her. "Guess I picked too many of her flowers that summer."

"Glenn Yves, so that's where you got all those flowers." She shook her head at him and smiled. "I remember you used to send them to me in a bundle along with a note. And you'd hooked it up to some kind of rope and pulley—"

204

"Which was attached to my tree house." Glenn grinned. "I was very resourceful."

"Yes, you were. I never did figure out how you attached that apparatus so near my attic window."

He gripped the arm of her chair. "So, you *do* remember me, then?"

"I do now. But you look so different, I didn't recognize you before."

"It's probably best. I was quite a gangly little kid, and my head was too—too big for my body." Glenn stuttered on his words a bit. "Well, some would say I've *still* got the big head." He let out a snicker.

"Why didn't I see you at school? You moved again, didn't you?"

"Yes, we moved into your neighborhood at the beginning of the summer, and then we moved *out* of your neighborhood before the school year started. My family couldn't seem to stay put. So I never got to talk to you." Glenn folded his arms and looked at her intently. "And as I recall now, that turned out to be one of the disappointments of my youth."

Clair touched his arm. "I saved every one of your notes, but you never signed them. I never knew your name."

"I was trying to be mysterious. Guess it came off looking a little ridiculous."

"Not at all." She smiled. "I wanted to respond to your notes but never had the courage."

"I wish you had." He took her hand and gave it a squeeze.

Clair drew in a deep breath and offered him a beseeching expression. "The night at the party. . .did you have it all planned out to meet me?" She looked into his eyes. "It's okay. I just need to know. I could never be angry with you. You've helped me so much. I will forever be grateful to you."

"No, I can assure you, it was a God thing, nothing contrived. When I met you at the party that night, I had no idea who you were. I can honestly say I was drawn to you, though I couldn't explain why. When you disappeared so quickly, I was alarmed, and that's the only reason I came after you. Presumptuous, I know."

She offered him a weak smile. "But nice. Kind."

"It wasn't until the limo pulled up in front of your house that I realized. . .it had to be you." He shook his head. "At least, I hoped. . .prayed it was you."

Clair's mouth went dry. "Is that why you offered to help me, why you went to so much trouble for me? Was that your way of coming back for me like you said you would do in your note?" *But why do I need to know? What does it matter?* She licked her lips.

Glenn rose from his chair and slipped his hands in his pockets. "I never totally forgot about my last note to you, though I had tucked it away in the recesses of my mind." He sat back down and looked at her. "Then when the Lord brought us back together the night of the party, I thought of it as a gift. I started falling in love with you all over again. I felt as if it were a miracle. . .us meeting again the way we did."

She felt compelled to ask more. "So, there really was a Walter Sullivan who helped you?" *Did Glenn actually say he loved me? How can this be?*

"Yes, Walter is real. . .although he passed away years ago."

"I'm sorry to hear it." Clair took in a gulp of air. "But why didn't you tell me who you were?"

"I don't know." Glenn gave her a mirthless laugh. "Well, I guess I *do* know. I was always ashamed of my family's poverty. I found it humiliating." He wrinkled his brow. "As a kid, I felt as if I was born into my family by accident. I was a king in a jester's house. Pretty cocky, huh?" He shook his head. "Just like Drew said."

"I thought you were sweet. Those bundles of flowers you sent me were the only ones I've ever gotten." She squeezed his hand.

Before she drew away, Glenn covered her hand with his. "Oh, now that *is* appalling. I'm surprised men haven't showered you with roses." He tilted his head, looking regretful. "I'm sorry you found out this way. I intended to tell you soon. It's just. . .the time never seemed right." His expression grew more serious. "This stepfather you mentioned. . . Did he harm you?"

"No. But I guess you could say he hurt my heart. Children do have this intense need to be loved."

"Yes, they do. And rightly so." Glenn sighed. "And the attic? You weren't up there just for play, were you?"

"No."

"I wish I'd *done* something. . .told someone." Glenn's head drooped against his chest.

She knew he was grieving about her past. Without thinking, Clair took hold of his face and gently tilted his head to look at her. "I doubt anyone would have believed you anyway. My stepfather could be chameleon-like at times. And it's all over now. All is well. Okay?" In the silence, she could hear the clock in the back room chime away the hour.

"Okay." Glenn gazed into her eyes as if he were memorizing every nuance of her face. "I had intended to surprise you tonight. I wanted to make this moment romantic in every way. All the things you deserve—candlelight and violins. But I'm going to be selfish and just come out with it." He took in a deep breath. "I've fallen in love with you, Clair."

The words still sounded foreign to her, coming out of his mouth. Anyone's mouth. "How can this be?" What had Glenn said at the restaurant? *"Sometimes the surprises of life will take us by storm."*

"You're stunned." He lifted her hand to his lips. "And I don't blame you."

THE LOVE SONG

Once again Clair felt lightheaded. *God, is this a sign?* Had she fallen in love with the wrong man? Then she recalled the promise in Glenn's final note. She understood now. He was just trying to fulfill a childhood vow. "The note. I would never hold you to it."

Glenn shook his head and his eyes grew misty. "What I've said today has nothing to do with that oath. I'm no longer a boy with childish notes and self-indulgent emotions. I'm a grown man, and these feelings couldn't be more real."

Clair felt his tenderness and sincerity all the way to her heart, and yet she felt a profound weight of confusion in her spirit. "You've been kind to me in so many ways, but. . ." Her voice left her.

"Yes?" Glenn kissed her hand as he gazed at her with a look of expectancy.

What were the right words? What would they be? Telling Glenn the truth—that she didn't feel the same way—felt wrong to her, and yet returning his feelings seemed impossible.

Falling in love wasn't supposed to be mystifying like a puzzle with missing pieces. Was it?

A flicker of pain crossed his face. "You're in love with someone else?"

Clair lowered her gaze.

He let go of her hand. "Do you need some time to think about it?"

How could she break his heart? Glenn was a good Christian man. Clair faltered with uncertainty. She felt a displaced kind of ache, and she knew that feeling was connected to a man in a guitar shop only a few doors down. *How ungrateful you are, Clair. You want too much.*

She reached over and touched Glenn on the cheek. "You are so good to me. Maybe I just need a little time."

He looked away for a moment. "There is a party tonight. As your mentor, I would love to show you off." He smiled at her. "I mean, look at you. Beauty. Intelligence. Grace. You're amazing."

Clair wanted to disagree, but perhaps that approach wasn't as humble as it was impolite. "Thank you."

"But you know, you've always had all these gifts inside you. You just needed someone to help you unwrap them."

"And you did." She gripped the arm of the chair. "I so appreciate all you've done for me."

"Believe me, it was my pleasure," Glenn said. "So. . .will you go out with me tonight?"

Clair hesitated.

Silence fell between them. "What is it you want from life, Clair?" he whispered.

"Sometimes I don't know how to. . .just be. I guess that makes no sense."

Glenn cleared his throat. "You want to know what I think?"

"Yes, I do."

"You haven't given me the details about the attic, but I get this feeling your opinions and ambitions got locked away in there. A bird cannot take to the air in a cage." Glenn took hold of her hand again. "For instance, do you know what your favorite things are. . .like your favorite ice cream?"

"I don't know. I usually just eat chocolate or vanilla."

"One day you must remedy that. But maybe I should ask you this—what is the essence of Ms. O'Neal? What is it you'd do if nothing could stop you?"

"But I'm just Clair."

"No." He flinched. "You are indomitable."

"I know now I'm capable of more than I ever dreamed possible. But I still feel I can't choose whatever I like. We mortals do have some limitations." Clair grinned.

"I know that kind of thinking from personal experience, and you don't want to limit the Creator." He released her. "Don't let other people choose your path. Not even me."

"Would I be able to sing?" *Why did I let that slip out of my mouth?*

"You can sing?" He leaned back, looking astonished. "You never mentioned it before."

Clair winced, wishing she hadn't bought up the subject. "I love music."

"But why didn't you tell me this? I had no idea."

"I barely knew myself. You were right. I've hardly thought about my own life."

Glenn took a book from the shelf and stared at it as if it were an adversary. "The shop. . .it was Ima's dream, wasn't it?"

"I cared for Ima. . .very much. So I thought I should do it because of love."

He slid the book back among the others. "That might seem like the honorable thing to do, but it will make for a miserable existence. . .living other people's lives for them. And you've had more than your share of unhappiness already."

"Yes." Clair felt such relief, knowing people dearest to her would allow her to release the bookshop into more capable hands—hands that were meant to take over for Ima. She looked back at Glenn, her heart aching with gratitude. "I owe you so much. I wish I could repay you."

Glenn turned the onyx ring on his finger and grinned at her. "Well, you could always tell me you've fallen in love with me, too. That would be a good start."

Clair squeezed his hand. *Lord, please give me courage.* "I wish I could. But God has other plans for us both." She leaned over and kissed him on the cheek. "I have a great fondness for you, but. . ."

"Yes." Glenn held up his hand. "I understand. I do." He looked down at the floor. "You shouldn't go with me tonight. It wouldn't be fair to either of us." After a long pause, he rose. "Well then. . ." He slid his hands into his pockets and walked to the door.

Clair followed him. When he stopped at the door, she physically turned him back around to face her. "But to be loved and cared for in any way—even like a brother—is a good thing. Isn't it?"

"Yes." He held her gently by the shoulders. "Love is always good, always welcome."

"And you not only kept the promise you made to Walter, you kept *your* promise to me."

"I did?"

"Yes, you also said someday when you were grown, you'd come back to set me free." Tears stung her eyes. "And you did, Glenn Yves. The Lord used you to set me free."

He touched her cheek. "Set you free. . .to love another."

She wished she could take the sadness from his eyes. Oh, how she cared for him—like the brother she never had. She reached up and hugged him. "I will always remember you, always think kindly of you wherever you are." Tears filled her eyes.

Glenn pulled out a handkerchief from his pocket and wiped away the tears now spilling down her face. "Promise?"

Smiling back at him, she grasped the lapels of his jacket. "Yes. I promise."

Chapter 20

Once Glenn crossed the street, Clair bolted the door and sat back down on the chair to absorb what had happened. Suddenly all the good things in her new life seemed to have vanished.

I said no to a marriage with a fine Christian man. I've chosen to run away from Ima's dream. I will move from the only home I've ever known to live in an apartment. And I will never be able to marry the man I truly love.

All seemed utterly lost or, at best, misplaced. Nothing remained, except a bit more confidence. She rarely chewed on her lip or twisted her clothes anymore when she got nervous. Her shoulders were straight and her outfit fashionable. But without love and a home, what did she really have left?

Clair smelled the lingering scent of his cologne in the air. *Glenn Yves.* She thought of his kindness to her in their youth, the way he'd grasped her hand with such affection and his grave countenance when she'd refused him. How could she deny him? Maybe she could go to the party after all and tell him she'd changed her mind.

But what can I really give Glenn? Were affection and fondness enough to last a lifetime? She knew the truth: Glenn deserved to be loved as deeply as she loved Hudson.

Love. She couldn't escape that word. She loved Hudson, and she loved him in the marrying way. There was no turning back from those feelings, but they were sentiments she could never take pleasure in.

Just as Clair had always done in the midst of life's sorrows, she started singing one of her favorite songs. This time, it was "Amazing Grace." When she finished, an idea came to her—Hudson had not been allowed to make one of the most important decisions of his life. And the flash of pain she'd seen in his eyes as she left the café with Glenn had been almost unbearable. No doubt she'd caused Hudson great pain, but Clair had become so convinced the decision would help him in the end she'd been blinded to the facts. Wasn't Hudson old enough and wise enough to choose his own way?

What a fool I've been. What have I thrown away? Like the settling of cement, resolution hardened in her mind. She would make things right again. *And I won't waste another minute.*

A familiar-looking woman in a purple hat jiggled the door handle and then pattered lightly on the glass. "Yoo-hoo. Mabel Sugar here."

Clair let her inside. "I'm glad to see you, Mabel."

"Oh, it's good to see you again, honey." The older woman looked over her reading glasses at Clair. "Have you had a chat with the good Lord about my offer?"

She didn't want to hurry Mabel out the store, but Clair felt determined to see Hudson right away. "I have," she started, "but unfortunately, I have some personal business to attend to right now. Could you meet me tomorrow around noon? We can discuss the sale of the bookshop." She almost wished Glenn could see her now.

"Thank you, Jesus." Mabel gave her hand a little wave in the air. "I would not only love to meet you, I will treat you to lunch. Do you like the River Grill?"

Clair smiled as she answered. "Yes, that sounds wonderful."

"You've got it. Lunch tomorrow. Noon at the River Grill. I'll see you then." Mabel smiled broadly and exited, humming a gospel tune.

Clair waited for Mabel to cross the street, and then she quickly locked up and strode toward Hudson's guitar shop. Her only fear was that he'd changed his mind—that he'd given up on her.

As she stepped into the guitar shop, she breathed in Hudson's world. A wide assortment of electric and acoustic guitars hung on the walls and a checkout counter stood in the middle of the big room. There were rows and rows of sheet music and books on the how-tos of playing the guitar, and someone could be heard strumming an electric guitar in the back. *Students, maybe? I can't believe I've never been in this store before.*

A young man at the counter, who'd been watching her, suddenly hollered, "Yo, over there. Something I can do for you?"

"Yes." She strode over to him. "I would like to speak with Hudson Mandel, please." Clair gripped the handle on her purse until her fingers throbbed.

He made an open-palm gesture with his hands. "Oh, sorry. Just missed him."

"Really?"

"He left for a wedding." He leaned on the counter, looking at her a little bug-eyed.

"A wedding? Surely not his own." Clair's heart skipped a beat.

"No. One of his friends is getting married today."

Clair sighed audibly.

"You one of his friends?"

"I hope so. I'm Clair."

"Ohh. Are you *the* Clair?" He flipped his long hair behind his shoulder. "From the song?"

"Yes."

"Awesome. It's really cool to meet you. We were beginning to think you were a figment of Hudson's imagination."

She reached out to shake his hand. "Clair O'Neal."

"Leroy Goldstein." He shook her hand like a water pump. "Yeah, awesome." His head angled like he was mulling something over. "Listen, Hudson got there really early for a sound check, so if you want to stop by, it'd be a good move. Grace Cathedral. It's not far from the capitol building."

"Yes, I know where it is." Clair headed toward the door. "Thank. . .very much."

"All right." He lifted his arms in a gesture of victory. "You go for it!"

Clair strode out of the shop toward her car. How many minutes would it take to get there—how long to make things right? Her stride broke into a run.

Once she'd arrived at the church and scurried up the steps, she halted at the double white doors. How would she explain her recent behavior without turning Hudson against his sister? She paused for a moment to give herself time to think. Clouds of what-ifs and warnings entered her mind like swarming bees, but this time she tried not to listen. Instead, she pulled open the door and eased herself inside.

She stood in the foyer, which appeared empty and silent. Deathly quiet, in fact. *Where is everyone?* Had she gone to the wrong church? She slipped off down a side hallway, in search of Hudson.

Just then a door burst open at the far end of the hallway. Girls and young women and older ladies dressed in pastel finery all burst out of the room as if there were a fire. The last woman to emerge was adorned in heaps of white satin and tulle. The ladies formed a hugging, laughing gauntlet for the beaming bride. Clair stepped out of their way.

The bride stopped in front of Clair. "You seem lost, hon."

"I'm looking for someone."

"Maybe I can help." The other ladies bustled on their way as the bride took hold of Clair's arm. "Walk with me."

They strolled down a hallway as the bride's luscious gown swished alongside of Clair. *What a lovely sound.*

"Now who are you looking for, hon?"

"Hudson Mandel."

"Why, he's one of my husband's friends. He's playing at our wedding." The bride took a good, long look at her. "Ohh, you must be Clair. I'm so glad you could make it. Last time I asked Hudson, he didn't think you'd be coming. By the way, I'm Susanna Cartwright." She gave Clair a hug. "Well, I'll be a Cartwright for a few more minutes anyway." The bride-to-be wiggled her eyebrows.

Clair chuckled, feeling overjoyed Hudson would mention her to his closest friends.

"Let's go this way." Susanna led Clair through another maze of hallways until they reached a door that led into the main sanctuary. She pointed through the doorway to the stage. "There's your man."

Clair blushed.

"There's plenty of time before the guests start arriving. Now go after him." Susanna winked.

"By the way, I hope you have a wonderful marriage."

"Oh, I'm sure we'll see each other again. But thanks." Susanna gently nudged Clair forward and then swished away in her bridal gown like a swan taking off from a lake.

Clair eased her way into the sanctuary and gasped. The church overflowed with yellow roses and ivory candles. *Oh my.* Then her eyes searched out Hudson. There he stood—hooking up his guitar to an amp. She watched him for a moment. A familiar voice in her head told her she didn't belong. *No, that's not true. I belong with Hudson.* She took a tentative step forward.

Hudson turned toward her as if he sensed her presence. "Clair." He almost lost the grip on his guitar. "Why. . .what are you doing here?"

She swallowed hard. Hudson wore a light gray tuxedo and looked more handsome than ever. *I hope he's happy to see me.* She circled her arms around her middle for comfort. "I came. . .to talk."

"I'm just really surprised to see you." He set his guitar on a stand and strode over to her.

"I know this isn't the best time to say this, but—"

"No, this is the perfect time," Hudson said.

"I don't really want to say good-bye." She moved a little closer to him. "If that's okay."

Hudson let out a deep sigh. "Oh, that's more than okay."

"I want to start where we left off at the park."

"I think that can be arranged."

Longing filled his eyes, and another sharp pain of remorse coursed through her. *How could I have hurt him so?* Between the intoxicating aroma of roses and Hudson's nearness, she felt she might do something a little impetuous. "And I want to begin right here." She kissed her fingers and then reached over to softly touch his lips.

Clair could feel his breath on her hand as its ebb and flow increased. She placed her hand on the back of his neck, drew him to her, and kissed him full on the lips. Her fingers gently tugged on his hair as she intensified the kiss. When she felt satisfied Hudson had a keen understanding of her regret in leaving, she drew back.

He tried to catch his breath. "Whoa. Do you think you could leave me and come back again?"

Laughing, Clair tried to calm herself as well. She wasn't used to being so forward. . .or so happy.

Applause and whistles exploded near them, startling them both. They glanced around, looking for the ruckus. To the side, the bridal party, including the bride herself, clapped and grinned with gusto.

"You go, girl!" Susanna hollered.

For once, the only heat on Clair's face was the warmth left by their kiss. She nodded and smiled at Susanna.

When the commotion and laughter settled down, Hudson turned to Clair. "Tell me, what changed your mind?"

Clair had known that question would come, but she still hadn't figured out an honest reply that wouldn't incriminate his sister.

"I think I know." Hudson frowned. "I called Leslie right before I came here, and she sounded unusually guilty. Please tell me, has my sister been playing in the wrong sandbox?"

Chapter 21

C lair opened her mouth, but nothing came out.

"So, it's true," Hudson said. *Leslie's out of control again.*

"Your sister was only watching out for you." Clair squeezed his arm. "She loves you."

Hudson couldn't think clearly when Clair stood so near. He took in a deep breath. "Okay. What did my sister do *exactly*?" He found himself gripping his guitar pick until it hurt his palm. "I can tell you don't want to say anything, but this has been going on too long. And it stops here." He took hold of Clair's hand. "Please, before the guests start arriving, we need to talk. In fact, will you be my date for the wedding?"

She touched the jacket on her silvery gray suit. "Am I dressed okay?"

"Yes, you certainly are." He leaned toward her, kissing her lightly on the cheek. "There's something else you need to know about my sister." Hudson cleared his throat. "Let's sit for a minute."

After they'd settled themselves down on a front pew, he said, "You know, I'd do anything for Leslie. We Mandels stick up for each other. Always have, but. . ."

"Yes?"

"I can't let her go on manipulating my life." Hudson leaned forward, resting on his knees. "It all started when our mother got sick. I was a kid then, and Leslie was ten years older. Mom put her in charge of me for a while." He looked back at Clair. "Actually, I have to give Leslie credit. She did a pretty good job helping out. But I'm a grown man now, and she keeps forgetting that."

"I can't imagine having a sibling who cares so much."

He thought of Clair's lonely youth and realized she might not understand older sisters who could be overbearing at times. He leaned back gazing at her. The look in her eyes could stop a raging battle and warm the coldest heart. "Yes, but—"

"Mr. Mandel!" someone hollered from behind them. "Ready for a sound check."

Hudson groaned. "Excuse me again," he said to Clair. "I guess this isn't the best time for an intimate talk."

She touched his hand. "Are you sure I should be at this wedding?"

Hudson leaned over and brushed her cheek with a kiss. "I am *very* sure."

After the ceremony, the guests flooded toward the reception, which was being held in a conservatory-like room adjoining the church. Hudson held hands with Clair as they maneuvered through the crowd.

"I've never seen a room like this before," Clair whispered as if in awe. "A glass ceiling and growing orchids and a piano in the middle of it all."

"The church uses it for all kinds of functions. Sometimes they have weddings in here as well."

She looked around. "It's so enchanting."

He loved watching Clair; she was always so full of wonder and innocence.

Then, as if too much bliss could bring some kind of wrath down on them both, he saw a sight he'd been dreading. His sister and Tara Williamson were walking toward them from across the room at an alarming pace, and the look on Leslie's face wasn't one of merriment. He'd always hated confrontation. *But I will make my position clear to them. Right now.*

Leslie approached them first, wearing a bizarre pink feathery garment. Hudson couldn't help but notice that, with her skinny legs, his sister looked just like a flamingo.

"Well, *there* you are," Leslie crooned with a slight edge in her voice.

"You were wonderful," Tara said to Hudson.

"Clair." Leslie's eyes grew wide "I love your outfit. Another gift from Glenn?"

Hudson's eye began to twitch. He mashed his finger against his eyelid to stop the spasm. The pianist started playing something cheerful, but he was no longer in a festive mood. "Leslie?"

"Yes?" Leslie batted her eyelashes with a comical air.

"May I see you in private?" Not waiting for his sister to respond, he took hold of her arm. "Please excuse us," he said to Clair and Tara. "We'll be back in a minute." Hudson then shepherded Leslie off to a private corner.

"How dare you herd me over here like a toddler? What's this all about?" Leslie jerked her arm free.

"You are a good woman. But what has made you into this ever-circling vulture looking for innocent blood?" Hudson rebuked himself, wishing he'd used a little more finesse with his language. "I'm sorry. That was my anger talking. But you know what I'm referring to—the game you're playing at Clair's expense." He crossed his arms for effect. "And when Clair refused to go out with me, I had no idea it was your fault."

"*Moi?*" Leslie shrank back with her hand over her throat.

"I'm thirty-one years old. I know when you're lying. You get this twittering thing going in your jaw."

"Twittering? Great word. I'll have to use it somewhere."

Hudson shook his head. "You know, Leslie, you were a great help to Mom all those years ago when she needed you. You were terrific, in fact. But don't spoil those incredibly selfless acts by continuing to pretend I'm a child. I know you think my life would be perfect with Tara, but—"

"It would be."

"How can you say that?" Hudson looked at her incredulously.

"Because I know you better than anyone else does."

"Obviously not." He shook his head in disbelief. "If you really knew me, you would know that I would never be interested in a marriage without love. I like Tara. I like her a lot. But I *love* Clair, and I'm praying she'll marry me someday. So, you have a choice here. You can continue to push Clair away. . .and make me miserable. Or you can trust me to make a wise choice about my own life and be happy for us."

"Well. . ."

"You know, if you'd love having Tara for a sister-in-law so much, then maybe you could marry Tara's brother, Jerold. His praise of you is inexhaustible."

Leslie suddenly looked lost in thought. "Is that true about Jerold?"

Hudson nodded.

"Hmm." Leslie's frown melted like butter.

"Come on now." Hudson smiled, hoping to make the most of the mellow moment. "You'll love Clair once you get to know her."

Leslie shifted her weight, balancing her stiletto heel on the marble floor. "You're incredibly talented, and I just want the best for you."

How can I get through to her? Leslie is so much better than this. "Clair *is* God's best for me. I've never been more sure of anything in my life."

Leslie arched an eyebrow.

"Your opinion has always mattered so much to me," Hudson continued. "And you've been there for me every step of the way. That's why it's so important to me now that you see God's hand in this."

She gave him a pensive stare.

Hudson opted for a different approach. "Look, your novels are full of characters who are courageous and noble. People love your characters. *I* love your characters."

"You do?"

"Of course I do." He lowered his voice but remained firm. "But we need a little heroism off the pages, sis."

Leslie clicked her tongue. "Well, I guess my little brother has finally grown up."

"He did a long time ago. You just needed to acknowledge it."

"Okay, okay." Leslie raised her hands in mock defeat. "I'll try. I really will." She patted Hudson's cheek, and with a cheerless expression, sauntered toward the piano.

Hudson turned and bumped into Tara as she came around the corner. "Tara?" He pulled back in surprise. Had she been standing on the other side of the wall, listening to them? "So, how much of that did you just hear?"

Tara flipped her dark hair back. Even though she looked nonchalant, there were tears in her eyes. "I heard most of it. But the only words I remember are, 'I like Tara, but I love Clair.'"

Chapter 22

Hudson realized the time had come to put an end to Tara's misguided hopes. "You know, it's been some time since we dated."

"I know." Tara smoothed her already perfect suit.

"I thought you'd moved on," Hudson said gently. "Weren't you dating Peter McKinney from church?" Tara's heavy perfume made him take a step backward.

"It's been over for a while." Her mouth curved up on one side. "I found out no one else was quite like Hudson Mandel." She glanced in a mirror nearby and adjusted her strands of pearls. "And well, I'm not used to being cast off."

"We both agreed to stop dating. No one was cast off."

"Well, I've had second thoughts about our agreement. But I guess you haven't." Tara nodded in Clair's direction. "You've moved on quite well, I see."

"I'm truly sorry for any pain I've caused you."

"Oh, I'll recover." Tara smirked. "I come from a long line of survivors. And I've discovered something—my daddy's money really does soften the blows of life."

Hudson had no idea what to say, so he decided to let her talk it out. He just hoped Clair didn't mind waiting a bit longer.

"I'll go on a singles' cruise around the Greek isles. Should take the last little sting out of things." Tara sauntered away and then suddenly turned back with a forlorn expression. "I will miss the music, though. I loved your music. And you don't look too bad in that tux either." She blew him a kiss and, without looking back again, strode swiftly out the door.

Hudson wondered how he could have ever found Tara interesting enough to date. What had been the attraction? She was stunning but way too smug. Surely he hadn't been small-minded enough to date her just for her looks. Or had the career promises from Tara's family caused him to hang around a little longer than he should have? He searched his heart, hoping he wouldn't find anything too devious or shallow.

As he continued to muse over his past, Hudson glanced around, hoping to find Clair. He strode back to the section of the conservatory where he'd left her, but she wasn't there. Had Clair driven home? *How can I blame her?* He'd convinced her to stay as his guest and then he promptly abandoned her.

Hudson turned toward the piano and saw the most amazing sight; Clair stood on the other side of the conservatory, having a lively chat with several people. He observed her for a moment. She had all the same wonderful qualities as when he'd first met her, but she had more confidence. Then he remembered Glenn Yves, who'd mentored her. Even though Glenn may have been competition for Clair's affections, he'd made a genuine difference in her life. *What can I give her but my love?*

Suddenly Clair's gaze met his from across the room, and he felt a rush of joy. She waved without appearing upset in the least.

Hudson made his way around the clusters of guests to join her. Clair circled her arm through his, and they strolled toward the bride and groom.

"Is everything okay?" Clair asked.

"Yes." Hudson covered her hand with his. "I'm sorry about that scene back there. It was rude and totally uncalled for."

"I'm all right." Her smile looked a little anxious. "But I don't want to hurt your relationship with your sister—"

"First of all, no matter what the enticement, I don't want to marry Tara. And Leslie. . .well, she'll come around. Once she decides it's her idea for us to be together, then you won't find a more loyal subject."

Clair seemed to study his face, and then she leaned her head against him. "I've always wanted a sister."

Hudson kissed her forehead, taking pleasure in the softness of her skin.

A burst of laughter drew their attention to the newly married couple. Susanna and Brad were giggling and feeding each other hunks of the wedding cake as cameras flashed all around them. Every movement they made together looked like a snapshot.

Hudson silently rejoiced with his friends and then wondered how Clair would respond to a proposal of marriage. "We're having a family get-together at my parents' house tomorrow evening. If you came with me. . .well, it would be a great way for me to introduce you to my family. And it would give Leslie a chance to get to know you better."

Clair took in a deep breath. "Yes, I would love to go."

"Good."

"Do you think your parents will like me?" Concern shadowed her lovely face.

Hudson put his hand on the small of her back. "They will adore you. As you know, Leslie has issues, but some of it is because she's eccentric. You know. . . writers." He rolled his eyes, grinning. "The rest of my family is normal."

"Hey," Leslie said, appearing at his side, "I heard that."

He reached over and gave his sister a peck on the cheek. Within days, he predicted, she and Clair would be the best of friends.

Chapter 23

Clair slipped on one of her new dresses—a luscious ice-pink linen. Hopefully, it would help make a good first impression on Hudson's parents.

As she stared in the mirror, she also saw the other gift Glenn had left her—a sureness in her stance. In fact, sometimes when she saw her reflection, she still had trouble recognizing herself.

Just as she turned her attention to her shoes, the doorbell rang. *Hudson?* She looked at a clock. *Too early. Maybe it's the Realtor.* She trotted to the front door and opened it. "Glenn?"

"Hi, Clair."

Glenn brightened her doorway with his one-of-a-kind smile—the same one he'd worn the evening she'd first met him. But surprisingly, he was dressed casually in jeans, a pullover, and loafers.

He whistled. "You look spectacular in that dress, like a string of pink diamonds."

"Thank you." She wanted Glenn to feel welcome, but she wondered what Hudson might think of his presence.

Glenn looked around. "I just came by to tell you something. I'm moving to LA."

"Really? Why?" Clair wondered if declining his proposal had anything to do with his move.

"I need a change. I have some friends out there. And, well, I shouldn't have any trouble finding work as an image coach in LA. Although, I did have plenty of work here, it's just. . ." His voice trailed off.

Clair could see the sadness in his eyes, even though she knew he tried to hide it.

"Listen, I know it didn't work out for us. But I hope. . ." Glenn choked on his words. "But I hope we can always be friends."

"Always." Mist filled Clair's eyes. "You changed my life in such a good way. Walter Sullivan would be proud of you."

Glenn chuckled. "Yeah. If he could see you, he'd be proud of us both."

"Thank you." Should she tell him she was indeed selling the shop and her home? The time didn't seem right.

Glenn looked across the street. "This neighborhood. . .it's kind of surreal standing here. Brings back a lot of memories for me. Good and bad."

"I wish you and your family had never moved away. I would've liked to have had a friend."

"You did. And you still do." Glenn smiled. "I just want you to promise me. . .if you ever need help of any kind that you won't hesitate to call. I won't be too hard to find."

"Okay." Clair chewed on her lower lip.

"Well, I *almost* broke you of that habit." He gestured to her lips.

She chuckled.

He tilted his head, looking at her with eyes full of emotion. "You say your life's been changed. But you're not the only one." He lowered his gaze. "You showed me the right kind of love, the real thing, is possible. And I'm glad to know it." He looked back at her, clasping his hands tightly and then letting them drop to his side.

To her, Glenn looked like a boy again, timid and restless, and her heart nearly broke.

"Well, good-bye, sweet Clair." He turned to go.

" 'Bye," she whispered. She reached out and hugged him. "I will miss you."

Glenn held her for a moment. He touched her chin and then released her. "Would you like to know one of my regrets as a kid?"

"Yes?"

"I wish I'd sent more flowers to a girl named Clair O'Neal. You know, with my little rope from the tree house."

Clair grew serious. "You made me feel less alone that summer. And it meant more to me than you'll ever know."

"Thanks." Glenn smiled. "Well then." He bowed slightly and then walked toward his car.

She waved good-bye to Glenn as he drove away, but moments later, the tears began to flow. She clutched her heart. *He loved me, and I could not love him back.*

After a long cry and an even longer prayer for Glenn, Clair cleaned up her face in the bathroom. She'd done the only thing she could think of—release him into the loving hands of the Almighty and pray that God would bless him in every way imaginable. . .especially in love.

The doorbell came to life again. *Hudson?* But when Clair opened the door, she saw an Indian gentleman on her steps holding a peach-colored urn filled with a zillion kinds of flowers. A bee followed the man, buzzing around his head.

"These are for you, miss."

"They're so lovely."

"Oh yes, but I am wishing the bee did not think so, too," the man said in a lyrical Indian accent.

Clair chuckled, wondering who would have sent them. Hudson? Glenn?

The man waited for the bee to fly away and then placed the huge bouquet in her hands.

She placed the flowers on the entry table and then handed him a tip. "Thank you so much."

"Oh yes. You are very welcome. I hope these flowers bring you much pleasure. It is what we endeavor to do," he said and then bustled off toward his floral van.

Clair stood over the enormous bouquet, breathing in the heady fragrance and sighing softly to herself. Except for the ones Glenn had given her from Mrs. Plow's garden, it was the first time anyone had given her flowers. *I've certainly had a lot of "firsts" lately.* The card simply read, "Lovingly, Hudson."

Just as Clair pushed on the door to close it, she saw Hudson coming up the walk. Her heart's tempo picked up a few extra beats. "Hello."

Hudson stopped at the door. "Hi."

Thinking it was time she gave away some compliments instead of just collecting them, Clair said, "You look very handsome in those khakis and that blue silk shirt."

"Thank you." He grinned, leaning closer to her. "And you look lovely."

She reached over and kissed his cheek. "I got your flowers just now. They're so pretty."

"I have to be honest, sending you the flowers was someone else's idea."

She wondered what he meant. "Whose idea was it?"

"I got this anonymous note left at the Silver Moon Café. It read, 'Clair should never be without flowers.'"

She knew instantly who'd written the note. Glenn. If he couldn't buy them for her now, he'd make sure Hudson did. Mist stung her eyes.

Hudson smiled but looked uncomfortable. "Glenn sent the note about the flowers?"

Clair slowly nodded.

"He fell in love with you." Hudson said it as a statement and not a question.

"Yes, he did." Perhaps Hudson had known all along.

"Hard to blame him. You're very easy to fall in love with."

What did Hudson mean? Maybe she should explain a bit more about Glenn. "He was my neighbor when I was a little girl. I mentioned that neighborhood boy to you, but at the time I didn't know it was Glenn Yves. It was quite a surprise when I found out. As you know, he'd been kind to me during some rough times growing up."

"So Glenn turned out to be the neighbor kid you talked about. Amazing." Hudson touched her arm. "I must thank him someday. . .for all his help."

Clair looked at him. "Glenn came by to tell me he's moving to LA."

"I wish him well." Hudson looked at her with a tender expression. "But do you mind if I ask what your feelings were for him?"

She breathed a quick prayer for the right words. "I'm grateful for his help, and I'm very fond of him. . .like a brother."

Hudson let out a puff of air and raked his fingers through his hair. "Well, I guess you should know that makes me feels good"—he rested his hand over his heart—"right here."

"I'm glad." She reached up and stroked his cheek with her fingertips.

He grasped her hand and kissed it.

Clair wasn't sure how long they stood there, looking into each other's eyes, but time didn't seem to matter. At all. She wondered if she should tell him she'd accepted an offer on the house and about Mabel and the shop, but somehow all her news seemed unimportant at the moment.

A short ride later, they sat in front of Hudson's boyhood home. Clair took in the loveliness of it—a two-story Victorian house painted blue with dainty shutters and a white picket fence. "It's so quaint and pretty."

Hudson leaned forward, staring at the house. "My mom loves all things Victorian. I guess you can tell." He looked at her. "Are you still anxious about meeting my family?"

"I'll be fine." *The old Clair is gone. God, help me to remember.*

"It's okay if you're scared. If *your* parents were still alive, I'd be terrified."

Clair laughed. "Really?"

"Oh yeah. Listen, maybe it would help if you knew a few things about them. My dad loves golf and building furniture. He's hard of hearing, so he winces a lot when he's trying to hear you. My mother likes gardening and reading, but mostly she likes mothering, so she'll immediately take you under her wing until you feel completely smothered with attention."

"It all sounds. . .wonderful."

"Then you're at the right place." Hudson's eyebrows creased. "And then there's Leslie. What can I say, except somehow I think it'll be all right." He pointed toward the house. "Speaking of family. . ."

A middle-aged woman, wearing a dress in robin's-egg blue, came toward them. Clair opened her car door.

"Ohh, you must be Clair," the woman said, reaching to take her hand.

Hudson hurried around to Clair and helped her down from the pickup seat. He made some introductions, but Mrs. Mandel had already pulled Clair into a warm embrace.

"I've heard so much about you. I'm so glad you're here. Come right on in. I've made some chicken and dumplings. . .from scratch. . .and some cherry cobbler. Edwin, Hudson's father, just loves it when I have company because he gets everything homemade."

Clair allowed the older woman to circle her arm through hers as they walked up the path to the house. She noticed Mrs. Mandel had a soft touch, smiled a great deal, and smelled of fresh dill.

Soon Clair was whisked into a world of warmth and beauty. She glanced around, taking note of the touches of blue in the pictures and the pillows and the circular rugs. To the right was a large living area with a stone fireplace, and to the left, a long oak table in the dining room. She wondered if Hudson's father had made it. A cuckoo clock went off somewhere in the house. There were homey touches all around her that spoke of cozy times with the family. *What must it be like?*

As introductions were made, Hudson's father shook her hand vigorously, and then Clair was escorted into the kitchen, where a myriad of homemade smells filled the air. She drank in the moment. "You've made such a lovely place to live. And I like all the blue."

"You do? Eddie thinks I've gone a little overboard," she said loudly. "But—"

"Overboard is right. She dresses me in blue, too." Edwin grinned at Clair as he handed her a steaming cup of coffee.

Just as Clair thought she'd arrived in paradise, Leslie appeared in the doorway like a long, dark shadow. *"You prepare a table before me in the presence of my enemies."* Clair stared at her and offered up a smile. *Dear Lord, please help me. What should I say?* She started with the obvious. "Hi."

Everyone turned toward Leslie. All bustle in the kitchen stopped, and for a brief moment they all seemed suspended in time. Did they know about Leslie's attempts to be rid of her? *Are they waiting for my reaction?*

Before Leslie could utter a word, her mother smothered her with kisses and hugs.

Leslie melted into grins. "Okay." She pulled away and held up her hands in a pretend tragic posture. "All right. The desperado has died. The real Leslie you all adore is back." She stuffed her fingers through the loops of her lizard-green slacks.

Family cheers broke out, leaving Clair stunned and silent. *What does this mean?*

Hudson slapped his sister on the back, and then Leslie gave him a good-humored slug.

Clair felt helpless, watching the spectacle. Was that the way families operated? Could problems turn into amusement as easily as ice melted into water?

She took a sip of her coffee.

"I'm afraid I've behaved rather badly," Leslie said to Clair. "Like my heroine, Marionette, in *The Bush Master*, too intensely possessive. . .to the point of losing her good sense."

Mrs. Mandel looked at her daughter with a pensive air. "Yes, but Marionette had many good qualities, too." She kissed Leslie's cheek.

"I read *The Bush Master*," Clair said, deciding to go with the family flow. "I loved Marionette. It was hard not to admire the passionate concern she had for her family."

"Mmm. Please tell me more," Leslie said.

Clair's fingers tightened on the cup handle. "In the end, you could forgive Marionette for everything because you would want to know that kind of love."

"You're quite clever. . .the best subtextual dialogue I've ever heard." Leslie chuckled, leaning on the counter. "So, you liked *The Bush Master*?"

"Very much," Clair said. "I've read *all* your books."

"Really." Leslie slid a plate of chocolate biscotti in front of Clair. "Mmm. Might be nice to have a fan around. No one else in the family is."

An uproar arose, each one announcing in his or her own way that Leslie couldn't be more wrong.

Clair laughed, taking in the scene before her. She wondered what they would think if they knew this was her first encounter within a real family.

Leslie picked up a piece of biscotti. "And I've never seen Hudson as happy as when he's talking about you, Clair. I got to thinking. . .that has to be worth a lot."

"It's beyond price," Edwin said. "And it's still the way I feel about your mother after forty-one years."

A warm feeling spread through Clair. Perhaps she'd finally come home—a place she'd imagined hundreds of times but had never known. . .until now.

After the hoopla died down, Hudson ushered her out onto the back porch, which was lined with large glass windows and soft couches in a wide assortment of blues. "Ahh." He shut the door. "Alone at last."

Clair looked out over the huge backyard, which contained a garden complete with a waterfall and a wooden bridge. A pathway of gray stone meandered through flower beds frothing with daffodils and pink tulips. "Oh, your mother must love this garden."

"Yes." Hudson moved a few steps nearer to her, his voice deepening. "I believe she does."

He'd come so close, she could smell his cologne. *Mmm. Just like the outdoors.* But in spite of the romantic moment, she felt a sudden need to tell him about the bookshop. "I had lunch with a woman named Mabel. She wants to buy the shop. Has always wanted to buy it, actually."

Hudson sat down on a wicker chair near her. "I'm glad, since I think your heart wasn't really in it." He looked up at her with an earnest expression.

"This woman, Mabel, seems perfect. She came out of nowhere one day. It's like I was waiting for her." Clair sat next to him. "I've decided to sell it to her at a reasonable price. I think Ima would be pleased someone so capable and devoted would be running her store."

"And do you know what you want to do now?"

"Yes, I *do* know." Clair took in some extra oxygen and decided, sink or swim, to make the boldest announcement of her life. "I want to sing. . .with you."

Chapter 24

Hudson's mouth dropped open.

Clair panicked, thinking she'd been too hasty in making such a presumptuous request. *Maybe I should tell him I plan to find another job as well.* "That is—"

"That is just what I've been praying for." He gathered her hands in his and kissed them. "There is nothing that would make me happier."

Relief filled Clair at his response, but she couldn't help but wonder how the decision would affect the future. Their future.

Hudson looked out at the garden. "Let's take a walk." He guided her from the back porch into the warm air of spring.

They ambled through the winding paths. The sound of ducks could be heard somewhere on the grounds. Finally they came to the middle of the little bridge, and Hudson turned around to face Clair. "My parents call this the kissing bridge."

Clair slid her hand along the smooth redwood railing, hoping Hudson would take full advantage of the bridge's nickname.

"I've been waiting for just the right moment. I hope this is it." Hudson looked at her as if he were collecting his thoughts. Then he pulled a small box out of his pocket and knelt on one knee.

Clair felt like she was dreaming. Could this really be happening?

"I have fallen so in love with you." Hudson's face shone with tenderness and affection. "Clair, I promise to cherish you all the days of my life." The velvet box crackled open, revealing a marquise diamond ring.

Clair's hand went to her heart. "You're asking me to marry you?"

"Yes. I believe I am."

Her eyes filled with tears. She wasn't prepared for the wild mixture of emotions inside her—gratitude, elation, and a fear she might wake up. "I'll say yes quickly just in case this is a dream."

Hudson rose and slipped the ring onto her finger.

"It's so lovely. This can't be happening. . .to me."

He placed his hands on her shoulders. "This is no dream." He pulled her into an embrace. "When I hold you. . .it's like you were always meant to be here."

She eased away and traced the contours of his face with her finger, lingering

228

on his cheek. "This is all such a gift."

Hudson closed his eyes and kissed her tenderly on the forehead. "I accept this gift, Lord, in thankful awe." He then cupped her face with his hands, and with mist-filled eyes, he leaned down to kiss her.

Clair returned his sweet affections. *No more dark corners. Only light and love.* She laced her fingers around his as her heart overflowed with joy. Home at last.

⟨⟩

Three weeks later, Clair and Hudson held hands as they mounted the stairs inside the Silver Moon Café. Clair knew she was not only walking up to the stage, but to a new life in so many ways. She felt an excitement in the air—an electric sort of anticipation for what would soon come. She could hardly believe it. *I'm about to sing with my fiancé!* She glanced at the room full of people and at Hudson's family, including Leslie, all seated around a table, looking animated and happy.

"You're not nervous, are you?" Hudson whispered in her ear.

"Should I be?" She mirrored his smile.

He shook his head. "No, not at all."

Clair had wondered, in fact, over the past weeks why she hadn't been anxious about her first appearance, but she decided to count that stillness deep inside as one of God's mercies to her. She'd lost so much over the years, surely now was a time of restoration.

Clair knew she'd have no problem recalling her part of the song. Over the past three weeks, they'd practiced "The Love Song" to perfection—a song Hudson had written for their upcoming wedding.

Once they were on stage, they reluctantly let go of each other's hands. Not used to the spotlight, Clair winced a bit as her eyes got used to the brightness.

Hudson adjusted a microphone for Clair, pulled out a guitar pick from his pocket, and sat down on his wooden stool. "Good evening. I'm Hudson Mandel."

His fans rewarded him with an enthusiastic round of applause. "And I'd like to introduce Clair O'Neal. . .a new voice in Little Rock. Someone I think you're going to like. I'm also happy to say, she's my fiancée." Cheers went up all over the hall.

Clair could feel her face getting warm, but she didn't mind. She smiled at Hudson. His announcement felt good all the way to her toes. She only wished Ima were alive to share in her joy.

She gave him a nod, and then he began to pick out the intro. They looked at each other as they sang the song that made their voices and hearts melt together.

"When I thought love was lost
And the stars had all gone out,
Your love came and found me,
Lit my world, my life, my heart."

Clair's clear voice harmonized with Hudson's velvet one, flowing out as one river of sound, filling the Silver Moon Café.

The waiters and waitresses stopped to listen and murmured among themselves.

Clair scanned the Mandels' table just in time to see Leslie's mouth fall open. She tried to concentrate on the lyrics.

As the song came to a close, Clair sent a prayer up to heaven, thanking the Lord for the chance to sing. She also praised Him for the gift of love, which He had so freely poured out upon her over the past several weeks. He had led her—wounded little lamb that she'd been—through the valley and onto the mountaintop. Oh! Would her heart ever be able to contain the joy?

Clair startled from the next sound—the thunderous and unexpected applause from the audience. "Thank you," she heard herself say into the microphone. She took in a deep breath and looked over at the love of her life.

Hudson gazed over at her and mouthed the word "Beautiful."

Epilogue

On a crisp fall morning in the sanctuary of Grace Cathedral, Clair slipped the gold band onto Hudson's finger and said the words she'd been longing to say. "Hudson, with this ring, symbolic of what is never ending, I promise you my love all the days of my life."

In hushed reverence before the Almighty and all those gathered, more vows were exchanged, which told of their tender affections and faithful devotion. When the minister said, "You may kiss the bride," Hudson lifted the delicate veil that covered Clair's face.

She smiled at him as he leaned down to her mouth. The kiss was tender and stirring and filled with promise.

Hudson whispered, "I love you."

Her heart swelled with joy and her eyes filled with mist.

"Surely goodness and love will follow me all the days of my life, and I will dwell in the house of the Lord for ever." The words to the familiar psalm added a gentle amen to the moment. Clair smiled and breathed a prayer of thanks to the Lord for His overwhelming goodness.

Following a brisk walk down the aisle and a brief session with the photographer, they headed toward the conservatory for the reception.

After meeting hundreds of happy guests in the receiving line, Clair readied herself behind the four-tiered ivory wedding cake. She sliced out a gooey piece and lifted it up to her husband. Hudson took a huge bite, making Clair laugh.

Cameras flashed. Applause and joyful noises rose up around the newly married couple, but their hearts and ears were tuned elsewhere—to the melodious enveloping sanctuary. . .of their own sweet love song.

CASTLES
IN THE AIR

Dedication

To the brave men and women of our United States military,
who stand in harm's way that we might enjoy the freedoms we hold dear.
Anita Higman

To Courtney and Andy—both sweeter than candy.
Janice A. Thompson

Acknowledgments

Gratitude goes to my husband, Peter, for his boundless help and support.
Anita Higman

Chapter 1

The tiniest scream rose inside Nori. She tucked the desperate feeling away as she watched a cozy-looking duo through the coffee shop window. The pair held hands and kissed, making a tight little circle of love.

Not wanting to torture herself, Nori moved on down the sidewalk and turned her attention to a display window at Simon's Book Shoppe. A title on one of the covers grabbed her attention: *Guerrilla Tactics for the Romantically Challenged.* She shook her head in disbelief as another book title ground into her psyche: *Why You Aren't Dating—Put Down That Chocolate!*

Nori rolled her eyes and slipped the candy bar she'd been eating into her coat pocket. Apparently, the author was uninformed that the cocoa bean was good for the heart.

The last book in the display clutched at her heart. *When Love Never Comes.* How much more could she stand? She forced a chuckle, but somewhere deep inside, where little girls grow up dreaming of happily-ever-afters, she knew her aloneness was getting to her.

A tear spilled down Nori's cheek. She glanced around, embarrassed. Swiping at her eyes, she started her usual pep talk. *Remember who you are—a successful entrepreneur. The newspapers call you "The Candy Shop Queen."*

A gust of icy air nipped at Nori's exposed skin. It seemed extra cold for mid-March. She pulled her coat collar up around her neck and strode to her car.

Nori's pace slowed. She glanced back. What if one of the books had even one idea in it that could change her clichéd life? She'd be foolish *not* to buy it. Right? Desperate times—desperate measures.

Nori turned around, and before she could change her mind again, she charged into the bookstore. She drew in a deep breath. The shop smelled of peppermint and coffee.

"I'll be there in a minute," a women yoo-hooed from the back room.

Not wanting to be embarrassed with unnecessary queries, Nori reached around into the small window display and pulled out a book entitled, *Finding Your Dreamboat.* She hadn't noticed that one before. Hmm. The book might have potential, but the cover nearly screamed, "Find out now why the whole world considers you undatable."

She flipped open to the contents page and scanned it. The book appeared to be set up with long lists of ideas. *"Tip Number One: Surround yourself with romance. Talk romantically. Dress romantically. And the greatest secret of all is to—"*

"Excuse me," a stranger whispered in her ear.

Nori screamed. In that instant the book became airborne, ricocheted off some shelves, and made a nasty landing on the wooden floor.

"Mmm, so you're the anxious type." The woman raised one heavy eyebrow. "Oh, I see you have one of our newest arrivals." She scooped up the book and glared at the crushed corners.

"Don't worry," Nori said. "I'll buy it."

The bell over the door jangled, and a man with some serious good looks ambled inside. Lots of Grecian angles and lustrous hair with highlights. *The guy is prettier than I am.* He glanced over at Nori and caught her drooling.

"Gertrude!" The bushy-browed clerk hollered loud enough to summon emergency personnel. "Somebody just bought that how-to-trap-a-man book in the window. You know, *Finding Your Dreamboat.* Can you bring me up another copy?"

Nori wanted to crawl under something. She might as well slap on a sandwich board with the word *desperate* and strut all over Hot Springs. "Uh, maybe you could just put the book on hold for me," Nori whispered to the clerk as she edged toward the door.

"There's no waiting whatsoever. You can buy this one. Actually, you *should* buy this one since you mangled it."

She wondered what Mr. Dazzle thought about that announcement. Or maybe he hadn't been paying attention.

On her way up to pay, Nori noticed a coffee-table book on the art of making homemade Christmas candy. Maybe she could sell a selection of books in her candy shop. She scribbled a note on her hand to remind her.

Back at the counter, the clerk frowned at Nori's check. "I'll need to see an ID, please. I can't be too careful for Melody. I'm just helping her out tonight for a few minutes." She glanced at her watch. "In fact, I'd better get back. I really belong next door in the nut shop."

What more could Nori possibly add to that thoroughly accurate statement? She paid for the book, slapped on the sweetest smile she could conjure, and fled out the front door.

Ahh. The arctic air felt revitalizing. But as she took off toward her car, an age-old question came back to haunt her—was there really a man somewhere out there who was meant to love her? No answer whispered back to her in the cold evening wind. When had falling in love gotten so complicated? Her own parents had fallen in love and were still happy. And what about all those dear elderly couples at the assisted living center where she'd volunteered? They'd found soul mates and were blissfully growing old together.

Huge flakes floated down and lighted on Nori's face. She looked up. The thick clouds seemed expectant. Tonight she might choose to tuck herself in with a blanket of self-pity. She knew a gloomy attitude wouldn't get her very far, but flying free from the constant yearning to have a family seemed nearly impossible.

In fact, she recalled the moment the seed was planted. Her mother had given her a wedding doll on her sixth birthday, and she playacted a hundred different kinds of weddings as she grew up. Breezy hilltop weddings. Cathedral weddings. Outdoor gazebo weddings. Then she'd create detailed lives for her lovebirds with careers and houses and kids. But sadly, her elaborate dreams were only built in her imagination. Only castles in the air.

She sighed. Life would be easier if her customers weren't escalating the situation by making suggestions. People tried to be helpful, but their encouragement and suggestions left a residue on her spirit, reminding her that she was on the spinster side of nuptial bliss. And that time was slipping away.

Nori scooted into her older model Mercedes and started the engine. As she waited for the heat, she looked into the rearview mirror. She touched the corners of her eyes. No wrinkles or sags. She hadn't turned into a gargoyle. Yet.

She leaned into the reflection. *Okay. Not bad at thirty.* Shoulder length, blond hair. A little washed-out, but all natural and no gray. Clear hazel eyes. Perfect oval face. None of that distracting bone structure like on magazine models. Surely she was still datable.

She knocked the mirror back in place. But she was still twenty pounds overweight. One of the hazards of loving dark chocolate truffles and owning the finest candy shop in Arkansas. Nori brushed at the bulging folds of fabric above her stomach as if to sweep them away. They'd been part of her life for ten years, so they weren't about to disappear overnight. But couldn't true love transcend a mere twenty pounds of flesh?

Nori looked out through the window across the empty parking lot and released a long breath. She wondered if God had taken notice that her sighing had recently increased. Did He keep a count of people's sighs and tears as He did the hairs on their heads?

God, I know You're listening, so here I am yet again with some more questions. Am I still going to be kissing the mirror when I'm creaking with arthritis? You've crowned me the princess of the friendship date. In all these years I have never even had a kiss I could call a real kiss. Only lips brushing across a cheek and little pecks on the forehead. I want a big juicy kiss! Can I say that to You, God? And I want our passionate kiss to mean something. Something real and lasting. A forever kind of kiss. And God. . .if it's not too much to ask. . .the next wedding I attend, I'd like it to be mine.

Silence. Seemed like there'd been a lot of that lately, too. Or maybe God wasn't saying what she wanted to hear.

Suddenly Nori noticed that Mr. Dazzle from the bookstore was trotting in her direction. She leaned in toward the windshield for a better look. Could the book have worked its magic by merely purchasing it? Or was the guy going to try to steal her car?

The stranger came toward her waving a book in his hands. Nori saw her purse on the passenger seat—no book. *Oh, great.* She'd left her purchase sitting on the counter. Mr. Dazzle had her book. Nori let her head fall forward against the steering wheel as she closed her eyes. *Is there no end to my humiliation?*

Chapter 2

Nori looked up to see the stranger's knuckles about to give her window a rap. She pushed a button on the side panel. The glass glided downward as she looked up at him, feeling grateful that the shadows of the car hid her embarrassment. "Hi, there."

He offered her the book. "You forgot this."

She tried to swallow her pride, but it felt as pleasant as gulping down a walnut. Unshelled. She reached out through the window for the book. "I really appreciate it."

A tiny cross swung around his neck on a silver chain. "Good luck," he said.

"Excuse me?" Nori felt her heart do a little two-step.

"You know," he said. "Good luck finding your dreamboat."

Okay, so how many shades of embarrassment are there? Flaming scarlet. Lobster-pink. Fuchsia fandango. Nori released a nervous giggle. "Thanks."

"It took me two years to find mine," he went on to say. "I'd recommend starting with a sailboat if you like adventure. Nothing else like it. Leave your cares behind." He appeared sincere.

And people have the nerve to make fun of female blonds.

"Yeah, I got a great deal on Serendipity. It's the name of my boat." He flashed his pearly whites as he flipped his collar-length hair back. "I found her in the newspaper. Sort of an unforeseen blessing. By the way, I'm Blake Lawrence."

She shook his warm hand. "I'm Nori Kelly. It's nice to meet you."

He paused for a moment as if wanting to ask her something. Then the moment dissipated along with the cloud from his frosty breath. "Well, I guess I'd better get going. It's pretty cold out here." He stomped around as he blew into his hands. "Hey, look, it's snowing. Now that's a surprise."

Nori stared upward and saw a few large and lacy flakes float around him. The snow had started sputtering again. "Yeah, life is full of surprises."

Blake chuckled as he looked at her. He stuck his hands into the pockets of his leather jacket. "Take care, now. Okay?"

"You, too."

Mr. Dazzle bowed like a nobleman and then bid her adieu.

Nori watched the man walk away. Blinking a few more times, she tried to take it all in. *That was different.* She rubbed her hands but realized she was

239

already warm. She paused for another moment or two and then sped off toward her apartment, grateful for a cozy place to be lonely and crazy. But she had to admit, the man tonight was not only cute but friendly. And she was glad he hadn't "gotten it." Otherwise the moment would have been awkward instead of sweet.

Hmm. Too bad Blake hadn't been in the mood to buy her some cocoa in the nearby coffee shop. Cocoa reigned supreme as the beverage of choice for a snowy evening, especially with those soft marshmallows bobbing their little heads around on top. Oh yes, mocha moo in a mug. The brew should be savored around stimulating conversation, but if alone, a book and a cup of the sweet charm could always be her escape and comfort. And a man who took the time to appreciate cocoa was a man worth taking another look at.

Blake Lawrence. Too bad. Nice name. Sounded a little fake, like a character from a romance novel, but nice anyway. Well, if there'd been an opportunity in that brief moment, it was gone now.

Nori started singing anything that came into her head—anything to get her mind off her spiraling thoughts. She was still humming when she parked her car, rode the elevator to the second floor of her apartment building, and strode down the hallway to her front door.

Oh no. She noticed her neighbor, Zachary Martin, emerge from his apartment as if he'd been waiting for her.

"Greetings." He appeared to study the floor.

"Hi." Nori wondered why Zachary was the only one in the known galaxy to greet people that way.

He raked his fingers through his short brown hair, which made a couple of his locks rise up like antlers.

Nori squelched a chuckle. She knew he was stalling, trying to think of something to say. If she hadn't been so tired, she would have given him a few rounds of chitchat. Instead she jangled her keys to give him a hint.

Zachary stuffed his fists in his pockets, making his polyester pants rise even higher. His white socks emitted a glow as if lit by a black light. "Hope your evening has been. . .good. . .so far."

"I think it has been. . .so far." Nori smiled, sliding her key into the lock.

"The National Oceanic and Atmospheric Administration says there's a 20 percent chance of snow tonight." Zachary stroked his palms together.

"It's already snowing." Nori tried not to have a condescending tone.

He shuffled his feet. "Oh."

Nori turned her door key. She didn't want to be rude, but her feet throbbed from working all day. "I've been out window-shopping this evening," she said, trying to throw him a preserver so he wouldn't drown in their silence.

Zachary puckered his eyebrows. "I do that all the time, too. Well, I window-shop. . .online." He snickered.

When she didn't respond with laughter, he recoiled as if to censor himself. *I think I was supposed to laugh.* Nori felt sorry for Zachary. He'd been her neighbor for a whole year, and yet they'd never once connected even as friends.

Zachary shrugged with his palms in the air.

Nori noticed the ink scribblings on his hand. He apparently had the same habit of writing notes on his hand as she did.

Silence crawled between them again—the prickly kind.

These gawking and quiet elements of his personality made Nori nervous. Plus his body gestures made her think of Mr. Potato Head when some of the parts were put back wrong. She certainly wasn't up for the stress of jump-starting their weekly hall conversations. "Well, I guess I'd better go on in." She opened her door and waved. "Good night."

"Sure. Thanks for talking to me. . .Noreen."

Nori paused and then turned to him again. "I do wish you'd call me Nori. The name *Noreen* makes me feel old."

"Noreen Kelly is an Irish name." Zachary had a faraway gaze. "From the land of flaming dragons and fair maidens," he added with a brogue.

Nori tried not to look too baffled.

"Oh. It's from a fantasy trilogy I've been reading. It's set in Ireland. You know, Land of the Flaming Dragons." Zachary stuck his elbow out as if to lean against the doorframe, but his aim was so off, he stumbled and fell against the wall.

"Are you okay?" Nori wanted to help him, but he'd already grabbed the door-frame and pulled himself up.

"Yeah." He raised his arms. "I'm good."

"Are you sure?"

He nodded, his face red. "Yep."

"Well, okay. Good-bye." Nori glanced back.

She caught him mouthing, "Good night." He said nothing more, so she smiled and eased the door shut.

Once inside her cocoon, Nori busied herself by hanging up her coat in the entry closet, but her thoughts remained on Zachary. Had she been unsociable? Perhaps. Here was a guy who'd actually showed some real interest, and she'd shut him out. Maybe she was being too picky. But she had hoped for a partner who was in the same species. *Oh dear.* Guilt clouded over Nori like the murky sky outside. She sent up a sincere apology to God, grabbed her teddy bear, and plopped down on her overstuffed couch with a sigh.

Zachary wasn't so bad. Really. A handsome face when he didn't scowl.

He had quite a mannish body, but the clothing could use some work. Same age and height as her—thirty and short. And on more than one occasion he'd mentioned how much he loved his church. All in all, he appeared to be a kind and thoughtful Christian man. That all rang up well. But one iffy issue really stood out—Zachary was a geek.

But then again, Nori reminded herself, she'd also had some endearing moments with him. Zachary never looked through her as so many other men did. He took the time to listen to her—to really "see" her. She wondered if there wasn't something about him undiscovered or perhaps misunderstood by people. Something one had to quietly seek, instead of just tossing out quick assumptions and dismissals. Had she been guilty of the latter? She gave her teddy a squeeze.

Nori ambled over to the kitchen counter with her bear, trying to imagine herself falling in love with someone like that. She wondered what he did in his cave with all his alone time. Just read medieval fantasy novels and play with his calculator? Sounded boring. She hardly ever heard a peep from his apartment next door. *What is he doing right this minute?* Funny how she'd never thought about that before, and he'd been next door for about a year.

What would her parents think of Zachary? Nori chuckled. They would like him. They'd adore anyone who'd marry her. Oh well, things to muse about some other day.

Nori reached down into one of her sample bags sitting on the counter and popped a few of the new chocolate-covered raisins into her mouth. Fine dark chocolate with a hint of orange. Mmm. Okay, this would sell to all of those female customers, including herself, who loved specialty chocolates almost as much as a good date. Almost.

She'd need to order some of the new treats but not without first allowing her best customers to sample them and decide. With no paper handy, she wrote out the reminder on the palm of her hand. She'd transfer the note to her memo pad later. Hmm. Maybe what she really needed were some hobbies beyond sampling chocolates. She chuckled. All her extra time went into the candy shop, so it had seemed almost impossible to explore any leisure pursuits.

Nori's gaze latched onto the slick hardbound book she'd just bought. *Finding Your Dreamboat.* Ignoring the almost condescending book title, she scooted the book closer and then cracked it opened in the middle as if some magical air might escape. The thirteenth chapter began: *"Makeup is an essential. Your skin is like a primer coat, so don't forget the paint. Without color, you're like a rose without its petals."*

"That's ridiculous," Nori mumbled. "I've never needed more than blush." She pulled up the sleeves on her turtleneck sweater. Out of curiosity, she read on: *"Try wearing liberal amounts of lipstick in the hue of pomegranates. Men are attracted to this ruby color—the color of ardor and romance. You don't need to flirt. Let your lips do it for you."*

Nori laughed. *Is this a joke?* But in spite of her doubts, she headed to the bathroom and rummaged through her makeup drawer for the tube of lipstick someone had given her for Christmas. The bottom of the tube read "Carnival of Rubies."

Hmm. Well, that name certainly didn't inspire confidence. She rolled up the lipstick from the container. Amazingly, it looked pretty close to the color of pomegranates, but once she smoothed it all over her lips, "Carnival of Circus Clowns" came to mind. *Oh dear.* "So much for desperate times—desperate measures." In an effort to attract males, she'd become no more than some animal preening her plumage. Nori released a prolonged sigh.

She set the gold case down on the counter and puckered her lips. Well, at least it was a *new* look. She decided she'd go ahead and give the fruity, flirty lip color a try the next morning. Besides, nothing else had worked. So what did she have to lose?

Chapter 3

After pacing the halls trying to think of impressive things to say to Nori in the future, Zachary retreated to his apartment and eased his front door shut. He let his head fall against the wall in frustration. He knew that gently thumping his head against the Sheetrock was futile, not to mention juvenile, but it felt good for some reason. Why had he acted so absurdly in front of her? In trying to kid around, he'd had some kind of intellectual blackout.

Hearing a crinkling in his pocket, he reached in and yanked out his latest paycheck from South Gate Oil and Gas. He slung it into a drawer in the entry table. He had more money than he could spend, but it couldn't buy him what he really wanted—the love of his life, Noreen Kelly. The woman had everything. Good teeth. Brains. A Mona Lisa smile.

Ah yes, his Nori was as fair as any maiden he'd ever read about. And sometimes when he got lost in her smile, he'd come close to just reaching out and touching her face without thinking.

In fact, he could easily recall the moment he'd fallen in love with her. One evening after work when he'd stopped in to buy his favorite candy, Nori was holding a baby girl while her mother shopped. She cuddled and sang to the child about Jesus until both Nori and the baby took on the most angelic countenances he'd ever beheld. He'd known in that moment he was smitten—for life.

Zachary groaned. Such amorous sentiments, and he couldn't even summon the courage to ask her out. He knew he lacked certain social skills, but he didn't need any coaching to see Noreen had "no" written all over her face. At least now he knew to always call her *Nori* in the future, since she seemed to dislike her given name. He couldn't understand why, though, since her full name made a sound as melodic as water gurgling over stones and moss.

After squeezing the bridge of his nose and adjusting his glasses, he glanced around. At least his domicile wasn't holding him back from settling down. His dwelling looked like a class act with all its contemporary furniture and technology. He had plenty of food, a more than comfortable income, and an expensive apartment. Of course, wooing was more than just dangling possessions in front of a woman, he reminded himself, but his financial status wouldn't hurt his chances.

Zachary gave a light whack to the model of the solar system sitting on the table. He liked the peculiar whirring noise it created. He watched the tiny planets lose their order as they flew out of control.

Maybe he still lacked some piece of the puzzle. He'd always been good at figuring things out, and now as a grown man, he certainly knew about geophysical interpretations, computer analysis, and physical models. But love and the female psyche seemed impossible to decode. In fact, no real solution came to him because there were no right answers.

Lost in thought, Zachary lumbered over to his telescope and touched the eyepiece. He wondered if Galileo had gone through as much trouble wooing a girl. Flustered, he dismissed the subject and stumbled into the kitchen to make a homemade cup of cocoa.

Once he had the brew poured into his cup from the pan, he took a cautious sip of his concoction. The heady steam curled upward and calmed him. *Good stuff.* Just the way his dad used to make it. "Top secret ingredients," his dad used to say with a wink. Dark chocolate and marshmallow cream. Those days seemed like an eternity ago—when his parents were still together. But those times were gone now, and he'd moved on.

An Irish tune came to him, and, wanting to be free of the melancholy, he made an instrument out of his spoon and began clinking it against the cup to the rhythm in his head. When the song played itself out, he picked up his new calculator and began fiddling with it. He already had three on his desk at work, but the new one could do three-dimensional graphics. Well worth the money. If only love could be as simple as an equation.

Zachary glanced up at the book he'd bought at Simon's Book Shoppe the day before and crossed his arms. *Courtship for Idiots.* He'd circled the aisles in the bookstore about fifty times before he bolstered his nerve to buy the thing. Now it sat there on the shelf, face forward and almost sneering at him.

He picked up the book and read the endorsements on the back: *"I found my wife with the advice from this book. What better endorsement is there?" "These ideas will change the course of your life. Buy it now, and let the journey begin."*

Zachary wondered if the overly glowing plugs were just made up by the author or submitted by close family and friends. He opened the book to the table of contents. It seemed to be set up under character types. "Teaching the Shy Guy to Say Hi." "Bob, the Pompous Snob." "Let's Meet the Freaky Geek."

Before scanning the next chapter titles, Zachary flipped to the geek chapter out of curiosity. He frowned and then read on: *"If you live in geekdom, your first task toward balance is to expand your reading materials to something besides technical journals."* He certainly wasn't guilty of falling into that trap, since he also loved reading science fiction and fantasy.

Zachary skimmed the author's reading list suggestions and then read a passage out loud. " 'Here are two more starter survival tactics. Pitch, cut up, or flush those nerdy white socks. And drive your shirts to the dry cleaners so they don't make you look like you slept in a dumpster.' "

He scooted his chair back to stare at his white socks. *Humph.* But white socks could be bought in big packages like bulk toilet paper. It was much more economical and logical to buy socks that way. And laundries were for sissies. He looked at his shirt. Not many wrinkles. Was it really necessary to iron clothes? They seemed to come out of the dryer sort of ready to wear. Didn't they?

He slapped the book shut in irritation and then took another sip of his cocoa. *Geekdom?* He wasn't truly a geek. Granted, he'd been called that term from time to time, but he'd never acknowledged it. He read the next sentence out loud. " 'You may be in denial.' "

Shocked, Zachary dropped the book as if he'd been electrocuted. After pacing the room, he finally picked it up again to take another peek. He read:

If you're in denial, don't fret. Just acknowledge your status as a communal outcast and then take heart. Geeks also control some serious cash, because of their superior brain power. That counts for a lot more than the guy down the street who has more hair-care products than brain cells. With your keen intellect, you'll catch on faster when it comes to tweaking the persona. So let's get started.

Zachary knew the book was idiotic, but the bright spot of encouragement egged him on to the next page. " 'Okay, listen up. Another news flash. Women don't like guys who wear thick glasses. Get contacts. You can afford them.' " He pulled down his glasses and rubbed the bridge of his nose. He'd worn eyeglasses all his life. They'd become like an appendage to his face. He wasn't even sure if he could let go of them. Then he thought of lovely Nori again. He pushed his glasses back up and vowed to make an eye doctor's appointment for contacts.

Okay. What could possibly be next? Zachary read on, " 'Women like the unexpected. In other words, if you're a geek, consider each thing you do and then do the exact opposite. Think *surprise.*' "

Could he really make all these modifications? Or would he always be a communal outcast, as the book implied? And why had God made him so different?

After a weird night of wrestling with the sheets and dreaming he was Gollum in *The Lord of the Rings,* Zachary woke up with a wicked cramp in his neck and still very much in love with Nori Kelly.

Zachary threw on his robe and staggered into the kitchen, where he gobbled down his usual frosted peanut butter protein bar, three jumbo prunes, and one half-liter of hazelnut coffee. After showering, he climbed into the pair of khaki pants that he usually saved for church and put on his only unwrinkled shirt.

While fumbling in his closet, he came across a chunky bottle of cologne that his parents had given him when he was a teenager. Except for deodorant, he'd never taken the time to use anything with a scent.

Hmm. New territory. Zachary gave the bottle a dubious look. Surely he could handle it. The name of the cologne was Legends. Sounded pretty decent. Of course, bad things became legends, too.

Zachary shook the bottle, making the amber liquid slosh around in the container. How much of this stuff was he supposed to use anyway? Since he had no idea, he just opened his shirt and splashed a generous amount of the fluid all over his chest.

Then he gagged. *Way too much.* Zachary grabbed a washcloth, soaped it up, and tried scrubbing off the scent. But the smell seemed to be embedded in his skin. Permanently.

After a few more frustrating attempts at improving himself, Zachary gave up and waited by the front door. He smashed his ear against the wood, waiting for the sound of Nori as she left her apartment. She always made the same noises. He knew them by heart. She always locked the door, zipped up her purse, sighed, and then exactly five seconds later she'd come back to make sure she'd locked it. It was yet another connection he had with his Irish maiden. They were both serious checkers.

Yes, he heard the *click*, *zip*, and then her stride back to the door. His cue. Zachary exited, minus his white socks and rumpled clothes. With the new mantra buzzing in his head, he smiled over at Nori.

Remember, "Women like the unexpected. Consider each thing you do and then do the exact opposite. Think surprise."

Chapter 4

Nori checked the door to make sure it was locked. Then she heard Zachary coming out of his apartment. *Oh no.* How did he always know when she left? He was like a human motion detector. She looked down the hall at him. "Hi."

"Good morning, Nori." Zachary smiled, and then without another word, he headed down the hallway toward the elevator, a book tightly clutched in his hand.

Hmm. That was different. Nori followed Zachary at a safe distance, looking him over. Something had changed about him. He didn't look so desperate or pitiful. And his clothes weren't crumpled. But what was that smell he left in his wake? After another whiff she realized *herbicide* might be a better word.

Ivan Wentworth, another bachelor apartment dweller, joined Nori and Zachary on their march down the hallway.

"Hi, Ivan," Nori said, trying not to be too obnoxious by puckering her lips.

"Morning." And then Ivan went back to talking into his earpiece.

Zachary turned to give Ivan a little wave but kept walking.

After they all boarded the elevator, Nori went up and down on her tiptoes, hoping someone, anyone, had noticed her lips. She had indeed decided to wear two layers of pomegranate lipstick. Even though Ivan was now off the phone, unfortunately he'd soon busied himself by fiddling with his Blackberry. And Zachary, who never read in the elevator, had his nose buried in a book. *So much for letting one's lips do the flirting.*

The elevator doors slid open, and the two men fled as if they were in a footrace.

Nori stood gaping, wondering why men were so unpredictable. And scattered. And insensitive. In fact, a long list of vivid adjectives came to mind. What a farce.

Zachary popped his head around the elevator door and offered her a tissue. "I noticed your lip was bleeding. Hope you're okay."

Nori accepted the neatly folded tissue. She opened her mouth to speak, but Zachary disappeared around the corner. She mashed her floor button a few times, rode the elevator back to her apartment, and stared at herself in the bathroom mirror. The lip color had smeared under her mouth, making her lip appear cut and bleeding. In fact, the sticky crimson goo had also gotten on her teeth, which made her look like she'd been hanging out with vampires. The color of romance, indeed.

After cleaning herself up and starting the day again, she drove over to her shop. She swung open the door and took in the aroma of every kind of wonderful treat. Sweet Nothings Candy Shop—her dream come to life. A quaint sign swung over the door, a black-and-white checkered floor lit the store with pizzazz, and magic waited in every jar of candy. *Ah yes.*

She lighted her fingers on some dainty bags of her famous Little Chocola' Rocks. *Mmm, mmm, mmm.* How could men compete with sweets, especially chocolate? She chuckled to herself.

Lizza Langtree, her manager, effervescent as always, stood behind the counter in her rainbow overalls schmoozing the customers until they were all helplessly buying several kinds of candies. A mom and her giggling children strolled out with a diverse assortment of goodies—watermelon worms, which were all the rage with the kids; homemade maple walnut fudge, good for buttering up dads; and the delectable caramel chews, which were a superb choice for apple-dipping even though the time for autumn treats had passed.

"Hey, girl." Lizza gave Nori a hug.

"Looks like you're already busy satisfying our tourists this morning." Nori hugged her back. Lizza had always been big on hugs. Even with her slender frame, she'd mastered the big bear squeeze.

After they discussed the inventory for Mother's Day, Nori tied on her rainbow apron over her navy pantsuit and did her usual round of cleaning.

Two hours later, Nori changed out some of the candies in the display window while Lizza refilled a few of the candy bins. "You know, you can handle the store so well, I barely even need to show up."

"Now aren't you glad you hired me?" Lizza turned around and winked at Nori. "It was a good day, wasn't it. . .the day I came to work for you?" She raised her hand for a high five, her blue eyes twinkling.

"Best day of my life." Nori slapped Lizza's hand and chuckled. Lizza loved high fives almost as much as bear hugs.

"I still can't believe your grandmother gave you the money to start this place. My grandma doesn't even bake me cookies."

Nori grinned. "Well, Grandma Essie didn't bake me cookies either, but she did believe in my dream. While I got my business degree, Grandma knew I wanted to own a candy shop someday. So when I graduated, this was my present."

"You gotta love that. Talk about faith in your granddaughter."

"Yeah, and I will be forever grateful." Nori remembered her grandma's pep talks and her letters of encouragement. "Grandma never wanted me to do all the work by myself. She said she was afraid I'd burn out. You see, Grandma believed in my dream, but she was also desperate for great-grandchildren. Since I was the only one who could give them to her, she was hoping I'd use my surplus time to find a husband and have babies." Nori sighed.

"Too bad she went to heaven before she saw you married."

"Well, even if Grandma *had* lived, there was no guarantee that she was ever going to see me get married."

Lizza spread her hand over her heart. "The love of your life is out there. I can just feel it. Right here. And Mr. Wonderful—that is, *your* Mr. Wonderful—is somewhere out there. Just waiting for you to dazzle his life. In fact, even as a little boy he was yearning for you, calling out to you—"

"Okay, you'd better quit while you're ahead." Nori smiled. "Where do you come up with this stuff, anyway?"

"I watch a lot of historical romances on cable." Lizza shrugged. "But I *did* mean what I said. *Your* Mr. Wonderful might live right here in Hot Springs. And he might be the next man who walks through that door."

The bell jingled over the door, making them both jump. Nori and Lizza stared at the front door.

Nori felt the hinge on her mouth let go. *I cannot believe this.* Zachary Martin, dressed in a cowboy hat and boots, stood in the doorway tipping his hat at her.

"Now there's an interesting-looking man for you." Lizza looked back at Nori and made a lasso circle with her finger. "Yee-hah," she whispered. "Wait a minute. I recognize that guy. Isn't he your next-door neighbor? He's the one who comes in for chocolate-covered coffee beans."

"Yeah, he's a real candy lover," Nori said out of the corner of her mouth.

"Well, I've never said this, but I think he's cute. And—"

Nori placed two fingers over her own lips and pinched them together, trying to give Lizza the hint to be quiet. Fortunately, it didn't appear Zachary had heard them since he was busy bumping into things. *Must be because he forgot to put on his glasses.*

Zachary leaned over, checking out a silver tray of samples. He made one of his obscure hand gestures and then stared at the pastel mint candies as if he had them under a microscope.

Nori thought he said "Nice," as he tossed a handful of mints, one by one, into his mouth.

"Hi." Nori strolled toward him. "Did you come in for a little dessert?"

Zachary didn't reply. Instead, panic washed over his face. His hands grasped his throat as his face turned dark red. And then blue.

"Hey, he's choking!" Lizza screamed.

Nori looked at Lizza and then back at Zachary. His hands still clutched his neck.

Heimlich. Now. Nori got behind Zachary and threw her arms around his middle. She clasped her hands together in a ball and gave Zachary's chest a firm thrust with her fists. Nothing happened.

"Lower," Lizza yelled. "Move your hands down!"

Nori slid her hands downward and gave Zachary another hard push. A small round piece of mint sailed out of his mouth. In the midst of the drama, his hat flew off and tumbled across the floor.

Zachary gasped for air and coughed a few times. Then he leaned over with his hands on his knees.

Must be trying to get his bearings. Nori patted his back and breathed a prayer of thanksgiving.

Zachary sucked in some more air and then looked at Nori. "This isn't what. . ." His face flushed crimson.

"Are you okay now? I can't believe I almost killed you with my mints." Nori wanted to make him laugh, but she realized her comment might have come off clumsy.

Lizza rushed over and hugged Zachary. "I'm Lizza Langtree, by the way." She released him from her hold. "I'm glad you're alive."

"Me, too." he gave her a half smile. "I'm Zachary Martin."

Lizza shook his hand.

Zachary turned his attention to Nori. "You saved my life. Thank you."

"I would have done it for anyone." *Oh, that didn't come out right either.* "Please choose anything in the store. The candy is on the house." Nori certainly didn't want her customer and neighbor to go away unhappy. "Please tell me, what would you like?"

Zachary brightened. A little. "I'd like some. . .well, I'm addicted to. . . chocolate-covered coffee beans."

"Milk, dark, or extra dark?"

"I think I'll have dark today. Thanks."

"Good choice. Coming right up."

"Really appreciate. . .you know." Zachary opened his mouth to speak and then shook his head. He seemed to be holding a conversation with himself in his head.

Nori shoveled a few large scoops of her best beans into a clear plastic bag. *That should take care of him for a week or two.* She tied up the bag with a twist tie and handed it to him with a smile.

"Thanks. I hope you have a good life. I mean. . .you know. . .a good week-end." And with those rather uninspiring yet seemingly genuine words, Zachary went out the door.

Nori just stood there for a moment, absorbing the situation. She wasn't sure what just happened, except that Zachary had choked on one of her candies. Pretty terrible stuff. *I mean, what if he'd died?* She decided not to chase that thought too far. She took in several deep breaths to calm her heartbeat.

Then Nori suddenly wondered why Zachary had been wearing a Western outfit. Was it somehow for her benefit? But sometimes he seemed more irritated around her than romantic, so what was up with that? She shook her head, feeling totally clueless, but so glad she was able to save his life.

"Oh man, I'm sure glad the shop was empty." Lizza blew a strand of hair off her face. "Your neighbor looks like he might not recover from that kind of embarrassment."

"How true."

Lizza tied another peach satin ribbon around a miniature box of gumdrops. "Zachary seems like a lonely guy. Makes me want to bundle him up and stick him in my pocket for safekeeping."

"Yeah, maybe." Nori helped Lizza stack the dainty boxes on a display table.

"I don't know. I always say that about people who look sort of lost. Like he doesn't know the secret."

"What secret?" Nori asked.

"That every person is wondrously hand-designed by God. I think the reason people don't turn out so well sometimes is because no one has ever told them that."

Nori thought if she told Zachary that he was wondrous, he would never stop pestering her. Hmm. But *was* he bothering her? She no longer knew for sure. In fact, this time she'd felt nervous and tongue-tied.

"And like I said, I think he's charming." Lizza gave the top box a little pat.

"He usually wears glasses, so I'd never noticed his eyes before. They're nice." Nori realized she was thinking out loud. The disclosure surprised her.

"Yes, they *were* nice eyes. And I think the real reason he came in was to ask you out. But he was too busy choking to death." Lizza winked.

"Please don't say that. I feel terrible as it is." Nori shook her head and grinned at Lizza. "And I don't think he came in to ask me out."

"Isn't that a bit negative?"

Nori placed her hands on her hips. "At *my* age, I'm just being realistic."

"Hey, don't say it like that. We're about the same age." Lizza jiggled her eyebrows. "So, you're interested in him after all."

"He's not my type. He's a very nice nerd. But even though I'm lonely sometimes and I'd like to start a family before I buy nursing home insurance, I don't want to spend the rest of my life having one-sided discussions about quantum physics."

Lizza leaned back on the counter and whistled. "Where on earth did you get such a gloomy view of nerds? Haven't you heard? They rule the world."

Before Nori could answer, a teenage boy opened the door. He had a smart-alecky grin on his face and a ferret sitting on his shoulder.

"Hey, buddy, he's cute, but we don't allow zebras or ferrets in the shop," Lizza said to the kid. "They just can't stop eating the licorice."

The boy rolled his eyes and then headed back down the sidewalk. The moment he disappeared, lightning flashed outside the window. Thunder exploded through the shop, making the lids on the candy jars rattle.

Lizza chuckled. "Wow, that came out of nowhere."

"We've certainly had some unexpected storms lately." Nori shivered.

Then, like the thunder, Zachary burst back into the shop.

Chapter 5

Forgot something." Zachary snatched his hat off the floor and then shuffled out before Nori could say anything to him.

"Mmm. That's what I love about the candy business." Lizza's mouth curved up at the corners. "Never a dull moment."

My, my, my. I will never understand that guy. Nori squeezed the top of her head, wondering if she had a headache coming on.

Lizza massaged Nori's neck and shoulders as she whistled a Broadway tune. "You know, girl, there's no reason why you shouldn't have dates. *I* have dates."

"That's because you're gorgeous," Nori said. "You have sassy, short blond hair, cobalt blue eyes, and baby-soft skin. You're thin, you dress like a model, and you always have that smirk that must drive men crazy."

Lizza laughed. "Well, I wouldn't know about that." She released Nori with a pat on the back.

"Thanks." Nori scrunched up her shoulders. "That feels a lot better."

"Good," Lizza said. "Now, you want some free advice?"

"I can't guarantee I'll use it."

"Fair enough." Lizza got in front of Nori and caught her gaze. "If I come off pretty in any way, I have to give some credit to God and to. . .well. . .good makeup."

"You don't wear a lot of makeup."

"Yes, I do. You should see my bathroom cabinets and counters. I'll show you sometime. The trick with makeup is patience. You know, figuring out your best colors. How to apply it right. It takes some practice."

"Practice?" Nori raised an eyebrow. "Like rowing a boat or playing the clarinet?"

"Yeah, like anything you want to be good at. Why don't you get one of those free makeovers at the cosmetics counter at the mall?"

"Hmm."

"And. . .now this I would only say to someone I love."

"Oh no." Nori scrunched up her face. "Something bad. Right?"

"No, not *too* bad. Look, for some reason your dear mother didn't tell you to straighten your shoulders when you were a girl."

"I slump?"

"Yes, you do. It makes you come off as if you don't have any confidence, which couldn't be further from the truth. And I think you'd enjoy using that gym membership you bought."

"I'm chubby?" Why had it come out as a question? Nori was more than aware of her elephantine frame.

"You just need to tone up your softness a little."

Nori laughed. "I'm chubby. You can say it." She took in a deep breath and thought about all the advice. "I suppose there is some merit to your suggestions." She stared at the tiny boxes of chocolate-covered strawberries. She'd always taken great care that the fruits were fresh and sweet. Then she'd dip each ripe berry in the finest chocolate with a drizzle of white. "Perhaps I've taken more care with my candies than I have with myself."

"Tragic. Perhaps someone forgot to tell *you* the secret, too. You know, that God made every person wondrous."

Nori straightened her shoulders and smiled. "Perhaps."

A man strolled by the shop. Lizza and Nori both stopped to watch him stare at the treats in the window.

"Wow. Will you just look at that? I didn't think men were made that way anymore." Lizza shook her head with a dreamy expression. "He's like Adam coming out from the Garden of Eden. . .well, with clothes on."

"What do you think he's staring at in the window? I'll bet he's wanting to soften up Eve with a box of those pralines. She's mad because he wouldn't let her name any of the animals."

Lizza chuckled. "Good guess, but no cigar. Look at those worry lines around his brow. He's troubled because his mother's in the hospital with inoperable bunions, and he thinks some old-fashioned divinity would cheer her up."

"No way."

Before they could continue their game, the subject of their musings suddenly popped his head in the door and yelled, "Hey, do you all carry any canine treats? I'm looking for puppy truffles for my sheepdog."

Chapter 6

Zachary trudged to his office. He took off his cowboy hat and stomped on it until it was no more than a horizontal piece of brown felt and a very bad memory.

He dropped into his chair and let his head slump down on his desk. The thud rocked his skull, but the sound was a relief compared to the screaming accusations in his head. How many things had gone wrong? *Let me count the ways.* Besides nearly choking to death, why had he bought those stupid clothes? Nori hadn't said a word about his attire. Likely she was too embarrassed for him and didn't want to add to his humiliation.

And that would be the last time he'd try to be *so* impulsive. Perhaps the book on courtship had good ideas, but when most men hear "surprise," they think about flowers. He'd somehow convinced himself that dressing differently would get Nori's attention. In a good way.

He lifted his aching head. But foolish as it was, in spite of the day's tragedy, he still wouldn't mind wandering back to the candy shop on his lunch break. Not just for his favorite candies. . .but to take another glimpse at the sweetest woman who ever lived.

Zachary swiveled around and stared at his computer screen, but his mind wouldn't let go of the disgrace he'd just suffered. The outfit had not only been a failure, but he'd come off as helpless instead of manly. In fact, Nori had been forced to save his pathetic life. Not very romantic.

Okay, repeat. I have an IQ of 160, so I'm not an idiot. I have an IQ of 160, so I'm not an idiot. Still, he felt like one. After all, he'd barely managed to speak a sensible word to Nori.

Wade, a coworker, strolled into Zachary's office. "Hey, how's it going?"

"Well, I'm here." Zachary rubbed his head.

"Women problems, eh, my man?" Wade eased his portly frame into one of Zachary's chairs, making its wooden limbs moan with what sounded like dread.

"How did you know that?" Wade had some bizarre intuitive thing going. He always popped in, made offhanded and wild speculations, and then usually guessed right. The encounters were starting to annoy Zachary.

"You looked kind of miserable. Had to be a woman."

"Right."

"How true," Wade said. "I *am* always right."

While Zachary waited for his coworker to leave, he straightened the items on his desk for the thousandth time. Fortunately Wade didn't notice his obsessive-compulsive disorder, since he was too busy combing and smoothing his thick mustache into what looked like an otter pelt.

His coworker appeared to be settling in for a while, so Zachary decided to ask, "You're happily married. So how did you get your wife to like you?"

Wade laughed. "Well, you can't *make* them like you. But it'd be so much simpler that way, wouldn't it?" He laughed. "I do have one secret, though."

Did he really want to know? "Oh yeah? What's that?"

"I softened Hallie up before I asked her out."

Zachary pulled back. *Yeah, you're a real Mr. Smooth.* "So, how did you soften her up?"

"I dazzled Hallie with surprises." He lifted the lid off Zachary's candy jar and helped himself to several wrapped chocolates.

"I'm afraid surprises have been my undoing." Zachary hoped Wade wouldn't slip half the jar of chocolates into his pocket like the last time. Good thing he didn't know about his private stash. "So what did you do?"

"Well, I found out Hallie liked Shakespeare, so I bought her the complete works bound in leather. And then on another week, I sent flowers anonymously."

"But what if she didn't know who sent them? Somebody else could get the credit."

"Risk, my man. That's what it takes." Wade laced his fingers together over his stomach. "Love is like radioactivity. In other words, unstable atoms decaying randomly."

Zachary winced. Well, *that* certainly sounded like the stuff romantic legends were made of. He couldn't tell for sure, but he thought if Wade were a sandwich, he'd be mostly baloney.

Wade rose from the chair, making it groan with relief. "Basically, you have to be willing to jump off a cliff for the woman you love. Figuratively speaking, of course. You don't really have to jump. But they like to think you're willing to. You know. . .sacrifice. That's the key."

"Sacrifice?" Zachary considered that word.

Wade hurled another chocolate in his mouth. "Owwee. Now these puppies are good."

"That's because they're Swiss. Dark chocolate with almond paste." Zachary tapped his finger on the desk.

"Guess I'd better have another one for the road." Wade took three more candies from the jar. "Got to keep up my strength."

Zachary frowned as he secured the lid on the candy jar.

"So, hey, was this a dress-up day or something? Why are you wearing a Western shirt and a bolo?"

Zachary shook his head. "Don't ask."

"Oh, right. By the way, if this girl ever knew how smart you were, she'd fall into your arms. Brilliance equals good income potential, and that equals security for women. That's what they crave. Security and. . .well. . .romance."

"Is that what your wife said?"

"Yes." Wade rocked his head. "*After* we were married. A woman won't tell you her secrets until that gold band is snugly on her finger. And I—"

"But I thought you said sacrifice was the key to a woman's heart."

"Did I say that?" Wade laughed so hard he stretched his clothes beyond their limits, making his shirt snap open while simultaneously propelling a button across the room. He looked down at the empty buttonhole and chuckled again. "My wife has an endless supply of these little guys at home. See ya later."

After his coworker finally left, Zachary wrote on his palm: "Sacrifice, security, and romance." He figured that even as ridiculous as Wade could be, he may have hit on some honest answers to his dilemma. But what could he sacrifice for Nori, and how could he let her know she was secure with him? And what was romance, really? Flowers and poetry? Or was there more to it? Watching over terabytes of data was easy, but romance was not a known quantity.

Zachary flipped through the phone book and looked up the number of a local floral shop. He'd always liked lilies. They looked like trumpets about to announce something wonderful. Perhaps he'd send her a huge bouquet of them. *Wait a minute.* What was the flower his mother hated because the smell was so intense and awful? Surely it wasn't lilies. Maybe he had them confused with carnations or orchids.

With that last thought, the decision was settled in his mind—he would send lilies to Nori. He picked up the phone and, with renewed confidence, called the flower shop.

Chapter 7

The following day, Nori decided to skip lunch and head to the gym. Lizza was right. What would it hurt to tone up some of her softness? Besides, her gym membership had gone unused far too long.

Nori made her way into the large workout room, looking around in awe. A large crowd of men and women busied themselves, sweating on elliptical machines, trudging along on treadmills, and lifting weights. Not only had the place been overhauled, but so had the crowd. Since when had humans gotten thinner? And more angled? Where were all the rounder, gentler frames to make her feel at home? Maybe they were busy grazing at an all-you-can-eat pizza buffet. Sounded good, actually.

She let out a sigh but then raised her chin in resolve. Soon she would join them, but right now she had some shopping to do. After a quick visit to the sportswear shop at the front of the gym to select proper workout clothes, Nori slipped off to the changing room to put them on. She cocked her head at her reflection, studying the blue shorts and top and then giving herself an approving nod in the mirror. Hmm. She might not be a goddess, but she was far from a gargoyle. Maybe the workouts wouldn't be too painful or humiliating after all.

She headed back to the gym, ready to begin the toning and shaping. Where should she start? Ahh. There appeared to be a free elliptical machine, right next to a nice-looking guy who was busy flexing his muscles.

When Nori drew nearer to the stranger, she realized that it was the same guy from the bookstore. *Blake.* She wanted to walk the other way, but not wanting to give in to her nerves, she took her place on the machine.

Blake turned with a glance, his face lighting in a smile the minute he saw her. He brought his machine to a stop. "Hey, it's you."

Nori's face got tickly. "Yeah, it's me." She gave him an embarrassed nod and then tried to figure out how to get the machine to work. Apparently, she was smashing all the wrong buttons.

After a moment of watching her struggle, Blake leaned over and flipped a small switch.

"Thanks," she mouthed.

Within seconds they were both working out in unison.

"It's good to see you, Nori. I thought I'd never see you again."

"Really?" *This man named Blake cared about that fact?* Mind-boggling. Especially considering he was handsome enough to reduce even the most level-headed woman to a helpless state of blather. But he sounded so heartfelt. "I'm glad to see you, too." In spite of herself, she giggled. *Oh brother, Nori. Don't get too excited.* Blake appeared to have such an eternally cheery temperament that he'd probably be ecstatic over a pile of clean socks.

Nori and Blake made light conversation while they worked out together. After a few minutes of exercise, though, Nori slowed her pace, hoping Blake wouldn't notice. A few times she felt out of breath, but in spite of her gasps and her already aching muscles, she was very pleased to discover they had two mutual friends through his church.

When they were finished, Blake cleared his throat. "As you may have heard, Grace Fellowship is having their annual spring festival and potluck dinner next week, and I was wondering if you'd like to go with me. Or maybe we could meet for coffee somewhere."

Nori blinked a few times, trying to find her voice again.

"Is there something in your eye?"

"I'm fine." Nori chuckled. The last thing Blake needed to see was her voracious appetite at a potluck dinner. "Coffee sounds. . .wonderful." She wanted to say unbelievable, but that would come off too pathetic.

Blake smiled again, showing his straight white teeth. "Well, how about I pick you up tomorrow evening at seven thirty, and we'll go to that coffee place on Central near Simon's Book Shoppe."

Nori nodded. "Sounds good. Very good. I'll give you my card when we're done."

"Good deal."

He followed her to the StairMaster and then to the stationary bikes. When she was worn out, Nori headed off to the changing room, promising to meet him up front with a business card in hand. She took a quick shower, slipped her work clothes back on, and practically sprinted to the front of the gym.

When Nori spotted Blake, she handed him her business card. "Here you are." Fortunately, she'd remembered to write her home phone number and address at the bottom.

"Thanks." He stared at the card. "So, you work at a candy shop?"

"I do. I own the place, in fact. Best candy in town."

"Not as sweet as the owner, I'll bet." He winked, smoothed his hair in a wall mirror, and then made his grand exit out the door, leaving her in a wake of designer cologne and some very welcome flattery.

Nori did her best not to holler, since others were looking on, but she did do a quiet little jig around the room and chanted to herself, "Yes, yes, yes." She knew she looked silly, but she didn't care. She had a date. A real one. One she could brag about to Lizza. One she could dream about on a cold evening when no one was around to offer her cocoa. And a date she could remind herself of when she felt like a frump.

The word *frump* seeped into her pile of worries. She thought of all the improvements Lizza had suggested. *Sometime soon, I think I'll get a makeover at the mall.* With renewed resolve, Nori straightened her shoulders and strode toward the door.

She made the drive back to work with an irrepressible grin. Candy never looked so good, and the rest of the day at Sweet Nothings floated by on a cloud of blissful expectation.

After opening the door to her apartment, she kicked off her shoes and wiggled her toes. For some reason, her feet no longer ached. Ahh. Dates worked like endorphins.

Just as she was about to fix dinner, the doorbell rang. She walked to the door and looked through the peephole. Nori saw a young woman with a giant bouquet of lilies. She opened the door. "Hi."

"Are you Nori Kelly?"

"That's me."

"Then these beauties are for you."

"I can't believe it."

"Well, enjoy." The young woman's nose twitched a bit as she handed Nori the vase of lilies.

"Oh, I will. Thank you." She gave the woman a generous tip. "They're so beautiful." But the second the door went shut, Nori sneezed. Five times. *Oh no.* And what was that pungent odor? Something smelled like smoldering garbage. The lilies.

She held her breath as she poked around the bouquet for a card. Hmm. Nothing. Whoever had sent them was sweet, but the smell was unbearable, so she placed the urn of flowers on an end table in the corner.

Then Nori sat down on the other side of the room, sighing and staring at the bouquet. In spite of the bizarre fragrance, the flowers were exquisite, and she certainly didn't want to be caught complaining since they were the first flowers any man had ever given her.

Blake must have sent them. Perhaps it was a new custom to butter up a woman before he took her out. She hadn't dated in so long, men might be sending gifts of shrubbery and small goats for all she knew. But then she wondered how Blake could have known she'd say yes to his invitation to coffee. She thought he must be a very confident guy. Or at least a guy who wasn't used to hearing the word *no*.

Zachary paced his apartment, a nervous wreck. Through a crack in the door, he'd watched the delivery take place. Lilies had been the perfect choice, at least from his vantage point. Not too personal. Not too intense. Just right for a girl like Nori.

Surely she would have to agree.

He rubbed his hands together, energized. He'd done it. He'd actually sent flowers to a woman. Soon he would work up the courage to let her know he was the one who'd sent the lilies. Then, about the time she opened her mouth to thank him, he would ask her out on a date.

Chapter 8

The next day at Sweet Nothings, Nori just stood back and watched as Lizza told all of the regular customers about the big date with Blake. In fact, Lizza was delighted to repeat the story loudly over and over to Harvey, who was a little hard of hearing. Evelyn, another customer, got so excited she celebrated Nori's good fortune by buying chocolate truffles for everyone in the store.

When Lizza had them frothed up, they started pelting Nori with advice like rice at a wedding. A middle-aged woman who frequented the shop said, "When you're out on your date, act unassuming. But don't be *too* inconspicuous. Just a down-to-earth kind of shyness. That's how I got my husband."

"Who said anything about a husband?" Nori asked.

Another woman waved off the suggestion. "No, no. You've got to be bold these days. And offer to pick up the check. That's how it's done if you want to stay in the game."

"Game?" Nori flinched. "But—"

"You *do* want to get married someday, don't you?"

"Yes, but. . ." How could she share her heart in front of a roomful of people she barely knew? Of course she had longings to marry, to have a family. But talking about the date openly would only make the sting more severe if something went wrong.

Another young woman, recently heartbroken, listened in with a somber look on her face as she ordered a pound of chocolates. "What's the point?" she asked. "They're just going to break your heart anyway." With a sigh, she ordered an extra half pound—for the road.

In spite of the wildly assorted responses, Nori could hardly contain her excitement. It seemed like every few minutes, something—or someone—reminded her of that fact. She was going on a date with Blake, and she felt like a windup toy on its last turn, ready to whirl. And what a wonderful specimen Blake was. He seemed to embody almost everything she could hope for in a man.

Around noon, Zachary Martin arrived at the shop. Today, he appeared to be dressed in more normal attire. Well, normal for him. He still looked a bit on the geeky side, but his smile warmed her heart. Then again, everything seemed to warm her heart today.

Zachary surprised her with more conversation than usual. In fact, he started with something quite flattering. "You look nice today." Zachary's eyes sparkled with anticipation.

She glanced down at her apron, covered in powdered sugar. "Mmm. . . thanks."

"That's a really nice *floral* print." He pointed to her blouse.

Nori shrugged and thanked him, but she couldn't figure out why he would notice such an ordinary and rather faded blouse. She tried to turn her attention to other customers, but Zachary kept appearing at her side, asking questions, commenting on the decor of the shop, especially the flowers on the tables. What was up with this guy?

After the crowd thinned, Lizza approached with a gleam in her eye. "I have the perfect idea."

"What's that?"

"You need a shopping spree—to get ready for your big date."

"Oh no, I can't. I'm working. Besides"—Nori lowered her voice so that the customers couldn't hear—"we're just going out for coffee. It's not that big of a deal."

"Are you kidding? You should take full advantage of this. Go to the mall. Get a makeover." Lizza raised her hands like she was directing an orchestra. "Seize the moment!"

Nori rolled her eyes, trying not to get too worked up. What if Blake's real plan was to ask her to join a multilevel marketing venture, or something crazy like that? "Maybe he just needs a chubby friend who looks sympathetic," she said to Lizza. "One who looks like she has extra softness to help her friends absorb the blows of life. You know, like those yellow bumper guards on the freeway."

Lizza erupted in laughter. "You're hysterical. Do you know that? But you gotta stop putting yourself down."

As Nori shrugged, she couldn't help but notice Zachary's penetrating gaze. Was he listening in on their conversation?

"This is going to be the best date of your life," Lizza announced in a voice far too loud. "So get out of here. Go shopping."

Nori shook her head, grinning, and then pulled off her apron. Yes, she would go to the mall. For Blake Lawrence, she might even go to the moon.

~⌒~

After Nori left out the front door in a whirl of happiness, Zachary slumped down onto a chair in the shop. He slid another chocolate-covered coffee bean between his lips. He no longer nonchalantly tossed candy into his mouth, since he was apparently a wimpy kind of guy who easily choked on candy.

He moaned to himself. How could things have gone so wrong? Not only had Nori *not* taken his bait about the lilies, she apparently already had a date with another guy. Someone named Blake.

That name sounded like an iron kind of dude who heaved timbers with one arm behind his back and wrestled Brahma bulls just for fun. Zachary was certain he wasn't a guy who choked on girly mints. He could picture Blake now—tall, bronzed, with fitness-center biceps. The kind of man who made most women lose all their good sense.

After sitting for a moment or two longer, he quietly slipped out of his seat and made his way to the door. The jingling of the bell was the only indicator he'd moved on. But move on he must. If Nori had her sights set on someone else, it would be wrong to ask her out now. Wouldn't it?

As he walked back toward his office, Zachary spent some time in prayer. He gave the situation to the Lord, realizing how wrong it would be to pursue a relationship with Nori if the Lord hadn't ordained it.

By the time he reached the office, Zachary's heart was broken in two. How was it possible to lose something you'd never won in the first place?

With a deep sigh, he dropped into his chair, ready to push that question—and all thoughts of women—out of his mind.

Chapter 9

After slipping into a blue linen dress and giving herself yet another touch-up with her new makeup, Nori felt ready to share some serious caffeine with Blake Lawrence. At least she wouldn't embarrass him. She glanced in the hall mirror again. Not bad. The sapphire colors in the dress enhanced her hair and skin tones rather than washing her out, and her eye shadow, lipstick, and blush were actually in the right places—this time she hadn't colored outside the lines.

Dressed and more than ready for her date, Nori waited for Blake by the door. Twenty minutes later, she started fiddling with her purse—opening and shutting the clasp, checking her lipstick, popping a breath mint, and generally wilting like a pile of tissues left in the rain.

Maybe the invitation is a hoax. Maybe one of his friends had talked him into asking her out as a joke. But Blake's face had been so kind. He didn't look like a guy who would fail to show up for a date unless something terrible happened—like broken limbs or a plane crash or maybe an abscessed tooth.

Nori watched the second hand on the big clock on the end table. With each stroke, she felt as if her life was pouring out of her. She had no idea where her spirit was going, but she felt drained and suddenly old. A single tear rolled down Nori's cheek. She wiped the wetness away and rose from her chair to change her clothes.

Just as Nori made it to the bedroom, she heard the doorbell ring. Hoping Blake had finally come, she swung open the door and let it bang against the wall, which confirmed the fact that she was feeling a little too eager and way too upset.

Blake raked his fingers through his hair. "I'm really sorry for being late."

Nori nodded. "Sure." She knew he must have gotten held up with some-thing dreadfully important. "Is everything okay?"

"You'll never believe this." He tugged on his hair. "I was in the middle of a haircut, and this girl starts tossing and whacking my hair like she's making a salad."

Should I laugh or weep or console? Nori compromised with a grin.

Blake seemed satisfied. "I had to find another salon and get a *real* haircut. So. . .I mean. . .what do you think? Do I look ridiculous?"

Nori swatted at the butterfly of sarcasm that flitted through her head. She chewed on her lower lip to think of a *real* reply. *Was I almost stood up because of hair?* She found her vocal cords. "You look great. Would you like to come in for a minute?"

Blake relaxed into a smirk and ambled through the door. "Sometimes I have highlights done, but I thought I could get by this time."

"Oh?" She'd naively guessed his highlights were natural from being outdoors. Nori didn't want to imagine Blake sitting in the salon chair with tinfoil spikes coming out of his head. She winced, trying to shake the vision from her mind.

They sat down across from each other. For a moment neither one of them said anything, so Nori did a casual inspection of his attire. She had to admit Blake radiated splendor like the sun in his designer denims and tangerine shirt. In fact, she knew few men who could pull off that color with such panache.

"So, what are your thoughts?" Blake suddenly asked.

"My thoughts? Uhh. . ." Nori panicked, thinking she'd missed something.

"You know, should I have gotten the highlights this time?" Blake puckered his brow. "What do you really think?"

She sighed. *I think quantum physics is looking good.* "You made a wise decision to wait," she finally got herself to say. "No sense in overbleaching. It will ruin your hair." Her words just sort of evaporated along with her hopes of a promising evening.

Blake nodded as if she'd said something profound.

After more conversation about hair and grooming products and salons, they headed out to the coffee shop. A few minutes later, they were seated at a cozy table with two cups of steaming coffee.

Nori inhaled the aroma of homemade pastries and fresh coffee as she admired the homey room—tables trimmed in gingham and vases filled with roses. What an ideal place for a first date. She took a sip of her cinnamon latte.

Glancing around, she also noticed that women were staring at Blake. And not just a fleeting look or two. They gawked with big dreamy eyes like they were groupies and he was their rock star. She wondered what that felt like to be born so pretty that everyone couldn't stop looking and admiring. Perhaps people thought if they were close enough to someone beautiful, they would somehow be more beautiful. A validation thing. *Is that what I'm doing?*

Maybe she could still salvage the date with a change of subject. "So what do you do for a living?"

"Oh, I do all kinds of odd jobs. I've been a waiter and a tour guide and a salesman. I also do some modeling. It pays really well when I can get the gigs."

Nori took another slow slurp from her cup.

"But I feel kinda guilty getting all that money for just standing around." Blake fingered his cup. "You know, I've been thinking about the name of your candy shop, Sweet Nothings." He raised a provocative brow. "What does it mean?"

Nori felt her face heat up a little. "Well, sweet nothings are. . .you know, the things lovers whisper to each other. You've never heard that saying before?"

"Yeah, I have. I just wanted to hear what you'd say." Then Blake laughed. One of those big horsey laughs straight out of a cartoon.

Nori took in a deep breath, trying to focus on reality and get her eye to stop twitching. Then she took a paper napkin and dabbed at the perspiration on her forehead.

"Are you okay?" He gave her a curious stare. " 'Cause sometimes you look like you're in pain."

"I'm fine. Really."

Blake grinned. "Good deal."

Nori thought she might as well ask the ultimate question. "I was just curious. . . . I always love to know what a person's favorite candy is."

Blake picked up a saltshaker and rolled it around in his hand. "Mmm. Heavy question." He shook his finger. "Oh, I get it. You're trying to figure out what kind of guy I am from the candy I eat. Right?"

"Yeah." She guessed he'd buy some kind of gelatinous candy. Maybe something in the family of gooey animal-shaped treats.

Blake brightened. "Well, I like those little gummy candies that are in different shapes and colors."

Nori almost choked on her latte.

"You okay?"

She nodded.

"The blue-and-white sharks are my favorite." His brawny shoulders went up in a shrug; then he puckered his brow. "I'll bet that sounds pretty stupid."

Nori decided to take the high road. "Well, it can make you come off like you're not afraid to be childlike. You're man enough to be whimsical, and—"

"Yeah, that's it." He pointed in the air. "That word you just said. That's what I am."

"Uh-huh." Nori took an extended swig of her brew as her gaze drifted over to the second hand on the wall clock, which appeared to be moving with agonizing slowness. *And they say time doesn't stand still.*

Blake took a tentative sip of his vanilla cappuccino. "Owee, that's still pretty hot." He pointed to his lips. "Gotta be careful not to burn these babies. One time, I nicked up my chin helping my mom with some yard work, and I lost a modeling gig." He moved his cup out of the way and leaned toward her. "So, missy, what do you think is the best candy of all time? I mean, you can choose the best. Right?"

Nori straightened up and took in a deep breath. With some effort, maybe she could give the evening one more try. "Well, I do have one favorite candy that is quite exceptional and rather pricey. It's—"

"You know, most of the girls I've dated are way too skinny and kinda blank. But you're different."

"Blank?"

Blake reached over to Nori and moved a strand of hair from her cheek. "You're smart. I mean, you'd have to be pretty intelligent to own a business."

"Thanks." Nori powered up for a smile. She wanted to say, "Yeah, us chubbies have all that extra fat to fuel our brains," but instead she replied, "By the way, thank you for the flowers."

Blake leaned in. "Now this is a time for you to see what an honest guy I am."

"Why is that?"

"Well, it sure would be easy for me to take credit, but. . .I can't." Blake grinned.

"Really?" Nori tapped her fingers on her cup. "So, you didn't have lilies delivered to my apartment?"

"No." Blake laughed. "I would *never* send lilies to a woman. They stink."

❧

The rest of the evening didn't improve. In fact, Nori found herself glancing around and squelching a yawn.

She liked Blake. He was a kind man but also a simple man, and perhaps a bit too self-absorbed. Nori thought she must be out of her mind for such thoughts, since she had no right to be choosy. At all. And Blake was as handsome as any man could get. And yet, no matter how hard she tried, she couldn't force an attraction anymore than she could change the direction of the wind.

Later, after what seemed like a long journey home, Blake stood at Nori's front door. He leaned on the door-frame and gave her a heavy-lidded look like she'd seen in the movies. Dead giveaway. He was going to give her a good night kiss. What should she do?

"I'm not sure if I mentioned it before, but I think you look nice this evening. Very nice," Blake added, his voice going down a couple of octaves.

"Thank you." Nori reached in her purse for her keys. "And thanks for the coffee. It was good."

"Yes, it was. It was all so good." Then Blake went quiet.

Nori held her breath, wondering if a kiss might put a better glow on the evening. Perhaps Blake just wanted to say thank-you for her pleasant company.

Or maybe he would just kiss her on the forehead like a small child.

The waiting and pondering was over the moment Blake leaned down and placed his lips over hers.

Nori closed her eyes, praying her first real kiss would be apart from all other sensations and feelings. Would it send her flying off into space? Indeed, the kiss was warm and not altogether unpleasant, but something was missing. In fact, as the kiss intensified, the stirrings became. . .what? Comical? Instead of soaring into space, she rose only a few feet off the ground—in a toy rocket. The plastic kind that fizzles and plummets to the earth. *Cut it out, Nori. This is difficult enough.*

They both pulled away at the same time and then stared at each other. Another awkward moment came hovering over them. Then, at the same instant, they both burst out laughing.

"Tell me what you're thinking." Blake touched her sleeve.

Nori covered her mouth. "I can't."

"Yes, you can. I think we're both thinking the same thing."

She circled her hands around her middle. "But it might hurt your feelings."

"You mean worse than when you laughed after our kiss." Blake chuckled.

"But you laughed, too. . .even harder." Nori's face heated in embarrassment. "But I'm sorry if it hurt your feelings. I really—"

"Come on, you're stalling. Just say what you want to say. I'll try to be man enough to take it."

Nori touched Blake's arm. "It's like. . .well. . .like we're just friends or family."

"I noticed it, too. But I think it's a good thing. You see, I'm an only child, and I've always needed a sibling." Blake covered her hand with his and knelt down. "Nori Kelly, would you be my sister?"

Nori laughed. "I would be happy to be your sister."

After they chatted for a moment or two longer and he'd given her a brotherly hug, they parted for the evening.

Before Nori shut the door, she saw someone back away into the shadows. Someone had seen Blake kissing her. And that someone looked like Zachary. Likely, he was walking to his apartment from the other direction, saw them, and didn't want to interrupt a private moment. Or maybe they'd embarrassed Zachary, and he'd taken off. Regardless, the whole thing felt awkward, especially in light of the way the date had turned out.

Nori locked the dead bolt and sank into a chair. "Well, I'm still princess of the friendship date." She looked upward past the ceiling. *Lord, why do I have such an intense desire to marry and have a family? If You put this need in me, then please fulfill it or give me the patience to wait for it. But if this dream would cause me a grief*

I cannot comprehend, then please take this desire away. I'm getting so weary of it.

And then revelation came to Nori—Zachary had sent the flowers. It all made sense now. He had been trying to drop hints at the candy shop—all those references to the floral print in her blouse and the flowers on the tables.

Hmm. Zachary Martin. Maybe, in spite of his clumsy efforts, Zachary was really trying to romance her. But why? He'd never even asked her out. Mysteries were abundant, and they all seemed to be taking up residence in her ordinary life.

❧

Zachary slumped on his couch—a couch which sat next to Nori's wall. He knew he was torturing himself, sitting there with the hope of being nearer to her, but he felt like a good wallow in misery was in order.

The facts felt devastating, since he'd witnessed Nori kissing another man. Must be that Blake fellow. And sadly, he was as good-looking as Zachary had predicted him to be. He wondered how long they'd been dating. Were they in love? Were all Zachary's chances to win Nori gone?

He looked at the receipt for the flowers and crumpled it. To say he felt let down was such an understatement. He was so disappointed, in fact, that he tossed his copy of *Courtship for Idiots* out the window. Well, not exactly out of the window. That would be littering. He stuck the book behind the curtain, hoping it would gather dust and eventually disintegrate into subatomic particles.

And yet, he couldn't blame anyone or anything. What claim did he have on Nori? None at all. And hadn't he prayed about all of this, giving it over to the Lord?

Maybe what he needed was time to get his thoughts together, to come up with another workable plan. Tomorrow morning he would do just that.

Chapter 10

The next morning in the clear light of a new day, Zachary decided his "workable plans" hadn't been too impressive or effective. Maybe what he'd been missing was some fresh air and a chat with God.

He snatched up his car keys and drove to one of his favorite hiking places. After parking his car and zipping up his jacket, he started the mile-long walk to the Mountain Tower. Zachary saw no tourists, so he prayed out loud as he hiked up the paved road.

"Lord, maybe I'm getting ahead of You, trying to force a relationship with Nori that's outside Your leading. You know how much I love her, and yet I know any relationship outside of Your will would only be a distraction."

Regrettably, in spite of his best intentions, Zachary found himself side-tracked rather quickly. His thoughts kept shifting to Nori's date. No matter how Blake appeared on the outside, he didn't really think he was Nori's type. And that ridiculous laugh of his. How could Nori stand it?

He slowed his pace and reality hit. "Why am I always trying to manipulate what I can't control? It's like I'm always trying to convince God what's best." Zachary surrendered himself to the peaceful solitude of the moment and to what God might have to say to him. *Yes, to get ahead of God would only complicate things.* If there was to be a relationship with Nori, it would have to be in the Lord's timing.

He picked up a rock and studied it. *Sandstone. Pretty typical for the Ouachita Mountains.* Probably from an ancient beach or river. He pressed the stone inside his hand, letting his palm and fingers mold around its solid mass.

His thoughts turned to the recent hours he'd spent in the Word of God, thumbing through the pages, looking for the Lord's take on love. "That's the kind of love I want," he said, "one rooted in faith." And so, as he walked, he committed himself once again to a deeper relationship with the Lord.

As Zachary continued hiking up the hill, he realized that even though the spiritual side was the most important part of his life, he also had a few things he could work on in the natural. Maybe it was time to focus a little more on his appearance. He'd gotten sloppy over the past few years. In fact, he'd almost given up on himself. But no more. Some simple changes along with a little discipline would put the wheels in motion. Wasn't that how he handled things at work, after all?

He finished his hike and looked up at the tower, which promised an amazing view of the town as well as the woods and lakes and hills he'd grown to love. Suddenly, a squirrel caught his attention as it scampered up high in a tree. The branches above him had already budded out, which lit the woods with a pale green luster. A cardinal, stark against the blooming dogwood, rested for a moment and then fluttered away, deep into the forest.

Zachary breathed in. The crisp breeze gave courage to his plan. "First, I will lay low and give Nori some space." Peace settled around him as he spoke. "Secondly, while I'm busy lying low, I'll make some necessary enhancements without making myself into a fool. If and when the time comes. . .Nori deserves the very best."

As the days passed, Zachary was good to his word. He dealt with the basics. He got a new haircut—nothing spiky or too trendy. He made a habit of wearing only pressed shirts and pants without white socks, and he was fitted for some contact lenses. The red indentations on his nose, which were made from wearing his glasses, began to fade. At times he barely recognized himself.

Next, he decided he should expand his mind. He should go to Simon's Book Shoppe and buy something inspiring or literary or romantic. Or all of the above. He would be able to understand Nori better if he could get inside the head of a woman.

One evening after dinner, Zachary locked up and made his way down the hallway to the elevator. He heard Nori coming out of her apartment and turned back to her. "Hello."

"Hi." She smiled at him.

A nice smile. Not the usual obligatory grin, but an expression that appeared genuine and inviting. Should he make a move now? No. He wouldn't get ahead of God. He would wait. Zachary reminded himself that "lying low" were his watchwords. *But she's never smiled at me like that before. Ever.* Yes, he should do it now. Or maybe not. He stood in front of the elevator in a fit of indecision. He waited for Nori to catch up to him before he pushed the button. "Uh, Nori?"

"Yes?"

Oh brother. Now he was committed to talking. Should he thank her again for saving his life? "I'm going to Simon's Book Shoppe."

"You are? Sounds good. I like that store."

Nori certainly is friendly. That was new. Maybe now *was* the time. "You want to come along?"

"I'd like to, but I've got this meeting to attend. It's with some of the small-business owners." Nori licked her lips. "But maybe another time. Okay?"

He nodded. "Absolutely."

The elevator doors opened, and they rode down together.

Zachary stood next to Nori, basking in the glow of her sweet smile.

Moments later, at Simon's Book Shoppe, Zachary stood perusing shelves and shelves of novels. He picked out a historical romance, paid for it, and then settled himself in one of the cushy chairs.

Soft classical music ebbed and flowed around him, providing a pleasant ambience for reading his book. As he looked over the dedication, which was a tribute of devotion from the author to his beloved wife, Zachary recalled something from Proverbs he'd recently read: *"Let love and faithfulness never leave you; bind them around your neck, write them on the tablet of your heart."* Had he been loving and faithful in all things, not just in his feelings for Nori? He wasn't sure, but he hoped so.

Thoughts of Nori made him think of Song of Solomon. A brief passage came to mind. . . . *"Your hair is like royal tapestry; the king is held captive by its tresses. How beautiful you are and how pleasing, O love, with your delights!"* Ah yes. Nori was indeed delightful in every way. He sighed as he stared at the book title in front of him, *Fields of Amber Light.* He read the opening lines:

> *I always knew I would love her. She had a smile one could never forget: soft, welcoming, transcendent. She was the winsome creature of my child-hood, and now to know her love in return was unfathomable joy. I know, as I have always known, that our love will warm the earth. It will sustain the stars. It will summon the songs of angels.*

The words moved him, making him wish he could be creative and expressive. Perhaps that was what poetry and novels were for—to articulate the feelings of a common man like himself. He pondered the words "winsome creature" and "unfathomable joy" and thought the author did very well in mirroring the fervent prose of the love verses in the Bible. *Beautiful.*

Zachary heard someone walking toward him, so he glanced up.

Nori stood in front of him wearing a pale green dress and a smile that rivaled the sun.

"You changed your mind?" he heard himself murmur.

She crossed her arms. "I decided I didn't want to waste my life sitting in meetings."

Zachary tried to keep his cool as Nori sat down next to him. "You look different. In a good kind of way."

"Thanks." Nori folded her hands in her lap, looking suddenly shy.

"And you have makeup on." He tried to enjoy her beauty without gaping.

"I just hope I didn't go overboard with the blush and lip gloss."

"You're absolutely radiant. . .like Sirius." *Oh boy. Talk about going overboard.* He meant the praise, but he knew men just didn't blurt out things like that.

She leaned her elbow on the chair and looked at him. "And what is Sirius?"

"The brightest star in the sky."

Nori looked down at her hands. "Thank you, Zachary. I think that's the finest compliment anyone has ever given me."

"You're welcome." He thought their banter was going better than expected. He couldn't help but wonder about Blake. Perhaps her date with him hadn't worked out.

She looked down at his book. "What are you reading?"

He held up the novel. "*Fields of Amber Light.*"

"What kind of book is it?"

Zachary cleared his throat. "It's sort of a historical literary. . .romance."

"I haven't read that many romance novels."

"Really?" Zachary set the book down on the arm of the chair. "But I thought women read them all the time."

Nori looked at the cover again. "It looks fascinating."

"Well, this is my first." Zachary felt his underarms start to sweat. "Do you want to hear some of it?"

She nodded. "I do."

"Okay." Zachary almost forgot where he was. In fact, as he got caught up in the romantic moment and gazed into her eyes, he almost forgot *who* he was.

He gathered his senses and opened the novel somewhere close to the front. He cleared his throat and began reading:

We first met in a field of clover, found by the sun and lit with gold. She and I escaped our dins of clamor to partake of those amber lights. Bees took to the air while we laughed about all things that gave us delight and all things that made us humble. When the amber lights had faded and the bees had made their honey, we returned to our worlds, lost in heart but found in love.

Zachary looked at Nori.

Nori clasped her hands over her heart. "That was delightful to hear out loud."

"Yes, it was." Zachary realized his eyes had filled with mist. His face went hot as he sniffled a bit. To Nori's credit, she didn't laugh at him. "Some of the fantasy novels I've read are written in this literary technique. A poetic style sort of gets to the heart of things in a roundabout way, and then when you least expect it, the meaning sort of steals your heart." *Did I actually say that? Am I still alive and breathing? Thank You, God.*

"That's true. And beautifully said." Nori shook her head. "I've been so busy running my business, I haven't taken enough time to read. I've missed a lot. And I'm embarrassed to say, I've even skipped my devotion time with the Lord." She sighed. "Well, my excuses are weak, but my determination in returning to it is sincere."

Zachary felt fresh out of words. He panicked a bit.

"So, you said you read fantasy novels?"

"I read science fiction and computer manuals." Well, that came off as exciting as a disposal full of sludge.

Nori touched Zachary's arm. "By the way, thank you for the flowers. They were. . .well, *pretty* to look at."

He looked at Nori's hand, the one that still touched his arm. Zachary hoped she wouldn't notice his erratic breathing. "Uhh. . .you're welcome." Things were going so well between them, he thought maybe he was dreaming. "But I'll bet you like roses better."

She pulled away. "Why do you say that?"

"I don't know. I think because you have so many pictures of roses all around your candy store."

"Oh, you noticed. I do like roses. Especially bridal pink."

"Trust me. I *will* remember that."

Nori raised an eyebrow. "I'm sure you will."

She's flirting with me. Zachary leaned forward in his chair, now feeling euphoric. What were the chances of Nori sitting with him tonight, talking about her favorite kind of roses? It all seemed impossible.

Nori's cell phone came to life. She looked at the caller and then at him. "It's my mother. I'd better get it."

Zachary nodded for her to take the call.

⌒⌒⌒

Nori wondered what could be wrong. *Mom rarely calls me.* "Hi. What a surprise. How are you?" She remained silent, absorbing her mother's news, which became graver by the second. "But I don't understand. Why would either of you do something like that?" She clutched at her heart. "Why can't we talk about this now? Okay. All right." Nori tried to calm her breathing. "I'll call you later tonight." She closed her phone and let out a long puff of air.

"What is it?" Zachary asked.

"My parents." Nori's arms went limp as her eyes filled with tears. "They're getting a divorce."

Chapter 11

M y mom and dad. . .they had a good marriage." Nori latched onto the armchair and squeezed until her fingers ached. "In fact, they'd gone to Paris to celebrate another wedding anniversary. They just got home." She felt her stomach go woozy. *Stay calm. You're not going to throw up in a bookstore.*

Zachary shook his head. "I'm so sorry."

Nori nodded and then plummeted back into her fears. Her parents had always loved each other. Hadn't they? "I don't understand. I thought they were having a wonderful vacation." Tears ran down her cheek. "What could have gone wrong?" She wasn't used to showing so much emotion in public, but somehow decorum didn't matter to her right now.

Zachary reached out to her.

Nori noticed his hands shaking. *Why would he be so affected?*

"I wish I could do something for you." Zachary blushed and pulled away.

"I do, too." Nori rested her head in her hands. How could this be? Even when most of the people around her were cutting themselves into bits on the sharp edges of divorce, she had always consoled herself with the idea that one couple would always remain steady. One couple, by the grace of God, would stay intact—her parents. "My mother and father didn't have the perfect marriage, but I'd held them up as an example of real commitment. I'd put my trust in them." Nori turned to him. "When so many good marriages in America die, what hope do people have in love?"

Zachary looked stunned with the question. "I think there's still hope. There's *always* hope."

Nori stared at her hands, which were now trembling. "Are your parents still married?"

He lowered his gaze. "No."

Something inside of Nori shifted—something that moved her toward a helpless anguish. More tears came. They were real, and they weren't going away anytime soon. She dabbed the wetness away with the sleeve of her dress. Several book browsers drifted by, but she didn't care who saw her.

Zachary pulled a handkerchief out of his pocket and handed it to her. "Do you want to go over to the coffee shop? We could talk about it." He leaned toward her, worry covering his face.

Nori blew her nose. "No, but thanks. I'm not sure talking will do any good. My mom sounded determined."

"Maybe you could discuss this with your parents," Zachary said. "And pray they change their minds."

"I *will* pray, but my parents have this thing called free will." Nori shook her head. "I really need time to think. Time alone." She rose from her chair and picked up her purse. "I'm going home."

Zachary stood up next to her. "You shouldn't drive when you're this upset. It isn't safe. Why don't you—"

"I'll be fine. Well, at least my drive will be."

Zachary stuffed his hands into his pockets, looking bewildered.

"Well, then"—Nori touched his sleeve—"good-bye." She looked at him one more time and then walked out into the night.

She drove home as the shock of her mother's news seeped deeply into her spirit like a slow-acting poison. How could something like that happen? Was no marriage secure? Did love and commitment mean nothing anymore?

Nori shut her apartment door and trudged into the kitchen, her feet feeling as though they were dragging ten-pound weights. She took the tinfoil off a deep-dish cherry pie and dug into it with a big serving spoon. The bite was gooey sweet, but it did nothing to ease her pain.

Even when her life had been fraught with loneliness, she'd always managed by keeping herself busy with work. But this? Now another piece of her life was whirling out of control. She could always petition the Almighty, but even He couldn't force her parents to stop the divorce proceedings.

She clutched at her dress, twisting the material into knots and feeling abandoned and scared. Did her parents have a terrible fight? Had they fallen out of love? Maybe one of them was having a mid-life crisis or an affair. Her endless questions brought no answers.

Nori felt the walls of her sanctuary, solid and sure, collapse around her. Even as a little girl she'd always gathered her dolls together for weddings, all in the hopes of recreating the marital joy she thought she'd seen in her parents' eyes. Had she imagined their love for each other? Or had they only been pretending?

She dug into the pie again with her spoon and brought another large chunk of the pastry to her mouth. *What does it matter if I try to lose weight to catch the attention of the opposite sex?* Nori shoveled a few more bites of cherry pie in her mouth until her cheeks were packed with pastry. Cherry juice dribbled down her chin. She wiped it off on the sleeve of her dress.

Disgusted with herself, she dropped the spoon on the table, promising herself to get in shape for her own health and benefit. Nothing more. She shoved the pie to the other side of the table but pushed too hard. The pie dish landed on the ceramic tile floor, crashing and making a crimson splatter of glass and berries.

She just stared at the mess. Soon tears gave way to heaving sobs as she lowered her head to the kitchen table. *What I'd always feared is true—love really isn't enough. Please, God, You are more than welcome to jump in here and intervene. Anytime, Lord. I know You're here with me. I have believed that ever since I came to know You when I was a girl. But right now, I don't feel Your presence. I feel frantic with all this news. Please, Lord, take these troubles away. I don't think I can handle them.*

Finally, when her tears slowed and her despair eased a bit, Nori raised her head from the table. She glanced at a greeting card she'd stuck on her fridge. A frog with bulbous eyes stared at her from the front of the card. The comical amphibian was Lizza's reminder that she might have to kiss a pond full of frogs to find her prince. She released a gloomy chuckle. "Well, Lizza, I'm no longer interested in frogs or princes."

Nori picked up the phone and tried calling her parents, but no one answered. Just as she pushed in the numbers again, a knock interrupted her. She dragged herself to the front door but wasn't sure if she'd answer it.

Zachary stood on the other side of the door with a lost puppy expression that would normally make her feel guilty. But now she felt nothing. She stood there, waiting for him to go, but he didn't move. *Maybe I should at least open the door.* He was no longer a prospective date, but he was still a fellow human being.

Nori decided not to check her eyes, even though she thought they must be red and bloated and festooned with black rings of mascara. Didn't matter to her, so she just opened the door.

"Hi." Zachary had a casual pose, but he appeared uneasy.

"What's up?"

A look of pain crossed his face. "You know, when my parents told me they were getting a divorce, I got pretty messed up," he said. "I held everything in, and that was pretty dangerous. I was like this walking time bomb ready to detonate at any moment." His eyes got big, and his fingers contorted into claws.

Nori was on the verge of a smile but wasn't about to give in so easily. "I know you want to come in and listen to my story and then give me advice. I appreciate that. I really do. But I don't know the story. They won't tell me any details. I think they're afraid I'll try to talk them out of it."

Zachary lowered his gaze as if he was praying, and then he looked up with more confidence. "I have this thing I do."

Nori groaned inside. *What can he mean now?* She just wanted to go lie down and sleep for maybe a month or two. "What is it?"

"Well, I have this ritual. . .for when I get upset about something. Or I'm disappointed. I have these ingredients that come together to make a pretty impressive cup of cocoa. I know it's maybe a little simplistic. But there's something about cocoa. . .that's settling. If you come over, I'll make you some."

Nori swallowed, her throat making a funny squeaking sound. How could he have known that cocoa was her favorite beverage of all time? Good for comfort, reflection, and camaraderie. But as always, Zachary's timing could not have been more haywire. "I don't know. . ."

"You won't regret it. And I promise I won't pressure you to talk about. . .you know. Anyway, I'll let you just drink the cocoa in peace and go home."

Oh well, what did she have to lose? Her only plans were to cry her heart out until she fell asleep from exhaustion. Homemade cocoa sounded like at least a temporary reprieve. "Maybe just for a few minutes."

Zachary's face lit up.

She already regretted her decision. "I should clean up my face."

"You don't need to. You look beautiful."

Oh come on. Nori wanted to roll her eyes but didn't. But she ignored the cleanup after all and followed Zachary to his apartment.

Ivan Wentworth, a bachelor she'd been curious about for months, locked up his apartment and strode toward them. "Hello."

Nori didn't turn away, even though she knew she looked like something approaching ghastly. "Hi."

Ivan stared at Nori for a moment as he passed by, his face flashing with horror as if he'd seen the headless horseman. Then Ivan hurried down the hallway.

In regular times, such an incident would have bothered Nori. First of all because of her hideous appearance, but secondly, because everyone on the floor of their apartment, especially the gossips, would soon say that she and Zachary were dating. And that they'd been arguing, since her eyes were all puffy and red. But why should she care? Why would it matter now? She had no interest in Ivan or Zachary or anyone.

Nori walked through Zachary's living room and looked around. Impressive. He didn't have a lot of decorating skills, but she was startled at all the expensive furnishings. Maybe Lizza had been right—perhaps geeks *did* rule the world. "You have a nice apartment."

"Thank you." Zachary blushed at her compliment. "Why don't we go into the kitchen? That is, you know, if you want to. Would you like to?"

Come on, Zachary, don't start up with the nervous routine again. It's a waste of your valuable time. I'm not going to marry you, so let's just settle down and maybe we can be friends. "Sure. The kitchen sounds fine."

"The kitchen is the best part of any abode."

"What do you mean?" Nori wasn't sure if she was up to hearing all his comments on kitchens.

"I guess when I was growing up, anything good that was happening was always in the kitchen. You know, baking, eating, talking. . .science projects." Zachary smiled at Nori as he led her into the kitchen. "You can have a seat right here while I make your cocoa." He pulled out a chair for her as if he were a nobleman and she were his lady.

Nori sat down and waited. She glanced around his kitchen. It looked somewhat empty, and yet there were personal touches here and there. Things that didn't look at all that kitchen-y but items that must have meant something to him—a framed poster of some of the characters from the original *Star Trek* shows, shelves and shelves of books, an old-fashioned telephone dismantled and set out in pieces on the counter, and to her surprise, a notable array of copper pots and pans. Even a cast-iron skillet.

"So how do you make your cocoa?" She hoped hearing Zachary chat about her favorite beverage might rest her mind.

He got out all his ingredients and set them in perfect order along the counter. "I start with dark organic cocoa. I use whole milk, raw sugar, vanilla, and then I top it with a little marshmallow cream."

Nori nodded. "Sounds good." She watched him as he puttered around the kitchen. He set out napkins and spoons on the placemats. His shoulders relaxed and that cringing expression that sometimes crossed his face had melted away. She realized he seemed different in his own home. Nori let her body relax as well. Maybe Zachary could be another friend like Blake.

When Zachary had finished his stirring and pouring, he set a steaming mug down in front of her.

She waited for him to sit down, and then she blew on the drink and took a tentative sip. Rich, dark creamy goodness rolled down her throat. Satisfying and even better than her cocoa. "It's good. And the marshmallow cream is perfect on top."

Zachary didn't try his drink but seemed to focus all his attention on Nori's reaction. "I'm glad you like it." His whole face lit up as he placed the jar of marshmallow cream in front of her. "Please, take it with you."

"Thanks." He looked pretty close to handsome when he smiled like that. Nori took another sip. The beverage was like drowning in decadence. It didn't take away the pain of the day, but it did soften the moment. Here she was, finally with a man who not only loved cocoa but who fixed her a gourmet cup. It was almost a shame to fritter away such kindness and generosity. But what could she do? Her faith in matrimony would need a great deal of nurturing. And she had no idea how many years of encouragement it would take before she could walk down that aisle.

"So, later, would you like to watch a movie?" Zachary fingered his mug, which was unexpectedly painted with monster trucks.

She could tell Zachary was trying to be nonchalant, but that flinching nervousness had come back. He seemed to be forever preparing himself for a blow like a dog that had been kicked one too many times. She looked into his eyes as he sipped his cocoa, and she saw something she hadn't noticed before. Not love, perhaps, but something serious, and something she was no longer ready to pursue. To keep from hurting him in the end, she would need to be candid. Friends, just friends. That's all she could give him.

"Zachary?"

"Yes?" His face filled with eagerness and affection.

Nori's heart ached for Zachary, since she didn't want to give him even more cause to cringe at life. But what else could she do? "I want to be honest with you." She cleared her throat. "I'm hoping we can just be. . .friends. Okay?"

Chapter 12

Zachary lowered his gaze. When he raised his head, his expression had changed from anticipation to distress. "I understand."

A pang of guilt seized Nori. Since she, too, had known rejection over the years, it was hard not to feel his disappointment. "It's just that after today's news, dating just doesn't look as good to me as it did when I first got up this morning." She covered his hand with hers. "But then maybe you were just being a good neighbor by offering me the cocoa. Maybe I'm making too much of this." She noticed how warm and sturdy Zachary's hands were. Good hands, capable of kind deeds.

"My invitation was more than just being a good neighbor." Zachary stared at her hand.

"Thank you for your honesty." Nori knew how hard those words must have been for him to say, particularly since she hadn't returned his affection.

"When my parents got their divorce about ten years ago, I felt the same way you do now. But things changed in my mind. As time went on, the need for companionship eventually outweighed the fear of repeating my parents' mistakes." Zachary let out a breath of air like he was glad to have gotten those words out of his system.

"Yes, I can appreciate your experience, but I'm not sure when I'm going to feel like that. I've had quite a shock. And I need to work things through. It would help so much to talk to my parents. . .to understand what happened."

Zachary took a sip of his drink. "This must be very hard for you."

"It is."

He rose from his chair. "Do you want more cocoa?"

"No, but thank you. It was the best I've ever had."

He grinned at that.

Nori pushed her mug away from the edge of the table and then gave it a few more inches for good measure. Then she moved it again but wasn't sure why.

"That might get worse." Zachary looked amazed as his own comment.

"What will get worse?"

He sucked in some air and looked all around like he was frantic to change the subject. "Oh well, I was just mumbling."

Nori massaged the back of her neck. "But I want to know what you meant."

"Your compulsive disorder. It can get worse with stress, but you'll get through it. I promise." Zachary looked even more worried with his words. "I have the same problem, but we don't have to be embarrassed about it. Since we're going to be friends, I think it would be okay for us to talk about it."

Nori wasn't sure whether to be upset or inquisitive. "How did you know I have that. . .problem?"

Zachary reddened. "Well, we both leave for work about the same time each morning. I can hear you locking your door and then coming back to check it. And then talking to yourself about locking it."

Feeling suddenly vulnerable, Nori hugged herself around the middle. "Well, lots of people do that."

"Yes, but not every day. . .unless. . ." His voice died away.

"What else can you hear in my apartment?" Nori tugged on her earring, trying to appear calm.

"Not much. A little music once in a while. You like jazz, I think. And some folk music."

"I do," Nori said. "I like that new artist in Little Rock. . .Hudson Mandel. He plays at the Silver Moon Café there." Nori thought changing the topic might be easier on her already tense emotions. "I heard him about a year ago when I was in Little Rock. Have you heard him?"

Zachary shook his head. "No. Haven't had the pleasure."

After a moment of silence and a few seconds to rethink her change of subject, Nori thought maybe discussing their disorder might be a relief instead of a strain. They were, as he just affirmed, friends who should be able to talk without censor. "So, you've got obsessive-compulsive disorder, too?"

Zachary nodded.

"Do you know how you got it? The OCD?" It was hard for Nori not to be curious. She'd never known anyone else with the disorder.

Zachary took in a lungful of air. "I can't remember one defining moment when I suddenly had OCD. The problem came on gradually. My guess is that it came on from a buildup of a lot of little things." He tensed his fingers around his mug until his knuckles were white.

"I see." In spite of her own problems, Nori found herself concerned about his life. Instead of asking him more specific questions, she decided just to wait and listen.

Zachary cleared his throat. "I think people get the idea that if they're careful enough about everything no one can hurt them. But that's ridiculous." He looked at her. "The only way not to be hurt in this life is to be dead."

Nori chuckled and then felt her face get hot. "Oh, I'm sorry I laughed. That wasn't funny. It just surprised me to hear you put it that way." She hoped her new stance on dating hadn't worsened his problem.

"But I've kept my problem under control well enough that I've never needed medicine or therapy. What about you?"

"What do you mean?" Nori asked.

"Your compulsive behavior? Do you know when it started?"

"Oh, well, I've never known for sure. The first time I noticed the problem was in grade school. I'd forgotten to take my homework to school, and I freaked out about it. I wanted to impress the teachers, and getting a zero on my homework was more than my little heart could take. Anyway, after that, I started checking my backpack. Then I'd wonder later if I'd *really* looked, so then I'd say out loud, 'I have my homework in the bag.' That sort of thing. You probably know what I mean." The memory made Nori flinch as she recalled the misery of always checking things.

Zachary nodded. "Yeah, I know exactly what you mean."

"And then this pattern of behavior started seeping into other areas of my life. But it's kind of like yours. I can dismiss it often enough that it hasn't been a great hindrance. Just a little pesky at times." She attempted a weak smile.

Zachary made no gestures of disgust or surprise. He just seemed to be listening. That part felt really good to Nori.

"I guess I should be going." She rose.

"Okay."

Nori waited for Zachary to protest, but he didn't. She appreciated the fact that he'd kept his promise not to pressure her into staying longer than she wanted to. *Good man.*

As she made her way out of the kitchen and through the living room, she happened to see herself in a mirror. She stopped cold. Raccoon smudges of mascara circled her eyes, and spikes of hair shot up around her face like palm fronds in a hurricane. And her dress was still soiled with cherry juice. "I look terrible. Why didn't you say something?"

Zachary looked puzzled at her comment. "Because you don't look terrible. In fact, you look wonderful."

Well, he's either blind or lying. Or maybe he was just being kind. "Thanks for the cocoa."

As Zachary walked Nori to the front door, she felt her heart beat out of rhythm. It pounded hard and then skipped some beats. She placed her hand over her chest.

"Are you okay?" Zachary asked.

"My heart. I feel funny."

"Here, rest over here." Zachary led her to the couch, and she sat down. "Do you need for me to call 911?"

Nori shook her head. "No, I just need to rest for a minute." She stretched out on the couch, hoping the odd sensations would pass. "I'm sorry to be so much trouble."

Zachary knelt beside her. "It's no trouble at all." Without faltering, he took hold of her hand and squeezed.

A tingle, unexpected and warm, trickled through her. In spite of herself, she squeezed back. Then she noticed it—Zachary no longer looked downward but gazed straight into her eyes. And those eyes. . .they were the same color of the chocolate-covered coffee beans he loved so much.

He released her hand and sat on the chair next to her. "Maybe it was the stress of the day. Some sleep would do you good."

Nori studied Zachary's face. He seemed more confident than usual. She liked it. It felt safe somehow. "Yes, sleep. I need to go home. I should be home." Even as she said those words, she could feel herself getting uncontrollably drowsy. Her mind continued to float until her eyelids became heavy. Soon she was overcome with sleepy thoughts and pleasant things, so she followed them. Maybe she'd let herself doze off for just a moment. . . .

Zachary watched Nori as she drifted off, thinking how lovely and peaceful she looked. But he wondered what he should do. Let her sleep until morning? Wake her up in an hour so she could go home? He had no idea.

He thought of Nori's comment about being no more than friends. The idea pierced him through, and yet she had indeed sustained quite a blow with her parents' sudden plans for divorce. But would she ever change her mind? Perhaps Nori would never love him. In spite of the opposing arguments, he would be a dependable friend to her. No matter what.

He picked up *Fields of Amber Light*, which he'd been reading in short intervals, and started where he'd left off:

> *The wait became a desolate winter. I loved her, and I could no longer live without her gaze, her hand brushing my cheek, or the pledge my heart ached to give her. How would I endure these cold days of March, these days of never-ending sorrow?*

After a few more minutes of reading, Zachary closed the book again. The words seemed too close. Too real. The only way he could handle the story was to read it in small increments, though he couldn't help but hope the author had written a happy ending.

Zachary gazed over at Nori. Her breathing intensified to a light snore. He grinned. She was so close to him just now, and yet soon she'd rise and leave. *And she might never come back.* He admonished himself, thinking how unwise it might have been to tell her about his OCD. Would the admission make him look more human or wimpy? Probably the latter. He didn't know women well enough to know what pleased or repelled them. And yet, if they were friends, true friends, couldn't they discuss anything?

Nori stretched her head back. "Please, no," she said in her sleep. "Why?"

She's having a nightmare. Zachary touched the sleeve of her dress. "Nori?"

"What?" She roused, looking around. "Where am I?" Her brows furrowed.

"You're in my apartment." Zachary wanted to take her into his arms and comfort her, but knowing how unwelcome that would be, he just waited by her side.

Nori glanced at him. "I guess I was pretty tired. Sorry."

"There's no reason to apologize."

"Was I talking in my sleep?" She sat up.

"Yes."

Nori rubbed her neck and smiled. "Did I reveal any dark secrets?"

"You were having a nightmare." Zachary leaned toward her.

"I guess I was—about my parents." Nori looked at him. "Thank you for being so kind to me, Zachary Martin." She took his hand and gave it a squeeze.

If there were such a thing as a body blush, Zachary thought he just might have had one. He never knew when Nori was suddenly going to render him speechless.

She released his hand and looked at his book. "I do love that title. *Fields of Amber Light.* How is it?"

"Good."

"Would you read a few lines out loud? It's like candy for the mind. . .with no calories."

Zachary chuckled. He let the novel open in a random spot and began to read again:

The cold air warmed the instant I saw her face. She had chosen to surprise me, and surprise me she did. My whole being rose like the eastern sun, and I kissed her smiling face.

"You brought spring with you. Shall we celebrate?" she asked.

"I know of a field that just might remember us." I said. "But this time, we should dance to a wedding song."

Zachary stopped before his voice betrayed his emotions.

"Thank you." Nori seemed to study his face as she rose from the couch. "My heart feels fine now. And I guess I'd better not trample on your hospitality an longer."

If only you knew. I wish you could stay forever. But Nori didn't know that. Sh only thought he'd wanted a date. "It's been a pleasure. Well, not the part abou your unhappy news or the flutters in your heart. But just you. . .being here."

Nori smiled and walked to the door.

Zachary followed her, feeling his own "desolate winter" coming on. Th chance of her ever coming back for cocoa was as likely as seeing Halley's Comet *Why does love have to be so complicated?*

The time they'd spent together at the bookshop seemed surreal and won derful. He hadn't even known he was capable of being so happy. For a momen he'd lived something truly amazing. But it had only lasted for a moment.

"Thanks. . .for everything," Nori said. "Good-bye."

Why did she always have to say good-bye like they'd never see each othe again? "Good night, Nori. Come over anytime you're in need of a friend or som cocoa."

She touched his face. "You are so dear."

Zachary watched her until she'd gone into her apartment for the night. H placed his hand on his cheek. On the very spot she'd just touched. His skin heate up—considerably—and he wondered about the chemical reactions. Surely if h could explicate these sensations, he would be more immune to them. He chuck led, wondering if love was no more than a combination of compounds colliding And yet, there were so many irregularities, too—things science would never b able to fully explain.

He pulled out the *Courtship for Idiots* book from behind the curtain and se it out on the entry table to remind him to glance through it one more time. H wouldn't allow the advice to rule his life, but he thought it still might be good fo a tip or two. Just as he was making his way to the bedroom, he heard a loud ra at the door. *Nori?* He headed back to the door and opened it.

Nori stood in front of him again, smiling. "I forgot my marshmallow cream.

"That's right." Zachary retrieved the jar and handed it to her, wishing h could think of something to prolong her stay.

"Thanks." She held up the jar. "I promise I'll use it." Nori pointed to th book on his entry table. "Oh, I see you've got the book *Courtship for Idiots.*"

Zachary's face blazed with the heat of a hundred red-hot suns. *So much fo controlling chemical reactions.*

Chapter 13

Nori realized she should have kept her observation about the book to herself. *I'd better put him out of his misery.* "I saw that courtship book at the store, too." She offered her sincerest smile. "I ended up buying *Finding Your Dreamboat* instead. Totally worthless, though. I intend to use it for kindling." She chuckled, thinking how liberating it felt to no longer hide things from the opposite sex. No more reason for airs if one wasn't actively pursuing a husband. All could be given openly without worry of repercussions or rejection.

"Really?" Zachary asked. "I guess some parts of life are confusing. I figured a little help wouldn't hurt."

"Well, when you come across the right woman, Zachary, self-help books will be useless. I hear love erases all need for formulas. At least that's what my mother *used* to say." She sighed and said good night.

As she left Zachary, she saw such intensity in his eyes. Had she upset him in some way? Had he loved once and lost? She breathed a prayer for her friend and walked to the front door, clutching her keys and his jar of marshmallow cream.

When Nori had readied herself for bed and slipped under the covers, she realized she felt a little more at peace. Zachary really had been a friend to her in a time of need. Her parents' divorce still seemed shocking and unbelievable, and yet she was calm enough to consider the news in a more reasonable way.

As Nori drifted off, she wondered if she'd dream about Zachary again. When she was resting on his couch, one of her dreams had been about him—it was the one dream she hadn't mentioned to him.

Much later, while enjoying her deep slumbers, Nori heard a noise. She jolted up in bed. What was that? *The telephone.* She shook off her sleep and glanced at the clock: 1:10 a.m. After another ring, she picked up the phone. "Hello?"

"Noreen?"

"Mother? Is that you? Are you okay? Where are—"

"I'm downstairs."

"What?"

"I couldn't remember if your apartment number was 203 or 205." Her mother sounded exhausted.

"It's 203. I can't believe you're here. I'm glad." Nori reminded herself to breathe.

"My flight was exhausting, but after I got home I wasn't able to sleep. Thought I'd drive over to see you."

All the way from Forrest City in the middle of the night? "Come on up. I'll see you in a minute." She threw on her fluffiest robe and scurried around the apartment, trying to make things tidy.

They hadn't seen each other in a long while, so Nori wanted their reunion to be lovely in every way. And yet that was impossible now, since she wasn't sure how she could avoid a confrontation about the upcoming divorce.

Nori tightened her robe. She loved her mother and she'd always dreamed of a close relationship, but for some reason it had always eluded them. In high school, they'd connected when she'd won an award in home economics. Her mother had seemed so proud of her when a local reporter came to the house to interview her. Nori had experienced a brief and wonderful attachment to her mom that week. In fact, it had been the best week of her life. But no matter how hard they had both tried since then, something always seemed to come between them.

The doorbell rang, jolting Nori from her daydream. She ran to the door, and with her hands trembling, she opened it.

Her mother stood in the hallway, still tall and stout, but looking weary-eyed and older. "Hello," she said.

"Hi." Nori stepped into the hallway and gathered her mother into a hug. She smelled of baby powder, a scent Nori had almost forgotten.

Her mother pulled away first, and then she patted her daughter on the back. "Well, it's been a long time."

"Yes. Too long." Nori picked up her mother's suitcase and led her into the apartment.

"My, my, my." She looked around, shaking her head. "I'd forgotten how nice your apartment was. *And* how expensive it must be."

Nori hated for her mother to think that she was wasting money, especially since she lived well within her means. But to keep from sounding defensive, she said, "The shop is doing very well."

"Oh really." Her mother raised an eyebrow. "That *is* good. I'm sure your *grandmother* would have been pleased." She picked at the material on her pantsuit.

"Yes." Nori stuffed her hands into the pockets of her robe, already wondering what she could say next.

"Funny, after all this time, and considering what you do, I've never known what your favorite candy is." Her mother seemed to wait for an answer.

"Well, actually there is one candy that I love above all others. It's—"

"Oh boy, do I need to take a load off." Her mother eased onto the sofa, leaned against the back of the couch, and closed her eyes.

Nori sat down next to her. *Poor Mom.* "You know, maybe tomorrow afternoon we could go to one of the spas. I think you'd really enjoy it. Everything they do is so rejuvenating. And it'll be my treat."

Surely she wasn't asleep already. Couldn't tell. But her mother had so many times tuned her out simply by shutting her eyes. "By the way, I can sleep out here, and you may have my bed."

"Thank you, dear."

Nori sighed. So she wasn't asleep. "Are you hungry? Or maybe you'd like something to drink. Chamomile might help you to rest."

Her mother raised her head, looking bleary-eyed. "Maybe some good strong coffee. I've still got jet lag."

Strong coffee? Nori couldn't imagine how loads of caffeine just before bed would help with jet lag, but she headed to the kitchen anyway.

Nori counted out the scoops of coffee, but then when she was finished, she wasn't sure how many she'd put in the paper cone. She poured the granules back in the package and started over. After several more attempts, she got the scoops right, poured the water into the machine, and turned it on. *Finally.* She marveled how she could even run a candy shop with such an annoying and time-consuming disorder. But for some reason the only time her compulsiveness became truly unmanageable was when she was with her mother. Nori breathed a quick prayer for strength. When the coffee machine beeped, her mother came through the door and sat down at the kitchen table.

For a moment Nori felt helpless, wondering what to do with the elephant in the room that they were both trying so hard to ignore—the upcoming divorce. What could she say that wouldn't start an argument?

"I know what your quiet is all about," her mother said. "I just want you to know, we both agreed to the divorce." She crossed her arms. "Nobody's hurting."

But what about me? I'm hurting. Nori kept her face toward the cabinets. She pressed her finger against her lips to help keep her emotions in check. "But why, Mom? Why now, after decades of marriage?"

"I'm really sorry." Her mother stared into space.

"But I thought you and Dad were happy." How could she have misunderstood all those years? "Were you only pretending all that time?" Nori gripped the edge of the counter until her fingers throbbed.

"Your father and I didn't want you growing up in a broken home." She raised her hands. "Now, I'm not blaming you. I'm just saying you're grown now. You've got a good career. And, well, we need to move on."

Her mother had said the words as if she were talking about hiring a new lawn service. Her casual and detached manner angered Nori. Trying to control her emotions, she busied herself by setting out cream and sugar and pouring them each a cup of coffee. There were a thousand things to say, and yet she wasn't sure what to ask first.

They sat for a while, sipping from their cups and chatting about the brand and flavor of the coffee. While they talked about everything and nothing, Nori took note of other changes in her mother. Her green eyes had lost some of their gleam, and her blond tresses showed hints of gray. But most noticeable was the change in her mother's temperament, which was now more tentative and melancholy.

When all the light chitchat had played itself out, they fell into silence.

In spite of the distress she felt for her mother, Nori could stand the wait no longer. "I'm sure you know. . .I have questions. I really—"

"I'm sure you do, dear." Pain shadowed her mother's face. "But I'm awfully tired right now. If you don't mind, I'm going to bed." She jerked up from the table, making the chair fall backward against the tile.

When Nori came to her mother's aid, she saw the sadness in her eyes and the tremor in her fingers. "Are you sure you're—"

"We'll feel better in the morning. Won't we?" Her mother's voice sounded hoarse with emotion.

Nori decided to let the anxious moment unwind. "You're right."

Her mother rinsed the cups and set them in the sink.

She hoped her mother was right—that after a good night's sleep, things would look better in the morning. Or at least clearer.

And yet, her mother's expression left her with a sense of dread. Was something else wrong? Perhaps something her mother was still hiding from her?

Nori woke with a start. Then she remembered she'd slept on the couch. The night had been riddled with night sweats and dreadful dreams. And the couch had been lumpy and the blankets itchy. Not a good combo.

She glanced over at the wall clock: 7:12 a.m. She rose from the couch feeling stiff and miserable. She rubbed her stomach, which still felt sour from the late night coffee.

Before showering, Nori padded into the bedroom to check on her mom. She stared at the empty bed and the rumpled sheets. "Mother?" Nori looked in the master bath. Empty as well. The sense of dread she'd felt the night before washed over her. She ran through the whole apartment, flicking on all the lights as she went, but the reality had already hit. Her mother was gone.

Chapter 14

Nori checked the front door. Her mother had closed it, but she'd left it unlocked. *Glad my apartment building is a safe place.*

She opened the door and looked down the hallway. No one was there. All quiet. Maybe her mother had just run to the store for a few toiletries and hadn't wanted to disturb her sleep. But even as she thought it, she knew something else was at play.

She went into the kitchen, and while pouring herself some orange juice, she noticed a note next to the vase of flowers. She picked up the note and read it:

> *Noreen,*
>   *I'm going on a cruise, so I had to get up early. Sorry I left before saying good-bye, but I thought things might be easier this way.*
>   *Love, Mom*

The note fell from Nori's hand. She hadn't seen her mother in ages, and now she'd vanished again. When would they ever get to talk? Not just dance around their real feelings with coffee chatter. Nori had hoped they could get to know each other better over the next few days. Find some common ground. Maybe talk about the Lord or friends or anything. Then maybe once they'd formed a closer bond, perhaps her mother would feel comfortable enough to explain the whys of the sudden break-up of her marriage.

Nori eased to the floor and let her head fall back against the cabinets. All this time, she'd naively thought her parents were busy enjoying the beginnings of their golden years: traveling, gardening, and learning to cook together. What a crock that was. She picked up her mother's note again and stared at it, trying to discover any nuances or hidden meanings.

Then Nori groaned, remembering her own questions as well as an accusation or two. Instead of waiting patiently for her mother to talk about the divorce as she'd hoped to do, she'd started the inquisition too soon. But what had she expected her to say with such shocking news—"I'm happy for you?"

The tears came. She clutched her nightgown like a lifeline, hoping for some reprieve. None came. She shook her head at romance and marriage and love. What kind of dreamworld had she been living in?

Oh God, please, I need Your help. And my parents do, too. Please guide them in all things, even if they don't want Your help.

She reached into the pantry, snatched a wad of napkins off a shelf, and blew her nose. After a shower and some whole-grain toast, she dragged herself out the front door. She couldn't imagine greeting customers in her foul state of mind, but it had to be done.

Zachary emerged from his apartment.

Oh no. She wasn't even in the mood for friends. "Hi."

"Hi there." Zachary cleared his throat. "I wanted to let you know I'm going to be gone for a little while."

Nori turned to him. "Gone?" Why was everybody leaving?

He caught up with her. "Well, I won this. . .this award, and so I need to go to a banquet."

"An award? What kind?"

"Geophysicist of the year." He blushed.

"You mean statewide?" Nori tried to act interested. She might be feeling as low as dirt, but she wasn't going to hurt Zachary's feelings.

"No." He looked away. "It's a. . .national award."

Nori's mouth fell open. "That's incredible. Congratulations."

Zachary smiled. "That means a lot to me. I mean, you saying that. Thanks."

She had to admit, his humility seemed real as well as endearing. Most people she knew would take kudos like that and make the most of it—like mentioning it coolly every few seconds. "So where do you fly off to?"

"Denver. I'll be gone about two weeks."

"Oh?" *Two weeks?* Nori felt disappointed. She hadn't expected that much sentiment. Her eyes misted over, but she squelched her emotions before they could be detected.

"I haven't had a vacation in five years, so I thought it'd be nice to do some hiking while I was in Colorado."

"Do you hike a lot?"

"I've been hiking every weekend for a while now." He grinned. "I'd like to expand my horizons."

"That sounds good." Nori locked her door. "Why didn't you mention the award yesterday evening?"

Zachary fiddled with his picture ID, which dangled from his belt loop. "Well, with the news you got yesterday, it didn't seem like the right time to mention it."

How selfless was that? Nori tried not to stare at this man named Zachary. She was lucky to have him for a friend. "Thank you."

"You're welcome. Do you feel better today?"

Nori wanted to pour her heart out to him, but she knew it would take all day. Maybe all year. And she didn't want Lizza to think she'd abandoned her at the shop. "Not totally. My mother showed up last night, but we didn't get a chance to talk very much. At least not about anything important. And then she left early this morning for a cruise."

"I'm sorry." Zachary moved toward her. "I can cancel my trip if you need me. You know, as a friend."

"Cancel? Oh no. Your award. I would never ask you to do that."

Zachary smiled. "Well, that's what friends do."

Yes, it *was* what friends did, or so she'd heard. Nori had never known anyone within the male persuasion, or anyone for that matter, who possessed such a noble heart. "I'll be okay. But I *really* appreciate the offer." She reached out and touched his arm.

Zachary nodded, looking embarrassed but pleased.

They rode the elevator together and then, after a heartfelt good-bye, went their separate ways.

Nori drove to work, gathered up her courage, and hauled herself into Sweet Nothings. Lizza was ready for business and looked chipper, as always. Nori shook her head, feeling disappointed and hurt over all the recent events. One minute she had her act together, and then the next it was like somebody had tossed the pieces of her life in a bag, shaken them up, and then dumped them on the ground. What a mess.

"S'up? You look like you need a handful of jelly beans. Doctor's orders." Lizza winked.

"No thanks. I'm not hungry, but I do have a story to tell you. A lot has happened. Too much, in fact." Where in the world would she begin? With Blake or Zachary or her parents' divorce? She took in a deep breath and began her tale.

While they worked, dipping strawberries in molten chocolate, Nori continued with her dismal highlights. "Anyway, Zachary and I are just going to be good friends. And I think that's a good thing."

Nori didn't dare ask for her friend's opinion, especially since the date with Blake had gone so strangely. But she could tell Lizza was busting with queries. And advice. Nori cleared her throat. "And my parents are getting a divorce."

Lizza froze, her strawberry still poised in midair. "Excuse me? Your parents are getting a *what?*"

"A divorce." The words still seemed impossible to Nori.

"Oh no. But this cannot be." Lizza set her berry on the wax paper and placed her hands on her hips. "But I thought they had—"

"I know, we both thought they had a good marriage, but apparently they didn't."

"It's so hard to believe." Lizza gave Nori's back a gentle rub. "I'm so sorry. Oh, but the word 'sorry' gets used for every little thing, doesn't it? I wish I had a better word." Lizza placed her palm over her heart. "I feel a better word right here."

"Thanks. Really." Nori took in a deep breath as she went back to dipping the strawberries into the chocolate.

⚊⚊⚊

After a day at work that felt more like a month, Nori trudged back home. She slid onto the couch and let her mind hash through all that she'd kept at bay. Questions, one after another, poured out until she felt like she was drowning in them.

Just as Nori began sharing her troubles with God, she heard a soft tapping at the front door. *Mom?*

Nori found Zachary standing at her door. "When is your flight?"

"Early tomorrow morning."

"Do you want to come in?" Nori hoped he'd say yes, even though moping for a while sounded pretty comforting, too.

Zachary shook his head. "That's okay. I just wanted to give you this." He offered her a book.

Nori accepted the gift—a rich brown journal trimmed in gold.

"It's a journal," he said. "You know, for writing things down. Important things and. . .well. . .not so important things. I use one all the time, and it helps me. I can better see where I've been and where I want to go. When I like life and when I hate it." He grinned. "That sort of thing."

Nori noticed Zachary's relaxed demeanor as he talked about journaling. She was fond of him like that—when he stopped trying so hard and was just being himself. Her fingers traced the gold trim. "It's beautiful. And the most thoughtful thing anyone has ever given me."

Zachary nodded, looking pleased.

Nori no longer kept her expression in check but let a smile warm her face. With the pressure off to constantly be on a manhunt, she could allow herself to unwind a little. Then she could spend all her excess time worrying about her parents.

"Well, bye," Zachary suddenly said.

"Good-bye." Nori didn't want to, but she let him go. "Have a safe trip." She closed the door and sat back down on the couch, taking in the beauty of the leather-bound journal. She lifted the heavy cover and noticed a sticky note on the first page. The note contained a quote by Ralph Waldo Emerson—*"A friend may well be reckoned the masterpiece of nature."* Nice saying. *Really* nice.

Nori flipped through the rest of the journal. Each page appeared to have a note with either a quote or a scripture. Zachary had taken the time to write out words of encouragement. Nori shook her head, smiling. *Amazing.* She already knew what her first entry would be: "I don't deserve a friend like Zachary Martin."

The doorbell rang, and she found herself hoping it was Zachary. When she opened the door, Blake stood in the hallway sporting a toothy grin, a denim shirt, and a few flips of freshly highlighted hair. "Howdy-do."

"Hi," Nori said, trying not to show her disappointment. "What are you doing here?"

Blake leaned on the doorframe. "Wow, you look thinner or something."

"Thanks." Why, why, why, she wondered, was Blake always leaning on everything? And why did it bother her so much?

"Well, hey, I hadn't seen you in a while, and I was in the neighborhood. So I thought maybe you'd like to share a meal with me since you're going to be my sister."

Nori took in some much-needed oxygen. "I'd love to, but I need to stay home tonight."

"That's okay. Maybe I could go buy us some groceries and we could fix it right here. But I have to warn you, I'm one lousy cook." Blake lowered his head in mock shame.

"So am I."

"No way."

"Yeah, I'm afraid I'm a typical single, too. I'm a terrible cook, and all I have in my fridge right now is orange juice, a carton of expired milk, and some veggies that are one stage away from penicillin." She shot him her chirpiest smile, trying to imagine what in the world Blake would say to that.

"But I'm allergic to penicillin."

Nori chuckled, but then she realized he wasn't joking.

Blake just stared at her. "Uh, I thought all you gals stocked food supplies and were good at cooking and stuff. Weren't you all kind of born that way?" He waggled his eyebrows.

"Not really. Are all you guys born with the know-how to replace a car muffler?"

"Well, *I* sure can't. That's why I have a good mechanic." He donned a sheepish grin. "Oh, I get it. I think you're just trying to say no. That's okay. Maybe another time."

Blake had such a dejected look that she felt sorry for him. "You're welcome to come in for a bit. I could make cocoa."

"Naw. I've never liked hot chocolate. Makes me think of what ladies drink when they're old and lonely." His expression warped into panic. "Oww, boy.

Guess that came off bad. Sorry. I hope I didn't hurt your feelings."

"No. You're fine." Nori grinned.

"I'd better get going." He stuffed his hands in his pockets.

"Thanks for dropping by."

"Same to you." Blake gave her a big-eyed grin and then meandered down the hallway toward the elevator.

What was that all about? Nori closed the door. Was Blake's spiel just a weaseling way to get her to fix supper for him? Had that been the real reason he'd asked her to be his sister? Maybe not. Maybe she was just seeing the worst possible scenario since she was tired enough to sleep under the sink.

Nori decided to go to bed before somebody else showed up for a seven-course meal or a back rub or maybe some free financial planning.

Chapter 15

Over the next two weeks, Nori threw herself into her work at Sweet Nothings, worked out at the gym with rabid determination, and found herself losing some of her fascination with food. She guessed it was one of the benefits of despair.

Her father hadn't returned her calls to talk about the divorce, so she assumed he was lying low in fear that their conversation would turn into a moral debate. She was in no mood for a quarrel, so she let the confrontation go. For now.

Nori milled around the shop doing all the usual things, but her thoughts were elsewhere. Zachary had been gone for two whole weeks and a day, and Nori realized that was part of the problem. She missed her friend.

Feeling preoccupied and lonesome, Nori thought some fresh air and window-shopping might do her some good. So, during her lunch break, she ambled out of Sweet Nothings and then strolled along the sidewalk on Central Avenue, gazing at the shops and pretending to be one of the tourists. She never tired of the town's old-world quaintness and its eclectic mixture of architecture.

A crystal chandelier in an antique shop caught Nori's attention. She thought the fixture would look stunning in a big dining room. But that couldn't happen without buying a home of her own since her apartment dining room wasn't very big or formal. And the landlord probably wouldn't appreciate her changing all the light fixtures. The yearning to settle her life in a more permanent situation tugged at her heart. She had to admit that in spite of what her parents were going through, she still longed for a home and family.

Nori continued walking past hotels, art studios, restaurants, and bathhouses and then made her way back to Arlington Lawn at The Promenade. She stood in her beloved spot, looking over the hot springs, hoping the waters and the sun's warmth could revive her. It always astonished her that she lived and worked next to a national park.

She leaned over the railing and watched the rising steam curl into ribbons while the rest of the thermal waters tumbled over the boulders. Nature's music. The sights and sounds were simple blessings but ones she was deeply grateful for. And especially now in early spring. . .when everything seemed to affirm and declare that God was still in the business of caring for all He'd created.

Nori took in the view of the historic district, the verdant hills cradling the town, the stately magnolia trees, and the many families below dipping their feet in the thermal waters. The village had always made her think of something magical, especially now with all the blooming flowers. *I could never live anywhere else. Spoiled for life, I guess.*

Her mind drifted to other fine things. Zachary. She wondered when he'd fly in. And against her better judgment, she began to compare Blake and Zachary. Both were so very different. God had never made the same man twice—that was certain.

She thought of the first time she truly "saw" Zachary—when he'd ditched his glasses and his wrinkled clothes. *Oh dear.* She felt a familiar twinge of guilt. *I didn't notice Zachary until he'd made himself "pretty."* She lowered her head, thinking how shallow and predictably human she was. And yet, somehow he cared for her. Deeply. Perhaps even unwisely.

Someone caught her attention out of the corner of her eye. The man who'd filled her head and heart was walking straight toward her.

Zachary.

Chapter 16

Zachary took in the wonder of Nori. She looked gorgeous in a pair of black jeans and a gauzy blouse. How wonderful she looked—had always looked. And she was standing in his favorite spot, smiling at him. Did life get any better? He moved toward her. "Hello."

Nori made up the distance between them, hugging him. "I'm glad to see you."

Okay, that was better than he'd hoped. So much better. Zachary returned Nori's embrace. She felt soft and warm against him, and as he imagined, she smelled of all things sweet. Then, suddenly, the moment was over and they released each other.

"How did you know I'd be here?"

"I stopped by the shop. Lizza told me."

Nori clasped her hands together. "So, tell me about this award."

"Well, it's etched in green glass. It's nice. I'll show it to you sometime."

"Was there a big crowd? Did you have an acceptance speech?" Nori's voice sounded a little breathless.

"There were about six hundred people at the banquet, and I said I was pleased to receive the award. That was about it." Zachary chuckled. "I was a little nervous."

"I would have been, too."

"Really?"

Nori nodded. "And did you go hiking while you were in Colorado?"

"Yeah. It was great." He rested his arms against the railing and looked out over the town. "There's a quiet about it that gets to you. Makes me more attentive to the things I usually ignore. And then the sounds and sights and smells suddenly seem. . .well. . .miraculous."

Nori stared at him with a new expression—one he hadn't seen on her before. Somewhere between astonishment and delight. He liked it. A lot.

"Hmm. Sounds like an excellent pastime. And it burns calories." She smiled. "I've always needed a good hobby, but I just haven't. . ." Her voice trailed off before starting again. "So is that where you got your tan?"

"Mostly from the skiing. It's a—"

"You went skiing, too?" Nori looked surprised.

"Yeah. I love the hiking, but I have to admit the skiing is a little. . . unpredictable."

Nori chuckled. "Yes, it certainly is."

"But it was good for me. . .to try something out of my comfort zone. By the way, there are a bunch of good hiking trails around here. Maybe you'd like to go with me sometime." *Wow, that was pretty bold.* Usually after a statement like that he'd plummet headlong into an abyss of mortification. Instead, he decided to smile.

"Okay. That sounds nice."

"Good." He hated to spoil a perfect moment by asking about the divorce, but he wondered how Nori was doing. "So, how have you been?"

"I'm still pretty confused and hurt about my parents' divorce. But I'm dealing with it. . .one day at a time." She looked at him. "Thank you for asking."

A family with cameras and lots of enthusiasm marched up the stairs toward them. The children were chattering about the thermal waters while their parents took snapshots. One of the children, a little girl with auburn ringlets, reached up and took hold of Nori's hand.

"Hi," Nori said to the girl.

The girl glanced up at Nori with a look of terror and then scampered back to find her mother.

"Guess she needs to pay more attention whose hand she's holding," Nori whispered to Zachary.

"Kids. They're a little random and messy," he said in a low voice. "But I'd like to have a few anyway."

Nori chuckled as she seemed to study him. "Well, I'd better get back to work. I'd hate to make Lizza think I've deserted her. Why don't you drop by the shop later for something sweet? It'll be on the house."

"I'll try not to choke this time."

"That's good. I prefer my customers go away happy. . .and still breathing."

They chuckled and then walked down the steps toward the street.

Zachary wondered what it would feel like to reach out and take her hand like the girl had. He imagined the experience would be intensely satisfying, though he didn't discount the perilous side of such an exploit. All the things that could go awry. . . And yet Zachary wished he could toss caution to the wind and simply reach out to her.

❧

The second his watch read 5:00 p.m., Zachary rose from his desk and sprinted out to his car. In five minutes, give or take a few seconds, he'd be in the presence of Nori. The thrill of seeing her again, especially now that she didn't loathe him, outweighed anything he'd ever done—watching *Star Trek* marathons or meeting his favorite science fiction authors or even going hiking in his favorite places. Nori surpassed all things wonderful.

In a burst of confidence, Zachary sped over to Sweet Nothings, strode to the shop, and threw open the door.

Nori said good-bye to several customers, and then she locked eyes with him. *Nice.*

Almost on cue, Lizza disappeared into the back room.

Nori strolled over to Zachary. "Well, do you see something you would like?" she asked with a sweep of her hand.

Zachary tugged on his collar and blinked. If she only knew. "Well, how about some maple sugar cakes? Those are always good."

"What an interesting selection." Nori tapped her finger against her cheek. "Does it mean anything?"

"Yes, I think so. Women rarely buy it. Maple sugar candies are usually purchased by men who like the outdoors. Men who are comfortable with themselves. The discerning man."

Zachary straightened his shoulders. He was feeling better by the minute. "Really? You can tell all that from maple sugar? I guess I just thought I liked the flavor."

"Candy is a very individual thing." Nori raised her chin. "People take their sweets very seriously."

Zachary had no idea there was so much study behind the selection of candy.

Nori took out a few small boxes of maple sugar cakes, placed them in a decorative Sweet Nothings box, and held it out to Zachary. "There you are. Candy collected from the finest maple trees in Vermont. Enjoy."

"Thank you."

Their hands touched in midair. Zachary felt a warm rush. In case his face looked ridiculously red, he glanced away at a row of candy bins. "I see you have plenty of chocolate-covered coffee beans on hand."

"Well, we do try to remember what our customers like." Nori smiled. "You know, it's that personal touch that's so important."

Yes, without a doubt, Zachary liked the personal touch. "I'm sure they've come to appreciate it."

"Who appreciates what?" Lizza said, bustling back into the room with a huge bag of taffy. "Spit it out. I must know everything."

"We were just talking about getting to know our customers and what they like."

"And what they don't even know they like. . .yet." Lizza winked. "Hi, Zachary."

"Hello there."

"Listen, I've got something I need to ask you both," Lizza said. "My sister's wedding is tomorrow evening. And she said they had a few cancellations for dinner and she hated to waste the food." Lizza turned to Nori. "Anyway, she wondered if you would like to attend. It'll be a lovely wedding with an elegant dinner. Oh, and she said you could bring a date. So that means you could invite Zachary."

Right at that moment, Zachary would like to have given Lizza a thousand dollars. He looked at Nori to gauge her response. She looked a bit green, if women could be that color.

"Well, that's a thought." Nori hesitated. "But a very good thought."

He noticed Nori giving Lizza one of the female gestures that only women could decode, so he couldn't tell if that was a good sign or bad sign. But he knew he wouldn't push it. This had to be her decision.

Nori approached Zachary with a girlish grin, which made his heart feel like it was hammering itself into pieces. "Would you like to go to the wedding with me. . .as my dear friend?" she asked.

Zachary nodded with eagerness while trying not to come off too dorky. He hoped her "friends only" position would evolve into something more through the evening, and the word *dear* did sound promising.

"Okay." Nori turned to Lizza. "We'd love to accept your sister's invitation."

"It's 7:00 tomorrow evening at Forrest Heights Chapel. And then afterward, there'll be a reception and dinner. Well, I'm glad that's settled. I'll see you guys there."

"Say, shouldn't you be getting ready for the rehearsal?" Nori asked.

"No problem. It's at seven-thirty. Plenty of time." Lizza went toward the back room again, whistling a merry tune.

"I hope that didn't pressure you into something you didn't want to do," Zachary said to Nori in a low voice.

She shook her head. "Not at all. It just surprised me. I've never even met Lizza's sister. I'm sure she invited me because Lizza works with me, but still, it was very nice of her."

Zachary took a peek at his box of maple candies, thinking of the hands that put them there. Then he gazed over at her. "I've only been to two weddings. And they were a long time ago."

"Really?"

"How many have you been to?"

"Quite a few," Nori said. "I think you'll enjoy yourself."

"I know I will." Zachary tried to keep the amorous tones from his voice. "What are we supposed to wear?"

"You can wear a nice suit. But I think I'll go to the mall tomorrow morning and find a new dress."

Zachary saw the light in her eyes. He was glad for the wedding invitation, not only for himself but for Nori. He thought it might give her a rest from worrying about her parents' divorce. And it wouldn't hurt for her to see a couple deeply in love—a sight that might inspire her to think beyond friendship.

A group of noisy and hungry-looking customers suddenly barreled into the shop like a herd of buffalo.

"I'd better let you take care of your customers. I know where Forrest Heights Chapel is. I'll be by your apartment at 6:30. Is that good?" Zachary asked.

"*Very* good."

Zachary left the shop in such good spirits that he ate every one of the maple sugar cakes. Then the rest of the day whirled by.

He found a suit that seemed to be a good style and fit even though the price was astonishing. It didn't matter, though. He could afford the extra cost, and he would do anything to sweep Nori off her feet.

Did men really do that? He was a little concerned about expectations on a date. He hadn't had a date in so long he wasn't sure what to do. Was he supposed to buy Nori a corsage, or were those outdated? He had no idea.

Maybe it was best they were going as friends for now. It did indeed take some of the pressure off. In the end he decided not to buy her a corsage since it might make her look like a member of the wedding party.

When Zachary had spent more hours grooming himself than he had in his whole life, he looked at the clock: 6:29. The time had come.

He locked his apartment and walked down the hall to Nori's door. He forced his hand to stop shaking as he rang the doorbell.

Chapter 17

*T*here's the bell. Right on time. Nori stopped to stare at herself in the entry mirror. She saw lipstick on her teeth, so she licked it off. Her eye shadow looked good, but then she'd had weeks to master the application. Cheeks... check. Hair...tolerable. Why was dressing up so traumatic?

Okay, she'd better get on with this. Nori opened the door.

Zachary looked at her and gasped.

Good response. Or not. Nori offered up her best smile.

"You look as pretty as an Easter egg," Zachary said.

Nori paused, trying to think how to respond.

Zachary blushed. "I didn't—"

"I'm sure you don't mean the oval part." Nori laughed.

"Not at all. You are color and light, and I don't think a woman could look more beautiful than you do right now."

Okay, now we're talking. "Thank you." Nori locked her door. "You look very handsome in that suit." Nori leaned toward him and touched the fabric. "Is that Italian?"

Zachary nodded. "Glad you like it."

Even though the date wasn't really a date, it felt like one to Nori. And to celebrate she decided not to recheck her door.

As they walked, her lavender dress made a swishing sound, her earrings swayed to the rhythm of their steps, and her perfume hovered in a delicate cloud. She knew the mood of the evening was suddenly becoming formal and datelike, but she also knew Lizza would want her to put aside her worries and enjoy it.

After a car ride up the hills and through a wooded area, they pulled into the parking lot of Forrest Heights Chapel. Moments later, they entered a circular-shaped receiving area with marble floors, a glass ceiling, and a Greek statue in the middle. The crowd of guests milled around, chatting and generally looking elegant.

To their right, a man dressed in a tuxedo opened the French doors and led the crowd outside through the covered breezeway.

Nori glanced around. Lizza was nowhere in sight, but then she remembered that her friend was in the wedding party and was most likely busy attending the bride.

With his hand gently at her back, Zachary guided Nori through the breezeway. She noticed his palm felt solid and sure against her, and she relaxed at his touch.

When they arrived in the chapel, an usher offered Nori his arm, and they headed down the aisle with Zachary in their wake.

The building didn't appear to be a conventional church but a chapel built just for weddings and special occasions. Nori had always dreamed of a traditional wedding in the sanctuary of her own church, and yet she couldn't help but admire the splendor and elegance of Forrest Heights Chapel with its high cathedral ceilings and glass walls. So inspiring. And to have all the windows overlooking a natural forest as well as a waterfall created a mood of hushed reverence.

While they were being seated along with all the other guests, the organ began to play a majestic tune. Was it Bach? Then the family members were seated, each of the two mothers dressed in apricot gowns and the fathers dressed in black tuxedos.

Soon the flower girl, a cherub with dimples and red curls, marched down the aisle, dropping white rose petals from her little basket. Nori felt the usual tug on her spirit but reminded herself that families, the best as well as the worst, could fall apart without a moment's notice. Nori chided herself for her dark thoughts and turned her attention to the wedding party.

The first bridesmaid walked in and then the second and third. Each time, Nori looked for Lizza. Then with a flourish, the organ played the wedding march and everyone stood up. *Where is Lizza? Is she ill? Isn't she supposed to be a bridesmaid?*

The bride marched in, beaming with joy and wearing one of the loveliest dresses Nori had ever seen—an ivory satin gown embellished with a full-length cape made of delicate lace. Her hair was left long but adorned with a dazzling tiara. The whole effect was breathtaking.

Nori looked back and forth at the couple's faces. Their smiles radiated such love and promise that she was indeed moved. No doubt the devotion was real, and yet she couldn't help but wonder how those holy pledges started out so hopeful and ended up so desperate. Why couldn't couples stay together? Did people forget about their vows before the Almighty? Was marriage worth all the agony it could create?

Nori chewed on her lower lip. *Oh dear. I've become a cynic.* She tried once again to concentrate on the ceremony. The couple turned to face the front of the chapel, and the minister began to talk about joining their lives together as one. A few minutes later, the bride and groom began exchanging their vows.

Nori was determined not to cry, but mist filled her eyes anyway. Weddings always got to her, even now amid the turmoil. She fumbled around in her purse for a tissue. Oh no. No tissue and her nose was running.

Without missing a beat, Zachary pulled a handkerchief from his pocket and handed it to her.

"Thank you," Nori mouthed. She dabbed her eyes and gently blew her nose. Then she listened again to the couple until all the lovely words were spent and all the promises made and the rings exchanged. Nori breathed a prayer for the couple, asking Him to give them both an extra measure of understanding and tender devotion toward each other and to guide and direct them all the days of their lives.

As the couple kissed, Nori suddenly recalled Lizza talking about her sister's curly blond hair. But the bride at the front of the chapel had long, wavy black hair. How could that be?

Oh no. Surely not.

Panic surged through Nori. Her mouth dropped open. She grabbed Zachary's arm. "I think we've attended the wrong wedding," she said in a hushed voice.

Zachary's surprise was tinged with a flicker of horror. "But how can it be the wrong wedding?" he whispered back.

Nori just shook her head and sunk a little lower in her seat. "I guess I zoned out when the minister said their names." *I've been crying over people I don't even know.*

After the song and a prayer, the minister introduced the couple as man and wife. They hurried down the aisle like they couldn't wait another second to start their lives together.

Guests rose to leave, but Nori stayed in her seat. She searched through her purse for the wedding invitation as Zachary looked on. Nori found the paper and scanned the words.

Zachary leaned over, looking at the invitation with her.

She pointed at the bottom line, which read: *"Forrest Heights Chapel—The Rose Sanctuary."* "I can't believe I missed that last part, the Rose Sanctuary." Nori stared out into space. "It's all my fault. We went to the wrong wedding."

Zachary stared up at the front of the chapel and smiled. "But it was a good wedding."

Nori paused for a moment and then burst out laughing. "I guess it was." She looked around. Everyone else had gone. "Oh my. Well, it's a good thing we didn't go to the wrong reception and dinner, too. It would have been a new level of embarrassment for me."

"That's usually *my* job," Zachary said.

"Why do you say that?" Nori leaned back in the pew.

"I don't think you really want to know."

"No, I do want to know." She glanced behind them. "There's nobody here but us."

Zachary looked at her as if to read her intentions. "Well, when I was growing up, awkwardness was so close to me it could have been a sibling. I guess you could say I was the odd rock in the pile."

Nori touched the padded seat near him. "How do you mean?"

"Well, anything that was different in school always stuck out. And *I* was different. I had the answers too quickly. My grades were too good. The teachers liked me too much. Somehow, that was objectionable. So I tried to hold back." He grinned. "Are you sure you want to hear this?"

Nori set her purse aside and turned toward him, wanting to make certain Zachary had her full attention. "I'm sure."

"Well, one time, when I was working on a science project, I realized it was going to be too technical, so I smashed the thing up and started over with an idea that was more. . .mediocre. I didn't want the grade as much as the approval. I tried to fit in, but it never worked. They'd already pegged me. It felt sort of like living in a suspended state. No one wanted Zachary, but no one would let him change." He fiddled with the button on his jacket. "Now I see how infantile that was, but back then, you couldn't have convinced me of it."

Nori remembered the kids in school being cruel at times, but she'd never spent time thinking about the sufferings of people who were brilliant. It seemed monstrously unfair to be ostracized for one's God-given abilities. "I'm so sorry that happened to you. That people couldn't just trust you with your gifts."

"Thanks. Was school ever hard on you?"

"Sometimes. I remember being very good at embarrassing myself. One time I tore my new clothes on a nail, and the accident exposed my undergarments to a whole gym full of kids." She shook her head. "That sort of thing seemed to happen to me more than the other girls for some reason. Anyway, after a while I began to assume that I'd embarrassed myself even when I hadn't. I'd find out later no one even noticed my blunder." She chuckled. "People are such strange collections of things. You know. . .all the miscellaneous hurts and fears we pick up along life's road. And then if we don't let go of anything, we find ourselves dragging all this stuff behind us."

"You, too?"

"Yeah. Me, too." She tugged on Zachary's jacket and grinned. After a bit more quiet had passed between them, Nori sighed. "Well, I guess we'd better go. We have a reception and dinner to attend. And hopefully, this time it'll be the *right* one."

They strode out of the chapel and back through the breezeway. When they arrived in the reception area, Nori noticed an archway with another sign that read THE ROSE SANCTUARY. She sighed. *Oh dear. Certainly too late now.* She just hoped Lizza wouldn't razz her too much about her faux pas.

Nori and Zachary headed down a hallway until they saw the opening to a banquet room. SILVERTON was displayed in front. "This is it. Lizza's sister married Anthony Silverton."

They gave each other a knowing smile and then chuckled in relief.

Zachary offered her his arm. "Shall we?"

She circled her arm through his, and they strolled into the banquet room. The word *splendiferous* came to mind. Crystal chandeliers dazzled the room, and gilded trim adorned all the wainscoting and chairs. Fine linen covered the tables, and white birdcages brimming with yellow roses served as romantic centerpieces. The bride had truly created a fairy-tale scene.

Nori raised her chin. She refused to let such a blissful evening be tainted with her own musings, so she guarded her heart as best she could. She busied herself, trying to spot Lizza somewhere in the crowd. She was certain they'd made it into the right reception, but she still didn't see her friend among the clusters of guests. Perhaps she was off mingling in another room or powdering her nose.

Zachary motioned toward the atrium. "Looks like they have hors d'oeuvres and something to drink in there. Are you thirsty?"

"I am."

Once again, being the perfect gentleman, Zachary touched the small of her back and gently steered her through the crowd, through the wafting mandolin music, and into the atrium. Nori ordered sparkling mineral water with lime, and Zachary requested a root beer with extra ice.

When they were situated with their drinks, they walked over to the fountain and watched the water as it flowed and sparkled down five tiers. The water continued its descent, narrowing into a stream and then collecting in a small pool, which was nestled in a tropical garden.

"How lovely," Nori said.

Zachary stared at the sight. "*Lovely* is a subjective term."

"Oh, is it?"

He released a grin. "Yes, it can be subject to opinion, false speculation, and irrational emotions."

Nori lifted an eyebrow, deciding to rise to the occasion. "So in your opinion, which is of course riddled with emotion and speculation, would you say that the fountain and garden are lovely?"

He stared at it. "They have their benefits."

"And what are those?" She batted her eyelids.

"They please you. And that's enough for me."

"That's nice, but don't you want something for yourself?" Nori asked.

Zachary looked at her. "I do indeed."

Chapter 18

Nori felt her face flush, wishing she hadn't asked the question quite that way. The moment had become unexpectedly intimate. But on the other hand, she wasn't about to shy away from it. She glanced his way again. There was something different about his expression—perhaps an understanding had grown between them.

She took a sip of her drink as she pondered the lives of married folks who'd made it to their golden years—the couples whose love was tethered so closely that it could not be undone. She guessed they died with a sweetness on their brow, knowing what it was like to be truly cared for. And truly known. Faithful love did exist; she knew that—and yet reservations persisted. But what could she do with these new feelings for Zachary except follow her heart just a little?

With a murmur and a nod between them, Nori and Zachary strolled over to a more secluded spot—a glassed-in alcove, which gave them a spectacular view of the heavens.

Nori loved the way the stars decorated the night sky, like cut crystals shimmering in a box of black velvet.

They sat down together on a wooden settee near the windows. "Ever since I was a little girl, I've been planning a wedding. My own wedding," Nori said without thinking. Perhaps she shouldn't reveal such intimate details to him. But she was in the mood to take a chance.

Zachary's eyes lit up with what looked like surprise. Or panic. "Really?" He took a sip of his beverage and then set it down on a small table.

"It's true."

He leaned closer to her. "I wish I'd been one of your friends back then. You know, maybe one of your neighbors. We could have played together, and I could have given your bridal dolls a ride on my Starship Enterprise."

Nori laughed. *Okay, this guy is sorta funny, too. So glad he wasn't upset with my revelation.*

"I hope what's happened to your parents hasn't wiped out all your dreams."

She thought for a moment. "They could never take away all my dreams."

Zachary nodded. "So, what was your ideal wedding? You know. . .when you did all that planning, you must have come up with something spectacular."

"I don't think you. . .I mean, guys don't usually want to hear about all the froufrou details—"

Zachary covered her hands with his and squeezed. "I do. . .want to hear it. All of it."

"Okay." Nori looked down at their hands.

Zachary released her.

A tingling sensation ran through Nori, starting with her fingers and racing all across her skin. "Sorry, what was I talking about?" She tried to gather her thoughts, but she felt distracted.

"Your dream wedding."

"Oh yes. Actually, I haven't thought about it in a while. Let's see. My colors were emerald and ivory for a winter wedding. Lots of greenery with ivory satin ribbons. Having more greenery than flowers would save money, but it would also look very elegant. And there'd be clusters of ivory candles, more than anyone could count. An organ for "The Wedding March," but a harpist to accompany one specially chosen song." Her hands closed together. "And a gown of Victorian lace with a scandalously long train."

"Sounds very nice. And what about the groom?"

Nori glanced away. "Well, I suppose a black tux is always stylish." She looked back at him. He wore an unreadable expression. The truth was, when she played wedding as a child, the groom part seemed too fanciful. Even as a young woman, she'd always had a hard time imagining anyone proposing to her. Maybe she should steer the topic onto a safer road. "I even used to bake little wedding cakes. Of course, my first ones were always made of mud."

Zachary chuckled.

His laugh made her grow warm inside. Nori noticed that Zachary's awkwardness and hesitancy were almost gone. Perhaps she'd made him more comfortable around women. Maybe he just needed some practice. In other words, he needed a female friend. But the stirring inside her didn't feel like mere friendship.

She studied Zachary's face. In the beginning, she had indeed misunderstood who he was. There was so much to discover about him—things that had to be quietly sought. Before she could censor herself, Nori spoke from her heart. "Zachary, I said I just wanted us to be friends. . .and that this evening was not a date. . ." She looked at him. "But I've changed my mind. Would that be all right with you?"

⁓

Zachary blinked a few times to make sure he was conscious. He could hardly believe what Nori had just said. "It's what I've prayed for all day."

Nori reached up and touched his cheek.

When she released him, he caught her hand and kissed it. *Oh wow.* That was pretty risky. They'd only made the date official by about five seconds, and he was already kissing her hand. Although he certainly wanted to do that weeks ago. Months ago. "So, if this is a date, do you mind if I ask you something...personal?" Zachary knew he might lose every inch he'd gained by continuing, but he had to have an answer to his query.

"I guess so."

"If you ever do follow through with your dream wedding, what *kind* of groom are you looking for?"

Nori went quiet for a moment. Extra quiet. Long enough, in fact, that he hoped he hadn't embarrassed her with such a delicate topic.

"Well," she finally began, "I would want to marry a kind and faithful Christian. Beyond that, maybe someone who's smart and funny, too." Nori looked away, fingering her evening dress.

Zachary thought those were all good qualities, but he wasn't really sure how Nori perceived him, except that she was with him now and she wanted more than friendship between them. He'd take that for a good sign.

"And what are you looking for...in a spouse?"

Zachary wanted to reply, "I've found the one I'm looking for," but he decided to say, "I'm looking for the same qualities you are."

He caught Nori with that faraway gaze again. The same way she looked when she talked about her perfect wedding day. Wistful, with childlike wonder. Happy. And utterly beautiful.

"By the way," he asked, "do you like dreams?"

"I like the good ones."

"Yes, well, last night I dreamed about you," Zachary said.

"You did? Tell me about it...that is, if it's good." Nori leaned toward him.

Zachary felt himself stepping into unfamiliar territory. Well, more like leaping into unknown waters without a boat or life jacket. Or the ability to swim. But with Nori, he couldn't help himself. "I dreamed I'd been dropped into a tunnel, dark and cold. I stumbled along for what seemed like days, and then just when I thought I might never escape, I turned a corner and saw a soft yellow light. Slowly the illumination morphed into something else."

"What was it?" Nori eyes widened.

"You. You were the warm light I'd been searching for."

"Oh my." A tiny gasp escaped Nori's lips.

"Is something wrong?"

"No, nothing's wrong. Except...I've had the same dream about you."

"Oh?" Zachary stroked his finger against his lip, thinking about divine assistance.

"How strange is that? I mean, this can't be. Can it? To have us both dream the same thing?" Nori gazed up at the stars and then back at him.

"I like to figure out things. I'm pretty good at it. But there are some things in this life, even with the help of science, that defy our understanding. Some things must be left to mystery. Such as the size of the universe, splitting atoms. . .love."

"So are you happy just to leave mysteries unsolved?" Nori asked.

Zachary raised his chin and spread out his hands in an attempt to be dramatic. "If there isn't enough data at the time to make a clear hypothesis, then what else is there but conjecture. . .or to revel in the unknown?"

Nori chuckled. "I suppose so."

He'd gone this far, so Zachary decided to take one more dangerous step. "Would you go out with me tomorrow evening?"

Nori gave him one of those pauses again—the kind that made him sweat.

"All right," she finally said. "What will we do?"

"Well, I thought you could come over to my apartment and I could make us some supper."

Nori pulled back, looking shocked. "You mean you actually bake things and fry things and roast things?"

He nodded. "I grill, too."

She cocked her head. "Are you sure you're not just trying to trick me into coming over to cook for you?"

"Never." Zachary placed his hand over his heart. "I like to cook. I love it, in fact. I could make salmon with rosemary, Caesar salad, and chocolate mousse for dessert. Anyway, after I feed you, I thought we could settle in front of my big screen TV. There's going to be a *Star Trek* marathon." Was that another grimace? *Oh, that last suggestion might have come off a bit peculiar.* Or was she upset about the salmon? Maybe women hated fish. "Or I could make you stuffed pork chops or filet mignon. . .whatever you'd like."

"Oh no, that's fine," Nori said. "I love fish. I just find it shocking that you cook. Do you want me to bring anything?"

He shook his head. "Just you. That's all I want." His face heated up. "Six thirty?"

Nori curled a strand of blond hair around her finger. "Yes, six thirty is perfect."

⸎

After congratulating the newly married couple and enjoying the wedding dinner to the fullest, Zachary deposited Nori at her door. He'd hoped to give her a good night kiss, but the moment didn't feel quite right. Their first kiss shouldn't be rushed or taken lightly. He knew little about women, but for some reason, on that one point, he felt certain. And then he remembered his prayer about not wanting to get ahead of the Lord. Yes, he would celebrate the romancing of Nori Kelly, but he would also let it unfold in a way that would please God.

Then Zachary did the only thing he could think to do before entertaining the love of his life—he microcleaned his apartment. He made certain the kitchen was sanitized and the bathroom was devoid of anything embarrassing.

At 1:00 a.m., exhausted from cleaning, Zachary fell into bed with all his clothes on. He stared up at the ceiling, knowing he was way too restless and tired to sleep. So he allowed his mind to focus on the wedding reception and dinner. *What an evening.* It'd turned out much better than he'd ever imagined.

He drummed his fingers on the sheet. *However,* when he'd dropped Nori off at her door, she'd paused, looking at him with a curious smile. Had she been waiting for a kiss? What would he do when the time *was* right? He couldn't think of anything finer than kissing Nori Kelly, but he'd never kissed a woman before. And he wasn't sure what to do. He'd watched couples kissing in movies, yet the process looked problematic. So much could go wrong. Too many variables. Where did one put one's hands? And then there was the matter of how much pressure to the lips. How long should a kiss last? And what did people say after a kiss? Were there secrets he was unaware of?

Zachary punched his pillow. How peculiar. He could manage twenty geophysical applications, but he couldn't manage a simple kiss. He'd probably end up slobbering all over Nori or saying something stupid, and she'd slam the door in his face.

The image of her being upset with him and banging the door in his face wouldn't play out in his head. She wouldn't be so rude, but she might disappear from his life. He could imagine that easily enough.

He hurled his shoes through his open closet door and then bounced on his pillow a few times. But all inclinations toward drowsiness eluded him. And he knew well what pebble of worry was rubbing his thoughts raw. *The wedding date had simply been too easy.* They'd floated around in an evening made perfect by a beautiful setting and expensive food. The environment was so splendid, Nori would have been happy next to a block of wood. But his apartment date would be an ordinary evening. *It will be a test.* He knew where he stood concerning his feelings for Nori, but if she didn't enjoy a regular evening in his apartment, how would he expect her to spend the rest of her life with him?

Zachary jammed his pillow over his head. Maybe his thinking was way off. In his mind, he was treating Nori like a pet he wanted to pamper and please so she wouldn't run off. But that wasn't how love worked. Was it?

He was fairly certain his parents' divorce had tainted his views on matrimony, and yet he still believed God could make a marriage last a lifetime. But first things first. He'd only had one date with Nori, and there was no acknowledgment or hint of love. Just the hope of it.

Maybe he'd better go clean the bathroom. One more time.

Chapter 19

The next day, when the hour of Nori's arrival approached, Zachary near lost his cool. He opened the oven door again and poked at the salmo with a fork to make sure it wasn't overcooked. Then he put on some ja: music and dimmed the bright lights.

Zachary checked the bathroom for the tenth time and realized his obsessiv compulsive disorder had reached an all-time high. "Calm down," he kept chantir to himself. *Do other men act like this?* He doubted it. Only nerds with compulsi behavior.

He groaned as he fingered his hair. *Oh no.* He'd slathered on too much g The strands had glued together, giving his hair the suppleness of molded plastic

Trying to figure out how to de-gel his hair, Zachary focused on the prol lem by rubbing his finger back and forth over his upper lip. *Oh no.* Stubble. glanced in the entry mirror. He'd forgotten to shave. How in the world cou that have happened?

Was he losing his mind over a girl? "I believe I am," he said. Well, at least h khakis were new and his shirt was as crisp as celery.

The doorbell rang, and all fidgeting ceased. He walked to the door, ar on opening it, he found Nori smiling, dressed casually, and looking ready for good evening. And to her credit she said nothing about his plastered hair or fi o'clock shadow.

Maybe all his intense worry was unnecessary. "Hi there."

Nori's face radiated warmth.

Zachary felt mesmerized by her presence and pondered how easy it wou be to gaze upon her face for a lifetime. Maybe he should stop gaping and s: something. "Would you like to come in?"

Nori stepped over the threshold and into his abode. She looked around th room, appearing to study each object on his wall.

I guess stuff on display was always the litmus test. Very telling. Earlier when she been in his apartment, Nori had been so distraught about her parents that sl hadn't gotten so up close and personal with his wall displays. He found himse holding his breath as she stared at his accomplishments.

"My, my. You were chess champion in college? And president of the mat club. And a magna cum laude graduate. And valedictorian. Look at all thes

316

awards. And now geophysicist of the year. This is incredible." She touched the award on the table and then looked at him. "You are one impressive man."

Zachary wanted to smile. No, he really wanted to do an arm pump and cheer. Or maybe laugh like a cage full of hyenas—but he just bit his lip instead and said, "Thanks."

Nori continued to look at all his memorabilia like it mattered—like she was making an effort to get to know him, understand him. After she'd asked about everything on the wall as well as the table, she slid her hands into the pockets of her pants.

Guess she was waiting for an invitation to sit down. Or was he supposed to offer her something to drink? "Are you hungry?" *Food. Oh no.* "I smell something burning." *The salmon!* Zachary ran to the kitchen and yanked the oven door open. Smoked poured out. He waved, coughed a few times, and then stared in horror at the sight. His salmon was not only overcooked, it'd become a fish-shaped cinder block.

Nori rushed in, grabbed the oven mitts, and pulled out the baking dish of sizzling salmon.

"Thanks," Zachary said. "I got kinda paralyzed just looking at it."

Nori stared into the baking dish and then poked at it with a fork. "You know, I think it's going to be okay. We'll just eat the middle part."

He sighed at the fish. The tree-like sprigs of fresh rosemary, which had been gingerly placed on top of the fish, now looked like the charred remains of a forest fire. "But the whole thing will taste burnt."

"Maybe not." Nori found a spatula in the drawer. "Let's hurry up and get it out of this pan."

They worked together for a few minutes to salvage whatever they could and placed a few chunks of salmon on their two plates.

He shook his head, staring at the mess. *Yep, dead, burned slabs of fish.* "I'm sorry. It's not edible."

"I'm the one who should be apologizing. I kept you in the living room too long. I should have asked you if I could help you in the kitchen."

How gracious was that? Zachary smiled at her. "It's okay." He turned his attention to the empty table and reached for salads and dressing, warm bread, home-made tartar sauce for the salmon, olives, cottage cheese, and anything else he could think of that would make his culinary disaster look a little less. . .well, disastrous.

When they finally sat down to eat, Zachary felt a lengthy but sincere prayer coming on, which he said out loud, asking God to not only bless the food to the nourishment of their bodies but to help it go down okay. Then he added a secret prayer that Nori wouldn't run away the moment the dinner was over.

Zachary watched Nori take her first bite of salmon. His leg bounced under the table as he waited for her response.

"It's good," she said. "It doesn't taste burned at all." Then she dug into the rest of the meal, making positive comments about the homemade bread and the salad.

He finally relaxed enough to eat. When they'd finished, Zachary rose to get the mousse from the fridge. He set one of the goblets in front of Nori.

"You made mousse? For me?"

Zachary nodded. "It's not too hard to make." He tried not to stare and chuckle as Nori raved and moaned over every bite of dessert. *Guess she likes it.*

Nori leaned her dessert goblet over and scraped out the last bite of mousse. "Well, now *that* was inspiring." She rested back in her chair. "I've never known a guy who liked to cook. Ever."

"Cooking is relaxing. Well, when I'm not burning things."

Nori chuckled.

"It makes me think about something besides work." Zachary picked up his dishes and set them in the sink.

Nori gathered her dishes together and followed him to the counter.

When he turned around, she was so close he almost started.

"You have a little mousse on the corner of your mouth." She reached up with her napkin and gently touched his face.

Zachary noticed that she had the same dreamy expression she'd worn the previous evening when he'd said good night. What should he do?

A lengthy pause ensued.

Should I take a chance and kiss her? He wondered what his odds were of success—probably 60/40 in his favor. But then again. . .

Before Zachary could go through an entire protracted debate in his head, Nori laced her fingers at the back of his neck and kissed him full on the mouth.

Oh, dearest, sweet Nori. Her lips—soft, moist, and inviting. If he'd known kissing Nori was going to be such rapture, the wait would have been agony. But now the wait was over, and so were his fears. He cupped her face in his hands and kissed her, hoping she could feel every bit of the love in his heart.

After a good long kiss, Nori pulled back, looked into his eyes, and then kissed his temples, cheeks, and chin.

Zachary closed his eyes to enjoy the full effect of her touch. Could life get any finer?

She placed her fingers over his mouth. "You have such wonderful lips. I never knew."

He chuckled and kissed the fingers that touched his lips. Zachary then slipped one hand around her waist and pulled her closer for another round of kissing. He wondered why he'd ever been so timid about kissing Nori. It was the most natural thing in the world. Natural and normal and yet extraordinary in every way. He felt as if he'd waited his whole life for this moment. He was home. Right here and now. With Nori in his arms.

When they let the kiss come to a tender close, Nori chuckled. "You know, I'd been wondering what it would be like to kiss you."

"Now you know," Zachary said. "And how was it?"

"Oh, I can assure you, it was all that it needed to be." Nori smiled. "And more."

"Well, I'm *very* glad for that."

"And what did you think?"

He looked at her. "You really want to know?"

"I do."

Zachary cleared his throat. "I think your kiss packs enough energy to cause a solar flare and enough celestial wonder to make an atheist believe in God."

Nori's mouth eased open, and her face lit up. "What an incredible compliment. I. . .uh. . .well, you've left me astonished." She released a nervous chuckle.

Even though Zachary would have loved to continue discussing the euphoria of her kiss, he suddenly felt self-conscious at his own frankness and fervor. "So, did you get plenty of supper?"

She paused, gazing at him. "Yes, thank you. It was *all* wonderful." Then Nori leaned over the sink and started to rinse off one of the plates.

Zachary lifted the dish from her hands. "You shouldn't have to do that."

"But I don't mind. In fact, when I fix you dinner, I'll make you help clean up." She winked.

"All right." He was so pleased to hear her talk of their future plans together that he couldn't refuse her. It was a good thing he made a fine income, because he knew he'd never be able to deny her anything.

They worked side by side, and when the cleanup was done and the dishwasher was softly humming, they headed to the living room.

Zachary pushed a button, and a large flat-paneled television rose up out of a mahogany cabinet.

"Oh. I've never seen a TV rise up out of nowhere before." Nori snuggled down on the couch like a bird in a nest. "Nice."

"You know, we don't *have* to watch science fiction. I also like other kinds of movies."

"Oh yeah?" Nori rested her chin in her palm. "Like what?"

"Well, I have one chick flick." Zachary pulled out a DVD and blew off so much dust that he coughed.

She grinned. "Only one?"

Zachary knew he looked a little sheepish. "Well, the truth is I ordered a sci-fi film, and they sent me this by accident."

Chapter 20

The evening with Zachary played itself out more beautifully than Nori could have ever imagined, and too soon, she thought, they were strolling back to her front door. "I had a great time," she said.

Zachary looked away for a second and then grinned at her. "You mean even with salmon that was burned beyond recognition?"

"Well, I'd say it was more fashionably *blackened*."

He chuckled.

When they arrived at her apartment, Nori wondered—hoped, in fact—that Zachary would kiss her good night.

After a moment of quiet expectation, Zachary moved closer to her. Instead of kissing her, he reached out and cupped her face in his hand. And then he let his fingers brush lightly across her cheek.

Nori closed her eyes, absorbing the warm and tender sensation of his touch. She couldn't help but notice the way he handled her—as if she were made of the most delicate china.

Ahh, no more princess of the friendship date. No more desperate times and desperate measures. And no more kissing the mirror!

Zachary continued to explore the contours of her face. "You are so beautiful in every way," he whispered in her ear.

How long had she dreamed of a man who would care about her like this? It seemed like forever. And now Zachary was here. He'd been so near, yet she'd never seen him. How could that be? *Well, I certainly see him now.* Just as she was about to open her eyes, Nori could feel his lips against hers.

After a tender kiss, Zachary eased away. "Boy, this makes geophysical interpretations seem *sooo* dull."

Nori laughed. "You're funny."

"I am?"

"The things you say. You're so honest and kind."

"That doesn't sound very funny *or* romantic."

She placed her hand over her heart. "Oh, it is to *me*."

Moments later, after a few more merry good nights, Nori closed the door and readied herself for bed. She realized that in weeks, even hours really, her impressions of Zachary had changed into something totally different. She found

320

him to be not only smart but loving and thoughtful and even funny in a sweet sort of way. And the biggest surprise of all was the gradual attraction she felt.

Gradual. She laughed. There wasn't anything gradual about the way she felt when Zachary first kissed her. Then Nori remembered that she'd kissed Zachary first. She was a little embarrassed about that. But not *too* embarrassed. She could tell he'd wanted to kiss her. Why he'd hesitated before she had no idea, but he wasn't faltering anymore.

Nori climbed under her comforter and scooted between the cotton sheets. She let their cooling softness soothe her wide-eyed emotions, and yet something untouched lingered in her spirit. Feeling too tired to explore all the emotions of the day, she snuggled into the pillow and closed her eyes, hoping for sleep.

Imaginings, light and airy, came to her like dangling willow branches swaying and dipping in the breeze. The little zephyr in her thoughts lifted her away into another world. She no longer had the will to hold onto her consciousness, so she released it like a kite on a wind-filled day.

Nori saw herself running in a field of golden clover. She had no idea how long she'd been there, but it felt like a lifetime. All was lovely and free and lit with sun. Happiness reigned in that place, and all was at peace.

Without warning, the autumn fields withered before her eyes and everything, all the flowers and bees and grasses, became laden with a gray wintry frost. Darkness spread over the fields, and an unseen oppression weighed heavily on her chest. Winds, biting and cold, lashed against her face until she could no longer breathe. A scream caught in her throat.

Then a hand, warm and strong, reached out to her, pulling her away from the peril. In one sweeping gesture, the fields of light were restored. She was home.

But in the midst of paradise revisited, she felt alone for the first time. But why? Who was her rescuer? Her hero? His face was in a shadow, his sweetness hidden from her. And yet she felt a familiarity when she'd touched his hand.

"Don't go," she heard someone say. "You must not go. Your time here isn't over."

Was she dreaming or living? She must find out the man's name and why he'd come.

Zachary.

Nori stirred out of a deep sleep, her heart racing and her body moist with perspiration. She rose up in bed, tossed back the covers, and looked around the room. The dream seemed so real. Too real.

Nori touched her palm and fingers where she'd felt his hand in hers. She knew her mind was playing tricks on her, but she could still felt the warmth of his touch. In spite of her flustered and whirling thoughts, the true meaning of the dream soon became realized.

I'm falling in love.

"How can this be?" Nori's heart made a few more hard and scary pounds before she calmed herself. *I'm still in control here.* She could take their relationship as slowly as she wanted to. He would wait for her. Wouldn't he?

She thought of Zachary and wondered what he was doing right now. Was he researching on the Internet? Making more chocolate mousse? Or was he also punching his pillow, curious as to why two ordinary dates had become like a surprise attack. Maybe he was scared and wary, too. Maybe that's why he had always hesitated in kissing her. He didn't want to get in too deep. Or too lost in love.

Too lost in love. She repeated the words out loud, listening to the sound of them. The word *lost* did seem appropriate since the feeling of losing one's heart to someone felt like being lost in a dark forest with no hope of light or rescue. She was lost in love, and there was no way out. But did she need a way out? Probably. Most likely. *I don't know.* But couldn't even the sweetest love eventually dissolve like melting snow?

She tried to fall asleep again, but thoughts of her parents plagued her. If they weren't getting a divorce all would look differently. She wouldn't be ruled by fear. But how could she fear what was so good and kind? With that thought, Nori let herself sink back into sleep.

⬿

Monday morning came softly, even though she'd tossed and turned all night. Nori rose, rubbing her back. She needed a new mattress. A new nightgown. And a new point of view. And she definitely needed some prayer. "Oh Lord, please help my parents to seek You first in all their decisions, and please help me not to be so injured from their choices that I miss Your will for my life."

Nori looked through the night table drawer for her Bible but couldn't find it. Had she misplaced it? She made a quick search through the apartment and finally found a copy in her closet. How sad and sorry was that? It had obviously been too long.

She sat on the loveseat in her bedroom and let her Bible fall open to her all-time favorite chapter, Psalm 121. *"I lift up my eyes to the hills—where does my help come from? My help comes from the Lord, the Maker of heaven and earth. He will not let your foot slip—he who watches over you will not slumber. . . ."*

How could she have forgotten some of God's most basic and loving promises? How could she have let that knowledge slip away from her heart even for a moment? She read further down into the chapter: *"The sun will not harm you by day, nor the moon by night. The Lord will keep you from all harm—he will watch over your life; the Lord will watch over your coming and going both now and forevermore."*

Could any scripture be more beautiful or comforting? It was hard to truly fathom His love and care.

He is watching me even now. He would take care of her needs. Every bit of confusion and fear and doubt. She embraced the book and thanked God for His Word.

Nori remembered how God used dreams to speak to people in the Bible and wondered if He was giving her guidance through her dreams about Zachary. Could God still speak to people while they were sleeping? He was God, and He was still in the business of miracles. All things were possible with the Lord. That she believed, too.

Placing the Bible on the top of her nightstand, she made a vow to herself and to God to reach out to His Word daily, not just when it was convenient or when she found herself in a tough situation.

Peace didn't flood over Nori, but she did feel a trickle. And it felt good. She decided to continue dating Zachary, but she would take her time—fall in love at her own pace. Of course at that speed, it might take years, but she was sure Zachary would wait.

⁓

Nori went through her usual morning routine—locked her door, checked it, and then headed to the elevator on her way to Sweet Nothings.

Zachary met her. They stood in the hallway mesmerized by each other for a moment. He reached out and touched her cheek.

The gesture felt so intimate that Nori felt her cheeks heat up. "Hi."

Ivan Wentworth emerged from his apartment.

Zachary and Nori grinned at each other as they joined Ivan in his trek toward the elevator.

Ivan looked back at her. "Nori?"

"Yes?" She caught up with Ivan but wondered what he could want. He was usually too enamored with his techno gadgets to notice her.

"I was just wondering if you'd like to go out to dinner sometime." Ivan slipped his Blackberry into his pocket and gave her his attention.

Zachary let out a puff of air that sounded like disgust.

Nori couldn't believe a neighbor would ask her out in front of Zachary—as if he were invisible. "I'm sorry, Ivan, but I guess I'll pass."

Ivan blinked a few times. "Really?"

They all three stepped into the elevator. The doors closed like a tomb, sealing them in together.

After Nori mashed the "G" button several times, silence seeped in, filling the small space like a suffocating, tar-like smoke. Nori wanted to cough but swallowed instead.

Chapter 21

Nori kept her eyes straight ahead, since she was too afraid to look Zachary in the eye.

"May I ask you why?" Ivan sounded hurt.

She winced, wishing she were somewhere else. Anywhere else. Like maybe in a den of hungry wolverines. How much should she say to Ivan? "I appreciate the invitation. But I'm dating Zachary right now." *Oh no.* How did that come out of her mouth? *Way too much information, Nori.* She should have stuck with "No."

Ivan glanced over at his competition and winced. "Oh, I see."

Nori was proud of Zachary. He'd crossed his arms in irritation, but he'd remained silent.

Ivan slapped the ground floor button like it was a mosquito. "There's something wrong with this elevator." When the doors suddenly opened, Ivan escaped with a weak smile and a wave.

Zachary held the door for Nori. "You okay?"

"Yes."

"So, I guess from the sounds of the conversation. . .we're involved." Zachary's expression told her he was more pleased than surprised with her admission.

"I do believe we are." Uncertainty and hesitation still lingered in her heart, but the moment called for a smile, and so she gave him one. A good one.

"I'm glad you feel that way." Zachary's voice held a cheerful lilt.

"But. . .I just don't know how much yet. I hope that's okay."

"I understand." He looked at her. "I'll see you later."

"I certainly hope so." Nori gave him a little salute good-bye. As she drove to work, her thoughts settled on to the shop.

The second she entered the glass doors at Sweet Nothings, Lizza was all over her with questions. "So what happened with Zachary at the wedding? We've barely had a chance to talk. Come on, tell me everything. Please. Please."

Nori put up her hands. "Okay, I surrender." She smiled. "Well, we ate. By the way, the filet mignon was the best I've ever had. Cooked to perfection. And that baked Alaska for dessert? What a unique idea. You're—"

"Yeah, the food was incredible. But what about you and Zachary?"

"Well, we talked, and we—"

324

"You know what I mean. I want the juicy parts. Come on. You gotta give 'em up."

"Zachary and I had a nice time," Nori singsonged as she walked around the shop looking for things to do. *I suppose she does deserve a few details, since she helped orchestrate the whole thing.*

Lizza gestured to keep going. "And?"

Nori wasn't sure how much to say. She decided to toss out one more point of interest. "We're dating, and—"

"I knew it. We have a touchdown." Lizza's arms shot up as she made crowd noises.

Nori laughed at her friend. "I'm taking my time."

"Girl, you're light-years beyond that."

"And how do you know?"

"Because I see something in your eyes." Lizza tilted her head and narrowed her eyes. "Something that wasn't there before."

"Probably just dust off one of the shelves."

"Hey, these shelves aren't dusty, and you know it." Lizza crossed her arms. "You've got a twinkle in your eye."

"A twinkle?"

"Yeah, you know, a sparkle, a glimmer of something that wasn't there before. You have the glow when a woman is falling. . ."

"Falling?" Nori asked.

"Yes, falling."

"It's probably more like bending a little."

"Sure it is." Lizza shook her head.

"Who can know love? For certain, I mean."

"Listen, love is a freight train. When you're hit, you know it."

Nori chuckled. "Well, what if it's a toy train?"

Her friend just sighed at her as she hid the feather duster and paper towels under the counter.

"I guess I'll mop the floor before the customers get here," Nori said.

"I already mopped the floor this morning."

"You're the best." Nori patted Lizza on the back and then headed to the cash register. "You're not a good shrink, but you're the best in every other way."

Lizza followed Nori. "I'm not giving up that easily. Not very long ago, you were so ready to fall in love. I know what's happening to your parents is bothering you."

Nori took in a deep breath, wishing Lizza would let it go. She wasn't in the mood to talk about her parents. "I won't deny it."

"Did your dad ever return your messages?"

"No."

"Boy, that's tough."

"He's not trying to be mean," Nori said. "Although that's the way it feels. He's just trying to avoid my lectures."

"And would you lecture him?"

Nori thought for a moment. "Well, it wouldn't start out that way. But sooner or later I know I'd want to ask a few pointed questions."

"But still, your dad should call you so you can deal with it."

"I've been *dealing* with it for weeks." Nori rearranged some jars of stick candy on the counter. And then rearranged them again.

"But have you? I mean, I know you've said you're obsessed about their divorce. But that's not the same as *dealing* with it."

Nori tried not to overreact. She felt like getting angry, but she got quiet instead. She didn't like having her remarks thrown back in her face, especially when she'd said them in a vulnerable moment. In fact, she would like to have told Lizza to mind her own business. But Lizza was a friend as well as an employee, and since they'd allowed each other certain inroads into each other's lives, it was indeed Lizza's business. "I don't know. You might be right."

"I wish you could talk to your parents. Maybe it would give you some closure. You know, so this doesn't ruin your life." Lizza placed a hand on Nori's shoulder. "I just hate to see *their* decision cause you to miss out on the joy you were meant to have."

Lizza's words were soft but piercing, too. *She's right.* "I know it takes a lot of courage to talk to friends candidly. I appreciate that." And then with that statement, Nori hoped the conversation had come to a close.

"Well, you know what else would help?"

Oh no. Not more advice.

Lizza wiggled her eyebrows. "Some of these buttercream truffles we got yesterday." She pulled a silvery box out from under the counter, opened the lid, and breathed in the fragrance. "Oh, I never tire of all these free samples."

"Yeah, that's because you have a waistline." Nori groaned.

"You do, too. You've lost a bunch of weight."

"Well, mainly because—" Their banter was interrupted by the bell over the door.

Zachary walked in the shop, his shoulders sagging and his expression twisted in pain.

They all said their hellos and then Nori strode over to him, alarmed. "What's the matter?" She hoped something terrible hadn't happened.

"This probably isn't the best time, but I felt you should know right away," Zachary said.

"Please tell me what's happening." Nori touched his arm.

"I'm being asked to move to Denver. Immediately." Zachary looked away. When he looked back at her, his eyes were misty.

Chapter 22

Denver?" Nori released Zachary's arm. "But why?"

"My boss just informed me that South Gate is moving its operations there. Everybody goes to Colorado, or we lose our jobs." Zachary thought this had to be the worst day of his life. Just when he'd formed a genuine connection with Nori. They'd have to try to develop a long-distance relationship. He'd rarely seen that option work among his coworkers, since the detachment usually meant a breakdown of the resolve to stay close.

"Denver is pretty far away." Nori's voice sounded bewildered.

"Yes, it is." Zachary knew one alternative that would solve their problems. Marriage. But that answer created new problems. Nori's business was successful, and he was pretty certain she'd never want to move. Nor could he ever ask her to make that sacrifice. "I could quit my job," he said.

"Do you have other job prospects here?"

He shook his head. "I wish I did. This isn't a big oil town, so there aren't that many opportunities. If I quit my job, I'm not certain I'll get another one here." Zachary realized his new plan wasn't going to fly the minute he'd thought it. How could he ask her to marry him if he had no job? He certainly wasn't going to let Nori marry a loafer.

"You can't quit your job." Nori shook her head. "I don't want you to."

From the back of the shop, Lizza cleared her throat. "I have everything under control. Nori, you go on with Zachary. You guys look like you need a minute."

"Good idea," he said. "Do you want to go for a walk?"

"Some fresh air. Maybe that will help us think more clearly."

Well, at least she was saying "us." That was a good sign. Zachary opened the door for her, and they strolled down the sidewalk toward their favorite spot—Arlington Lawn at The Promenade. Once they'd climbed the stairs and they were seated by the mist, Zachary took Nori's hand. It was time for some honesty. Some revelations. "I care about you, Nori. A great deal."

"I care about you, too," she said.

Zachary gazed at her. The surrounding light made Nori's eyes look like the color of the sea. But something else shone in her eyes. He hoped it might be love. Now that they'd shared some of their feelings, he couldn't imagine himself saying good-bye, even if they promised to build a long-distance relationship.

If he did propose to her, she would at least discover the extent of his feelings. Then maybe God would take care of the rest. Somehow He could work everything out. Did he have that much blind faith? He breathed in. "It's more than just caring. I love you. I have for a long time. . .from afar, I guess you could say."

"You love me?" Nori sounded confused, maybe even a little scared.

"Yes." Zachary looked around, grateful the park had emptied of visitors. At least for the moment. But the clouds above them had darkened, and he hoped they wouldn't be interrupted by a storm. With resolve and a feeling of urgency, he scooted off the bench and knelt on one knee. "Nori Kelly, would you do me the honor of becoming my wife?"

"Be your wife?" Nori looked down at their fingers, which were intertwined. "But we barely know each other. I don't mean to belittle what you've said. It's a generous and lovely offer, and I'm grateful. But. . ."

This isn't going well. Zachary tried not to panic.

Nori slipped her hand from his. "Except for the times we've spent together recently, we've only had bits of conversations outside our apartments."

He rose to his feet. "Love isn't subject to time. . .or anything else."

"I thought maybe we should date for a few months. To see if what we felt would grow. It's too soon." Nori stepped over to the cascades and looked over the edge.

Zachary sat down for a moment, begging God for some help and hoping Nori would come back to the bench. But she didn't come back.

He walked over to her and looked down at the steam coming off the rocks. Perhaps he'd gotten ahead of God. Once again. *Well, that feels familiar.*

He stood in silence next to Nori as he stared out over the battered rocks. The ever-rising water vapor always reminded him of something celestial—perhaps angels sweeping about, only half materializing. He wondered how Nori saw the mist. More importantly, he wondered what she was thinking about right now. What he wouldn't give to know all her thoughts—to be able to overcome all her fears by saying just the right words. Oh, to have all the perfect expressions of love in his mind, just waiting to be said.

Instead of rising to the occasion, forcing himself to conjure up a magical phrase or two, Zachary felt drained, as if he no longer could hold himself up. Did that dull side of his personality bother Nori as well? She had every right to worry about marrying a man who was as exciting as an empty jar of jelly.

"I just don't want us to rush into anything," Nori said after a long pause. "What if we were to make an error in judgment? You know. . .do something we'd both regret all our lives. We don't even know the basics about each other."

"What do you mean?"

Nori seemed to study him. "Like for instance, what's my favorite color?"

"Well, I think you can know people's characters and essences without knowing their favorite colors." Zachary didn't want to manipulate or make light of her doubts, yet he still found himself wanting to defend his love.

"See, you don't know what my—"

"Lavender." Zachary leaned over the railing, looking away from her. "Your favorite color is lavender."

"But how could you—"

"You wear that color twice as often as any other color. So I assumed it's your favorite." He laced his fingers together but didn't glance back at her.

"I wear lavender twice as often? How could you know that? *I* didn't even know that." She reached out and touched Zachary's cheek. "That is very sweet of you to notice, though."

Nori called me sweet. Not a good sign—probably what women say when they're trying to say good-bye. For the last time. Should he make the moment less painful for her by letting her walk away? Or should he keep trying to persuade her of his devotion? Even when she was frightened of the consequences? Was he being noble or selfish? Perhaps he would never deserve such delight. *God, please help me.*

Zachary waded through the awkward moment, but not without some perspiration and prayer. Then he decided to try and rescue the moment. "I may not know a lot about you, but I feel I know the important things." He looked straight into her eyes. "You have a kind face and a generous spirit. I love many of the same things you do, and we both love and worship the one true God. I know we come at life from different angles, but that's the beauty of it. We're like this prism. When the light hits it, colors stream out of it. . .separate and yet flowing together as one." He shut up then and wondered how he'd gotten himself to say such words.

"That was by far the most beautiful thing any man has ever said to me. Or will *ever* say to me." She chuckled. "You're making this so hard. I'm trying to set you free if that's what you need, and here you—"

"It's not what I need. Or want." Zachary took her by the shoulders. "Without you, I'd be lonely and miserable in Denver. But what about you? Can you let go of what we have that easily?"

She shook her head. "No. I think there'd always be a hole there. A place you filled that no one else can fill. There's no doubt I'd be a little lost."

"Only a little?"

"I don't know." Nori pulled away from him. "But even if I *did* know for sure how I felt, our choices are still pretty bleak. Quitting your job is not a good option. And if we dated, flying back and forth would be very hard. If we ever *did* marry, then I'd be forced to sell my shop. You see, even though my grandmother wasn't a wealthy woman, she insisted on giving me the money to start Sweet Nothings. She trusted me to follow my dream. The shop is finally taking off. I just can't walk away from the sacrifice she made. It wouldn't be fair to her."

"No, of course not." Zachary dropped his gaze. "I would never ask you to sell your business."

Nori's eyes filled with tears.

He felt terrible that he'd put that sadness in her face. He pulled out a handkerchief from his jacket pocket and dabbed at the wetness on her cheeks. "I'm sorry I made you cry."

"You know, I think I believe you now," she said in a soft voice. "You really *do* love me."

"Yes." Zachary lifted her chin.

Nori shook her head. "Why is the timing in life always so off? Why is everything that is good and right always so hard?" She took his hand and placed it against her cheek. "I like what we have together. I don't want to lose it. And yet, there seems to be this great and impossible fissure. . .where there's no bridge."

There was so much more Zachary wanted to say, but now perhaps it was pointless. Nori had made up her mind, and he would not continue to badger her or make her cry.

"When would you have to go?" she asked.

Her words jarred him back to reality. "The company moves everything in about six weeks." He winced. "But now. . .I guess I'll catch a flight out this afternoon and search for an apartment."

Nori's cell phone came to life in her purse. "I'm so sorry." She looked at the caller. "It's my father. I'd better take it. I'm sorry."

"It's okay. Go ahead." Zachary sat on the bench away from her, wanting to give her some privacy. He watched her from a distance as she answered the phone.

Nori held her finger over her other ear. She seemed to listen for a few minutes, frowning and sighing. It became obvious whatever her father was saying to her caused her pain. After a few more minutes, Nori folded up her phone and walked back to him. "It's my father, finally responding to my messages."

"You're upset. Do you want to sit for a while and tell me what's wrong?"

Nori sat down close to him. "He called to tell me the divorce is almost final. He said Mom mentioned something about possibly marrying someone else. And he's okay with that. I can't believe it." She placed her hand over her mouth.

"I'm so sorry." Zachary put his arm around her.

She rested her head against his shoulder but said no more.

What an awful blow for Nori. He spent the quiet in prayer for her. But in the midst of his appeal to God, he became aware of his own sorrow, since as self-seeking as the thought seemed, he knew this latest misfortune would affect his life as well.

Surely his chances of wooing Nori were over.

Chapter 23

Nori wasn't sure how long she'd been sitting on her couch in her bathrobe, just staring at the wall. Minutes, maybe an hour. She did feel badly, though, for leaving the store so early in the morning. But after she'd burst into tears, Lizza had insisted she go home to rest.

Oh great. Was that someone at the door? She slogged to the door and opened it. Her mother stood in the hallway, looking misplaced. "Mother?"

"Hi." She shuffled her feet. "Will you let me in?"

"Of course." Dad must have told her about his phone call. *So, Mom knows I know about her possible remarriage.*

This time Nori was pulled into a warm hug by her mother. The exchange felt good. Comforting. And long overdue.

"May I have some of that famous hot chocolate of yours?" her mother asked as she headed toward the kitchen.

"Sure." Nori followed behind her, wondering what she was going to say. And praying her own words wouldn't get too sharp or divisive.

They puttered around the kitchen together, gathering up the turbinado sugar, the unsweetened chocolate, and the milk and cream. When the cocoa was ready, Nori poured it into mugs and then garnished it with peppermint sticks and dollops of homemade whipped cream.

They both sat down and took careful sips.

Her mother dabbed at the whipped cream mustache on her upper lip. "This is good."

"Thanks."

"I suppose you know why I came."

"Well, Dad finally called me back."

Her mother fiddled with her napkin, folding it and unfolding it. "Well, I didn't tell you about the possibility of remarrying since it didn't seem necessary at the time."

"I love you. I'm your *daughter*. I would want to know."

"Yes, I see that now. Leaving for a cruise was silly. I felt like such a sneak that morning. Anyway, I ended up canceling my trip."

"Oh?" Nori wondered why she wasn't told. Why such mystery? She realized she didn't know her mother. Perhaps she never had.

"I want you to go ahead with your questions now." Somber creases lined her mother's face. "The ones you never got to ask."

"All right." Nori took in a deep breath, relieved for the chance to understand. "So, *you* asked for the divorce because you want to marry another man." She kept her tone respectful.

"Well, yes, I brought up the subject of divorce with your father, but he readily agreed to it."

"Really?" Nori looked down at her fingers, which had balled up into fists.

"Yes." Her mother licked her lips. "But there is something else you need to know."

Oh no. Can I handle more surprises? "Okay."

"Well, I need to just get this out." She shook her head. "Before I married your father, I was in love with a man named Roger Conley."

Nori gave her a smile, but inside she already felt weary of the discussion. "Then why didn't you marry Roger?"

Her mother pursed her lips. "Because my mother demanded that I marry your father. I didn't want to, but I had no say in the matter."

"But Grandma Essie was so sweet. I can't imagine her doing such—"

"She was sweet to *you*. She adored you, in fact. But she was quite the spitfire in her younger days, and she did a pretty good job of controlling my life."

"But why would Grandma Essie do that? Force you and Dad to marry?" Nori hugged her middle for support. She couldn't stand to think of her beloved grandmother doing anything so deplorable.

"She made us marry right away. . .because your father and I were going to have a baby."

Nori blinked a few times. "Me?"

Her mother nodded.

Okay, stay calm, Nori. She tried to steady her breathing.

Her mother scooted her chair closer to her. "Please understand. We'd made a terrible mistake. I know that."

"*I* was a mistake?"

"I'm not trying to say *you* were a mistake." She pushed her hair away from her face. "Surely you understand what I mean. It's just—"

"But why isn't Roger my father. . .if you loved him?" Nori realized her question might be getting too intimate. "You don't have to answer that."

"Thank you for not demanding an answer. You do have a right to know, but it's kind of complicated. And to be honest, after all these years, it's kind of hazy, too. Anyway, my mother wanted us to do the right thing, but marrying the wrong man just piled one mistake on top of another."

Nori wasn't sure what to say now. All her talks on devotion seemed diluted by the truth. God didn't like divorce, and yet He wouldn't force people into marriage. Confusion clouded her reason and resolve.

Perhaps she'd feel a little better if her mother stroked her hair and whispered to her that all would be well. Isn't that what mothers always did? Yet Nori couldn't even summon a single memory of her mother comforting her in such a way.

"Your father is okay with this decision. He's not hurting."

"But *I'm* hurting." Nori rose and splayed her fingers on the table. "Doesn't that mean anything?" She knew her words were selfish and insensitive, but the words still flowed out of her. *God, am I lashing out in pain or reprisal?*

"Of course it matters what you think. But in the end, I have to live my own life. I can't always be living it the way others want me to. That's what I did for my mother, and it didn't work." She reached out to Nori and clung to her arm. "I have a little time left for happiness. My mother snatched this joy from me. Please don't let it be my own daughter who keeps it from me when I have a second chance." Her voice became raspy. "I think that would be too ironic for this old heart to take."

"But. . .what does God want in all this?" Nori touched her mother's hand, which still clung to her arm.

"To be honest, dear, I haven't asked Him. I haven't been close to Him for a while now." She let out a long puff of air. "By now, I think maybe He's forgotten about me."

"That's not the nature of God. . .to forget. He could honor this commitment you've kept with Dad by giving you love. . .if only you'd ask Him."

"That's sweet, Nori, but isn't it kind of naive?" She released her arm.

"Anything is possible with God."

Her mother took another mouthful of hot chocolate and then looked at her intently. "I want you to know something. There's been no infidelity in our marriage. Your father and I have been faithful all these years. Do you understand?"

"I do."

"And someday when you marry, if you choose to marry, promise me you'll marry for love."

"I will." Nori dipped her head, feeling so many emotions that she wasn't sure what to deal with first. But when she saw the lifeless and remorse-filled expression on her mother's face, it tore at her heart. "I'm sorry it was me who got in the way of the man you really loved."

Her mother gave her a firm nod. "It's not your fault." She rose and rubbed her hands along the counter. "Although there was a time when I felt differently. And I've always wanted to talk to you about that."

"Oh?" Nori wondered what she could mean.

"When you were growing up, I think I resented you from time to time. Whenever I got to thinking about Roger and what could have been, well, somehow in the midst of thinking about my predicament I forgot how to be a good mother."

Nori stared at her hands, which were folded in her lap. "But what did—"

She put her hand up. "Please let me get all the way through this. I need to say these things. I've practiced this speech for years." She cleared her throat. "What I'm trying to apologize for is the way I treated you sometimes. I was too hard on you. You know, the way I made you do things over and over when you were little."

"Over and over?" Nori asked. "What do you mean?"

"Well, sometimes when I was upset about my circumstances, I would take my irritation out on you by telling you that you weren't doing things right." She ground her knuckles into the counter. "You'd make your little bed and then I'd come behind you and undo it, saying you didn't do it right. Or you'd make a stack of folded towels, and I'd knock them over and make you start again. Those kinds of things." She looked away. "I'm sure you know what I mean."

Nori searched her mind, and then one by one, some of the hurtful moments her mother spoke of came filtering back. She winced and hugged herself. "Yes. I guess I do remember a little now." Perhaps she'd blocked some of the memories since they were so painful.

"I guess they were acts of retaliation. But it was cruel to take out my frustration on an innocent child. *My* child. I can't believe I did the things I did. I'm so sorry." She brought her fists up to her forehead.

Like a lens adjusting its focus, Nori began to see why she'd grown up with compulsive behaviors. Somehow knowing, just knowing the truth, was a great relief.

Her mother turned to her. "Nori, please, will you ever forgive me?"

Nori rushed into her mother's arms. "Yes, I do. I forgive you."

They hugged for some time as a quiet reverence settled over them.

"You know what I've wanted over the years?" Her mother whispered into her hair. "Even more than Roger?"

"What?" Nori asked.

"This moment. When I could finally get myself to say those things. And then to hear you say that you'd forgiven me. It takes courage to admit such embarrassing things, and I've been a coward for a long time."

Nori could no longer hold back the tears. "I love you, Mom. I always have."

"And you're my greatest blessing in this life." She moved from the embrace and leaned against the counter, her eyes flooding with fresh tears. She waved her hands in frustration. "And here I was determined to get through this without crying." She raised her hands. "It's impossible."

Nori smiled. "I don't mind." She thought her mother had never looked so beautiful. And her hug never felt so comforting.

"Okay, so that I don't turn into a total fool here, why don't you tell me something happy? Something wonderful in your delicious, candy-filled life."

Nori knew this might not be the best time to tell her mother about Zachary, yet she felt compelled to continue their newfound camaraderie. "I *do* have something to tell you. . . ."

Her mother sat down. "Please tell me."

Nori laced her fingers together. "A man proposed to me today," she said in an excited whisper.

"What? Really?"

"Hey, don't act so surprised." Nori grinned.

Her mother chuckled. "I'm only surprised because I didn't even know you were dating anyone."

"Well, I haven't said yes. I wanted to give it some time."

"Do you love him?"

Nori released a puff of air. "I believe I do. But I'm a little scared."

"Well, you already know what my advice would be. Only marry him if you're sure." Her mother leaned toward her. "What's he like?"

"He's an exceptional man, smart and handsome. A wonderfully kind Christian man. I don't deserve him, but he loves me."

"Oh my. He sounds remarkable."

Nori clasped her fingers together. "He is."

She gathered her daughter's hands in hers. "I have one more word of advice. Do you want to hear it?"

"Yes, please."

"I don't want our divorce to scare you away from marriage. That would be the worst kind of torture for me. Do you understand? If you love him and this is meant to be, I'd hate to see you forgo your happiness because of what's happening between your father and me."

"Okay." Nori took a long drink of her cocoa. "And will you do one thing for me?"

"I'll try."

"Before the divorce is final, will you ask God about it? Just talk to Him about it. That's all I'm asking."

Her mother paused. "That's a hard one, Nori. But I give you my word." She grinned. "Now, please tell me more about this young man of yours."

Nori chuckled. "Sure."

After an hour of heart-sharing and a bite of lunch, her mother left with a promise to stay in touch.

Nori shut the door still wishing her mother would change her mind about the divorce, and yet her heart overflowed with gratitude for the forgiveness that had started a healing in their relationship. It had been a merciful gift from God and one she hadn't even asked for. In fact, perhaps she hadn't asked for the Lord's help often enough. Maybe God was trying to give her an answer about marrying Zachary and she was too busy to hear Him.

That still, small voice. Nori sighed. Had she taken the time to really listen? It was easy to forget that the Lord wanted to brighten every corner and crevice of her life—the already radiant stuff, the shadowy stuff, and the dark stuff. Had she forgotten how dazzling and piercing and calming His Light really was? *One way to find out.*

She remembered the new prayer chapel their congregation had just completed and decided to make use of it. Nori drove up to her church and parked near the stone walkway that led to The Chapel in the Woods. She strolled down the winding path through the stand of pines and gazed up at the building. The chapel had a quaint look to it, complete with a tiny steeple, an arched front door, and several stained-glass windows.

Nori tried the lever on the door handle. *Open. Perfect.* She headed down the aisle, passing by the short rows of wooden pews, and then sat down in the front row. As she took in the beauty of the chapel, her gaze traveled over the vaulted ceiling and beams, the beautifully carved altar, and the magnificent stained-glass window just in front of her. The glowing glass depicted Christ listening to a group of children who were gathered at His feet.

Her hands folded together as she meditated on the scene, wondering what the Lord would have said to the little ones who wanted nothing more than to be near Him. And how would the children have responded to His words? They must have felt safe enough to share their stories with Him. Yes, Jesus always was a good listener.

"Still is," a voice echoed in her mind.

Nori knelt at the altar. Without holding anything back, she poured out her heart like a child—emptying all the joys and worries and hopes to her Father, her Friend, and her Savior.

After a long moment of reflection and then a prompting in her spirit, she prayed. "Forgive me, Lord, for desiring that tight little circle of love to always be about romance and not about You. I acknowledge You as the Lover of my soul and the Someone who cares for me far more than any husband ever could. Help me never to forget these truths and to love You first, above all."

And then Nori wept. And waited. And listened. The Lord came near and comforted her. After some time had passed, she rose from the bench, feeling refreshed.

Nori walked out of the chapel with peace and an answer to the happy dilemma bursting in her heart. She would marry the man she dearly loved and move with him to Denver. She felt certain Lizza would buy the shop, and then all would be well. Zachary wouldn't have to quit his job, and she could start a new Sweet Nothings in Denver.

Once back at the apartment building, she rang Zachary's doorbell, hoping she could catch him before he headed to the airport. She paused for a moment and then rang the bell again. Nothing. Nori looked at her watch: 4:05 p.m. He'd already gone.

After a long wait with no response, Nori glanced up and down the hallway, wondering what to do next.

At that moment, Ivan the Not-So-Great emerged from his apartment.

"Ivan, have you seen Zachary?"

"Who?"

"Zachary Martin. You know. . .the guy who lives right next to me."

"Oh, you mean the geek you're dating?"

Nori winced. "Please don't say that."

Ivan looked hopeful. "So, you're *not* dating him anymore?"

"No, I mean please don't call Zachary a geek."

"Why not?"

"Because he's a wonderful man, and I'm in love with him." Nori surprised herself, saying those words, and yet she knew it was the truth.

Ivan pulled back. "Is that right? You love him?"

"Yep. That's right. So, have you seen Zachary?"

"Yeah."

Nori breathed a prayer of thanksgiving. "Where and when?"

"Well, I saw him this morning when we all got on the elevator together."

Her shoulders drooped. "No, I mean since then."

Ivan nodded. "Yeah, I did see him come back home."

"When was it? Did he leave again? Did he have any luggage with him?"

Ivan held up his hand. "Hold on. I'm trying."

"Sorry."

"He came home maybe ten minutes ago. But I don't know if he went out again. He did have a piece of luggage with him. I'm sure of that. One carry-on bag."

"Did he say anything?"

Ivan shook his head. "No."

"Did he look upset. . .at all?"

"Sorry, I wasn't paying much attention. Is everything okay?"

Nori took in a deep breath. "I'm going to make it okay. If I can."

"Good luck then." He smiled.

"Thanks. I appreciate your help."

"Sure." Ivan gave her a wave and went on his way.

Nori heaved a sigh of relief, thinking Zachary must not have gone to Denver after all. He'd changed his mind. But why wasn't he answering his door? Had he seen her through the peephole and then refused to let her in? Did he think she wasn't worth so much indecision and doubt? The flood of new concerns didn't win her over. Zachary's devotion appeared real and lasting. His love wouldn't be so easily discarded.

Nevertheless, Nori felt a need for some serious haste. Perhaps she still had time to make things right. She'd call Lizza at work and discuss the sale of Sweet Nothings. Then she'd give Zachary's door another sound rap. Surely her news of commitment would convince him of her love.

Determination mingled with her excitement as she swung open her front door and raced to the phone.

Chapter 24

Zachary unplugged his coffee grinder. *Wow, that stupid machine is loud.* Had he heard somebody at the door while he was grinding his bag of coffee? He listened. Nothing. Must have been noise from upstairs. He often heard pounding as if somebody up there was learning to step dance—somebody, in fact, who was a kinsman to Goliath.

With robotic efforts and zero enthusiasm, he cleaned out the coffee grinder, put the grounds away in a large glass container, and then decided not to make coffee after all. Caffeine wasn't going to make him feel any better. What he really wanted to do was bang his head against the wall, but he knew the act would prove itself too infantile and unproductive as well as painful. But what could be worse than the way he felt now?

He plopped on his couch and didn't move. His flight to Denver had just left, but all his inspiring self-talk wasn't enough to get him on that plane. What would happen now? He'd have to schedule another flight. But then the love of his life wouldn't be a part of his future. He had envisioned so many good things with Nori. Taking her to the jazz festival. Hiking all the trails together in the national park. Sharing their first Christmas.

What a disaster. How had he come to know such misery? He hadn't moved to the apartment with the idea of finding someone to love. But now there was no second guessing. No turning back. He'd have to live with the lonely truth. Love happened, and there was nothing he could do about it but suffer.

Zachary rested his head in his palms. If Nori was never meant to love him, then he must have taken a wrong turn somewhere. *But where?* Hadn't he prayed about the situation and felt a peace about it? Hadn't he gotten the green light? Maybe he was color-blind.

Zachary squeezed his temples. If only Nori's parents had waited to talk about their divorce. . . He and Nori could have married before the fallout. But then there was always the possibility she would have regretted marrying him, and that would have hurt even more.

Then a new scenario hit Zachary. Maybe there was more at play than the breakup of Nori's parents. Maybe Nori had other reasons for wanting to sever their connection. Perhaps he'd poured his compulsive behavior into their budding affections like motor oil into leaded crystal and Nori had decided one

341

person with OCD was more than enough.

God, if I messed up somewhere, could You please undo my mistakes? Clear the file? Is there any way I can have another chance?

He groaned, thinking of the worst possibility of all. "Lord, even though it's painful for me to even think of the other possibility. . .I still want Your will. If Nori was never meant to be my wife, then please help me to let her go."

Tears wet his skin, and he brushed them away. As he sat there, though, an idea formed. Maybe Nori was so focused on the fear of divorce that what she needed most from him was a sign of devotion and commitment. But how could he accomplish that?

Zachary rose off the couch. *I will quit my job, even without the promise of another.* He could always consider other career options, but he needed to stay in Hot Springs. That would prove to Nori he wasn't about to toss her off easily. That's what she needed. . .right? To know that he was determined and faithful and willing to sacrifice everything for her?

Zachary dropped back down on the couch in confusion. *And the whole plan could backfire on me. Big time.* Giving up his job could upset her. She might think he'd been foolhardy and impulsive in not talking to her first. That he'd presumed on their affections, and that he'd pressured her by taking such a drastic step.

He imagined himself sitting on the couch for the rest of his days, alone, without Nori. Unbearable. But was this new idea a prompting from God, or was it the pathetic ruminations of a desperate man? Unless the Almighty was going to come forth with some Old Testament-style writing on the wall as a definitive answer, then he just might have to go forth in faith and pray that the Lord would take care of the rest.

With renewed resolve and a sudden injection of calm in his spirit, he constructed a letter of resignation on his computer, printed it out, and headed toward the door.

Chapter 25

Nori hung up the phone. Just as she'd guessed, Lizza was happy to buy Sweet Nothings and overjoyed to learn why the shop was for sale.

She hurried back to Zachary's apartment and rang his bell. Nori caught herself giggling, imagining his face as she announced the sale of her shop. She placed her hand over her heart. *So this is what it feels like to be in love.*

Zachary didn't come to the door, so she mashed the bell a few more times. Maybe she'd taken too much time working out the details with Lizza. Was he still refusing to answer his door, or had he just left for the airport? What a comedy of errors, except the situation was far from funny!

Tears started to fill her eyes. *Stay calm, Nori.* Then an idea came to her. Surely someone at South Gate Oil and Gas would know his plans. She glanced at her watch: 4:45. They hadn't shut down for the day, so there was still time to call. After getting the number from Information, she quickly pushed in all the right buttons.

Nori counted each second as she waited for a receptionist to answer. Even though the passing of time hadn't altered, this was starting to feel like the longest day of her life. She drummed her fingers on the kitchen counter.

"Good afternoon. South Gate Oil and Gas. May I help you?"

Finally, a human being. Thank You, Lord. "I'm looking for Zachary Martin. Please."

"Mr. Zachary Martin?" a young woman's voice said.

"Yes. That's correct."

"Well, I think I saw Mr. Martin leaving the building maybe five minutes ago. Let me check on that for you. One moment please."

The woman placed her on hold. Nori waited, drumming her fingers.

"Yes, I was correct," the woman finally said. "Mr. Martin just left. I don't—"

"Was he leaving for Denver?" Nori tried to keep her voice in a normal vocal range, but she knew it was getting higher-pitched by the second.

"No, Mr. Martin no longer works here."

"Oh no." Nori's heart sank. "Are you absolutely sure?"

"From what I just heard, he won't be making the move with our company. He quit his job."

Nori clutched her throat. "I can't believe it."

"Well, I can," the girl said. "Just between you and me, some other people have quit, too. Some people just don't want to make the move."

"Thank you for your help," Nori said. "Oh, did he say where he was going?"

"You mean what kind of job—"

"No, I mean if he was headed home right now or somewhere else?"

"Sorry, I don't have that information. No, wait. He did say something about a favorite spot. But I don't know where that is."

"I do. Thanks for your help." Nori put the phone back. *This is my fault. That dear sweet man is out of work because of me.* She couldn't contain her anguish as tears spilled down her cheeks. She wiped them away. At least she knew where Zachary had gone.

Nori drove as quickly as she could without killing anyone, found a parking place, and headed up the stairs, which overlooked the cascades.

There was Zachary, just sitting on a bench and looking like the most dejected man on earth. "How could I do this to you?" she murmured. She breathed a prayer for courage and walked over to him.

Zachary looked up, surprised and very pleased. "You've come."

Nori sat down next to him. She wasn't sure what to say first. So much needed to be said. "I heard you quit your job. Why?"

"This place is home, and you're part of that. At least I hope this will allow us to continue to date. I want to give you all the time you need, Nori." He looked at her. "I'll find work. Somehow."

Zachary's earnestness ripped at her heart. "But I hadn't even said yes. I mean. . .that was taking quite a chance."

"I guess that's what love does."

Nori wanted to kiss that despair right off his face, but the time wasn't right. Not until she'd said what she needed to say. "You know, Lizza loves my shop, and the customers adore her. I just talked to her, and she's going to buy Sweet Nothings so I can start over in Denver. Maybe if you hurry, you can get your job back."

"No." Zachary rose, looking troubled. "You can't sell your shop."

"My love for you is more important than any company. And you were right. I got so caught up in the whirlwind of my parents' troubles, it kept me from seeing what was right in front of me. But I see it all clearly now." Nori placed her hand over her mouth, feeling choked with emotion. "How can this be?"

Zachary eased down next to her. "How can what be, Nori?"

"That I could be so fortunate. . .that you would love me. I've prayed a thousand prayers for a man to come along just like you. And there you were all this time. God must have one incredible sense of humor." Nori chuckled through her tears. "But He also has mercy. He remembered my prayers all these years, and

He gave me you, Zachary Martin. You are the present I want to open before it's too late."

Zachary's eyes misted over. "It's not too late."

Nori loved his passion. She loved *him*. Pure and simple. And now she had some proposing to do. "I have something else I want to say." She knelt down on one knee in front of Zachary. "You asked me a question here, and I turned you down. Well, now *I'm* asking." She took his hands in hers. And while jets thundered overhead and tourists ambled by, Nori said, "Mr. Martin, I once saved your life. Now would you please save mine?" She kissed his hand and smiled. "Would you do me the honor of becoming my husband?"

Zachary rose and lifted her into his arms. "Oh, how I love you, my dearest Irish maiden. The answer is categorically affirmative."

Nori laughed, thinking she'd never felt so wonderful or seen Zachary so happy. Then he kissed her—a real kiss. A big juicy one. The very one, in fact, she'd dared to ask God for. And it was a kiss that meant something. Something real and lasting. A forever kind of kiss.

Chapter 26

Seven months later

Lizza helped slip the ivory Victorian gown over Nori's head. If there was such a thing as bridal rapture, Nori definitely had it. *I'm getting married.* Finally—after years of hoping, praying, believing—she would walk down the aisle on her father's arm.

Lizza stepped behind Nori and zipped up the delicate dress, then fussed with the lengthy beaded train. Her best friend's hand went to her mouth as she stood back. "You're the most beautiful bride I've ever seen. And I'm not just saying that."

"Sure you're not." Nori chuckled and then turned to look at herself in the mirror. For a moment, the reflection took her breath away. She looked—and felt—like a princess. Just as she'd always dreamed. She ran her fingers along the delicate Chantilly lace.

Right away, she thought of the wedding doll her mother had given her on her sixth birthday. How many years had she played with that exquisite little doll, imagining the wedding she would one day have? And how many different types of ceremonies had she planned? Hundreds.

Oh, but today's would be the best of all. Not just because of its classic traditional style but because the man waiting for her at the front of the church was Zachary—*her* Zachary.

Nori couldn't help but smile as she thought of her groom. What was he doing right now? Fumbling with his bow tie, no doubt, reflecting on how much it reminded him of the magnetic field of the earth. She grinned at that thought. And maybe Zachary was sending another prayer of thanksgiving for his new job in Hot Springs as a geophysical consultant.

A rap on the door interrupted her reverie, and Nori glanced over as her mother entered the room with a black box in hand. "This is the pearl necklace I showed you a few months ago. It belonged to your great-grandmother, your grandmother, and then to me." She opened the box. "But now they are my gift to you."

"Oh, Mom, are you sure?" She bit her lip and forced back the tears.

"Very sure." Her mother placed the strand of pearls around Nori's neck.

"They're exquisite. Thank you so much."

They hugged each other, and her mother began to cry. Despite her best efforts, Nori quickly followed.

"None of that, you two." Lizza shook her finger at them and grinned. "Your makeup will melt like cotton candy!"

Nori chuckled and reached for a tissue. How she loved her dear friend and now business partner. She was thrilled that Lizza was about to open Sweet Nothings II in Little Rock. Lizza would have her own shop after all. What a blessing for everyone.

Lizza lifted the headdress of silk blossoms off the stand and carefully pinned it to Nori's upswept curls. She stepped back and straightened the beaded tulle as it cascaded down Nori's back, completing the picture. "Mmm. Like icing on the cake."

"Look at this. All grown-up." Her mother dabbed at her eyes. "I just can't believe it. My little girl is about to get married."

Nori gave her mother an inviting smile, feeling so very blessed that her parents hadn't signed the divorce papers after all but had decided to get marriage counseling instead.

"Oh, how I love you," her mother whispered to her.

Nori basked in the wonder of her loving words. "I love you, too."

Another knock on the door caused the ladies to turn in curiosity. A tentative male voice rang out. "C–can I come in?"

Dad! A knot rose in Nori's throat as her father stepped into the room. He took one look at her and reached to take her hand, tears slipping down his cheeks.

Nori looked back and forth between her parents and ushered up a silent prayer. *Oh Lord, thank You that they're both here for me.*

She turned to face her father and gave his hand a squeeze. "It's okay, Dad. I'm sure by the time this day is over we'll all be drying our eyes. I know I will be."

Lizza, still playing the role of organizer, handed out bouquets of red roses, each framed with greenery. They looked beautiful against the emerald green bridesmaids' dresses.

With joy overflowing, Nori took her Bible in hand, the same one that had guided her through her relationship with Zachary. Affixed to the front of the Bible was a spray of bridal pink roses. Nori pulled them to her face at once to inhale their fragrance. Then she looked at the special bouquet of bridal pink roses that had just arrived. Zachary had sent them. He'd remembered they were her favorite. She'd memorized his attached card.

> *To my Irish maiden,*
> *All of nature comes to life*
> *And celebrates our delight*
> *As we walk, so full of love*
> *In our fields of amber light.*

Ah, Zachary. He really did have a poet's heart. And he'd sent her a box of her favorite candies—lavender chocolate truffles from Belgium. He'd thought of everything.

Suddenly the familiar strains of Pachelbel's *Canon in D* drew Nori's attention to the open door that led to the sanctuary.

"I think that's our cue." Her father extended his arm to her. "Are you ready?"

"Oh, I am *so* ready." She gave herself one last glance in the mirror and then paused, remembering something. "Oh, just a second." Reaching into her beaded purse, she came up with a container of pomegranate lipstick, which she applied with care.

Funny how Zachary had fallen in love with the color during the months of their engagement. Funnier still as she realized the external changes they'd both made had nothing to do with their blossoming love for one another.

With Lizza, her maid of honor, and then her bridesmaids leading the procession, they all made their way down the hallway toward the back of the familiar church sanctuary. The doors swept open, and for the first time all day, she set her sights on her bridegroom.

Oh my. Zachary looked every bit like a prince in his tuxedo and silk vest. Okay, so his tie was a little askew and his hair stuck out a bit on one side, but his face lit up with expectancy, and all the more so when he caught a glimpse of her. Love poured from his eyes, and Nori fought to keep the tears from flowing.

The organist shifted with dramatic flair to the triumphant bridal march, and Nori's heart thumped in anticipation. She squeezed her father's arm, knowing the moment had come at last—the one she had dreamed of since childhood. The pipe organ seemed to beckon, wooing her to the front of the church.

"Are you ready?" her father whispered.

"Oh yes."

She took the first nerve-racking step with her right foot. Then her left. Then her right. Somewhere along the way, she and her father entered into a steady gait, walking in time with the music. They reached the altar area in record time, and Nori smiled as Zachary looked her way and mouthed a silent, "I love you."

Nori responded with a nod. Of course, the tears got in the way, but she didn't mind as she took her place next to Zachary. *Ahh.* The world was suddenly a much finer place. So fine, in fact, that Nori thought no confection on earth could ever be as sweet.

A Letter to Our Readers

Dear Readers:

In order that we might better contribute to your reading enjoyment, we would appreciate you taking a few minutes to respond to the following questions. When completed, please return to the following: Fiction Editor, Barbour Publishing, Inc., P.O. Box 719, Uhrichsville, OH 44683.

1. Did you enjoy reading *Ozark Weddings* by Anita Higman and Janice Thompson?
   ❑ Very much. I would like to see more books like this.
   ❑ Moderately—I would have enjoyed it more if _____

   _____

   _____

2. What influenced your decision to purchase this book?
   (Check those that apply.)
   ❑ Cover   ❑ Back cover copy   ❑ Title   ❑ Price
   ❑ Friends   ❑ Publicity   ❑ Other

3. Which story was your favorite?
   ❑ *Larkspur Dreams*   ❑ *Castles in the Air*
   ❑ *The Love Song*

4. Please check your age range:
   ❑ Under 18   ❑ 18–24   ❑ 25–34
   ❑ 35–45   ❑ 46–55   ❑ Over 55

5. How many hours per week do you read? _____

Name _____

Occupation _____

Address _____

City_____ State _____ Zip_____

E-mail _____

HEARTLAND HEROES

THREE-IN-ONE-COLLECTION

Three independent women encouter unexpected heroes of romance in Iowa. With God in the driver's seat, anything can happen.

Contemporary, paperback, 384 pages, 5⅜" x 8"

HEARTSONG
PRESENTS

If you love Christian romance...

$10.⁹⁹

You'll love Heartsong Presents' inspiring and faith-filled romance by today's very best Christian authors. . .Wanda E. Brunstetter, Mary Connealy, Susan Page Davis, Cathy Marie Hake, and Joyce Livingston, to mention a few!

When you join Heartsong Presents, you'll enjoy four brand-new, mass-market, 176-page books—two contemporary and two historical—that will build you up in your faith when you discover God's role in every relationship you read about!

Imagine. . .four new romances every four weeks—with men and women like you who long to meet the one God has chosen as the love of their lives—all for the low price of $10.99 postpaid.

To join, simply visit www.heartsongpresents.com or complete the coupon below and mail it to the address provided.

Mass Market, 176 Pages

✂ -

YES! Sign me up for Heartsong!

NEW MEMBERSHIPS WILL BE SHIPPED IMMEDIATELY!

Send no money now. We'll bill you only $10.99 postpaid with your first shipment of four books. Or for faster action, call 1-740-922-7280.

NAME _____

ADDRESS_____

CITY_____ STATE _____ ZIP _____

MAIL TO: HEARTSONG PRESENTS, P.O. Box 721, Uhrichsville, Ohio 44683
or sign up at WWW.HEARTSONGPRESENTS.COM